Millennium War

A Story of the Future of Mankind
3501 – 4501

Millennium War

A Story of the Future of Mankind
3501 – 4501

Ian Kincaid

cP
Aventine Press

Published by Aventine Press
1202 Donax Ave, Suite 12
Imperial Beach, CA 91932, USA

www.aventinepress.com

ISBN: 1-59330-166-9
Printed in the United States of America

Letter to the Reader

Dear Reader:

Thank you for reading this Limited First Edition of Millennium War. As a Limited First Edition, this book represents the first public presentation of a story that has been a big part of my life for over two years. Rather than as the final product, however, I see this version of the book as another stepping-stone on the long and fascinating journey that this project has become.

My primary purpose in producing this release is to give interested readers an opportunity not only to experience the story but also to have a chance to shape its future. So with that in mind, I hope that you truly enjoy reading this tale and perhaps, in some small way, join me on my journey.

Please email me at ian.kincaid@millenniumwar.com and tell me your thoughts about the book. Your input will help shape the future of this novel. If requested, I will make every effort to respond to your questions, keep you informed about future releases or post comments you may have to the book's website.

If you found the book a pleasure to read, I also ask that you share that joy and pass it along to a friend. Additional copies can also be purchased directly from me at the website: www. millenniumwar.com.

Thanks again for giving me a little of your time. Good reading.

Sincerely,

Ian Kincaid

To Catherine, for the love and acceptance to make this book a reality.

To Theresa and Jamie, my greatest blessings, may all of your dreams come true.

To Paul, for the encouragement that made this book possible.

To Jane, for taking some time to add a little polish.

When we think about the future,
we change the present.

Table of Contents

Chapter 1

Prologue

3501
Earth

It was a golden age for Mankind; the time of the great generation ships. All of humanity celebrated a thousand years of peace and prosperity on Earth. The problems that had hindered the planet throughout most of her past: famine, disease, environmental catastrophe and war, had been vanquished to the pages of history. The citizens of Earth enjoyed an unprecedented time of openness, freedom, security and wealth, under the protection of a single, unified and democratic government.

Human life, once confined only to the surface of Earth, was now spreading throughout the galaxy. The construction of great generation ships consumed the energy of the entire race. Not since the building of the great pyramids, had the output of an entire civilization been so focused on a single goal. Interstellar colonies had been established stretching out for light-years in every direction from our birthplace on Earth. It seemed that the eternal existence and prosperity of Mankind was now assured.

And then, somewhere in the darkness of space, something changed.

Chapter 2

The Incident

3503
Omega Theta Colony
Over 50 Light-Years from Earth

It began with a faint signal sent across trillions of miles of empty space. That signal was destined for Omega Theta, a small first generation colony just over fifty light-years from Earth. With a population of a little less than a thousand, scattered over three small colony stars, orbiting a medium sized sun; she was the most remote outpost of Mankind. Yet like most of the early colonists, the citizens of Omega Theta were determined in their mission to spread the boundaries of man. Luis Rodriguez, like most of his kinsman, shared this dream but he could never understand how his particular job contributed to that greater goal.

Most of Omega Theta was focused on the tasks of driving production and operation of the mining drones that would tap the resources of their host solar system, allow them to expand their colony and eventually build and launch their own colonization mission.

Luis however, considered himself little more than a babysitter to an overgrown calculator. He had the tedious task of confirming the analysis of a computer system that to this date had never been wrong. Though based on technology a thousand years older than that being deployed on Earth, Omega Theta's central management and analysis system had done a flawless job, lasting for centuries and producing reliable results based on tried and true algorithms of mathematical and physical science. Luis failed to understand why a human mind, so feeble in comparison, was required to verify such an infallible system.

So it wasn't surprising that Luis sank his head and sighed as he activated his terminal to begin his work for the day, reviewing the incoming signal from a small, outbound exploration drone.

"Display signal data," he mumbled to the terminal.

The viewing screen in front of him flickered and displayed an unexpected statement.

"Exploration Drone Omega Theta Thirteen failed – Cause Unknown."

Drone thirteen was a deep space exploration probe that had been launched over one hundred years ago by the first generation to setup Omega Theta. It had been hurtling through space toward the Omega Theta's closest neighboring star and was almost half way there. Its mission was a simple one, to gather data about that system and the space that lay between. Its failure, though unfortunate, was not that unusual. The fact that "Mr. Perfect" didn't know the cause was.

"What do you mean "Cause Unknown?"" Rodriguez retorted.

"State specific request," the system responded coldly.

"Fine, display last ten entries of system maintenance log," Luis clarified.

The system filled the screen with ten specific entries of data that were sent by the probe. It became apparent that thirteen's last moments were busy ones. The log showed failures occurring one by one across the probe's subsystems at almost exactly the same time, immediately before the probe was completely lost.

"Show Graphic," Rodriguez requested.

The terminal displayed a three dimensional image of the probe, demonstrating the key systems failing all within a millisecond of each other.

"Particle Impact!" exclaimed Rodriguez delighted that he finally beat his nemesis.

"Negative," responded the system. "Momentum of probe not affected."

"EM pulse?" Rodriquez queried.

"Negative," responded the system again. "Disparate impact to probe's systems; non uniform failure. EM pulse eliminated as possible cause."

And so it continued for the next several hours, well past the end of Luis' normal shift, Rodriguez stepping through the data provided to him and the system shooting down all of the theories he could come up with. He was overjoyed the system couldn't resolve the problem for once but frustrated that neither could he. Finally he gave up, saved his work and deactivated his terminal. He needed a break.

For Luis Rodriguez, his favorite way to pass his free time was in the colony's one still functioning virtual entertainment gallery. Here he could join in any number of game systems that provided a lifelike recreation of a myriad of experiences. His favorite was a system that allowed the re-enactment of some of the air combat battles that had been fought throughout the twentieth and twenty-first centuries on earth. On this day he chose to pilot a Messerschmitt 109B over the skies of Great Britain during World War II. The experience was real in every way from the sensation of G force as he climbed and banked his fighter to the smell of the leather in his helmet; he loved the escape from his own mundane duties.

He played the game for a couple of hours, allowing the system to throw different scenarios at him. On his last sortie he found himself stuck to the tail of a Hawker Hurricane tearing it to shreds. He gritted his teeth with exhilaration as the wing of the Hurricane peeled away and suddenly it hit him.

"It couldn't be," he gasped to himself.

He fell to his knees as he scrambled to get out of the entertainment gallery and rush back to his terminal. Confirming his theory would be easy.

"Activate Terminal," he snipped. "Insert new data element," he added, before the system had even completed bringing his screen to life.

"Describe new data element," the system responded finally.

"Mark eight drilling beam drone within the vicinity of the probe," Rodriguez replied.

"Inserted," the system responded.

"Rerun analysis," he smirked, stretching his hands behind his head with confidence.

"Exploration Drone Omega Theta thirteen failed – Cause: accidentally targeting by drilling beam," the system pronounced.

"So the damn thing was shot down!" Rodriguez shouted jumping from his chair.

"Negative, drilling beam drone fictitious data element," the system replied.

Rodriguez just laughed, he had won. He had finally won and the damn system was nothing but a sore looser.

But the seriousness of his discovery soon began to sink in.

Three light-years from Mankind's very farthest outpost, an unmanned space probe had been destroyed by something or someone; something or someone that could produce a focused energy beam unlike any that had yet been found in nature in over fifteen years of space exploration and colonization. Could it be? Could it really be?

He knew who he had to call and it wasn't going to be fun.

"Contact Dr. Tzu," he instructed the terminal, sitting back down quietly.

"Dr. Tzu is in rest status," the system responded.

Rodriguez shook his head in a moment of hesitation then swallowed and responded, "Emergency Override". He gritted his teeth awaiting the response.

"This had better be good," came a gruff voice from the terminal, on audio only and barely awake.

"I'm so sorry to wake you Sir but I believe I've found something you have gotta' see," Rodriguez apologized, swallowing hard as he spoke.

Dr Chin Tzu remembered Rodriguez from his science fundamentals sessions. He hadn't been his brightest student but he wasn't a prankster either and if he thought he had something it deserved at least a review.

"Very well Luis, I'll be down in about ten. We better go over this together," Dr Tzu concluded.

The colony's communication system allowed them to share all the data and graphics they wanted to, communicating clearly about the concern, but there was still no replacement for face-to-face discussion. As the Doctor made his way down, Rodriguez remembered one of his former teacher's pet peeves. He hated unprepared students. Luis began a flurry of commands to the terminal.

He quickly took all the relevant material that he had gathered regarding the probe and compiled a presentation of his case. It ran through the failure itself in clear graphic detail and then presented all the possible failure scenarios that had been ruled out in his earlier research, presenting data eliminating each one. Finally he showed his own scenario, one where a powerful beam device was placed in the vicinity of the probe, just as he finished the presentation and saved it Dr. Tzu entered his workspace.

"Ok, Rodriguez let's see what you've found," the Doctor requested, still in his sleeping robes and wearing some comfortable, if old-fashioned, fuzzy slippers.

"It'll be easiest if you just watch this," Rodriguez responded, too nervous to even begin to explain what he'd found.

The Doctor sat quietly and watched the presentation unravel on the screen without expression. He then turned to Luis and quietly asked. "Well?"

His former student wasn't going to get off that easy. He was going to have to say it.

"It was shot down!" Rodriguez blurted, suddenly anxious that perhaps he'd missed some obvious and simple explanation for the event.

Dr. Tzu turned back to the screen and after a moment of silence and consideration put Luis' mind at rest.

"Yes, I believe it was," he stated and then smiled to the younger man.

"This will have to go before the council and that won't be fun," he continued. "We'll have to provide a lot more data than this when it does. I'm going to get cleaned up and then work on this from my lab. You should get some rest and I will speak to you later."

When Luis awoke in his quarters it took a moment for him to remember the previous days events but when it came back to him he once again felt his heart race. He turned to his personal terminal and uttered a simple instruction.

"Dr. Tzu please," he requested.

The response came back quicker than before.

"Well sleepyhead, how are you doing?" Dr Tzu responded with a tone of familiarity that Luis wasn't expecting. "Listen, I want us on the same shift so I requested your alarm be turned off to let you oversleep. You should be pretty well rested. Why don't you come down here and I'll show you what I've got."

It was then Luis realized that he felt a little strange, the kind of feeling you get when you realize you've been asleep for over twelve hours when you're used to six. It took him a while to get his bearings clean up and get down to Dr. Tzu's lab.

"Come in, come in," the Doctor smiled. "Quite a discovery kid. Let me give you a run down."

The surprises just kept coming. He hadn't seen his teacher this thrilled in the three years he'd known him. Dr Tzu had always been such as serious man but now Luis was looking at inspiration at work.

"See here," the Doctor indicated running a new presentation for Luis. "This shows the exact path the beam took across the probe as it hit. From the changing angle of the beam, we can tell that the direction of the source as it passed by the probe. The beam was extremely intense, beyond anything I've seen or we could produce here and extremely focused. It cut through the probe instantly but in a very narrow line. Very efficient indeed; it destroyed different components instantly as it hit them."

He gestured at the screen as he spoke.

"But here's the really bad news. If we study data from the sensor logs, we see a very high frequency signal trace here. That's a reflected harmonic from the primary beam as it hits the probe. Now, if we look at it later in the event, we can see a significant reduction in the frequency of the signal. It's unlikely the beam itself changed frequency, so we have to presume that is Doppler shift. The source of the beam is in fact passing the probe as the event occurs and traveling at very high speed indeed."

"I'm sorry Doctor but you've lost me?" questioned Rodriguez.

"Come on Luis, did you sleep through all of my sessions?" joked the senior scientist. "To make a long story short kid, in about fifteen years we're going to have a really nasty visitor".

"No, Sir, you must be mistaken, the probe was almost three light-years out and took almost a hundred years to get there," Rodriguez exclaimed in disbelief.

"Let's hope I am," the Doctor responded trying to soothe his tense young friend, "but that's what the data tell us."

"What do we do?" Rodriquez questioned, as his mind raced with possibilities.

"That's not our decision," the Doctor responded. "Come on the council is waiting. They're expecting us in about thirty minutes and the shuttle will be here soon."

Rodriguez hadn't realized he would be finding himself in front of the governing body of the colony within just a few minutes and wasn't really prepared.

"Don't worry," said the Doctor, as they walked down the hallway toward the shuttle together. "I'll do all the talking".

They climbed onboard the shuttle and strapped in, along with a couple other colonists that were moving between the colony stars with them. It would take them about ten minutes to make the journey from their colony star, number two, over to number one. Neither felt it appropriate to discuss the situation in the company of the other passengers so they both took a moment to look out of the shuttles windows and enjoy the sensation of zero gravity. The shuttle was too small to have rotational gravity and relied on old-fashioned harnesses to keep everyone in their place. Luis didn't get to ride the shuttle very often so he couldn't help but take a minute to watch the nutrition stick he'd been nibbling on drift from hand to hand. The professor looked over and smiled, wondering if his younger associate had yet really grasped the nature of this incident.

The shuttle jolted a little as it docked to the primary colony star and the small thrusters shut down. Artificial gravity resumed as the shuttle fell into the rotational path of the spinning colony. Dr. Tzu and Luis made their way to the door.

"Doctor, why do you need me here?" Luis questioned, his nervousness growing.

"You found it," the Doctor smiled at Rodriguez as the door opened.

"Perfect timing as always," said a smiling elderly man at the end of the council chamber, who Luis soon recognized as Dean Rogers, the senior of five educators in the colony and a

close friend of Dr. Tzu. He also recognized the colony chair,
Joseph Rothman, who sat at the closest end and who turned
and gestured to their seats without breaking a smile.

The twelve-member council was the governing body of the
colony. Though its law was based on the Unified Justice Code
that was created on Earth over a thousand years ago and had
served as the basis of all legal proceedings on and off Earth
since then, each colony, so far removed from Earth, had to
make its own interpretations and decisions about its welfare.
The council played that role. Formed from members of the
colony who also had other full time jobs within the population,
they served on a volunteer and elected basis to make important
decisions about the future of Omega Theta.

"Ok, Doctor, let's have it," requested Rothman, dispensing
with formalities.

Luis was a little surprised to see the council chair behave in
this abrupt way, as he been more use to his public face. Outside
of council chambers he presented himself as a pleasant man
and sympathetic listener, though it was widely known to the
more senior members of the colony that he was a shrewd and
calculating leader behind close doors. This balance of public
relations savvy and command of practicalities had kept in the
seat of chair for over fifteen years.

"It will be easiest to begin with a presentation of the data,"
the Doctor began.

Luis couldn't help but feel a little déjà vu as the presentation
began, wondering if the Doctor was feeling as nervous as he was
when he had first presented his theory but the data presented
now was far more thorough and convincing.

The screen of the council chamber came to life and stepped
through the incident in detail, first establishing the probe's
fate: shot down three light-years from the colony, then building
upon that by establishing the speed and direction of the source
of the probe's demise. The presentation closed with a piece
that Dr. Tzu had not yet showed to Luis.

It was a simulation of the beam that had destroyed the
probe directed at a colony star of Omega Theta. Luis for the
first time saw the stark reality of what they were dealing
with. This was followed by a sense of amazement at how his

instructor had showed such a passion for the science of the discovery while knowing the ultimate potential outcome of events. An eerie silence dropped across the room, as the screen showed the colony star rendered useless by the piercing beam in less than a second.

Luis was surprised at how readily the council seemed to accept the reality of what they had seen.

"How ouro can we he it's coming here?" came the first question from Rothman.

"Can't say for sure," replied Dr. Tzu. "I can only tell you that it's headed in our general direction."

"Any chance we can defend ourselves against it?" came the next question just as pointed again from Rothman.

"Well, everything has a weakness, so I wouldn't rule that possibility out. Unfortunately we're not able to gather any data on the source itself and its capabilities beyond producing the beam," replied Dr. Tzu.

"Can we be sure its intentions will remain hostile when it arrives?" came a new angle from the Dean.

"Can't help you there," he responded. Dr. Tzu was a physicist and an astronomer. He wasn't going to work outside his field.

"Anything else Doctor?" Rothman requested, drawing a close to the presentation.

"That's the data we have at this time," Tzu confirmed. "Of course, we'll keep working on it and see if there's anything we've missed."

"Very well. Thank you," the stern man responded, standing to urge Tzu and Rodriguez to depart. But just as the two almost reached the door, Rothman had one last comment.

"Rodriguez," he uttered to stop them. "Good Job," he complimented the young man before they left; Luis felt a sigh of relief come over him.

The two walked from the room in the silence for a while before Tzu broke the ice.

"Hungry?" he questioned.

"Yes, believe it or not I am," Luis responded, realizing that he was probably in a slight state of shock over everything. He still couldn't believe where the last couple of days had taken him.

"Good 'cause the food here's much better than at home and we've got two hours to kill before the shuttle," the Doctor stated. It seemed that he was intent on keeping an upbeat mood. With that they walked down the hallway a few doors down and turned into the colony's food hall. It was one of the only rooms in any of Omega Theta's colony stars to have an outside view. The side windows of the long room looked out past some of the closer asteroids directly toward the systems single red sun. Around the nearest asteroid, they could barely make out the shape of the mining drones circling busily around it, like bees coming and going from a particularly fruitful flower.

They sat and ate for a while in silence, enjoying the very rare treat of a dish that included some real meat, colony pork as it was known, a product of a distant relative of Earth's pigs, a creature specially bred as the second highest member of a space colony's tightly managed food chain.

This time it would be Rodriguez who would break the silence. "Is this for real?" he questioned his teacher.

"Honestly it's impossible to say. Clearly it's out there and it's coming this way but its intentions? We can only guess," he responded, not wanting to stress his associate further.

Before he could continue, Dr. Tzu was interrupted by his personal terminal. Luis couldn't see the image on the Doctor's wrist. He only heard him respond. "We'll do the best we can Sir."

"Congratulations," he said looking at Rodriguez. "You've been just been assigned as one of two inaugural members of Omega's Theta's first ever Department of Defense."

"And who's the other member?" questioned Luis.

"I am," Doctor Tzu responded, turning again toward the view of the stars.

Chapter 3

Foundation Voyager

3512
Foundation Voyager
In orbit of Jupiter

Far away from the events unfolding in the outer colonies, life for humanity was progressing as it had for the last one thousand years. Knowledge of distant happenings would not even reach Earth for several more decades. Mankind was instead, absorbed in the celebration of his accomplishments and the expansion of his realm out into the stars and for some, beyond. Dr. Frank Ryland was one man who had always thought beyond his time and place and today, as his private shuttle neared the end of its journey, was no exception.

His blood pulsed with anticipation as his shuttle came over Jupiter's Northern Pole and banked away from the solar plane. Foundation Voyager lay ahead, a few degrees off due North of Jupiter. Even though she was nothing more than a tiny white speck ahead in the viewing screen he could feel her presence growing nearer. He could have brought the view to zoom and seen the ship in all her glory but, instead, he decided to let the moment grow as he drew closer. Besides, he had seen images of his creation in a myriad of forms for the last twenty years. He had taken virtual tours of every nook and cranny of her gargantuan form. No: now he would let the reality of the moment play its course.

As she took form on the viewing screen in front of him, the tiny white speck began to grow into a white line and then the various elements of her structure began to take shape. Above all Foundation Voyager was an engine, the greatest and most powerful that Mankind had ever built. At her peak velocity she would carry her twenty five thousand inhabitants faster than any man had ever traveled. But even as she hurtled through space at almost thirty thousand miles per second she would still take over three hundred years to reach her destination. Dr. Ryland knew that his eyes would never see the distant sun that her children's ancestors would call home but that made the moment no less thrilling for him.

As the ship's details revealed themselves, the great fuel tanks that lay along side the central drive system became clear. Over eighty percent of her fifteen million tons of mass at launch would consist of the pure hydrogen contained in those tanks. It would be burned through a complex series of fusion and fission reactions until drained of its usable nuclear energy and ejected from her main drive at near the speed of light. This thin stream of super accelerated particles would push Voyager out into space and across the void. Her linear reactors weren't visible from the shuttle as they sat hidden beneath the massive tanks. The only element of the drive system itself that could be seen was the very end of the accelerator shaft that ran down the central axis of the ship.

As his shuttle grew close to her, it began to curve toward the head of the ship and the five colony stars that were her precious cargo. The name colony star was a glamorous word created over a thousand years ago, at the dawn of the galactic colonization, to entice Earth citizens to condemn themselves to a life of imprisonment aboard a generation ship. Though the structures had become a much more pleasant place to spend one's life they were still far from the glorious homes the name implied. The colony stars had more the shape of great drums each lined up like beads along the front of the ship, with the front end of the accelerator shaft threading through each of them. And at her very tip, like a great spearhead, Foundation Voyager held her protective shield, a bank of high energy beam generators used to smash even the tiniest particles of dust that would come into her path. Finally, just in front of the ship itself, lay his shuttle's destination, the massive preparation colony. Larger than the ships own colony stars, the preparation colony was a single facility that held all of the ships inhabitants in a single spinning drum while Foundation Voyager took form. Unlike its smaller cousins the preparation colony would not be going with Foundation Voyager, she would stay behind, her job done. But for now Foundation Station, as she was known, was a hum with activity and the first place where the children of Foundation Voyager would meet their Founder.

As the shuttle docked to Foundation Station, Ryland felt the shift in artificial gravity. His eight-day journey from Earth was over and his private interplanetary shuttle settled into standby mode. It gave up its own rotation and fixed itself to the outside of Foundation Station. Ryland stepped onto the airlock elevator and entered the station. Captain Jenkins met him at the door.

"Welcome Frank," the captain greeted his boss.

Dr. Ryland had found throughout his life that informality helped bridge the gap created by his wealth and position with those who worked for him. He insisted on it. Frank was not the type to dictate his desires to his employees and followers but rather to work to build consensus with his team. It was Frank's intelligence and respect for his fellow man that earned him loyalty more than the simple fact that he paid the bills.

"Is everything ready, Tom?" Ryland questioned the captain.

"Yes Frank, but wouldn't you rather have rested before making the speech?" Jenkins replied.

The captain knew it was too late to change any plans now and that Dr. Ryland had just had eight days of solitude and rest aboard his shuttle but was more curious about why the urgency to greet the colony immediately. The answer would still elude him.

"There's a lot for us to get done Captain, we must get started," Ryland replied.

"Very well Frank let's get you there then, the preliminaries will just be drawing to a close," Jenkins responded.

Captain Jenkins led Dr. Ryland down a wide corridor that ran in a circle around the inner circumference of the Station. Above them lay a curved transparent roof that allowed them to look out into space to both sides and see the far side of the station above them. Looking directly in front of them and up about thirty degrees, they could see their destination: the main amphitheater of the station. Dr. Ryland took a moment to glance to the right, at the orb of Jupiter, even from two million miles away the form of the planet was massive and took up much of the view of the right side of the station. Dr. Ryland smiled in a moment of gratitude to this God of Earth's heaven.

He knew that almost all the materials used to create the marvel that was Foundation Voyager had come from Jupiter and her moons.

The preliminaries, as captain Jenkins had called them, were just finishing as they entered the upper presentation area above the stadium, which for now was concealed into the ceiling of the facility. Foundation Station's amphitheater was indeed a stadium in all sense of the word, built to seat all twenty five thousand of the ships inhabitants at one time in comfort and able to host events of all kinds. Today, it had hosted a two-hour presentation of every aspect of the ships mission, from its launch to its final destination; everything had been covered in a spectacular manner. The citizens of Foundation Voyager already knew their roles and much about the ship. This had all been covered in their training. Now they would celebrate all they had learned and the mission that lay ahead.

As the festivities drew to a close and lights in the stadium dimmed, the announcer's voice came over the speakers.

"And now I give you, for the first time before all of us in person, our benefactor, our leader and our Founder: Dr. Frank Ryland." Cheers rose from below.

With that, the presentation area itself began to lower into the center of the stadium and the lights and monitors began to focus on the Doctor. Ryland was very comfortable in public appearances, they had always been a part of his life but comfort should not be confused with enjoyment. He still preferred to deal with people one on one and he saw large personal appearances as an essential part of achieving his goals, not an accomplishment in and of itself. His speech today was no different. It was a measured step towards achieving an important goal. The most important goal he or any man had ever set. The cheers began to subside and Dr. Ryland spoke.

"Today we begin a great journey," he began. "A journey that will bring our very existence to a new plane."

Though neither Captain Jenkins, nor any of the other thousands of listeners knew exactly what Dr. Ryland spoke of, he, like many of the colonists, felt a sense of joy at his words. He had joined the Foundation not because he longed to give up his life to captain a generation ship, far from it. He had joined the Foundation because he believed that Dr. Ryland was a genius and a visionary and he longed to be part of his future. He knew that if Dr. Ryland was building a generation ship it was not just to add another to the almost two hundred colonies Mankind had created, beyond our original solar system, no; something greater lay ahead. Unfortunately, it had become his and everyone's frustration to not know what that might be. He had only been able to conclude that if it required construction of the greatest generation ship ever built, that it was something that couldn't happen on Earth, or anywhere within the jurisdiction of the Unified Government.

All of Foundation's children felt privileged to be part of Dr. Ryland's vision. They had all felt anxious to have passed the intense physical, fertility, intellectual and psychological tests required to join the mission but not just because the very cost of their birthright was at stake but also their own personal longing to be part of something big. A something they knew nothing about and could only dream of.

Only the incredible cost of the project and, for some of the more perceptive colonists, their common philosophies, gave clues about what might lie ahead. Foundation Voyager was different than almost every other generation ship that was built before; she was funded entirely by the private wealth of its Founder. Most generation ships had been funded by birthright sale. The creation of a generation ship meant the creation of a certain number of new birthrights, which were sold on the birthright market to the millions of buyers who would rather have a child condemned to life on a generation ship than not have that child at all.

"And though it may not be clear to us all yet what form that greatness may take or where the road ahead will lead," Ryland continued, as if to deny some great crime.

He then took a moment of pause to look out at the audience. He smiled as the response came back to him in a powerful roar from the crowd. He then knew they were ready, his children, all picked in ways only he could understand from millions of candidates for reasons they themselves did not know, would succeed in their task.

"We will drive forward," he went on, "just as Columbus knew not when he would find land or even what land he would find and Armstrong knew not if his ship would disappear into the dust of the moon, we know our own mystery awaits us but we will drive on.   Just as Collins did not know if his colony would perish in the depths of space or survive man's first journey across the void. We will maintain faith in our mission and reach our goals."

And so the speech continued, rising and falling like a great symphony, speaking of challenges that lay ahead and the faith that they must always have that their purpose is good and their cause noble, that their colony would be something special. As the speech drew to a close the entire colony knew clearly that a new destiny awaited them but what that was they did not know and with two last words the journey began.

"Destiny awaits," concluded Dr. Ryland.

With that an ancient artifact of a glass bottle filled with a beverage bottled over fifteen years ago, was projected toward the head of Foundation Voyager. In a moment of silence it drifted across the space between the station and the ship and suddenly in a burst of light was smashed into smithereens by the ship's energy beam shield, each successive piece again being smashed in a brilliant flower of light till not one single particle of the bottle lay in the path of the great traveler.

It would normally have been thought foolish for such a large group of people to have so blindly followed one man. It was Dr. Ryland's life to that point, however, that had made his following a reality. He was one of only six survivors of the Saturn Four tragedy, a baby of six months of age drifting alone in space in an escape pod with a broken signal beacon. His life raft was ignored by the rescue ships, considered debris from the accident. He wasn't picked up until four months later, after auto sedation by the escape pod's life support system. Found in a billion to one chance it would come into the path of a materials freighter bound for Earth, it was almost vaporized in routine path clearance. Only the chance scan by an astronomy student passenger, warned the captain of the true nature of the debris. The young Ryland was brought onboard and nursed back to health. From that moment forward he became known as the miracle baby.

And Ryland lived up to his promise. He captivated the world with his brilliance breaking academic record after record during his childhood. At an early age he took an interest in the

failed science of Artificial Intelligence, a field that for almost
fifteen hundred years had been unable to deliver on its promise
of a truly thinking machine. Yes, computational science had
done astounding things for Mankind. It had made possible a
society where machines could do almost everything. The only
remaining challenge for Mankind in the thirty sixth century
was fighting boredom. Most humans indulged in some form
or other of artistic expression to fulfill their life, giving to each
other the one thing that computers had yet to provide: Human
creativity. Even politicians and judges, roles still reserved
for humans, were mostly judged by their artistic ability as a
measure of their intellect and as merit for their jobs.

Ryland was one of the few that chose a different path. He had
spent his life learning about computer systems and the variety
of ways the technology could be applied. His breakthroughs
had created the Advisors, systems capable of providing not
only analyzing data but also bringing information together
to determine its effect on the bigger picture. Politicians and
leaders now were able to see much of the results of their decisions
before making them and extremely large and complex problems
could be addressed with some foresight. As a consequence
of his work the company he had built, the Ryland Computer
Research Foundation as it was originally known but later
was referred to simply as The Foundation, had accumulated
unimaginable wealth and he became the most influencual man
of his time. But yet with all his power and wealth, Dr. Ryland
still had been restricted from achieving his most ambitious
goal and had come to see the Unified Government he had
helped so much, as an obstacle to his success and the laws
that he acknowledged were for the greater good of Mankind as
unacceptable constraints to his research.

And though none of them could speak of the possibilities
that lay ahead the children of Foundation Voyager had been
chosen based on the likelihood that they would become willing
participants in his cause.

An umbilical cord connected Foundation Voyager to
Foundation Station and now the colonists began to move down
the corridor toward the ship. Dr. Ryland led the way and
stepped on the ship without further ceremony. The colonists
followed behind branching out into the various colony stars

they would call home for the remainder of their life. Dr. Ryland let Captain Jenkins take the lead in front of him and they both headed for the control area of the ship as the other members of the crew joined him. To still call them a crew was almost a misnomer on this ship, they were little more than observers to its complex operation. They would merely give human approval to the committee of Advisor systems that would determine the fate of the ship.

As the crew settled into the control area and Dr. Ryland sat in one of the observation seats, he turned to Captain Jenkins and asked, "are we ready Tom?"

A little startled again by Ryland's eagerness to get underway the captain replied, "Yes Frank everything's set," then paused, "would you like to give the command?"

"No Tom, the pleasure is yours," Frank replied.

"Very well Frank," the captain replied and turned to the control console. "Advisor One you are authorized to proceed with launch."

The ship responded in a formal but pleasant tone, "thank you Sir, launch sequence initiated."

And with that preceded a series of steps that would lead to the ship's departure. First the linear reactors were brought on line each phase coming to life and producing the vital elements needed to drive the next. Fusion reaction followed fusion reaction then the fission phases began to engage and finally the particle reservoir began to fill. One by one all three reactors were brought on line and brought to full power. Finally the main accelerator engaged. Everything was timed to coincide with the ship's orbit of Jupiter so her orbital momentum, which had been carefully aligned with her pathway to the stars, was preserved and built upon. As the drive engaged, the system would push her into a wider orbit of the planet eventually breaking her free from the massive gravitational pull of the gaseous mass.

The acceleration of the ship was almost imperceptible. It would take over seven minutes for her to accelerate her mass by a mere sixty miles per hour. It was not the rate of acceleration but the duration of the burn that would take Foundation Voyager to her awesome final velocity. Her engines would burn without pause for twenty-five years.

Chapter 4

Dark Shadow

3520
Omega Theta
Over Fifty Light-years from Earth

Commander Rodriguez reached out with his finger and touched the letters engraved into the wall. The inscription read:

Dr. Chin Tzu 3393-3518

The Hall of Remembrance, as it was known, was the one place in Omega Theta Two where all of those who had walked its corridor's were honored, if only by a few simple words. Dr Tzu had chosen to be remembered by very few words indeed.

"We live life for our children not our elders," he had said to his young comrade before his transition ceremony.

It had seemed like a strange statement at the time coming from a man who had never contributed to a Birthright. As Rodriguez reflected upon it though, he began to realize that Dr. Tzu had considered all the young scientists of Omega Theta as his children in a manner of speaking. Though he was often harsh to their other sensibilities he always nurtured their scientific thinking and the events of his last fifteen years had made Luis his most important student.

Their mission had seemed an almost impossible one, to defend their colony against the likelihood of attack by an enemy of unknown origin and immense power. They had worked closely together over the fifteen years after the discovery of the Intruders to plan the best defense they could for the day when the visitors would arrive. The result had been the sentinel system that Luis now commanded.

It consisted of an array of sensor devices that orbited Omega Theta's sun creating a bubble of awareness, inside which the four colony stars of the system orbited. These sensors were then backed up by another set of orbiting weapons stations that held beam generators that could be directed by the sensor beacons. The weapons stations also had drive systems allowing them to be sent to intercept incoming threats. Beyond this, additional weapons stations were docked to the colony stars themselves and capable of launching to attack any Intruder that passed through the outer defenses. Luis and Chin had been proud of their creation, especially given that it had been built with little help from the colony itself. Perhaps because they believed the threat would pass them by, perhaps because they believed it couldn't be stopped if it came, the council had chosen to only allocate ten percent of the colony's resources to their endeavor and far less staff. Bringing their fourth colony star online had been a much higher priority.

At its peak their team had reached thirty individuals, their roles being primarily monitoring and strategic decision-making. The tactical combat responsibility, if it ever became necessary, would fall completely on the shoulders of the distributed computer intelligence of the weapons stations. Each one, once launched, would become an independent system programmed to inflict maximum damage on its target.

Luis thought about his old friend and mentor, wondering if he'd be proud of how he'd lead the team these last two years. It had been a difficult time. Not only had he now been thrust into the position of being wholly responsible for the defense of his people but he'd also had to do it during the time of greatest danger. The original estimated date of arrival had passed just two years earlier. That had been a tense time indeed. Every single electro magnetic anomaly and piece of oversized space dust that had been detected by the sensor system had sent them all into a state of alert, months went by where Rodriquez slept barely a wink. But now they had settled into a smooth routine and much of the team had even begun to believe that their services would never actually be required. So the commander didn't even raise an eyebrow when his moment of reflection was interrupted.

"We have a level two incident, Sir," a female's voice came over Luis' personal terminal.

"Very well," he responded. "I'll be up to take a look in a moment."

He walked into the command center and received a respectful nod from the first two defense officers in the room and was signaled over by a third in the second room, the female who had hailed him. Sandra Johnson was one of Luis' finest team members. He felt he'd learned as much from her as she had learned from him. That's probably the major reason he married her. They had been together for fifteen years now and had been honored with three Birthrights during their marriage but you never would have known from their professional interaction in the command center. Colonists were very used to separating their personal and professional lives. They had to, as they lived and worked in such close quarters.

"What do you have?" Rodriguez questioned as he stepped up to the console.

"Gravitational Anomaly," the Lieutenant replied. "Thirty-five minutes out and moving fast."

Luis knew his comrade was relaying distance information. The object that had been detected was thirty-five light-minutes from their present location. It was just entering their small solar system and was more than twenty-light minutes from their closest sensor beacon.

"Can you get an EM image?" he queried.

"Nothing Sir, I've been trying the whole spectrum." Then she paused, "wait what's this?"

The straight-line graphs on her screen suddenly spiked on almost all frequencies, then went flat again. Then a few seconds later, did the same thing again.

"Check for background sources," he instructed her, not wanting to get fooled by a distant pulsar sitting behind their target.

"Negative," she responded. "Black space background. I think we've got something here Luis," she said looking up at her husband.

"Let's take it slow Lieutenant," he replied. "We've been fooled before. Do you have mass and velocity from the gravitational readings yet."

"Yes.   Looks like she's about five million tons, moving about one eighth light speed and decelerating," she responded, resuming her professional tone.

"There she goes again," she blurted, as the electro magnetic readings spiked one more time.

This happened three more times in a row.

"I'll alert the council," Rodriguez responded calmly. "Keep tracking her."

With that he stepped away from the console, while Sandra continued to track the mysterious visitor.

"Come on, who are you?" she questioned to herself, still unable to get any continuous image reading.

As Rodriguez re-entered the room, she had collected enough data to determine the object's track through their system and was surprised by what she saw.

"It's heading straight for our sun," she informed her commander as he calmly placed his hand upon her shoulder in an effort to calm her nerves.   "ETA six hours and thirteen minutes, if she maintains present course."

"How close will she come to us?" Luis questioned, pulling up a chair next to her.

"She'll pass about six light-minutes out from us on her way in.   And she'll be about three million miles from the closest sensor beacon, the same one that's tracking her now," she paused and turned to him. "What did they say?" she asked, changing the subject.

"They don't want to push any panic buttons yet," he responded. "We still have no idea what the hell this thing is."

She turned back to the console and they resumed their work. The object continued to close in on the sensor probe and periodically at seemingly random intervals released another burst of electro magnetic energy then went quiet again. This continued for several hours, as they counted up to twelve of the events. An analysis of the surges showed each of them varied slightly in intensity.   The object drew closer to the sensor beacon and still no image could be found anywhere in the spectrum. The sensor continued to track the object as it moved across the solar system.

"My God," uttered Sandra suddenly breaking the silence.

"What!" responded Luis, a little shaken by her sudden outburst.

"Check the Visual," she instructed and with that Rodriguez looked to the left screen, as Sandra replayed the last few seconds of imagery. Luis could hardly believe what he saw. The object had passed an area of view covered by a few bright stars and it was as if a shadow, a great dark and silent shadow, had passed before them. He quickly went back to the scanners and replayed the same time period, nothing, not the slightest reflection. They were staring at five million tons of invisibleness streaking toward their sun at over fifteen thousand miles per second. They sat in silence and watched as the object tracked across the sun, revealing its shape clearly in the monitor, a long thin black elliptical form moving silently across the face of their sun and soon disappearing into the sun's mass. As mysteriously as it came the target was lost. Its mass merged with that of the sun, making it impossible to detect by itself. Even the image of the strange shadow disappeared as the outer shell of the sun swallowed it.

"It's gone," Sandra concluded.

"Monitor the sun carefully," Luis cautioned not wanting to get caught off guard.

The suspense didn't last long as the monitor flashed a new reading in front of them.

"New target," Sandra confirmed. "Much smaller and much closer."

Picked up by the same sensor that had traced their strange shadow through the system, the new anomaly was a little less than ten tons and only two thousand miles from the beacon. Like its bigger cousin it also lacked any visible image. Though Luis couldn't say why there was something about this new visitor that made him very nervous.

"Go to Battle Stations," he commanded. "Target new anomaly. Hold Fire till my command."

With that the weapons stations burst to life and began to accelerate toward the new signal. There were three weapons units in close proximity to the sensor beacon and each began to close in.

"Closest weapon station twenty-two thousand miles and closing," Sandra updated.

"Damn," she continued, "I've lost the sensor beacon."

"Engage enemy," Luis responded not waiting for confirmation of the source of the kill.

The weapons stations opened fire on the last known position of the target but their bright red energy beams just seemed to streak off into empty space. The sensor beacon was gone and the more distant attackers were not equipped to detect a gravity anomaly.

Leaving his assassins to do their job, Luis sat down at a neighboring terminal to confirm his fears.

"Show me last ten entries of sensor beacon's maintenance log," he instructed the terminal.

A dreaded sense of Déjà vu' filled his mind as the system responded. For a moment he felt himself in his old lab seventeen years ago. The sensor beacon had been killed with the same deadly accuracy as the ill-fated deep space exploration drone.

"Are we transmitting?" he questioned Lieutenant Johnson.

"Yes. Everything we're seeing is going on the beam," she replied.

The beam was their colony's only link with the rest of humanity, sending a very tight and focused transmission signal out across the void, over fifty light-years back to Earth. The beam carried every scrap of important data from their world back to their distant relatives on humanity's mother planet. They knew that Earth could do nothing to help them. It would be fifty years before they would even know what was happening and another fifty before they could give so much as advice in assistance. Nonetheless, to let the rest of humanity know what was happening on Omega Theta was critical. In the bottom of his heart Luis knew that their little colony might just be the first battlefield in a long war.

"Contact Chairman Rothman," Luis requested his terminal.

"Yes, Commander!" responded Rothman almost immediately.

"We are under attack sir. Request we go to alert status one," he informed the colony's leader.

"Very well Commander," Rothman responded and as Rodriguez was about to disconnect, the Chairman threw out one last comment. "Good luck Luis," he closed, as Luis hit the emergency alert switch.

Throughout the colony his defense team scurried and assisted the colony in preparations that had been rehearsed many times before.

"New target," Sandra warned before Luis barely had a moment to look back at his terminal.

"Same object reacquired?" he questioned.

"Negative," she responded, "about the same size but coming at us from a completely different angle."

Luis reached forward to his terminal's control pad and gave an instruction that could only be given by fingerprint recognition.

"Full attack mode activated," responded the terminal.

From that point forward all new unidentified targets would be considered hostile and attacked. The pace of events quickened. New targets began to emerge on every front, closing in on their sensor array from every angle. One by one the sensor beacons were cut to pieces. The weapons stations closed in and tried to acquire their targets with what data was available to them but as the sensor array collapsed they were able to do little more than shoot blindly in the general direction of their targets. Every once in a while, it seemed they registered a hit on their monitors but the evidence of any real success was fleeting. Soon the weapons stations themselves came under fire from the attackers. Then the darkest revelation yet revealed itself.

From the edge of their sun a new target emerged but its familiar elliptical shadow against the background of the sun showed its true nature. This was the ship they had tracked into the sun before the attack began. Though they couldn't believe what they were seeing, the data was clear. This ship, this long dark destroyer, had not crashed into their sun but had merely skimmed around its outer shell using its huge gravitation field to reverse its direction and streak out of their system from the same direction it had entered. Anything manmade would have melted in the heat of the star but this thing came out like it had just taken a bath.

The picture was now clear to Luis. This great dark monster was some kind of carrier ship. Transporting a deadly cargo of smaller and even harder to detect attackers of some form.

Their shape and nature was yet to be revealed. The flashes of energy they had detected had been the ejections of these killers, decelerating them to a velocity that allowed them to take up station within the system. They had then set about the task of destroying any evidence of technology they could find. It was almost as if Omega Theta was some kind of infestation being exterminated.

"Prepare to initiate emergency procedure Delta," Luis solemnly instructed his team through his terminal.

He sat down beside Sandra and let go of his command role.

"Go take care of the children," he instructed her.

She leaned forward to him and kissed him gently on the lips as a tear welled up in her eyes. He reached up and caressed her cheek and then reiterated his request.

"Go," he said, almost in a whisper.

He turned to the terminal as she stood from her chair and left the command center.

"Chairman Rothman," he beckoned the terminal. The Chairman's face appeared on the screen.

"I'm sorry Sir, there's not much hope," he informed his leader resolutely.

He had to admire the strength of the response.

"Damn good try Luis. Damn good."

The terminal screen went back to the tactical display but then suddenly flashed and sparked and went dead. At almost the same moment a brilliant white beam cut across the room and sliced across his arm in the process. The smell of burnt flesh suddenly filled the room. Luis fell to the floor clinging his arm, then reached up and hit a large red button on the side of the command center. With that, the entire colony star shut down. All systems were brought to a halt and all power taken offline. The room went dark.

Luis lay in the darkness for a moment. Listening carefully, listening for any indication of further impacts on the colony star. There was nothing, only silence and the hissing and spitting of the console as it smoldered. It had worked. At least it seemed.

For just a moment he reflected on his old friend and how after tireless hours in their lab pouring over the data from the ill-fated exploration drone, they had noted something about its demise. The force that had destroyed it had particularly targeted its technology systems. Any and all components of the system that used or transmitted power had been destroyed with surgical precision. This had led them to create the final defense protocol of the colony star, turn everything off, everything.

Unfortunately the colony stars of Omega Theta simply weren't designed to operate without power They needed power to drive all the recycling systems that kept everyone on board alive. The first problem would be Carbon Dioxide. Deadly quantities of this simple gas would fill the entire colony within hours. The colonists had been equipped with simple breathers but these would only buy them a couple more hours. The population of Omega Theta was, without power, doomed.

Luis Rodriguez had to put the time he had left to good use. He slowly stood up and reached for a panel on the wall. He fumbled around in the dark to open it and found what he was looking for, a chemical light stick. He squeezed the stick and it lit up casting red light across the room. Next he reached into the cabinet and pulled out the medical supplies. He squirted a treatment gel all over his arm and rubbed it in. The green liquid provided a combination of pain relief, disinfection and healing stimulant to the injured area. It would be enough to keep him going for what he had to do next. He then, quickly wrapped the wound and made his way out of the room. The hallway was eerie in the red glow of the light stick. Black lines scarred the hallways where the Intruder's beams had cut through the structure of the colony. A hissing sound told him that the colony star was loosing atmospheric pressure. He tried to hurry his pace down the hallway to some long cabinets. He opened them and donned the pressure suit that hung loosely inside. The suit had been specially modified to use no power elements. It relied on old-fashioned screw-on seals to maintain its pressure. A canister of nitrogen oxygen mixture was attached to the suit. Unfortunately powered breath recycling would not be option. He donned the suit and checked its valves.

He then slowly made his way down the rest of the hall to an airlock chamber and broke the seal on the inner door. Once inside he checked his suit one more time and then released the seal on the outer door. As the air pressure in the chamber dropped and the vacuum of space filled the room, he turned to a large metal box that had been attached to the inside wall of the airlock. An identical box had been fixed in every airlock on the colony and Luis had already carefully rehearsed what to do. He opened the front panel of the box and found in front of him was a crude looking device about the same size as his air tanks and similar in shape. On the outside of the canister was the distinct and ancient symbol that indicated the contents of the container were radioactive. He pulled a cord that extended crudely from the top and then began to count. He then took hold of a small data disk that was attached to the inside wall of the box and closed the box again. He knew that he had approximately three minutes to complete the rest of his mission. He remembered how Dr. Tzu had cautioned him that the crude chemical timers they had created would not be exact. He reached outside of the structure of the colony star and exited onto the outer wall of the rotating drum. The next part of his journey would be the hardest. He had to climb slowly on rungs that had been built especially for this purpose to the inner opening of the structure. The artificial gravity rotation of the colony star was pushing him away from his destination and it was difficult to climb in the suit especially with his wounded arm but he made it to the top of the makeshift ladder. He heaved his weight onto the top of the structure and sighed. He was now standing on roof of the colony star, on its inner circumference, above him was the opposite side of the drum-shaped structure and the rotation of the whole thing kept him stuck where he was. He slowly began to walk to the far end of the colony star and stopped at a large transmitter dish that had been fixed to the structure. He opened up a panel on the side of the dish and inserted the data disk he had collected earlier. He leaned forward and looked through an optical sighting device that was attached to the dish. He remembered how Dr. Tzu had trained him to point the dish the right way without the assistance of powered aiming. Once the dish was pointing the way he wanted he sighed and activated the device.

"I just hope someone's listening," he said to himself, as he brought the transmitter to power.

"Come on, come on," he gestured as he waited for the indication his message had been sent.

He sighed as a small light on the device flickered from yellow to green. Then looked up and gasped. It was as if a hole had opened up in space at the far end of the colony and all the stars had been sucked into it. But he knew it was his invisible enemy come to shut down his little radio station. The ominous black orb was floating perhaps a hundred feet from him.

"Too late," he smirked, as the cutting white beam of the attacker shot straight through his abdomen on its way to its target.

The power unit of the dish turned to a cascade of sparks and flying metal as the signal was silenced. As Luis Rodriguez gasped his last breaths he hoped that he was not the only one who was going to be silenced. His last thoughts were of Sandra and his children, hoping she had been able to bring them some comfort before the end.

Luis would never know if the blast that killed him had harmed his enemy, or if his last message would be heard by anyone, far away, in the cradle of humanity, on Earth.

Chapter 5

Last Breath

3537
Foundation Voyager
Deep Space, two light-years from Earth

Jenkins sat across from Ryland in his suite and looked at the man he had come to admire more than he believed he ever could, pleading with him not to proceed.

"I beg of you Frank, not yet, you have so much left to give the colony," he stressed.

"Don't you see Tom, it's essential that the experiment move forward while I'm still relatively young and healthy? I must have all my faculties when I do this. I'm already one hundred and thirty-two years old and we are not going to get any more ready," Frank replied.

Jenkins couldn't argue with him. He really had only a cursory understanding of all the science involved in the great journey on which Dr. Ryland was about to embark but he wasn't going to give in that easy. In his desire to convince his mentor not to move forward he began to reflect back over the accomplishments of Foundation Voyager since its departure from Jupiter over twenty-five years earlier.

First, the ship itself, she had performed flawlessly and had turned out to be the true marvel of science that everyone had hoped she would be. She was now moving through space at peak velocity, her main drive system shut down and placed into dormancy to be awakened in two hundred and fifty years, when the ships deceleration would begin. She was now drifting freely through space faster than any manmade object had ever traveled before.

Foundation Voyager's children were also doing well. Life on a generation ship was still difficult even after one thousand years of colonization. The basic equation was still that if large amounts of mass were to be devoted to supporting living beings, those living beings couldn't just be cargo. So colonist had roles to perform on the ship, roles that on Earth would have been performed by robots. Redundant mass was avoided. So everyone had a job to do. Keeping the ship's recycling and food chain systems intact, replacing components as needed and sending old pieces to the workshops for refit were all tasks performed by the colonists. Everything flowed in an endless circle. Both organic and technological, everything was recycled. But despite these challenges the colony was strong and optimistic. They felt a sense of worth in their mission. Their population had swelled to its maximum of thirty-five thousand and there was now a six-month waiting list for new Birthrights. Maintaining a stable population was a key sign of health for a generation ship and this lady was bursting at the seams with bouncing baby colonists.

Also, the ship's true mission was still very much a secret to most of her population but some significant clues had already revealed themselves. The first was political. Relatively early in her journey, shortly after her Council had entered into their second term, an interesting debate had been brought before the Council, a debate that hadn't seen the light of day on Earth in almost a thousand years. The validity of the Biotech Laws had been brought up for challenge. Like any generation ship, Foundation Voyager was ruled by the Constitution of the Unified Government but she could challenge that law where it was deemed her own survival was at stake and the required changes would not threaten Mankind as a whole. Anywhere else in the realm of man, these most sacred of man's laws would not have even come up for casual discussion let alone be challenged in Council but Foundation Voyager was unique in this way. Ryland himself had made sure of that. He knew his colony would have to be progressive and his selection process had ensured that would be the case. A challenge to the Biotech Laws was a key step on the path he had defined for Foundation Voyager.

The Biotech Laws had existed since the end of Great Wars that had taken place on Earth in the late twenty-fifth century. They had been the answer to one of man's greatest questions. 'Should humans who wish to enhance their physical bodies through integration with technology be allowed to do so?' This was a question that had first arisen when the science of nerve integration had been perfected over two hundred years earlier in the late twenty-second century; as a result almost all human disability had been permanently removed. The creation of a replacement leg, arm or even an eye had been simply a matter of manufacturing a sophisticated technological equivalent and integrating it with the patient. People were left better than normal in many ways.

The problem for human society began to emerge when able-bodied humans began to use the technology to improve their own bodies and the improvements themselves began to include integration with powerful systems. Citizens involved in difficult and dangerous roles would elect to have their natural body parts removed and replaced with superior biotechnical replacements. Security forces in particular became a mixture of robot and human. Eventually two classes of humankind evolved. The first, known as the natural humans, made up the vast majority of the planet's population but a growing number of enhanced humans made up the second group. Due to their common traits of biotechnical enhancement they began to form their own separate culture.

Throughout all of Mankind's history differences between people had formed the root of conflict. Whether it was a difference in the color of one's skin or the God one worshipped, it seemed impossible to find a time when at least someone wasn't willing to go to great lengths or even sacrifice their own life in order to harm others they considered different. It was in the twenty-fourth century, after the greatest period of peace that humanity had ever known to that point that the greatest differences had emerged. People had now become physically different in drastic ways. Soldiers became an integrated component of the war machines they commanded. Pilots were part of their aircraft and sensors in their wings let them truly feel the wind, it was a life that natural humans couldn't even begin to grasp and like differences of the past, it caused conflict.

Natural humans began to react, though the enhanced humans had for the most part served Mankind well, saving lives, improving security and doing jobs that normal humans couldn't do and in many cases neither could independent technology. Perhaps it was an underlying jealousy that sparked the conflict or perhaps it was a desire to defend the value of our natural form. Whatever the reason, tensions grew until the population as a whole was forced to take action. The first of the Biotech Laws were created restricting the level of direct integration between man and machine. But this new and strong culture of the enhanced humans wasn't willing to be the last of their kind and they fought back.

Two billion would die to determine the future of Mankind, whether we would become integrated with our machines, or forever separated from them. Though outnumbered over ten thousand to one the enhanced humans fought for over fifty years. They first took the entire world by surprise when they united and smashed the world's space based security grid and then launched massive strikes against production and industry across the globe. Their goal was simple to separate their enemy from its technology, gain control over it and force natural man into submission. They came close to succeeding but were eventually defeated.

Once victorious, natural Mankind showed no mercy. Biotech culture was forever vanquished from humanity. Direct integration between man and machine was forever forbidden. Medical science was limited to only restoring the natural form of any human.

The Council of Foundation Voyager would be the first to challenge that law. The culture of the colony was one uniquely chosen for this task. They were picked because of their progressive views on the future of man, because they shared a sense, that man had somehow trapped himself in his past. None of them wanted the Great Wars to happen again but they wanted their colony to be unrestricted by the mistakes made before their time.

The specific aspects of the Biotech Laws that Ryland had challenged, dealt not with the physical integration of man and machine, but the mental integration. Certain aspects of the laws had dictated that machines could not be produced that mimicked the thought structures of man, or that recorded actually human memory. It was this wall that Ryland wanted to breakdown. During his development of the Advisor systems, he had experienced constant scrutiny of the government and seen applications of his technology that were not possible under their watchful eye. It was this experience that had led to the construction of Foundation Voyager.

Foundation's council had paid him back well. They had voted almost unanimously to amend the Biotech Laws such that machines could now use human thought patterns or store human memory if it permitted them to better serve Foundation Colony. These enhanced systems would also never be permitted to leave the colony and they would be kept a secret from Earth so as not to create trouble for the colony. These restrictions had no impact on Ryland's needs and the changes still laid the political groundwork for his continued research.

Over the next fifteen years, the major accomplishments of Foundation Voyager were very much a secret to most of the colony. In a secure lab in colony star five, Ryland assembled a team of brilliant scientists to resurrect a dead science. The team worked in two groups each dedicated to a specific piece of Ryland's plan. The neural capture team had made the most progress.

The goal of the neural capture team had been to devise a method for capturing the contents of the human neural system. To do this they had relied on nanite technology. Nanites were tiny machines built of organic materials, they were no bigger than an organic virus and capable of working within the body, even within human cells. This team had designed a nanite machine with an amazing capability. The Neural Interpreter, as it was known, was capable of entering a human nerve cell and recording its contents by passing the molecular code of the RNA and other important molecules it found, the very memories of that cell, out as electrical pulses. Once it had completed that task, it would then mutate into a second phase, one that allowed it to identify the linkages that neuron had with those around it. Its final act would be to devour the insides of the host cell and use its material to build new Neural Interpreters that would spread into the neighboring cells. The shell of the cell would be left behind as conductor of the data collected by its children that would forge ahead into the neural system of the host individual. The process would be repeated millions of times over and over again, feeding data back to thousands of entry points where the seed Interpreters had been placed. Eventually the entire contents of the human neural system, our very memories and feelings, would be captured and stored in a massive electronic data storage system.

Or so went the theory.

Of course, the problem was a simple one. The subject would be killed in the process. His nervous system itself would be eaten away from the inside.

Death was a certainty, life after death only a glimmer of hope on the distant horizon.

It was for this reason, that Dr. Ryland considered himself the only plausible subject for his experiment. Unwilling to take the life of another as part of the process and admittedly unwilling to let anyone share its possible future, Dr Ryland would walk this path alone. Many of his followers had volunteered but he had forced his research team to take an oath he would be the only subject of this great experiment until it was proven a complete success. On the day of the experiment Frank Ryland as his followers knew him would be no more.

And that day had now come.

For Captain Jenkins, however, this was to be the day he would loose his great friend and mentor.

"Let me walk you down," the captain solemnly requested of his friend.

"Of course Tom, we'll talk along the way," Ryland replied as they stood and left the suite.

They talked as they spoke, Tom pleading with Frank to rethink his options and live out the remaining years till his transition. His attempts were futile.

"Tom, you know that I'm counting on you after I'm gone," Ryland continued. "Foundation Colony is strong and Voyager is doing us all proud but this generation will need leadership when I'm gone. They must keep the faith. They must always know that their future is a great one and they," he paused and turned to face the captain, "we, must make our destination."

The captain had exhausted any argument he had against continuing and finally conceded to his dear friend.

"We will not fail you Sir," Jenkins responded.

Ryland wondered when the last time his good friend had called him that but forgave him the formality knowing to a lifelong deep space captain it was a term of endearment. Their conversation continued to lighter matters as they walked toward the lab, Ryland asking about the captain's wife and children. Tom let him know they would all miss him dearly. He had become like a wise old uncle to his entire family and he knew things would not be the same with him gone. Soon they reached the entrance to the lab shook hands and smiled at each other. Jenkins watched as Ryland entered the lab and closed the door, his heart pounding the way it does only when we are fighting to change the very reality of the moment in vain.

The demeanor of the lab staff was quite different. They had worked their whole life for this day and though they were going to loose their team leader they knew this was his desire and were supportive of him in that end. They were scientists and believed that their Founder was going on the greatest voyage of scientific discovery Mankind had yet taken.

"Are you ready Frank?" asked the leader of the team as Frank entered the room.

"Yes Francois, let's get started," Frank replied.

The entire team knew Frank preferred to dispense with any ceremony, so none had been planned.

Ryland simply took off his clothes and lay flat on the lab's operating table. Sensors were placed over his heart and lungs and a cover was pulled over him. He was given a tablet to swallow and began to feel sleepy almost immediately after taking the pill.

The procedure began.

The skull cap was removed by beams, carefully targeted to expose the upper area of the brain and one by one tiny needles were inserted into various areas of the exposed grey material. Each needle was a tiny hollow tube, with a Seed Neural Interpreter in one end, linked by bioelectrical cord to a tiny photoelectric repeater. This tiny device would send a signal down a thin transparent fiber that ran upward from the operating table into a computer interface that was built into the ceiling of the lab.

"Initiate signal test," the senior lab scientist, Francois Dubois, signaled.

"Signal test initiated," a polite computer voice responded from above, there was a pause and then an update, "test successful."

"Plant Seed Interpreters," Francois continued deliberately.

"Planted," the computer responded.

And with that the experiment began. The needles all moved forward slightly into the brain and released their deadly cargo. The tissue around each needle began to turn from grey to white, as the Interpreters did their work and replicated throughout the brain.

A monitor on the wall indicated a rise in Ryland's heart rate and an instruction was given.

"Stabilize subject," Dubois instructed.

With that the system issued a signal to the tiny pill that had now lodged itself into the stomach wall with a needle that penetrated directly into Ryland's heart. Further sedative was injected into his system and his heart rate stabilized. The experiment continued for over two hours. Periodically the body would become slightly unstable and further measures would be taken.

Eventually the full contents of the brain had been absorbed and Frank Ryland was a mindless body, still functioning but with no thoughts or memories.

Fighting back the emotion of the moment that overcame his scientific sensibilities, Dubois stuttered as he issued the last instruction.

"Terminate subject," he solemnly requested.

The room seemed to freeze as Ryland's body jolted slightly then sighed its last breath.

"Data file name?" interrupted the system.

Dubois knew of only one response.

"The Founder," he replied.

Chapter 6

War Council

3570
Earth

Joanne Foresythe couldn't believe her luck. She sat as still as she could on the moss covered rock, watching the scene unfold before her, trying not to make a whisper. She watched the female move slowly between the saplings, barely making a sound. The skilled hunter didn't take her eyes off the prey for a second as she navigated through the maze of small trunks and exposed rocks. Further up the hillside, to Joanne's right, the younger male was closing the escape route. Joanne was astounded by the teamwork displayed before her. It was a beautiful scene. She reflected on how it had played itself out time and time again, on these rocky hills, over the last few thousand years, with only a few recent interruptions.

The North American Timber Wolf had been a native of this region for thousands of years until its extinction from the area in the very early twentieth century. Its prey, a young female white tailed deer that had straggled from a group of larger does, had been more successful. It had been an inhabitant of this region, living side by side with man, until its obliteration, along with almost all life in the area, in a single and horrible moment in 2496, a moment that also saw the loss of over forty million human lives. But now, over a thousand years later, nature had worked her miracle and restored the area to much the way it had been before man's disruptive influence. Left undisturbed and with a little assistance in the reintroduction of her dominant natural predators, the western edge New York Area Wildlife and Historical Preserve had become a pristine paradise for addicted hikers like Joanne.

Though she had been watching the moment build for quite some time now, she couldn't help but be slightly startled when the two wolves suddenly charged their prey. Within moments the doe was boxed in. She turned and kicked at her attackers but her struggle was short. Within seconds the female had sank her teeth into the doe's hind quarters and brought her down. Almost before the deer hit the ground, three nearly grown pups emerged from the undergrowth and began to taunt the fatally wounded animal. Old enough to follow on the hunt but not quite strong enough to make the kill, the youngsters had been hiding, waiting to feel safe enough to come out and learn from their older kin.

For a less experienced nature enthusiast observing a moment like this might have been intimidating but to Joanne it was pure rapture. She knew that she was in absolutely no danger. First the wolves, had they spotted her, would have been more afraid of her than she was of them. Secondly had they threatened her in any way, a quick tap on the pendant around her neck would have released a hypersonic burst that would have sent the animals fleeing. Joanne knew the reality of the moment. The most dangerous predator on this hillside was the observer.

Again the moment was disrupted but this time by a subtle vibration from her pendant. Joanne tapped the device in response. Immediately, the velvety ball uncurled, sprouting tiny monkey like hands and a tiny but friendly robotic face. The little companion quietly crawled up Joanne's shoulder and wrapped itself around her ear. Joanne's robotic personal companion had always been an invaluable tool, but she wasn't pleased to hear from it right now.

"Sorry Jo, but I've been asked to prepare for immediate return to active status. An Aero shuttle is inbound to your position to provide transport to central command," the tiny friend whispered in her ear.

Joanne couldn't believe her long planned hiking vacation was being interrupted and was certain it was someone's idea of a bad joke to schedule a drill while she was on leave. She stood, revealing her position to the wolves below. Both the adults turned to face her and snarled, the younger ones taking cover behind them. Joanne was not stirred for one moment.

"I'm sorry my friends but I have to go," she said to the wolves, as a whirring sound emerged and quickly began to grow louder by the moment. The wolves were startled and confused by this new visitor that came from above and scattered from the area, leaving their prey unfinished between the trees. Joanne sighed and looked up to see the shuttle approaching.

The triangular shape of the shuttle descended into a clearing about twenty-five yards away from Joanne. As it came down, she could clearly make out the downward air-stream of the three control turbines located one in each corner of the craft. Each of the rapidly spinning devices sent out jets of air, on which the craft hovered about ten feet above the ground. It held its position steady as three supporting legs extended down and made contact. Once the padded feet of the support structures reached the ground, the turbines slowly wound down. When the whirring was gone, the passenger pod, a mostly transparent spherical structure, about eight feet in diameter, lowered to the ground from the center of the craft. A sliding door opened beckoning Joanne to enter the pod. As she did, the door closed.

"Simon, put the shuttle on manual," Joanne instructed her personal and omnipresent Advisor.

Like all of her associates Joanne was assigned an Advisor. The highly sophisticated Artificial Intelligence system was not actually on board her shuttle. It resided deep within the bowls of central command and at various other redundant locations but through the sophisticated communications system that Joanne was linked into, Simon was available to her anywhere she went and was able to control most things around her.

"Will do Jo," Simon responded, "was your vacation enjoyable?"

"I'm going to pretend it's not over," Joanne smirked back.

Simon's sophisticated human interaction capabilities, tuned to Joanne's personality, took that as a clear signal to give its master control of the craft and solitude. A small soft panel popped out from the side arm of the seat and changed form to create an impression perfectly shaped for Joanne's hand. She placed her hand on the panel and with slight adjustments of the pressure in her fingers was able to maneuver the shuttle easily. The transparent passenger pod of gave Joanne an almost three hundred and sixty degree view above and below her as she gave the turbines power and lifted out of the woods.

As she came over the crest of the hill where she had spent the morning hiking, the river where she had canoed the day before came into view. She scanned the shoreline and quickly located her canoe and tent still sitting on the sandy banks of the river.

The Delaware River had flowed through these hills for millions of years and had recently served to create borders between various provinces and states of man's society. Now it served as the Western Border of the Preserve. Looking west Joanne could see the glittering domes and towers of the Pocono Mountain residential zone, the place that Joanne called home, nestled amongst the hills and trees. Directly below, she could now see the Gap, one of nature's many wonderful creations. The Gap was a place where it seemed the river had just decided to say "no" the natural order of how rivers were supposed to flow. It suddenly and drastically cut right through the hill line as if it had decided to take a short cut to the sea. Joanne promised herself she would be back as soon as possible.

She turned the craft East and headed out across the Preserve. She was pleased that the decision had been made to keep the area pristine after its environmental rehabilitation. Over a thousand years later, it still served as a reminder of the terrible price man had paid for his failures.

Below her she could barely make out the remnants of one of the great transport lines that fed the great metropolis of New York. The transport tubes that once carried millions of people each day at hundreds of miles per hour to and from all the incredible structures of the region. Like Rome, New York had symbolized the pinnacle of era. From the mid twentieth century until that terrible day over five hundred years later she had served as the financial and cultural center of the world. During that period, she had been attacked many times but always recovered and regained her stature. Now ahead on the horizon Joanne could see the great obelisk that preserved her place in history. It rose like a needle directly out of the almost perfectly circular harbor that was once Manhattan Island but was now a massive water-filled impact crater.   The obelisk rose ten thousand feet from the surface of the water and to this day was the tallest manmade structure on the planet. Constructed of the structural crystal that was first invented around the time of the city's demise, she stood as a symbol of the loss Mankind had suffered and a reminder of the need for constant vigilance. Though technology was available to build structures of almost limitless size, it had been mandated by law that nothing on Earth's surface could exceed the obelisk's height.

Joanne was approaching the great structure from the West, as the sun was dropping behind her. The light of setting sun was creating cascades of rainbow colors reflecting off the surface of the brilliant structure. It was a sight that stirred the soul. Joanne thought for a moment how lucky she was to have lived a thousand years after the creation of this hallowed structure and the terrible destruction that its construction marked the end of. In contrast, her time was one of strength, peace and prosperity.

As she passed over the marvel and began heading out over Long Island and the Atlantic she sighed and accepted the task at hand.

"Ok Simon, what's this all about?" she queered turning over control of the shuttle to her Advisor.

"I'm afraid that data has not been authorized for transmission over the net," Simon responded. "But don't worry Jo, I'll get you to central as soon as I can so you can get all the details," he responded, programmed to ease tense nerves.

"Don't give me that crap Simon," she fired back. "Under what authorization is data being withheld, is this someone's idea of a bad joke?"

"I wish I could say it was," replied Simon, still trying to sooth his master's nerves. "But as you know, only a security threat level Alpha can cause data to be withheld from communication over a secure net connection."

Joanne knew very well what Simon was implying, a possible extinction level threat had been assessed and she was being called to duty to help with the analysis and planning of a response. That being the case, she wasn't going to let security procedures stop her from going to work.

"Anything else worth noting?" she questioned Simon.

"No, not yet," he replied, not having to tell her that in response to her question Simon had performed a myriad of observations regarding activity across the globe. He had listened in to any live entertainment and information events for tones of stress in the voices of the performers and announcers. He had checked the weather net, the military alert status and even scanned for geo-thermal or astronomical anomalies. He knew to look for anything that might relate to a global security issue that Joanne might be interested in.

"Keep looking Simon and give me an ETA to central," she continued.

"One hour and sixteen minutes," Simon responded and left her alone.

The shuttle climbed higher into the atmosphere as the towers of New Boston faded into the distance to her left. Out beyond the shoreline, she could just make out the glistening pinnacles of Atlantis reaching out of the ocean and remembered for a moment her childhood vacations on this manmade paradise.

Though one of the Planet's favorite recreation sites, the primary purpose of this amazing structure was more fundamental. Atlantis was perhaps the most famous of the hundreds of oceanic energy farms on Earth. Hidden away in the columns that soared out of the water and into the sky sat her massive generator turbines, quietly and harmoniously converting the energy of the oceans into the power that drove man's world. Even the energy that now powered Joanne into the sky originated in Atlantis or one of her many sister cities. It was an irony of man's technology that though powerful nuclear forces took us to the stars, the simple swell of the ocean turned out to be most suited to fulfill our needs at home. Free from radiation, chemical or thermal pollution these stations simply diverted the planet's natural energy to our needs for a while, until, like the downward wind that Joanne's shuttle generated, it was given back to the environment.

As her altitude and speed increased she felt a slight pop as she exceeded the speed of sound and headed for the upper atmosphere. She looked up through the transparent ceiling of the craft and stared up at the stars above her with a view far clearer than the highest mountains below.

"I think I may have found something," Simon interrupted.

"What is it?" she queered hoping for some valuable information.

"Omega Theta," Simon responded. "It appears that public release of the incoming beam is being simulated."

"And how long do they think that will work?" she questioned.

"It's likely the free media will pick up on the problem within a few hours when they correlate their beam data to the release version. Then they'll start asking questions," he replied.

Since its inception, the primary mandate of the Unified Government had been the security of Mankind and though the public now enjoyed freedoms far beyond those known in any previous time, it was still sometimes deemed necessary to deceive them for their own good. It was a privilege that the government rarely used. It was also a privilege that was difficult to utilize. The free media watched the government, much like the wolves that Joanne had followed that morning watched their prey. Even the slightest slip in adherence to their mandate was reprimanded harshly. Having reached the consensus after the Great Wars, that nations and individuals could no longer be trusted to possess the instruments of massive violence that had wrecked the planet, information was the only weapon left to keep humanity free from oppression and the people of planet Earth used that weapon without hesitation. It was for this reason that Joanne knew the information that had come from Omega Theta must be of the most serious and threatening nature.

"Can you tell me how long the data stream has been simulated?" she asked Simon.

"I can detect aberrations in the data that appear to indicate the signal has been one hundred percent simulated for approximately two hours. There also appear to be intermittent aberrations going back for seventeen years."

Joanne had only been signaled a little less than two hours ago. Whatever had happened, somebody in the Unified Government Security Services had been waiting for it and had hit the panic button in response. The Unified Government Security Services were all the Earth had left of the once plentiful military forces that spread across the globe and Joanne served in the civilian research and planning division of that organization. She thought through the types of scenarios she had reviewed in the past that would require this level of secrecy and only a few came to mind and only one of those could have affected a colony as distant as Omega Theta and be deemed a threat to Earth fifty light-years away.

"It couldn't be," she mumbled to herself. Suddenly feeling a strange sense of dread that she had never known.

"Ok, Simon," she instructed, "Give me everything you have on Omega Theta."

For the remainder of her trip, her head was filled with data on Omega Theta and the system it resided in. She learned of the colony's launch over nine hundred years ago, as one of the last of the Omega series of generation ships and its arrival at its host star six hundred years later. To this day the colony held the record for the longest generational journey. The ship had suffered tremendously during her trip, loosing two of her five original colony stars to debris impact and running dangerously low on critical trace elements during the voyage. The total population of the mission had been reduced to the less than five hundred when she arrived at her destination. The first two centuries of her existence in her new host system had been spent searching for the required materials to secure her population and begin growth. She had finally been successful in that endeavor and began a recovery. She had just celebrated the completion of her fourth functional colony star and her population had stabilized at over one thousand, when her signal had stopped. Simon searched for some evidence of the exact nature of the failure but could find none. Whoever had been covering this up had been doing a good job. But a completely simulated signal would be impossible to hide for long.

She was so engrossed in the details of this tiny outpost that the scene unfolding before her did not catch her attention. The shuttle sank from its high cruising altitude and began to head back toward Earth. Ahead in the distance the lights scattered about the slopes enabled Joanne to make out the shape of the mountains getting closer as she descended. Dwarfing the rocky hillsides where she had hiked that morning, the Swiss Alps stood majestically pronouncing the power of nature and seemed to come rushing up to her as her craft descended rapidly into their cradle. It almost seemed that she would crash into the side of one of the rocky giants but quite suddenly the rock face opened and revealed a hangar within. Her craft slowed and came to a rest in the hangar. But Joanne did not get up or even pause in her conversation with Simon.

There was a slight jolt as the entire passenger pod of the shuttle dropped from its triangular carrier that had brought it halfway across the planet. As it slid down toward the floor of the hangar, an opening in the floor emerged and the pod was dropped in. The ceiling closed again above and the pod began to move forward. The lights on the sides of the transport tube soon made it clear the pod was now accelerating down into the depths of the mountainside. At any other time, Joanne might have taken a moment to reflect upon the thousand years that these tunnels had served the Unified Government protecting one of their many command centers but for now she was too busy to notice.

Finally the pod slowed and came to a halt. The door of the pod slid up and Joanne stepped out. An older man stood in the hallway and greeted Joanne.

"Glad you could make it Jo," the older gentleman smiled.

"Speak for yourself," Joanne responded. "Now tell me what happened to Omega Theta Jack."

"I can see that Simon's been taking good care of you," Jack replied, "you'd better come with me, we have a council session scheduled in ten minutes. You'll get everything there."

Jack Thompson, who greatly respected his younger associate and admired how she'd escalated herself to the Section-two council at such a young age, was probably next in line for the council's chair position. He was a key player in the group's decision-making process. Joanne's insights would be invaluable as he worked to tackle this new crisis.

Section-two was the organization within the Unified Government Security Services that dealt with what were referred to as external and natural threats, i.e., those that did not originate from within human society.

Within no time, Jack and Joanne were ushered into a large room with a large elliptical table in the center and twelve large high backed chairs evenly spaced around it. Joanne took a seat

and Jack took the next chair. The three other members of the
council already seated smiled and nodded to their associates as
they joined the group. The remaining members of the council
filed in and everyone quickly took a seat. A man perhaps a
little older than Jack, probably in his late one hundred and
thirties began calling the meeting to order.

"With all members of the Section-Two security council
present, I call this meeting to order. Jack why don't you give
us an update."

"Very well Joseph, thank you," Jack replied.

Jack began to tell the tail of what they had learned about
events on Omega Theta. He told of the colony's discovery
of the cause of their lost space probe and then continued to
describe the events that took place when the visitors arrived at
the colony seventeen years later. A three-dimensional viewing
screen showed images of the great dark shadowy ship depositing
it's deadly cargo and then displayed details of the destruction
of all the colony's power dependent systems in a systematic
manner. It demonstrated how the life giving technology of
the colony stars had been surgically disabled with incredible
precision. Finally the presentation closed with a pre-recorded
message that had been sent in Omega Theta's last moments.
The room remained quiet as the image of a young man from
Omega Theta appeared on the screen.

The message began.

"My name is Luis Rodriguez and I am the defense team
Commander of Omega Theta. If you are receiving this message,
then it is most likely that our colony has been destroyed and
we are all dead. I hope that in our last hours we were able
to learn a lot about our enemies that will be of value to you.
The most valuable lesson of all, however, might be found in the
very fact that you have received this message. Our analysis
of our enemy has led us to believe that they only attack our
technology. Biological human life is not, for whatever reason,
something they target. Perhaps they simply don't consider us a
threat or perhaps they have some other purpose in mind for us,
we don't know. Whatever the case, it is my intention to send
this message to you only after powering down all the systems
of our colony and successfully surviving long enough to prove
the truth of our theory. Unfortunately that information will be

of little value to us, despite numerous attempts we have been unable to find a way to keep our colony alive for more than a few hours without power but to you, however, this information could mean the difference between the survival and extinction of the human race. We hope you will remember Omega Theta and we wish you good luck in the struggle that lies ahead," the message ended.

"Let's all be very clear about our predicament," Joseph added. "Humanity has been attacked by an alien force of tremendous power and that same force could strike again, with little or no warning at any human colony, including Earth. We have been listening to and exploring the galaxy for fifteen hundred years now and nothing led us to expect a threat like this. For this reason, we find ourselves completely unprepared for our defense. Our job is to start preparing that defense."

A moment of silence hung over the room as everyone at the table digested the information. Joanne was the first to speak.

"I'm assuming that our initial priority will be managing the public message to minimize negative impact from panic effect?" she questioned.

"That's correct Jo." Joseph responded. "The president will be addressing the planet within thirty-five minutes. His speech was prepared for him previously as part of the response scenario for this event. We have already reviewed and updated the speech based on the latest information we have and latest data regarding probable public reaction. However, once that speech is made, management of public perception of this issue will be a top priority. It's somewhat ironic but right now the threat of the reaction outweighs the threat from our new enemies. I am, therefore, putting forward the motion that Jack continue to take charge of interface to the Government Media Management Committee and get back to that immediately. Any objections?"

They sat quietly for a moment.

"Good, that motion carries," he continued. "Jack anything you need from the council at this point."

"No, I believe the response scenario will carry us through the first critical hours. Beyond that I'll need information regarding the specifics of our action plan."

"Very well," Joseph responded. "Why don't you get to work and we'll keep you posted."

Jack stood, nodded and left the room. He smiled to Joanne as he turned to leave.

"Now, unfortunately the second item on our agenda is a little less prepared. That is how exactly we intend to stop these bastards. Should they pay us a visit," Joseph continued.

"Is there any further data indicating an attack on Earth or any other systems may be imminent?" Jo asked, hoping she already knew the answer.

"None at all," Joseph responded. "The ship that attacked Omega Theta left from the direction it entered the system, which takes it away from any other colonized system and we have received no other reports of any systems encountering difficulties. We also continue to receive no signal of intelligent extra human origin from any of our listening stations in human domain. Unfortunately, however, we don't know how long that means we have. They could arrive tomorrow or we may never hear from them again."

So began a long debate of the council regarding the best course of action to defend humanity from this new strange and unknown visitor. The group interacted with each other and with their Advisor systems to reach an initial consensus regarding their approach, stopping briefly to hear the president's speech. His words reminded them of the gravity of the situation.

The president began, "today we received the news that a far away outpost of Mankind was attacked and likely destroyed by a previously unknown and obviously intelligent force."

He continued on to speak well of the courageous people who worked at the edges of human civilization and had so suddenly and terribly been lost, then slowly turned to the questions of how the event would impact Mankind.

"Today our lives are forever changed," he stated and spoke of the need for all of humanity to join together to ensure our survival.

"May the future speak well of how we face this challenge," he concluded.

As the speech ended, the council turned back to their debate with even more vigor and began to assign individual responsibilities to areas of the plan. The plan would break down the defense of Earth into four different components. The last line of defense would depend on the information they had just received from Omega Theta and would explore how well Earth might be able to get by without power. The second component would focus on the fortification of Earth itself, this would consist of the construction of a large defensive array that would orbit the planet. A third piece would deal with the defense of the broader solar system and tho final and fourth piece would fall on Joanne's shoulders. That would be the development of an interstellar contingent that would take the war to the enemy and see what we could learn. Joanne's mind turned like a laser beam on the task at hand and began to explore the options.

As the meeting broke up, Joseph turned to Joanne and put his hand on her shoulder.

"I'd like you to meet someone," Joseph indicated as they walked back out into the hall.

The subject of their conversation began to approach them from the other way before Joseph's words left his lips.

"Pleasure to meet you 'mam'," the stern young man introduced himself without breaking a smile. He rendered a quick salute then reached his hand out and gave Joanne's a firm shake, "Lieutenant Stone, UGSS."

Stone looked like he was barely out of school but the determination in his eyes went far beyond his years.

"Top scores at the academy. He'll be a good start to your team," Joseph concluded as he smiled and left the two in the hallway.

Joanne almost laughed to herself. She had a Navy to build and so far she had only one sailor.

As she and Stone went to work, Joanne reflected back upon her four legged friends who stalked the hills across the river from her home. She wondered whom nature would choose to dominate Earth's future.

Chapter 7

Glimmer

3662
Foundation Voyager
Deep Space, over 25 light-years from Earth

It had been a very long day in the lab for Dr. John Carmichael and his neck was getting very stiff. He had worked three hours passed the end of his shift and was ready to call it quits but he just couldn't end another day without making any progress at all. He decided to run the sequence one more time and try to find the problem.

"Reinitiate sequence," he instructed the lab's computer interface.

"Reinitiating Sequence," the computer responded and followed with a series of updates on the progress of the experiment.

"Data file loaded," the voice continued. "Activating neural network."

The silence was agonizing for Carmichael. He had spent his entire life living on Foundation Voyager as a member of the Artificial Intelligence Operations team and had performed AI neural network loads countless times in his career but this was different. Since being assigned to the Founder Project he was no longer working on Advisor systems that were nothing more than complex distributed software solutions built to aid human activity. Now he was working on something much more. The data file he was loading was the memories and feelings of a human being and not just any human being but his entire world's benefactor, the one person who had made his very existence and the existence of everyone on this great ship possible. Through the greatest personal investment made by anyone in all of history, the Founder had made it possible for the thirty-two thousand souls, who now inhabited this graceful one hundred and fifty year-old lady, Foundation Voyager, to have a place within humanity. Carmichael's sense of obligation to this man, a man who had died eighty-five years before he was even born, was unflinching. Perhaps this deep sense of obligation was the root of the stress he felt over his recent failures.

Then came the disappointing update he'd heard so many times.

"Neural network activation failed," the lab's system concluded.

Dr. Carmichael sank his head and pushed his chair away from the console. After a slight pause he stood, stretched his back and turned to leave the lab. He walked down the colony star's main hallway somewhat oblivious to the activity around him. The evening time period was drawing to a close and several of the younger adults of the colony star were making their way down the main hall toward the entertainment area. On a less stressful evening, Dr. Carmichael might have noticed the giggling and the laughter of the couples flirting as they walked. He may have thought about his own courtship not so long ago but his mind was elsewhere today. He simply couldn't understand why he couldn't keep the network stable and he couldn't get the problem out of his mind.

It wasn't long before he arrived at his family's quarters. His head was still hanging when he walked through the door. Samantha greeted him, smiled and wrapped one arm around his waist. In the other she held an electronic notepad that had a colorful hand drawn image on the screen.

"Greta wanted to stay up and show you her drawing but she didn't make it," she said, nodding over to the little girl curled up on the couch in front of the family console.

He looked down and saw the vague but lively shape of a fish with every color of the rainbow scribbled into it somewhere. He sighed, realizing he'd managed to miss dinner and any chance to enjoy some time with his wife and little girl, yet again.

"I'm sorry. I'll put her to bed," he said to his wife, kissing her on the cheek.

He walked over to the five year old and snuck his arms under her as she slept. Once he had her in both arms he picked her up and cradled her to his chest. As he picked her up, he looked down at her soft white cheeks and curly red hair. He didn't know what he'd done to deserve such a thing of beauty in his life and felt terrible that he hadn't spent any time with her again today. He carried her into her bedroom and laid her down on the soft mattress. Her eyes began to open slightly as he lowered her into the covers. She realized whooo face was hanging over her, woke up and smiled.

"Daddy, I miss-ded you," she said. "Did mommy show you the fishy I made?"

"Yes angel," he responded, "and so colorful! Now get to sleep baby girl," he continued, treasuring the moment but not wanting to let on to his wife that he had woken his daughter.

He bent down and kissed her cheeks as she closed her eyes and smiled. He then tucked the covers over her and turned to leave the room, looking back one more time as he turned down the light and pulled the door over.

His wife was already tucked in bed and asleep by the time he entered their sleeping area. He sighed quietly as he'd hoped to have a moment to share his frustrations with her before lying down but he could tell his tardiness had made her day a difficult one too. He got ready for bed as quietly as he could, turned out the light and lay down beside her. Thankfully the exhaustion of the day overcame the frustration he was feeling and he drifted off into an uneasy sleep. Unfortunately he would find no rest in his dreams.

He found himself sitting in his lab looking at the picture on the wall of Foundation Voyager. The great white ship was moving quietly through space against a background of stars and emptiness. As he stared at the picture it began to grow before him and he found himself no longer looking at a picture but in it. He was floating freely, staring down at the great lady as she floated on toward her destination. As the dream progressed, the ship moved past him and he found himself looking at her great accelerator shaft, now silent and black. Eventually the image of the ship became smaller and smaller. He was now floating alone in space, with only the brilliance of the stars around him. It was an astounding sight. In the coldness of deep space he could make out much of the detail of the galaxy around him.

The great long white cloud of the Milky Way shone brightly to his left side, stretching out both to his front and rear and to his right he could see many of the brighter stars of the outer galaxy shining brilliantly like great sparkling diamonds. Looking up, he could make out the shape of some of the closer galaxies in the cosmos. Only in the very depths of space, with even the lights of Foundation Voyager's viewing ports no longer visible could he have expected to see such brilliance with the naked eye. It was the strangest sensation but as always happens in dreams the image began to change. The stars and galaxies around him began to fade, growing dimmer and dimmer. Blackness began to steadily surround him. He strained to see if he could still make out one of the brightest stars in front of him but before long the blackness had enveloped him. He lifted his hand to see if he could see that but it too began to fade and then disappear. Leaving behind it only darkness. His heart rate began to increase and for a moment he began to break out of the dream into consciousness of fear. He reached for his face to see if he could feel anything and felt his fingers against his cheeks. He sighed in relief, falling back into the dream. He lifted his hand away from his face and again tried to strain his eyes to make out anything in the blackness of this vision. Still nothing and now he could begin to feel the sensation of his hand itself drifting away. It was as if his other senses were also fading out. He was heading into a complete blackness, a complete lack of any connection to the universe around him. He was fading into nothingness, he couldn't determine if even he was real or not. As the fear of the nothingness began to grow, the darkness began to turn to pain and the pain grew. Soon it covered him, suffocating him. This incredible pain of nothingness was all around him. He felt that he would drown, drown into a sea of non-existence.

He awoke and suddenly sat up in the bed. He reached up and felt his face. It was there. He was there. It was just a dream, a terrible terrible dream of nothingness. He sighed to catch his breath and reach to his side to touch his dear wife. She was already stirring, awoken by the sudden jolt he had given the bed.

"John, are you alright?" she asked, still half asleep.

"Yes, I'm fine," he responded, "I'm sorry dear. Go back to sleep." He rubbed her back as she closed her eyes again.

He couldn't lie down though. He quickly discovered his body was covered with sweat and adrenaline was pulsing through his veins. He couldn't get the vision out of his mind, the emptiness, the horror of the emptiness.

Thon it struck him like a shot through his mind.

"The Founder," he almost shouted but caught it and whispered to himself without waking his wife again.

"The emptiness he must have felt as his mind faded away. The emptiness he must be feeling, is feeling?" he questioned himself.

"My God," he concluded and jumped out of bed.

In a moment of despair he realized that perhaps the great neural network of the Founder Project was working fine after all. Perhaps it was the data itself that was failing, falling to pieces in a catastrophic neural collapse, a breakdown caused by a lack of the very connection to the universe that confirmed its own existence. It needed to be aware of itself and needed its senses to provide that awareness. Horror shot through his heart at the realization that a terrible and empty death had been playing itself out in his lab, over and over again.

He rushed through the quarters and out into the hall, throwing on his dirty clothes as he hopped to the door. He ran out into the hallway and bumped the wall as he turned the corner. He then realized he'd need some help and noticed he'd forgotten his personal terminal. He stopped at the first hall terminal and blurted at the system.

"Emergency situation contact Dr. Ahmed," he blurted.

Doctor Atef Ahmed was the top Neuro-Therapist on the ship and a good friend of John's but not part of the Founder Project. As the project was now dealing primary with a highly complex Artificial Intelligence System the neurological elements had been completed long ago. Now it seemed those skills would be needed again.

"John, what's the problem?" the voice came over the terminal.

"Sorry but not much time to explain. Please meet me at my lab as soon as you can." John replied.

He left the terminal, then rushed on to the lab. As he entered he began to realize, that time was the one thing he did have. The project had been underway for over one hundred and twenty-five years now. There was no practical reason for his sense of urgency. It was the sense of not knowing that was creating the rush, the feeling that something terrible had been happening that had to be rectified immediately.

It wasn't long before Ahmed arrived at the lab; fortunately he worked on a later shift than Carmichael so he looked much better than his friend when he arrived.

"What's this all about?" he questioned as he walked in.

"I need to develop a neuro-sensory data stream," Carmichael responded.

"A what?" his friend questioned.

"I'm sorry but I can't explain all the details and I'm not even supposed to be asking for your help without getting you clearance to join the project but it's an emergency. I need a recording of sensory input that can be fed into our network," Carmichael requested.

Ahmed cared deeply for his friend John and understood the secrecy that surrounded the Founder Project. It was widely known that the political freedom to deviate from the Biotech Laws was being exploited by the research teams but it also been deemed that the details of the project would be revealed on a 'need to know basis' to ensure that nothing on the homebound beam gave clues about what was happening on Foundation Voyager. Ahmed's sense of loyalty to the colony and to its Founder was no less than anyone else's so he decided to co-operate without question.

"Ok, Ok, I believe I have some recordings that might be useful to you. They are studies of neural impulses of patients under sensory depravation," Ahmed explained.

"Good, good," John responded, "that will be the best kind of data."

The two friends went to work taking the sample files that Ahmed had in his archive and converting them into the required format to interface directly with the neural network.

"What good will a set of human sensory signals be to a computer?" Ahmed couldn't help but ask as they continued.

"Hopefully, you'll see," John responded, knowing that he owed it to his friend to let him sit through the test.

They finished their work and Carmichael altered the test sequence to activate the neural sensory input prior to activating the neural network itself. As the network came to life it would be fed the sensations of a human lying in complete blackness in a soothing solution of body temperature fluid. The sensory input would be minimal but it would be there. He also created an audio channel allowing him to record his voice in the lab and feed it into the signal. Finally he linked the vocal nerve impulses of the neural network to an elaborate decoding routine that would translate the signal into sound coming out of the speaker at his console. A recording of the Founder's voice was used to achieve the right tone.

John sighed in anticipation and turned to his friend.

"Here goes," he said, crossing his fingers.

Ahmed was still confused about what was happening but couldn't help but feel a sense of awe looking into Carmichael's face. Something big was transpiring in this lab in the depths of space.

"Initiate sequence," John instructed the computer.

"System resources at maximum capacity," responded the system. "Maximum Neural Network will operate at one percent of real time."

"Slow but it will have to do," John fussed.

The Founder Project's neural network was the most sophisticated Artificial Intelligence system ever built, greater in complexity and purpose than even the most sophisticated Advisor systems on Earth. Its construction had used up every scrap of Optio Crystal on the ship. John wished they had been able to get more of the precious material but knew that security restrictions of the Unified Government on Earth had limited the amount of computing raw material that Foundation Voyager, or any private enterprise had been able to utilize. Computing resources were, in and of themselves, power and the Government knew better than to let anyone have more than their fair share. The components of the system were each designed to duplicate the process that occurred within a human neuron. Within their crystalline structure they would contain the ever-changing structures of messenger proteins within a nerve cell. There were no actual organic elements but rather an optioelectronic simulation of those elements. The update John had just received had informed him that with all the sensory management overhead that he had just added to the program, the network would now only be able to function at one percent of human brain speed. If John spoke for a minute, the system would take almost two hours to hear him.

"Proceed with load," he instructed the system, confirming acceptance of the reduced performance.

"Initiating load sequence," the computer continued.

Then came the agonizing delay that Carmichael had become to familiar with and this time much longer, with all the added data to be integrated into the network. John couldn't stand the silence.

"Can I get you something to drink?" he asked his friend anxiously as they sat and waited.

Ahmed wasn't thirsty but could see the nervousness in his friend's face. "Yes, that would be wonderful," he responded.

John got up and went to the drink dispenser in his lab; it served up a glass of steaming herbal tea in no time. John took the glass and walked it over to his friend, forgetting to get anything for himself.

"Data file loaded, activating neural network," the system updated.

This time Carmichael couldn't take himself away from the console. He just sat there and felt his heart pound. Ahmed reached over and placed his hand on John's shoulder.

"Neural network active but unstable," the system reported.

John quickly reached out and his hands flurried across the control panel of the console trying to pin down the problem.

"Increase sensory input amplitude," he blurted.

"Increasing," responded the system, "network stabilizing."

"Activate audio output," John requested.

"Activating audio output and translated to real time," the system responded.

John knew that if the network was going to give any kind of response it would take a few minutes for it to be recorded and accelerated to real time but the knowledge made the delay no less painful.

Then it came, like a ghost from the past, in the voice of a man dead for over one hundred and twenty-five years.

"Where am I?" the voice moaned from the speaker, clearly in pain and confusion.

Ahmed knew instantly that there was something more than Artificial Intelligence in that voice and he turned to his friend.

"Who is that?" he questioned, suddenly realizing the nature of the Founder Project.

"The Founder," his friend replied, with tears of elation streaming into his eyes.

Chapter 8

Transition

3664
Earth

It was hard to believe that Joanne Foresythe was the guest of honor at this Transition Ceremony. She looked twenty years younger than many of her guests and nothing in her mood conveyed that she was only a couple of hours from the very last moments of her one hundred and fifty year life. Both her physical and mental health were a clear argument for the extension of life allowance beyond the limitation it had been set to over seven hundred years ago. What was perhaps even more amazing was that Joanne had been able to maintain her great condition with only a minimal dosage of aging retardant. Though over ninety-five percent of humanity now reached their maximum allowed age, it was rare that someone reached that final day of their life in the best of health. Often, even with high doses of age retardant, mental deterioration began to set in after one hundred and twenty. This had been the main argument for the life allowance of the Birthright to be kept at the current level. Though physical health could be maintained to that point, mental breakdown would typically leave most people unable to live any kind of meaningful life, if their transition were extended. It was generally agreed that it was still best to pass the torch to the next generation at a century and a half of life. With the population of the planet restricted to ten billion as it had been for over a thousand years, every soul that passed through their Transition ceremony made room for a new birth somewhere else in the world.

The Birthright Laws had been a cornerstone of human society since the population crisis of the early twenty-second

century. This had been the period of the convergence of two
growing problems that humanity had been facing. First,
though population growth had slowed during the twenty-first
century the total population was still climbing. Second, the
global environmental shift began to accelerate. The result was
a catastrophe across the globe, massive crop failures occurred
across Europe and Northern America and large-scale droughts
hit equatorial regions. Worst affected were the nations of the
Asian Subcontinent, already the most populated region of
the planet. The dire humanitarian crisis that the region was
thrown into sparked a nuclear exchange between the nations of
India and Pakistan. These nations though at peace for almost
a century, were sparked into sudden renewed conflict by the
overall stress of the climate change and the massive population.
The world reacted quickly, neutralizing the military capability
of both nations and bringing an enforced peace to what was
left of the devastated region. Though starvation continued to
plague many of the overpopulated areas of the globe, the newly
formed World Government was able to stabilize the global food
distribution system and keep humanity together. Canada
and Russia became the great food produces of the world for
much of the twenty-second and twenty-third centuries until
global climate control was finally perfected in the late twenty-
third century. But the great legacy of the era remained, the
Birthright Laws.

These laws set the maximum population of the planet to
ten billion, the limits of the globe's food production capabilities
at that time. The limit was first implemented by a system
of incentives for people to reduce the size of their families.
The world financed massive programs to implement family
planning across the globe. Once the infrastructure was in
place to control the population, an ethical process was needed
to maintain it. From this evolved the Birthright. In the
Birthright system, a person willed, at the time of their death,
their right to exist to someone else, very often their own female
children but sometimes a female relative or friend. That
woman then had an additional birthright beyond her own,
which translated into the right to give birth to a new person and
endow that new child with the inherited Birthright. In theory
every human on the planet carried a Birthright. Of course,

early on it was a difficult system to implement, children born
without a Birthright couldn't be blamed for the transgressions
of their parents and so the Birthright Marketplace emerged.
The marketplace was a virtual trading environment where
the very right to exist could be purchased. People could sell
a Birthright they had received instead of having children of
their own and others could purchase that right. Those who
could not afford the cost but still wished to have a child could
turn to a wide array of charities that began to spring up but
rarely a parent would be incarcerated for violating the laws.
At first it had seemed a harsh system but when humanity had
been forced to face the reality of the limited resources of the
planet, limiting the population that relied on those resources
had materialized as the only plausible response.

At first Birthrights existed without limitation upon the
length of one's life but the invention of the first age retardant
pharmaceuticals in the early twenty-third century added the
age allowance to the system. Age retardants made it possible
for people to extend their life by delaying or halting the natural
aging process. Unfortunately, the effects of the medication did
not preserve the stability of the mind.   As it became more
common for people to live over one hundred years of age, it
became clear that the mind would still fail and the very oldest
would loose their sanity completely. It was for that reason that
the age allowance was introduced. First set at one hundred
and twenty-five it was later extended to one hundred and fifty
as the process for preserving mental stability improved.

The location of the Joanne's Ceremony couldn't have been
a more perfect place, nestled in Joanne's home country of the
Pocono range, the Blue Mountain House of Abraham was a
perfect location for this gathering. The completely transparent
roof of the facility stretched seventy-five feet into the air, tall
enough that the trees growing within the enclosure didn't
quite reach the ceiling. The facility stretched along the side
of the ridge about a mile and from top to bottom took up about
four hundred feet of the hillside at its widest point. Below the
enclosure at the bottom of the hill a lake stretched out beneath
them, where several pairs of mating swans swam gracefully.
On the far side of the small lake the hillside rose again from
the water, covered with pines, oaks and maples.

Within the enclosure of the temple itself, the landscape was a collage of natural elements. Waterfalls and ponds mingled with the massive flowing shrubs and towering trees. Tables and chairs were nestled throughout the greenery and babbling water gardens, pathways and footbridges tied the area together. Massive ornamental Koi of stirring colors swam in the ponds and white doves flew about the tops of the trees. The bright early spring sun shone through the structure but the cold air had no affect on the temperature in the enclosure. The facility was equipped to maintain the lighting and temperature of a warm sunny day any time of the year. It was truly a manmade paradise. Joanne might have preferred a ceremony in the actual outdoors but was not the sort to impose her own wishes upon all of her guests and her neighborhood House of Abraham was a location she knew everyone would enjoy.

This temple was one of the millions of facilities across the globe that belonged to this sixteen hundred year-old religion. Originally founded in the United States of America in the late twenty-first century, the House of Abraham had grown to be the largest religious organization in the world with over four billion members. Its Founders were three collegiate students of history who each came from the three main religions of the western world, Christianity, Judaism and Islam. They became great friends during their studies and began to wonder what they could do to end the conflicts that had raged between their respective faiths over the centuries. Violence had erupted again in the Middle East for the twelfth time in less than a century and a half and they were simply disgusted by the seemingly endless killing. They began by calling multi-faith peace protests calling for all the people of the region to recognize their common belief in the God of Abraham and their common belief in the sanctity of human life. Their first efforts were little more than a whisper on the battlefield but their message took root, at first in America but then across the globe. The principle of peace through unification began to win over against the curse of intolerance the region had known. The House took shape as a formal organization, after the high profile show down, between peace protestors and both the Armies of Israel and Palestine, in the historic town of Jerusalem.

Joanne was not a devoutly religious person herself and as her friends chatted throughout the gathering, they could not recall whether Joanne had ever given any of them a clue as to her inner beliefs. Had she been agnostic or even an atheist it would have made very little difference to this gathering. Like any House of Abraham this congregation would not judge its members on their particular beliefs but rather on their contributions to humanity. Those that gave greatly of themselves were the most honored in this place of worship and those who harmed humanity were thought of as lost souls in need of nurture. Judgment was a secular duty not for consideration by this gathering.

Though Joanne's life had not been without controversy the audience here today were her friends, those that had stood beside her through good times and bad. Joanne had risen to prominence upon the world stage shortly after the fateful day almost a century ago when Mankind had first learned of the Intruders and the terrible destruction of Omega Theta. She had been at the forefront of a vast array of change that had struck humanity. Galactic colonization had been stopped and with it the creation of new Generation Ship Birthrights. The construction of the great defensive array that now protected our solar system had begun, ships designed to travel the stars with weapons not colonists had been built and here on Earth much of humanity had focused on the construction of power-free shelters. At the peak of the development of this last line of defense, it had been believed capable of supporting almost the entire population of the planet. They consisted of both open air and great greenhouse domes that were capable of producing food with the help of mechanically driven windmill irrigation systems. They represented the technology of two thousand years ago re-implemented with modern building materials and engineering. With her own attachment to nature, Joanne thought of them not just as a defense against possible attack but as places of solitude and peace to escape the ever present hand of technology that seemed to rule life outside. As time had passed though and further intrusions from the void failed to occur, people had lost interest in these refuges and many of them had fallen into disarray. People even began to question the motives of those who had supported the great changes of the century and wondered if the Omega Theta attack had ever even occurred. Many of the advocates of defensive measures, Joanne included, had been forced out of positions of influence and human life had began to move back to the sense of security it had before the Intrusion. Colonization was re-initiated and further development of the defensive network was halted.

Though it was clear to anyone who had taken a close look at Joanne's life that she had done nothing but work tirelessly for what she believed was the best interests of Mankind, she like many of her fellow defense advocates were blamed for fifty years of lost colonization, stunting the growth of humanity.

Those gathered here today, however saw Joanne differently. To them she was person of unending persistence and true belief in her cause. After leaving office, in her single two-year term as President of the Unified Government, she had continued her work privately promoting an awareness of how nature and human ingenuity could interact without advanced technology and promoting military readiness. Looking at Joanne meander through the crowd chatting with her guests it was easy to tell that despite what anyone else may have thought, Joanne was proud of the role she had played during her life.

A soft and uplifting melody was murmuring through the trees as more and more of the guests entered and made their way to their tables. Joanne moved from table to table chatting with her friends and guests. She exchanged hugs and kisses on the cheek with many of them and would occasionally reach up and wipe a tear from a loved one's face and smile as if to say: "please don't be sad."

Joanne herself was not one for tears, even on this occasion, which was for many an endless stream of blubbering and crying as relative after relative gave a tearful farewell, Joanne demonstrated her ability to always see the beauty and joy in the moment and somehow miss the sadness of life. She didn't mind the sadness that was creeping in around her too much though. She knew it showed the love that everyone had for her.

As she approached her old friend and associate, retired commander J. T. Stone, who was seated alone, she took comfort from the deep respect he always showed to her. For Stone, however, who seemed a little out of place at such a social occasion, respect came in the form of a stern glaze that were it not for his current civilian status would have carried with it, a swift salute.

"Hello Commander," Foresythe greeted the man as he stood and gave her arm a firm shake. It might have seemed strange to an observer but the concern between them seemed to come from Joanne toward her junior associate. "How are things progressing?" she questioned.

"The trials begin in two months," Stone replied. "I wish you could be here to see us make this happen."

"You have my every confidence Commander, you always have," she responded, putting her hand to his face and smiling.

It looked for a moment that Stone might actually blush in response to the unexpected show of affection.

Leaving her comrade, Joanne began to move down through the crowd. In time she reached a large table in the center of the hall, filled with her closest family. Her younger brother Paul was first to greet her with a warm and strong hug. Softer of heart than his sister, a tear welled up in his eye as he felt his cheek against hers. He tried to brush it away before ending the hug but couldn't hide his feelings.

"Look at you," Joanne said smiling widely at her brother and holding his shoulders. "You're going to make a mess of that wonderful speech you wrote."

Paul couldn't help but laugh recalling how Joanne had picked on him endlessly over how he'd agonized over the speech he would give at this event. She had told him many times that he didn't have to say anything if he didn't want to and if he insisted on speaking she wouldn't be insulted if he kept it simple but he had insisted on giving a message worthy of the sister he was so proud of.

"But you're still so strong," Paul quipped, as if to suddenly question the wisdom of the Birthright system.

"What and have your great-granddaughter born without a birthright?" Joanne jested nodding to the younger woman at his, side clearly in her seventh or eighth month of pregnancy.

"Go on," she continued. "They're all waiting now."

Paul turned and walked toward a small podium that stood on a pedestal toward the front of the temple. Joanne turned to the younger woman and looked down at her tummy.

"How are we doing?" she asked placing her hand on her grand niece's round abdomen.

"We are kicking," exclaimed the lady, rolling her eyes.

Denise Rutland was Joanne's youngest grandniece and her favorite relative. She had enjoyed many long days with her, sharing many of her favorite hiking trails and natural vistas. Joanne had spent much of her younger life busy in politics and defense planning and hadn't had time to connect the younger generations till later in her life. Over one hundred years younger than Joanne, Denise was in the peak of her childbearing years and felt fortunate to be the named inheritor of Joanne's Birthright. To inherit a birthright was a great honor and by tradition obligated a parent to raise their child in a manner that would pay respect to their benefactor. Denise knew this was a tall order but felt a sense of elation at being given the task. She felt a warmth across her whole body as Joanne leaned forward and kissed her cheek, then placed her other hand on Denise's back and helped her down into her chair, leaving her hand on the younger woman's shoulder as they sat and turned to the podium where Paul was beginning to speak.

"First, I'd like to thank every one of you for coming here today and joining us in the celebration of my sister's life," Paul began. "I cannot stand up here and try to tell you that this day is not a very sad one for me, most of me is in denial of the fact that these are the very last hours I will share with Joanne. I promised my sister, however; I would not allow this to become a sad speech, so enough about how I feel and let's talk about why we are here."

"We are here today to celebrate the life of the most wonderful person I have ever been privileged to know. I say that of her not only because of the incredible things that she has done for all of Mankind but also because of the incredible joy she has brought to me as her brother. As you can all see by taking one look at Joanne today, she's a lady that never let anything stand in her way. Not even age has slowed her down. She is someone who no matter what the situation is always able to look at the positive and no matter what the challenge is always able to find a solution. Joanne has never wavered from her deep love of nature and her deep commitment to the good of man. Most of you know of the great challenges she faced in world politics but only few of you may know of the challenges she brought upon herself to protect the things she cared about. So I want to take a minute today to tell you a little story. It's a story I promised Joanne I'd never tell but I'm going to break that promise today."

"Just before Joanne began her term as President, during some of the toughest times for many of the programs she supported, she took a vacation to get her mind together for upcoming trials. She decided to go back to the New York Historical Preserve that she loved so much and spend time visiting a wolf family that she had made a hobby of monitoring over the course of several years. While engaging in her nature excursions, Joanne always took great care to follow all of the non-disruption guidelines of the parks and worked hard not to interfere with her wild friends. She'd visited them many times and learned how to blend in to the scenery and let them go about their lives."

"Unfortunately on this one occasion and this is the only time I know of, Joanne made a hiking mistake. She put her weight onto a rock that turned out to be loose and it gave way under her. She and the rock went tumbling down the hillside right into the clearing immediately in front of the wolves' den. Joanne had broken her left leg, as well as her right arm and was surrounded by some very angry North American Timber Wolves."

"Now had it been me, or any of you," Paul paused and pointed out across the audience. "We would have made quick use of our personal terminals, gave those wolves a sonic tone they'd have never forgotten and called for immediate medivac but Joanne didn't do that. You see even in the extreme pain that she was in, she knew that a disruption like that would scatter the adults and cause them to abandon their pups and Joanne didn't feel that her loose footing was the pup's fault and she wasn't going to let them get hurt, even if that meant being their dinner. By sheer force of will she managed to somehow convince the adults she was neither a threat nor a meal, just an unwelcome visitor that would be on its way. With one good leg and one good arm, bleeding extensively, she crawled over three hundred yards to a safe distance before calling for help, wolves snarling at her angrily much of way. When the medtech got his shuttle to the scene, he indicated that she had almost lost a fatal amount of blood and she was lucky he had made it there when he did. She made both that medtech and me swear to secrecy, a secrecy that I've kept till today. I only found out the truth because of my complaint to the medtech as to why it had taken him so long to get to her. He made her tell me the story. You see that's the kind of person that Joanne is and that is why the pain of loosing her is so great."

Paul paused again and raised his glass from the podium as a tear welled into his eye.

"To my sister, my hero, Joanne Foresythe," he called out raising his glass high into the air and then bringing it down to his mouth.

The reply came back strong from the crowd.

"To Joanne," they roared.

Much of the crowd turned to Joanne and began to cheer and clap but she wouldn't have any of it. She blushed and smiled and waved her arms downward as if to ask them not to make such a fuss.

Then she looked back at Paul as if to say, "you'd better quit."

Paul knew when he was getting into trouble so he finally moved on to the rest of the afternoon's agenda. Joanne had insisted the event be a celebration and so with a wave of Paul's hand to a control booth tucked away in the greenery far up the hillside the music resumed.

The rest of the event went much as Joanne would have liked it, there was music and food and drink for everyone and though many there didn't feel like dancing, Joanne wasn't going to let them get away with sitting all day long, so she moved through the many dance floors that nestled through the facility getting people to their feet. She set the example that people were to have a good time and as was usually the case when Joanne was around people followed her.

But as the afternoon turned to evening the moment drew near. Joanne had been born almost exactly one hundred and

fifty years ago and the time allotted to her by her Birthright
was drawing to a close.

Quietly without breaking the festivities, Joanne made her
way up to the podium and silence fell across the temple as
everyone began to notice where she was. All eyes were fixed on
the woman of the moment.

"I have to leave you all in just a moment but I wanted to say
a few words before I go," she began. "I want to thank all of you
for being here today and sharing my last hours with me and
trying so hard to keep a smile on your face but more than that
though, I want to thank you all for being a part of my life. With
your help, I have known more joy and satisfaction in my life
than I ever could have wished for. It is my belief that life is a
gift. A gift from who; I cannot really say but a gift nonetheless.
I have tried in every way I know how to make the most of that
gift. I have even had the opportunity, thanks to the wonders of
modern medicine, to make that gift last a little longer than it
should have and I am grateful for that and do not ask more. I
am honored to pass the torch to the next generation and hope
I have set a good example of how to use the precious gift of
life." She looked down at Denise and smiled warmly and then
continued. "There is one last thought I want to leave you with,
however, and that is this. Mankind has faced many challenges
in our existence here on earth and out in the heavens and we
will face many more challenges in the future. Perhaps those
of you here will know some of those challenges. Perhaps they
will be left for your children but they will come. When they
do I hope that you will know this. Mankind will survive. We
will survive because we are privileged to be one of the most
wonderful creations that God has ever made." The audience
gasped quietly having heard Joanne use the word God for
the perhaps the first time. "We are capable of survival, not
only because of our ability to adapt not only biologically but
culturally and technically to any challenge we face but also
because within us exists a goodness, an ability to put the needs
of our fellow man above our own and to ensure that we will
always go on. This is our secret weapon."

"I love you and thank you all," she concluded.

Then without pause Joanne stepped back from the podium
and entered the transition chamber that sat immediately

behind it. The chamber was spherical with a small doorway in the front, which opened automatically as Joanne got close. As the door closed there was no visible indication of what happened next but everyone knew exactly how a transition pod functioned. A sudden pulse of intense electro magnetic energy would instantly neutralize every single neuron in the body. The chamber then proceeded to cremate the Joanne's body and deliver her ashes in a small urn that appeared in a panel just beside the doorway. The entire process took a matter of seconds.

It took all the strength that Paul could muster to stand, take the urn from the chamber and begin a slow walk from the temple. One by one the guests filed in behind him.

Later that evening the wolves of the New York Preserve howled, as the ashes of their friend drifted down amongst them, from high above.

Chapter 9

Fire and Ice

3693
Reykjavik Colony
42 Light-years from Earth,
12 Light-years from Omega Theta

Hendrickson was frustrated. His people could have known about the potential nightmare that he was now trying to prepare for, over one hundred and fifty years ago but there was little that he could do about that now. The shortcomings of his colony's interstellar communications system weren't something that could be changed quickly. However, his colony's readiness for possible attack was and that was just what he had been doing for the last two years, ever since they had heard about the events that had transpired in their neighboring colony. Omega Theta lay just twelve light-years away but communication between these two remote outposts took much longer. The dynamics of communications at this range made it prohibitive for colonies to invest in the capability to speak to each other. Instead their communications systems transmitted data only to Earth's solar system. There, massive orbiting listening arrays, over one hundred times the size of the average colony star, would pick up the extremely faint signal transmitted across the stars. Information was then sent out from the cradle of humanity via high power communication beams over a thousand times as powerful as those that sent data inward. These stronger signals were more easily picked up by the smaller listening arrays of the outer colonies. The benefit of the system was the ability of the colonies to communicate with Earth for a smaller investment in resources. The downside: They could not speak to each other. For Reykjavik the problem was exacerbated by the fact that their single listening array spent seventy-four years out of each two hundred and fifty four on the dark side of their solar system, blinded by the static of their massive star and out of touch with Earth. When added to the ninety-two year round trip for information from Omega Theta this had left Reykjavik ill-informed of events that could have an ominous effect on her future and were being taken far more seriously than they were on Earth.

Like its neighbor, Reykjavik was a first generation colony. Its forefathers left Earth over eight hundred years ago in the first wave of interstellar colonization. It was now a little over three hundred years old and had been doing quite well until the recent news arrived. Also, like Omega Theta, the population of Reykjavik believed they had little chance of fending off an attack by the Intruders but unlike the former had a much better chance of surviving without the power technology that the Intruders seemed to consider a threat.

For most colonies, the possibility of existence without power was not an option and under the circumstances their only choice would have been to attempt a defense against attack. Most colonies were free orbiting colony stars that, without power, either solar or nuclear, would not be viable. Perhaps temperature variance would make them a deathtrap for human life, or the systems required to maintain food and oxygen would not function without power. The construction of a colony star that could subsist without power was possible but had not yet been attempted. Reykjavik was different though, it was a lunar colony and its host moon had a unique environment that gave its inhabitants a chance at survival, allowing for a different strategy.

Reykjavik was almost the same size as Earth and like many of the moons of our solar system orbited a large gas giant planet. Much larger than Jupiter, this great green gaseous monster, Thor, orbited its massive very hot host star every two hundred and fifty four years and Reykjavik, one of its five moons, orbited it, every six months. Reykjavik also rotated about its own axis every thirty-six hours. This complex sequence of changes relative to its closest star and its host planet made it a tumultuous place and produced its two defining characteristics: Fire and Ice. Named after a place on Earth that shared these same characteristics to a lesser degree, Reykjavik was a far more hostile place than the most hellish location on its namesake's home planet. During the three months it spent on the hot side of its host planet, surface temperatures exceeded the boiling temperature of water and in its coldest period when it circled the dark side of its massive neighbor temperatures dropped to a point far colder than the coldest spots on Earth. Yet, despite these extremes, Reykjavik was one of a handful of places man had found that performed its own special miracle. It supported life.

Extreme volcanic activity around the moon's equatorial belt had produced large networks of caves that provided the special environment needed to maintain biological activity. Whereas water on the surface of the moon went through cycles of being converted from vast ice sheets, to large gaseous clouds of water vapor, water in the caves, insulated from the drastic temperature changes of the surface, was able to stay liquid and sat in vast underground lakes deep within the lunar crust. It was within these lakes that the bottom of the pyramid of life had formed. Volcanic plumes delivered thermal energy and sulfurous gases into the lakes. Primitive organisms thrived on this energy and produced vast quantities of base organic material. This material was brought to the surface of the moon by the massive thermal geysers that dotted the crust and surrounded the many volcanoes. Then during the interim period between the peaks of the seasons an amazing transformation would occur on the surface of Reykjavik. In what had become known as Reykjavik's spring, when the great ice sheets would begin to melt and turn into vast seas that spread across the moon before being evaporated into the atmosphere. The entire moon would bloom a brilliant green. Dormant spores of primitive plants would burst to life absorbing the liquid water that flowed from the ice sheets. Shortly after that what might have been mistaken for strange looking rock formations would reveal their true forms, as huge fernlike features would explode around the shores of the great seas and then finally in her last miracle of the pyramid of life, various forms of plant eating and even meat eating life would emerge. Some of whom would lie dormant on the surface, while other larger creatures that had learned to retreat into the caves would come out to feed upon the abundant plant growth. Finally, as the cycle of the environment continued, everything would seemingly fade away as the water vanished into steam and disappeared from the surface. Then during her autumn, Reykjavik's miracle of life would start all over again.

This was the place that Greg Hendrickson and his fellow colonists called home. Reykjavik's fourteen human colonies were built on relative stable plateaus of rock that sat to the North and South of the volatile equatorial belt and relied and sprawling solar energy arrays to produce the energy necessary to keep them protected from the erratic temperature changes. Their great transparent domes allowed the sunlight to enter and feed the plant life they used as part of their food chain, plant life that would not have survived outside the domes but was ideal for the Earth like environment within the colonies themselves, plant life that was native to, or engineered far away, on Earth. The most amazing fact about Reykjavik colony, however, was that the airlocks of the colony domes were there as much to protect the native life as to protect the colonists. The air of Reykjavik, unlike almost anywhere in the realm of man, was breathable and much of the plant life was edible as well. To Hendrickson, this was the true miracle of the moon he called home. It was, with a little help, potentially capable of supporting human life.

Hendrickson and his thirteen fellow colony managers had created a simple plan. In the event of an attack they would simply turn off their colony's energy systems and make use of their exploration hover rovers to cross the plateaus to the nearest cave system. Then through tunnels that were currently being dug, they would head down and take shelter from the seasons. Food would be stored in the caves and could be replenished through foraging, conducted in spring and autumn. The plan seemed simple but a great degree of preparation was required.

First, a gravitational detection array was under construction and would soon be launched into orbit. Based on the information they had obtained from Omega Theta, they knew the Intruder ships could not be detected through scans of the electro magnetic spectrum. They possessed a powerful stealth technology that prevented that. They did, however, give off a gravitational signal that provided sufficient data to warn of their presence. The array would give them a few hours warning of impending attack. In addition to having the warning time needed to flee their homes, the colonist would also need tunnels constructed down into the caves. Many of the native cave openings were too small or too volatile to use. Finally, shelters would be constructed inside the rocks to house the refugees. Unfortunately, these preparations were at least six months from completion and, as the Colony manager of Reykjavik Four; Greg Hendrickson would not rest easy until this task was complete. The short autumn, which lasted only three weeks, was upon them. If they were attacked during winter and unprepared, they would be doomed.

Greg's reflection upon his predicament was suddenly interrupted.

"The power coupling is completely blown," came a deep rough voice from directly behind him.

Greg turned to see Tom Houston striding toward him, with the power module of a drilling drone held firmly in both hands. Tom was Greg's project manager in charge of cave drilling and one of his best men. This was the reason he'd been given the toughest assignment of his colony.

"We can pull one from liquid recyclers and rig it to fit," he responded to Tom placing his hand on the big man's shoulder.

"That was my thinking. We've got enough redundancy in the recycler to hold us over for now," Tom responded and strode away toward the fluid-processing center.

Greg went back to his thoughts. He looked up into the sky through the dome above him and wished he could freeze the picture. The giant green image of Thor that held them in its embrace filled the entire sky. Their sun had just set, making the site of the planet above them far more brilliant. Early evening during the Reykjavik Autumn was an amazing site. The orb of their host planet sat in almost perfect symmetry between its day and night. On the daylight side, the surface of the sphere was a brilliant swirl of various shades of green ranging from bright neon to deep forest tones. Just a little above the equator sat the great storm, a deep green ellipse, almost black, itself half the size of Saturn and far larger the Reykjavik. Actually a massive atmospheric storm, you couldn't help but think it might open up and swallow the moon whole. On the night side, the blackness was even more forbidding, occasionally broken by an electrical flash within the atmosphere, it foreshadowed the approaching winter. In a few days, Reykjavik would slip into the dark side and become enveloped in the ice she brought with her. Only the storm flashes in the planet above and the stars out in deep space would cast their light upon his home.

Greg's reflection was again interrupted but this time by a source far less friendly than his good friend Tom. The piercing white beam came out of nowhere and Greg knew in an instant what it was.

The Intruders had arrived and they were early.

"Damn it," he yelled, as a million thoughts shot through his mind all at once.

His first instinct was to make sure that nothing he was wearing was going to get him killed. He patted himself down quickly and realized his personal terminal was active and strapped to his wrist. He quickly unstrapped the device and tossed it across the courtyard of the colony dome in a direction he hoped would be safe. He had acted just in time. Before the device even hit the ground, it was incinerated by a direct hit from the thin white energy beam. He was now no longer a target but many of the people under his care were still in harm's way.

He cupped his hands together and began to yell over toward the main facilities. "Get clean and get out!" he cried, waving his arms toward him.

The energy beam continued to cut the colony apart, sparking fires and explosions as it hit various components of the structure. Several of the colonists had escaped from the closed in buildings and were fleeing toward the center of the dome. Here lay the greatest chance of survival. Though the main preparations for attack were far from completed, Greg had at least been able to take some tactical steps. He had built a shelter in the center of the dome, away from any of the powered components of the facility and in it stored supplies that might give them a chance of survival. Greg was fortunate that he had happened to be standing very close the entrance to the shelter when the attack had begun. As his friends came

closer to him, he lifted the door in the floor that covered the
entrance to the shelter. He began to guide the survivors down
into it. As the crowd began to grow around the entrance, Greg
struggled to keep order.

"Take your turn, young and old first, take your turn, don't
panic," he instructed.

Everyone suddenly ducked their heads for a moment as a
massive explosion indicated the main power storage module
had been blown wide open. The power module sat just outside
the dome of the colony and the explosion sent massive chunks
of structural crystal hurtling through the air. Several large
pieces could be seen, almost in slow motion coming down upon
the structure of the dome itself. As they crashed through the
roof of the facility they brought down many of the structural
members and much of the transparent skin with them. The
shattering sound was deafening.

"Take Cover," Greg yelled as he heard screams around him.

A sixth sense told him to look up as long as he could and
track the path of the largest pieces. Out of the corner of his
eye he noticed a young girl standing lost and screaming at his
side. At the last moment he dropped to the ground and covered
his head with one hand, grabbing the child and pulling her
beneath him with the other. Upon hitting the ground he felt
the debris fall upon him and prayed that he would survive the
moment.

He lay still upon the ground for another second and wondered
if he was still alive. An eerie silence surrounded him and a
strange new smell filled the air. The silence was broken when
the child he was sheltering began to cry out and many of the
people around him began to moan and wail. He lifted his head
and began to look around. It seemed the attack was over, at
least for now. All the power of the colony was dead and most
of the buildings around the perimeter were on fire. Several
of the colonists around him were climbing to their feet. He
was pleased to find he was able to stand up as well. He had
suffered some cuts to his legs and back but, for the most part,
he was ok. He felt particularly lucky when he looked to his
left and saw a large structural beam, embedded in the ground
perhaps a foot and half away. He began to notice that many of

the other colonists around him had not been so lucky but there was no time to focus on that. His first order of business was the living.

Another large structural beam had fallen directly upon the cover to the shelter and some of the colonists were already trying to get a hold on it and move it. He came over to help and waved some of the others around also. Together they were able to heft the load off the shelter door and get the shelter open. Hesitantly those trapped inside looked out, not sure if others were coming in or they were getting out. Greg looked down at the faces and gave some instructions.

"The attack appears to be over, come on out," he instructed.

As the survivors made their way out of the shelters, those that weren't immediately tending to the wounded began to gather in a semi-circle around him waiting for some kind of direction.

He looked at the faces and was relieved to see his trusted friend Tom Houston one of those staring back of him.

"Tom, I need you to immediately gather up a team and head for the caves. You're going to have to find us a way down, without the drilling probes," he ordered with a reassuring nod.

"I've got some ideas," Tom responded, which was lie but he knew it wasn't the time to be pessimistic.

"Healthy young adults only, take whatever supplies you may need. You'll need to move fast." He continued. "Everyone else, with me, we'll need to gather up survivors and whatever supplies we can salvage from the colony."

He made sure that he got close enough to talk softly as Tom made his way past him to recover the emergency supplies from the shelter.

"Tom, make sure there's a good male to female balance in your group," he whispered into his friend's ear.

Tom looked back at him puzzled for a moment, then realized what Greg was thinking. It was quite likely that only his advance party would make it across the plateau in time. It was going to get cold fast and they would need to move quickly. The young, old and wounded might not be able to make the trip.

"You belong with us," he whispered back to Greg, with the sort of cruel practical thinking that said, we could use your leadership even if it lessons the chances for the others.

"Bullshit," Hendrickson smiled. "I'd slow you down. Get going."

Tom realized he should have known better than to think Greg would desert the colony for one moment. He was a good leader even if that meant going down with the ship.

"Now get going, we'll catch up to you," he concluded and patted Tom sharply on the back.

The younger man moved on waving some of his team down into the shelter to gather up their equipment.

Greg turned to the rest of the group and began to look for those he could count on to lead the many difficult tasks left to him. As he began to scan the group, he felt a tug at his side. The little girl that had been by him when the dome had collapsed was now looking up at him with a look of helplessness and shock on her face. She had stopped screaming and now looked longingly at Greg for some type of protection. He leant down and picked her up.

"What's your name sweetie?" he asked the little angel.

"Jenfer," she responded, through her tears, not saying another word.

"Well Jennifer, I'm going to need your help, Ok?" he asked.

The little girl nodded in response and squeezed her arms tightly around him as if she'd never let him go.

With the girl still in his arms he turned back to the group. His next priority was to care for the wounded. He looked around the area and couldn't see either of the colony's two doctors but both of the nurses had made it through and were working feverishly on some of the more serious cases. They had already managed to draft some helpers on their own. He decided not to interfere but rather set up a channel of communications. He noticed Derek Johnson in the group in front of him and quickly tagged him the job, knowing the older facilities chief would be able to keep his head.

"Derek, could you check with Jane and Ann and see what help they'll need and keep us updated?" he instructed.

"Will do," Derek responded with confidence and purpose. It wasn't until then that Greg noticed Derek had his own fairly serious wound on his left leg but seemed to be coping with it.

Now to the really hard part: finding any survivors in the burning buildings.

He broke the remaining group into two teams and directed them to move around the perimeter of the dome where all the raised structures were and call out if they found any remaining survivors. Just as the search began he noticed Tom's group making their way toward the main airlock to the dome. He scanned the group with approval. Tom had made good choices on those in his team. None were too old and none too young. The only parents he noticed in the group were old enough to have their grown children by their side.   Tom looked back across the dome briefly as he left; Greg nodded as if to say, "Good Luck."

It was several hours later when they had completed a search of the facility. They were pleased to have found three survivors, relatively unharmed and trapped in the buildings. Many they found were far less fortunate. When the search was completed Greg made a mental count of his colony. Of the one hundred and sixty-four souls he was responsible for fifty-three were lost and twenty-five had left in Tom's team. He counted thirty-two wounded and fifty-one healthy survivors. Three were missing.

He made the difficult decision that the time it would take to conduct a second search of the facility would cost him more lives in the time he needed to reach the caves. He made no mention to the group of the specific count but everyone knew that some were still missing. They trusted their leader to make the right decisions though.

His next task was even more difficult. He asked the leaders of his search teams to begin gathering supplies, then made his way over to the makeshift field hospital that had sprung up in the center of the colony. Jane Franklin and Ann McCarthy were still working frantically on their patients when he walked up.

"How does it look?" he asked Jane, the more senior nurse.

"It's not good Greg," she responded. "Under normal circumstances I could probably save all of them but my supplies were mostly lost in the fire, both of my doctor's are gone and I can't use any of my equipment to treat them. I'll be lucky to save half of them and most of those that I can save won't be able to move for several days."

"We..." began Greg.

"I know, I know," Jane interrupted. "We don't have days." She paused for a moment then asked. "When will you leave?"

"As soon as we can," Greg responded. "Hopefully, within a few hours."

"I see," Jane sighed, hoping for just a little more time. "I'll get those that can travel together and make sure Ann joins you."

"What about you?" he asked, looking the older nurse in the face.

"Sorry Greg I never was one for long walks," she responded trying to make light of the moment.

"We need your skills," Greg insisted reaching for her hands.

"Ann is a good nurse, she's much younger and stronger than me and these people need someone to take care of them. My husband is trapped in this damn place somewhere and if it's alright by you I'd rather die close to him than out 'there' somewhere." She freed a hand for a moment and waved it wildly as if in disgust at the unforgiving surface of Reykjavik. "I've got a good supply of sedatives and I'll make sure that no one suffers. Now get going. I've got work to do."

As Jane laid down her way of thinking two things occurred to Hendrickson. First, that Dr. Ron Franklin, Jane's husband, and one of the medical doctors in the colony, was one of the three missing and also that Jane was right, their chances on the plateau weren't a whole lot better than their chances here in the colony. He looked hard at Jane's firm and resolute eyes, squeezed her hands firmly, nodded and turned to the rest of the survivors but then turned back with one last question.

"The girl, Jennifer?" he said nodding over to his little companion that stood looking at him not far away.

"Sorry, Greg, they didn't make it," responded Jane, letting Greg know that Jennifer was now an orphan.

Greg took Jennifer by the hand and headed back to his group. They had been busy.

They had already managed to gather up many of the supplies that were available from around the colony. They had brought a good supply of food, probably enough to last the journey across the plateau. They detached the helmets, burned power modules and breathing gear from several of the atmospheric suits, obviously with the intention of using them for warmth. Some had fashioned spears from structural rods of the colony and finally they had pulled together a good supply of miscellaneous items that might be used for burnable fuel. What most amazed Greg, however, was that they had managed to fashion together a few primitive carts to load the materials on. With the advanced power technology the colony's normal mode of transport had been the hover rovers. Without power these were useless and he couldn't think of one single wheeled vehicle the colony possessed. The colonists had, however, been able to fashion some of the hardware from the waste processing system conveyers into wheels and axles. Sections of building wall served as platforms for the cargo.

He evaluated the amount of supplies they were bringing and tried to determine if it was the right amount. Too much would slow them down and prevent them from reaching the caves until it became too cold, too little and they'd run out of supplies before their trip was through. As best as he could tell it looked like they were on target.

With the supplies loaded up they were ready to move out. As the makeshift caravan began to form up, he looked over at Jane, who was walking toward him with five of the wounded who looked like they were ready for the trip and her assistant nurse Ann. For the most part the group suffered from injuries to their arms or upper body and looked in good condition to walk. One young man had bandages across his eyes.

"Jack should recover most of his vision if his bandage is left over his eyes for another two days," Jane began.

"I won't slow you down sir, I promise," Jack interrupted.

"Don't worry son, we'll lead the way," Greg said taking him by the arm.

Jane gave a nod and headed back to the hospital area, Ann took Jack's other arm and they led let him to the back of one of the carts and placed his hand on the back of the platform.

Greg took a look around for his little companion and quickly found her, sitting quietly on a backpack.

"Are you ready to go little one?" Greg asked, picking the girl up again. Jennifer nodded quietly still not saying a word.

With that the group began to make their way out of the colony, with a few of them running to join after a last hug or a word with a loved one left with the wounded. Jane kept her eye on the group till they reached the threshold of the colony, then turned back to her duties.

Greg tried to keep the group focused on the journey ahead rather than on looking back toward the ruined colony as they made their way south toward their subterranean destination ahead. Had they taken a moment to look back though, they would have seen what was left of the dome of the colony glaring white in the Reykjavik dawn. The broken top of the structure looked almost like a broken egg buried half in the ground and still smoking a thick grey column into the air. What Greg did notice was the source of the new odor he had detected earlier. At first he had thought it might be the smell of some burning materials but it wasn't, it was in fact the smell of Reykjavik. It was an acrid burning sulfurous smell that was quite foul if you thought about it too much. Greg put it out of his mind, as he also tried to put out of his mind all the strange and foreign microorganisms that would be floating in that strange and alien air and what those little invisible creatures might do to him and his group. What he did try to focus on was the things he could control.

He began by making calculations of the pace he needed to maintain. He smiled to himself as he thought about how long the journey would take in a hover rover. Usually not more than an hour, perhaps two if you took the long way around and toured the active volcanoes on the way. On foot, however, he hoped they would be able to make it ten days or less and he was very concerned about how cold it was going to get those last few days. He had perhaps six or seven sunrises left before Reykjavik would fall behind the gaseous envelop of her parent planet and drop into her lunar winter. He also hoped that Tom's group had been able to get there in time and find a way down into the caves. He estimated the younger group would be able to move much faster and should get there within six days.

Having performed the required calculations to give his group the best shot at surviving the journey, he began to think about other dangers he would be facing.

He could not dismiss the danger that might be posed by the invisible black orbs that probably still loomed above, looking for and striking any sign of advanced technology on the surface below. He did a mental double check that the group had nothing that might draw attention to itself in its supplies. He was comforted to notice that it looked like his team had done a good job of cleaning everything they brought with them. Even items they had brought that might once have been able to produce or use power were ripped apart by the colonists if not by the attackers so they couldn't accidentally trigger an attack.

Finally his mind turned to the native life of Reykjavik and how it might feel about his little rag tag party. This time of the season the Snow Tigers would still be out, looking for any stragglers in the Sloth Worm herds. There was no question one of these great beasts would easily settle for a couple of members of his party as an alternative.

As he continued to hike, keeping an eye on his team as he did, he began to think further about what might be motivating the attackers to behave as they did. Surely, if they had the ability to pinpoint even small technology components with deadly precision and destroy them, then they could with ease have destroyed their owners. Why were they being left alive? It was as if the Intruders were saying, "you may live but you may not have technology."

He began to reflect back on his knowledge of the history of warfare. He reflected on how many of the most successful armies of Earth's past had learned how to take away their enemy's ability to fight back. Destroying an enemy's ability to resist had been found to be often easier and far more morally palatable than destroying your enemies. Once subdued, terms for coexistence were easily dictated. But perhaps those analogies were wrong. After all they were built upon a review of conflict within humanity itself. In many of these cases the opponents at least respected each other as fellow men, if not always as equals. It was this sense of decency, which, in all but the most horrid examples, saved the vanquished from the wrath of the victor. We were not the same as the Intruders though. They were strange and foreign beings with powerful technology, far more powerful than our own and with our technology destroyed we were little more than wild game to them, a part of the landscape little different than the native life of Reykjavik. Were we perhaps to be subdued, as Mankind had subdued the wild game of his planet tens of thousands of years ago, turning wild cattle into domesticated sources of food? Was that the future that lay ahead for Mankind to become livestock for the Intruders?

Greg couldn't think about it any more. He decided to focus his energies on the mission at hand: Staying alive and making it to the caves. As he brought his mind back to the here and now, he looked down at his little ward. Jennifer had climbed onto one of the carts and was now curled up in ball sleeping quietly on top of the supplies. He smiled as he noticed how the bumps and jostles of the rough ride didn't seem to interrupt her one bit. She just lay quietly, snuggled up between two of the warm atmospheric suits.

The group stopped briefly to eat and drink a little, after several hours of walking, then without a lot of fuss moved on. The conversation during the journey was minimal; everyone was working to save their energy. Periodically you'd hear a warning about a hole or a sharp rock and it seemed that almost everyone found a moment to encourage Jack and keep him safe.

"Watch out for that drop," or "slight step up" kept the young man feeling confident. He kept his ears peeled for the warnings and his fingers touching the back end of one of the carts.

Greg was most worried about the older members of the group, they were keeping up fine on the first day but he wasn't sure how they would be doing in a few days time. They would be hardest hit by the cold as well. He feared that more hard decisions might lie ahead.

They traveled for five days stopping only to eat, drink and sleep for short periods in the evening. The weather for the most part was kind to them. The Reykjavik Autumn was the one time the surface of the moon got rain and plenty of it. The vast quantities of water vapor that would hang in the atmosphere during the moons summer would cool and turn to clouds, then those clouds would release their moisture to the ground. First as a warm rain but as each day passed the showers would get colder. At first they wore ponchos cut from fabric to keep them dry but as the precipitation got colder, they put on the atmospheric suits. The suits made the walking slower but taking them off the carts made the cargo easier to haul. Their loads were also getting lighter as they went through their supplies. For the most part they had been lucky, the rains were not too heavy, the winds had remained quite still and so far the wildlife of Reykjavik had not threatened them. Things changed drastically on the sixth day.

The night had been a good one, the rain had let off and the winds had remained still. Despite the cold air, many of them had been able to sleep with their suits only loosely around them. In the early morning things took a turn for the worse though. As they began that day's portion of the journey, a harsh wind began to pick up from the South. The cold air blew dust into their face and made it difficult for them to walk. A hard cold slanting rain soon added its voice to the chorus and for the first time in their journey, turned to ice as it hit them with hard pellets of sleet. It then quickly turned into a blinding snow. What Greg wouldn't have done for a hover rover at this point in their journey. He had always enjoyed flying in the Reykjavik storms in the nibble little craft, thinking of them as friends to play with. Here on the ground there was nothing friendly about them. His group's progress for the day was cut in half and the night was not any easier. They did manage to find a rock bluff to shelter them from the driving wind and snow but the temperatures dropped further making it difficult to get any rest. They all huddled close together and tried to sleep the best they could.

The sun rose the next morning on what he thought would be the last day of the moon's autumn. Already the light reaching them was dulled to grayish green by the outer layers of the planet's atmosphere and the harsh storm that wasn't letting up, cut the light down to almost nighttime conditions. He knew though they were doomed if they stood still, so he gathered everyone up and tried to make some forward progress. Walking into the thick cold biting snow was almost unbearable and their pace was slowed to a crawl but the deteriorating weather wasn't the only hazard they were facing. Through the swirls of snow they began to see strange forms stalking them. Greg knew they could only be one thing: Snow Tigers.

The Snow Tiger, so named because of bristly spikes that covered their body that from a distance looked like fur, actually had more in common with Earth's Komodo Dragon than a large cat. Its metabolism was lizard like with its blood temperature varying widely with the environment but unlike Earth's lizards, the chemical composition of the creatures blood, if you wanted to call it blood, allowed them not only to endure the heat of the early autumn and late spring of Reykjavik but also enabled them to stay out in the environment during extreme cold. The bony spines that covered the body acted like insulation and slowed the loss of heat. A full grown adult was about twelve to fifteen feet in length and armed with sharp knifelike claws on the front two of its six legs. Greg's whole team knew the danger these creatures posed. Many of them had had the pleasure of watching them hunt from the safety of a hover rover. There was no pleasure, however, in knowing you were their prey.

Greg quickly gave instructions for the group to gather up and positioned the strongest members of his team in a perimeter with spears for defense. Unfortunately, he couldn't allow the fact that they were being stalked stop them, so the group kept moving forward, closely watching the shadows lurking in the storm.

As they progressed the hunters became more daring darting in closer to the group as if to test their defenses. Greg tried to keep everyone as close together as he could, hoping that the size of the group would deter attack. They would yell and jab out at the creatures as they came closer. Unfortunately the animals could not be kept at bay forever and finally they attacked.

One of the larger animals came straight at Greg. He held his position and lunged his spear at its frightening mass but the force of the lunge knocked him off his feet and left him lying in the snow. He looked up to find that he had managed to pierce his spear directly through the chest of the beast. It was still fighting though and managed to reach down with its massive claw and swipe Greg directly across the abdomen. He felt the sting of pain, as his suit and his skin were ripped open. At that moment his attacker jolted, as two of his fellow colonists plunged spears directly in its side. It screeched with the most hideous sound as it went down and Greg sighed half in relief and half in sheer pain.

He tried to get up to join the fight again but stumbled back to the ground and went dizzy, through his blurry eyes he saw one of his own taken into the mouth of one of the monsters and shaken about like a rag doll. His team went after this one to and brought it down like the first. It was clear there were others lurking in the storm but they seemed to fade away after loosing two of their pack.

Ann rushed over to him and instructed him to lie down. He felt the freezing cold on his body as she cut free the front of his suit; working quickly she bandaged up his abdomen and taped some new material across the front of his suit. He was then helped to one of the carts where he was instructed to sit and be pulled. He didn't want to be a burden to the team but several of his group told him that was nonsense and began to pull him through the storm. Jennifer snuggled up beside him and they both tried to stay warm in the blinding snow.

Greg was hoping against hope that they still might make it but chances were getting more and more remote. They were still perhaps three full days hike from the caves and at the pace they were moving that distance would take them twelve days at least. By that time the temperature on the surface would become so cold, that even in their protective clothing their blood would freeze. It was going to take a miracle to save them at this point.

They trudged on through the remainder of that day and the following night, stopping only to rest in short spans, trying to at least fulfill the need for physical rest. There were no more nights and days and the temperatures had dropped too low for them to get any sleep.

Finally, at least two full days hike from their destination, with darkness and winter storms all around them, and no real hope of reaching their goal, they stopped and gathered together. A fire was lit burning up their few remaining burnable supplies. Suffering from shear exhaustion and frostbite they couldn't move any further. Greg knew that it was helpless to even ask them to try. They had done their best. Everyone had done their best.

He was just about to call Ann over to discuss what might be done to ease the pain of their final moments when a startling event caught his eye. A great red and orange explosion burst into the Southern sky. Just on the horizon, on the ridgeline above the caves they were trying to reach, an eruption was now spewing molten lava down the mountainside.

The same thought struck everyone in the group immediately.

"Let's go everyone," Greg cried out to the group. "That's our miracle."

It might have been the only time in the history of man that the massive eruption of a volcano could have been seen as a life saving event but to the colonists of the Reykjavik Four, it meant one thing: heat and heat meant life.

He picked up Jennifer, kissed her on the cheek and placed her on the only cart they were still using. His stomach was still hurting but he found himself able to walk.

With the glowing river of lava flowing down onto the plateau the storm just didn't seem quite as strong. With some hope glowing ahead of them the group was able to move more quickly and it seemed that for every mile they traveled the lava river flowed two or three miles closer to them. It soon became clear the storm was having less effect on them as well. As they edged closer to the mountain range, small valleys began to emerge out of the ground in front of them heading up into the mountains. They chose one of the paths that the lava was following, looking to get as close as they could to the heat source.

Before long they reached the head of the fast moving river of molten rock. They made their way up the side of the ravine the lava was following, keeping perhaps fifty feet from the lava itself. That was close enough. Even at that distance the snow and ice was melting away into water and running toward the lava where it was quickly turned to steam. They sat for some time on a ledge over looking the life saving flow and warmed themselves.

Ann began to make rounds up and down the group inspecting everyone's fingers, toes and faces. Almost everyone in the group had some degree of frostbite, some of it quite bad. Ann spoke quickly to Greg, urging him to get everyone moving before the pain of the thawing extremities made it impossible for them to move. Greg heeded her advice and got the group moving.

Their luck seemed to come to an end when the ravine they were following narrowed such that there was no room for them to walk between the lava and the Cliffside. Their best luck yet came, however, when a rope dropped down from above and a familiar voice cried down.

"What took you so long?" the gruff voice cried.

Greg would recognize Tom Houston's booming shout just about anywhere and he couldn't imagine anything he would have rather heard at that moment.

It wasn't too much longer before they had helped everyone out of the ravine and made their way along the side of the mountains to a cave entrance. Four members of Tom's group had formed the scout team that had been sent out to find Greg's group, which Greg hoped meant the rest of the team was somewhere safe deep below the ground.

"You found a way down?" Greg asked anxiously.

"Of course, did you doubt us?" Tom asked jokingly, not really wanting to hear the answer. He put his hand on Greg's shoulder and then expanded on the details.

"We managed to use some of the base components of the energy modules on the drilling rigs to create chemical explosives. I had a good recollection of how far our drill holes sat from some of the higher cave areas and we just blasted our way through laterally. We could then use the passageways of the natural caves to get down the required depths. We think we've found a spot that will keep us sheltered through the winter. We'll take you straight down."

Then Tom continued.

"By the way, how did you like our welcome party?" he asked, nodding over to the erupting volcano behind them.

"You did that?" Greg asked.

"Sure, we thought you guys might need a little warming up, so we found some soft spots in the top of the dome and gave them a little help with the explosives we had left over," he explained, smiling proudly.

Greg smiled and shook his head laughingly at his friend thanking him silently for saving the lives of his group.

It took them a few more hours to work their way down into the rock through the maze of tunnels that Tom's group had uncovered. As they descended into the mountainside, the cold air of the surface drifted further and further behind. Tom and his team had made primitive torches to light the way and instructed Greg's group to leave their atmospheric suits in one of the chambers. They all felt relieved to remove the heavy clothes and to feel the warmer air against their faces. Before much longer they found themselves break out of a narrow passageway into a vast high domed cave that was mostly filled with water. The great underground lake must have been at least three times the size of the colony dome they called home a couple of weeks ago. Along the edge of the lake a flat area stretched away from the water and this was the spot that Tom's team had made their home for the last couple of days.

As they arrived members of Tom's group greeted them and brought them water and something paste like to eat.

Greg looked at Tom.

"We've been boiling water from the lake here and finding mushrooms that seem quite edible." Tom updated his boss. "But there is one problem we haven't got figured out yet."

With that statement, Tom led Greg over to the far area of the encampment to a group of three who were lying against the cave wall. Greg looked down and could see they were in a lot of pain and as he held the light closer, he noticed blue and green blotches that were appearing all over their skin. He had expected this but hoped he'd have more time to prepare for it. Reykjavik was fighting back. The human invaders who were contaminating her realm were now being invaded themselves. Tiny microorganisms in the air were taking advantage of their newfound hosts.

Greg turned away from the victims as Ann arrived to take a look at their infections. He walked down to the edge of the water and sat down. His little companion joined him and snuggled up beside him. He put his arm around her, kissed her on the forehead and then turned to look out across the lake.

The reflections of the torches danced across the still water
of the lake and the chatter of the colony bounced off the roof
of the cave and echoed back to him. The sensations made the
cave seem strangely warm and welcoming. Greg felt blessed to
have survived the day but knew the challenges for Reykjavik
colony were just beginning.

Chapter 10

The Soldier

3735
Earth

Michael Kelly flopped down onto the stone bench and looked down at his personal wrist terminal.

"Twelve minutes and thirty-two seconds, not bad," Kelly thought to himself. He took a few deep breaths, practicing a controlled heart rate slow down, and took a moment to enjoy the view below him.

The beach goers far below looked like little specs, dotting the white sandy beach. To the left he had a clear view of the marina and the pleasure yachts docked along the ornate wooden piers. The scenery was absolutely breathtaking. You simply couldn't have imagined bluer water or bluer sky and the ocean breeze flowing up the cliff toward him was exhilarating. Kelly, however, wasn't one for enjoying the view for very long. A view that someone else might have spent a whole afternoon soaking up, Kelly absorbed in a matter of seconds. His mind was now ready to move on. He took a closer look down the ancient stone staircase he had just climbed up from the ocean. He considered for a moment how he might have improved upon his time, knowing that like most of his self imposed training tests, he would only take this one once. Kelly believed that the best training was to expose his mind and his body to every new challenge he possibly could. Dealing with the unexpected made him ready for anything. Usually, he would be training in a location far less hospitable than the beautiful coastline of southwestern Europe but a family visit had brought him here and he wasn't going to let the relaxed environment slow him down. He had taken advantage of the opportunity to work on his swimming, climbing and running. But now it was time to focus on what would come next.

First he needed to take a look at his finances. A couple of taps on the screen on his wrist and up it came. "432.654 credits" the screen displayed. That would last him about a week. He was going to need some more money soon.

In thirty eighth-century society, there were several basic ways that folks paid their keep. The most old fashioned way was to have a paying job. In past centuries the vast majority of the adult population would have earned their living that way, or have been a member of a family that did. That was still the case in most of the outer colonies. On Earth, however, things were different. Only a small fraction of the population still earned a living by working and most of those worked in some type of decision-making or intellectual capacity, perhaps as a corporate decision maker, politician or high ranking civil servant. Most other tasks were performed by man's advanced technology. This left the vast majority of the population free to enjoy their lives. Many lived off the accumulated wealth of their ancestors. They would invest in the various markets of the complex financial system, taking a little off the top every now and again to support themselves. A few would even trade in their Birthright. Those who had decided they didn't want to keep their Birthright within their family would sell that right for an advance payment and could live much of their lives off that sale. A Birthright future was the most valuable trade-able commodity there was. The rest, those who did not want to work in a job, didn't have invested wealth or the desire to trade in their own birthright, could still live a comfortable life. They earned a living by learning things.

Over eighteen hundred years ago, Mankind had first discovered that the productivity provided by technology had created new challenges. The ability of a smaller number of people to produce a greater amount of goods left less for others to do. This created great poverty and desperation in much of the population in earlier times. Mankind experimented with various ways of dealing with this problem. First, entirely new economic systems emerged, replacing the age-old systems of inherited power and wealth that had served man since ancient times.

Communist and Socialist societies emerged. These systems attempted to rectify the problems of industrial society by guaranteeing everyone a job and thus directly managing the spread of wealth within the economy. This system, though relatively good at distributing wealth, proved highly flawed in its ability to create it. Without the ability to retain a good portion of the wealth created by their own innovation, people were motivated to simply follow the flow. Technology failed to progress. Corruption and complacency soon crept in and wrecked entire nations.

Similarly early capitalism had its own failures. Though very adept at creating new wealth, it suffered in its ability to distribute it. Those that were not needed by the economy at a given time were simply left out in the cold, called the unemployed, no one was quite sure what to do with them, especially the unemployed themselves. At first they were simply reduced to destitute poverty but in the mid twentieth century the more advanced nations of the planet began to experiment with remedies for this problem with programs like welfare, unemployment pay or doll. These systems were limited in their success, however. Societies soon found out that giving people something for nothing simply didn't work. People simply did not attach value to the precious gift they were being given. They were left feeling like lower class citizens, dependent upon the state. The result was crime, substance addiction and general unrest in the lower levels of the economic ladder.

Creative solutions to this problem began to emerge in the early twenty first century and became refined in later years. The trick was to create an environment where everyone had the freedom and opportunity to earn their keep but every keep was earned. The solution was not only to pay people for their contribution to the economy but also to pay them for increasing their ability to contribute to the economy. Those that couldn't find jobs applying the knowledge they had, could earn a living though the acquisition of new knowledge. The system became known as the knowledge economy and it had survived and been refined for over fifteen hundred years, existing side by side and as a symbiotic system to the free market capitalist world.

The knowledge economy began as a move by wealthy nations and global corporations to close the vast educational gap that existed between wealthy and developing nations. In a global treaty, signed in the early twenty first century, the signing companies and nations agreed to donate a tiny percentage of their revenues into the newly created knowledge bank. The signing companies were granted improved trading status within the signing nations to drive their participation.

The knowledge bank in turn invested in global digital access and a testing and certification program to educate the citizenry of the developing regions. The target audience was compensated for taking and passing tests and proving attainment of new knowledge.

From these small beginnings the basis of the future economy of Earth would evolve. Mankind would still depend primarily upon publicly traded, profit driven, companies to deliver most of the goods and services that people depended upon. Of all the revenue that a company earned, however, a percentage was allocated into the knowledge market. As always, another percentage went to the government to fund the few services still provided by the public sector. These included security, law enforcement and oversight of key global systems like the financial network, transport and healthcare. The knowledge market and the education it provided, however, was a non-government environment. The contributing companies themselves determined where to put their money and therefore what knowledge attainment they wished to sponsor. Its success in the developing world soon led it to supplement the state education systems of the wealthy nations as well. Before long the system was available across the globe to anyone who was not employed. Governments encouraged the program and it soon grew to replace the welfare and education systems of the past.

Knowledge attainment was broken down into levels and the market gave visibility to how many people had attained a given level in a given subject and how many were in a position to gain the next level. Companies invested their knowledge funds toward promoting attainment of knowledge they themselves might someday need. This created a virtual reserve workforce that companies could leverage in the future. The unemployed became known as reservists and gained a sense of self worth based on their educational accomplishments. Every reservist was able to earn a limited but very sufficient living by preparing to provide value in the future.

The greatest benefit of the knowledge economy was that it was a self-balancing system. It kept things from growing too fast or from stagnating. The balance was managed by setting a target for the size of the reserve workforce: the corporations who had signed the knowledge bank treaty and those that joined later defined this target. If the target was being exceeded, the percentage of funds allocated to the knowledge fund was reduced driving the reservists to find better pay by joining the active workforce. If the target was not being met, the percentage of revenue allocated to the knowledge fund was increased, creating an environment where members of the active workforce might find better pay learning rather than working.

As technology improved and productivity increased, the target percentage of the reserve work force steadily grew. By 3700 it had reached ninety-four percent, meaning only six percent of the earth's population still worked for a living. Given that a large portion of the population had acquired family wealth handed down from generation to generation and no longer participated in the knowledge market place, those that chose to earn an income from knowledge attainment had a lucrative market available to them.

Michael Kelly was one of those people. When his travels left his finances short, he would simply log onto the knowledge market and select a couple of certifications that would earn him the funds he needed. Whenever possible he would try to select certifications that might in some way enhanced the skills he cared about. A quick scan of his terminal found a couple of courses he liked: "Advanced Cycle Reactor Engineering Level IV" and the "Battle Tactics of Attila the Hun".

It wasn't that Michael Kelly wasn't interested in becoming part of the work force. He was in fact highly qualified in his chosen skill; it was just that there was very little demand at the present for what Kelly considered his line of work. Michael Kelly, by every fiber of his training was one thing: a soldier, a soldier without a war.

In earlier times being a soldier might have meant he was good with a sword, or perhaps a gun but in his time it meant something much more. It meant that he had an acute understanding of technology, physics and battle tactics and he had extremely well trained reflexes to deliver that knowledge. It meant that given an array of military assets and a myriad of attacking forces his mind and body were tuned to define the deployment of those resources to have maximum effect against an attacking enemy. Of course like most other things in the thirty-eighth century, waging war was something done, if it were being done at all, mostly by technology. Michael Kelly understood that, but was prepared to be part of and enhance, the capabilities of that system. Technology still lacked one thing: human creativity and it had been determined that even on the battle field that unpredictable ingredient was a valuable thing.

As valuable as his skills were, Kelly chose to remain a reservist, learning by himself, independently. It wasn't that there weren't jobs available for him if he'd chosen a different line of work. He constantly received offers to join the UGSS, or criminal reaction teams but this just didn't cut it for Kelly. He had trained his whole life to serve humanity in only one way, as part of the Interstellar Naval Command or INC. There was only one problem for Kelly: there was no INC.

The group had been formed in the late thirty-sixth century, during the Foresythe administration with its mission being to launch counter attacks against the Intruder force that had destroyed Omega Theta, as it attacked other systems. The force, however, had been dismantled forty years after its creation even before the launch of its first mission. Political favor had shifted and the general belief that the Intruders would ever return had faded. Their six warships had been mothballed, with most of them now dismantled and their components used in newly approved generation ships. Only one remained, The Avenger, and she was scheduled for disassembly in less than a year.

Kelly had seen The Avenger. He had even been on board. It had been a high point of his life. He had taken a tour shuttle out to Saturn where she sat in orbit and participated in a rare guided tour of the ship. Of course, when she was built, The Avenger was an unmanned ship. Unless she had been built as a generation ship there would have been no way to get a manned crew to her target destination and the decision had been made not to sacrifice weapons cargo space for people. In the hundred years since her mothballing, however, new Cryo technology had emerged that made it possible to include human creative capabilities into the weapons arsenal of any new interstellar warship that Mankind might chose to build. The Avenger, or more likely her replacements would now carry a crew with them. A small group of well trained combat experts would become part of the cargo, transported across the stars in a near frozen state, able to deliver, when needed, that vital element of human creativity to the powerful weapons array of their host ship.

For Kelly, however, he knew that his dreams of serving his people as a warrior, sent out across the stars, were probably no more than dreams. The INC would most likely remain a forgotten chapter of a different time. A time when at least for a few short decades, Mankind feared for its existence and heroes were in high demand.

Today, Kelly found himself sitting on one of the most beautiful spots on a planet that felt it had nothing to fear from anything. He was part of a global civilization that had reached a peaceful and prosperous high point in its long history and had only better and more glorious times to look forward to. Kelly was an anomaly, a man who believed we had enemies and had dedicated his life in preparation to challenge them.

After selecting the courses that met his needs, he decided it was time to get moving. He stood up from the bench and looked around for the nearest access point to the travel tubes.

The overlook was a cozy stone patio cut into the side of the cliff very near its top. Around its edge beautiful flowering bushes gave the spot a wonderful fragrance that lifted up on the ocean breeze. A gardening droid was making a pass of the plants trimming, watering and feeding them as it moved along. A couple of tourists were chatting on the bench across from him. In the back of the patio there was a stone archway integrated into the rock. In it sat what appeared to be a decorative wooden door that fit well into the rustic décor of the overlook. Engraved into the door was the word "Tube Station". Kelly walked up to the door, which opened automatically as he got close. From the rustic wooden appearance, you might have expected it to creek open like the doorway to an ancient castle, but no; it simply slid aside with a slight "whoosh".

Behind the doorway sat a much more modern looking room. On each side of the room were two more benches but this time they were bright in color and simple in design. Above them large display screens flashed images of some of the local products and services that Kelly might have been interested in. The abundance of outdoor equipment and physically intense activities presented, made it quickly apparent to Kelly that like any information display system the information was being tailored to him. The doorway he had entered just a moment ago, had not only opened for him but had also performed a biometric scan of his face and eyes to identify him, charge him for entry to the tube system and tailor its environment to his needs and desires. Despite the intelligent effort to grab his attention Kelly barely noticed the images on the screens. Instead he walked to the other side of the room where a large transparent tube filled the back wall. The tube was approximately eight feet in diameter and entered on one side of the room and left on the other. In the center of the back wall, at the mid point on the tube's traversal of the room, there was a bulge, a semi spherical outcropping with a small display screen attached to it. Kelly stood directly in front of this panel and spoke.

"Private Pod Please," Kelly instructed the panel.

"Yes, Mr. Kelly," the panel responded in a polite female voice. The system also knew that Kelly preferred a female voice.

Within a few seconds, a spherical object slid down the tube and stopped directly in front of him. It then slid forward and locked itself in a perfect fit into the docking point. Once locked in place, both the transparent side of the docking point and the sidewall of the ball-shaped transport pod swiveled to grant access to a comfortable looking circular couch that lined the walls of the cozy little ball. Kelly stepped in, sat down and gave further instructions to the system.

"Cairo," he said.

The Sahara Desert Preserve would be a fine place to train.

The side of the little pod, swiveled shut and it accelerated down the tube with barely a sound.

The tube system was an amazing creation and had served as the main transport system of Mankind for over fifteen hundred

years. Of course, the specific technology had changed many
times but the principles behind it had remained the same.
The tube system had its origins in the subway systems
of the twentieth century, more specifically in the Executive
Subway project initiated in New York in the mid twenty first
century. At that time problems of pollution, traffic congestion
and safety were still plaguing the road-based transport that
had served man for almost 100 years. Hydrogen fuel cell based
vehicles were solving the pollution problems and automated
driving systems attempted to make the system more convenient
but the fundamental constraints of the so-called "open road"
were limiting the evolution of the man's transportation. The
Executive Subway was an exciting alternative. Targeted at
the wealthy financial decision makers that were the kingpins
of the global powerhouse that was New York, the system was
an electric rail system than ran in tubes throughout key parts
of the city and into the suburbs but unlike the subway the
system was designed as a private transport system. Individual
private rail cars took a passenger wherever he or she wanted
to go and the closed tubes of the system allowed the cars to
reach speeds completely unsafe on the road. The system was
an instant success and soon expanded to connect many of the
cities of the Eastern U.S. Passengers could step into a private
car right in downtown New York and find themselves on the
capital steps of Washington within an hour. Copycat systems
sprang up in other cities across the world and soon the systems
became compatible and interlinked.
Technology advancements in the systems followed.
Powerless cars that were driven by air pressure in the tubes,
replaced the electrical railcars. Air was sucked out from in
front of the car and forced in behind. The new tube riders, as
they were known, traveled at speeds close to the speed of sound
and though still slower than the ballistic shuttles that handled
much of the long-range transport. They were far less brutal
on the environment. It was the environmental collapse of the
twenty second century that really solidified the tube system as
the transport network of the planet. Later innovations added
magnetic levitation propulsion to the system and changed the
tube riders to spherical pods. By making the tube riders ball
shaped and adding gyros to keep them upright, they could now

move vertically as well as horizontally and as such were able to take the passengers not only to their building of choice but right to their room. It wasn't until the fourth millennium that the final addition to the tube system came into being. With high efficiency electric technology finally making possible long range non polluting flight, the Aero shuttle came into being, allowing the transport pods as they had become known to be carried anywhere the tube system didn't go.

Unfortunately for Kelly, his budget rarely supported a private aero shuttle, so he stayed tube bound. Riding the tubes didn't bother Kelly at all though. He used the time to study. This trip would take him about an hour and a half. He would shoot down the central peninsula of Italian Southern Europe through an undersea tube into Africa and on across to his destination.

Across the pod on the opposite side from the semi circular couch that Kelly was comfortably lounging on, there was another terminal screen that took about three feet of the far wall. He looked at it and gave an instruction.

"Logon."

Within a moment the screen display came online mimicking the display on his wrist terminal but much larger. The system knew his voice and had logged him into his own tailored virtual environment. First he checked his finances once again to find out what his little tube ride was costing him. Like everything in the thirty-eighth century the cost of transportation changed every second, as part of a fluid and interconnected economy. Kelly knew whatever price he had paid was acceptable to him as he predefined the parameters of any negotiation in his personal financial profile. As expected the price was reasonable.

Next, he accessed the study materials for the course on Attila and began to delve into the fascinating history of this dynamic leader. He was pleased to find that the screen of this pod was in very good working order.

Unlike two-dimensional viewing technologies of ancient times, the viewing screen of the transport pod presented a three-dimensional image. This despite the fact the screen itself was paper-thin device spread across the wall of the pod. The trick: almost a thousand years old now but much more refined than its earlier predecessor, was the multi directional pixel. Like its ancestors, this device created an image through the use of millions of tiny dots that scattered across its surface. But unlike its more primitive descendents, the pixels of this screen were capable of emitting a different frequency of light in different directions. This allowed the screen to present a different image to an eye or a person viewing the screen from one spot compared to another eye or person viewing from somewhere else. If a face was displayed, a spectator on the left side of the pod would see the left side of the face and the person on the right the right side of the face. The result was magnificent, a perfect three-dimensional image.

As the screen displayed the details of a hunic bow, the choice weapon of Attila's horse born warriors, Kelly couldn't help but dream of reaching out and grabbing the powerful and ancient weapon. How he would have loved to have served with Attila. Though his nomadic people would never match the majesty of their Roman adversaries, their military prowess was the envy of their contemporaries and many military historians since.

Kelly's studies were suddenly interrupted.

"New job offer received," the screen displayed.

"Ok, I'll play along," thought Kelly, believing there was no way this could be anything more than a very clever joke. There was only one job position that Kelly was currently interested in and the INC wasn't hiring. They didn't even exist.

He opened the message and read it:

"Position description: Interstellar Naval Academy Cadet - further details: classified."

Kelly thought what the hell, he had nothing to loose.

"I accept," he proudly pronounced, expecting some corny 'just kidding' to follow.

The message disappeared and for a while Kelly thought the joke was over but then he realized his transport pod had taken a turn he hadn't expected. Through the transparent wall of the pod and the transparent tube, he could see he had been taken up to the surface and he hadn't expected that. From the scenery above him, it looked like he was still in Italy at least an hour away from the trans-Mediterranean tube. But he wasn't heading out to the undersea tubes. He was headed for an aero shuttle port. Sure enough, before long, his pod came to the end of a tube and was inserted into the belly of a single pod aero shuttle, which immediately took off and headed north.

He wasn't going to Cairo anymore.

There had to be an explanation for this. He looked back at the screen that had now returned to his study file and gave a new instruction.

"News," he snapped.

Kelly hated the news. He never watched it. He knew if anything really important happened he'd learn about it somehow. The endless gossip and sensationalism was nothing more than a distraction to him.

Sure enough, there it was, all over the news; Reykjavik. He knew it well. He'd studied this crazy little corner of the galaxy in the past. He'd even taken a course in its climate and native life. He wondered if anyone had survived. Very little was really known. It was mostly speculation. The only way they had been able to confirm it as an Intruder attack was through the maintenance log data of the communications array. The colony hadn't even been able to deploy a sensor array to warn them of the attack.

"Could this really be happening?" he thought to himself, tempted to pinch himself to see if he'd nodded off, only to wake up in Cairo.

It was enough of a surprise that another attack had occurred. It had been over two hundred years since the original attack on Omega Theta and most of humanity had become convinced that it wasn't going to happen again. The added surprise was that Interstellar Naval Command was already active and hiring and that he had been selected. It was one thing to work your whole life toward a goal. It was another to have it happen.

The shuttle climbed quickly and continued north. Below him Kelly could see the western coastline of the Italy and the Alps lay dead ahead. The flight was fast and short lasting perhaps ten minutes before he began to descend directly into the Alps. For a moment it would seem he would crash directly into the mountainside of the one of the more magnificent peaks but as he drew closer to the cliff, a vast opening appeared in the mountainside and his shuttle flew in. It slowed and came to a rest in the solid rock hangar. Kelly thought for a moment

that his ride was over but a slight jolt told him his pod was
dropping back into a transport tube.

It was difficult to tell exactly where he was headed as he
dropped deeper into the rock but it was clear to him that he
was going down. He knew he'd probably traveled several miles
before his pod finally came to a rest. The door swiveled open to
the most surprising part of the whole journey.

"What the hell are you waiting on slime bucket?" a very
large man in a simple grey uniform screamed at him, as he
scrambled to exit the pod.

This was unbelievable, INC seemed to be using intensive
human interaction stress training, a method of military
indoctrination used throughout much of history but now
considered obsolete. After a few seconds of confusion Kelly
realized that his strong sense of military history gave him a
good sense of what to do: stay alert, do exactly what you were
told to do, don't ask any questions and most of all don't show
any emotion other than the obligatory appearance of fear and
obedience. Exhibiting any other reaction would only mean
trouble. Most would be fighting back a sense of desperation
and confusion. Kelly, however, was fighting to stop himself
from laughing.

"I said move!" the loud man yelled, which was perhaps a
little unnecessary as Kelly was already moving quite quickly.

"Where the hell do you think your taking that?" the man
continued to yell, as he grabbed Kelly's pack out of his hand
and threw to the back of the room.

"I guess I won't be needing that," Kelly thought to himself,
still trying not to laugh.

"Through the doors two lefts, two rights and straight-ahead
then though the blue door," the man continued to yell. "Don't
make me repeat myself!" the screaming continued, again
unnecessary as Kelly had captured every instruction and was
already moving out.

He had not been specifically instructed to run but Kelly
knew the drill and double-timed it down the maze of hallways
and through the doors. As he ran, he found himself joined by a
couple of others who had obviously been similarly harassed as
they entered this complex. The three of them charged through
the doors and joined a group of about twenty others who were

standing in a long low room neatly at attention. They weren't given any more instructions but sensed the best thing to do was simply join the line and freeze. They heard the sound of the door slamming behind them then heard a new voice, even louder and more ominous that the first.

"About face!" the voice boomed.

It was a sound one might only hear once if their life, the kind of sound that commanded fear and respect instantly. Kelly felt chills rush down his spine and a whirlwind of emotions swept over him. It suddenly struck him that he had entered a completely new world. His life had suddenly and dramatically changed and would never be the same again. It was as if the ground beneath his feet had changed to liquid and sucked him down into a great vortex. He felt a rush of elation knowing he was part of a great and powerful machine: the sword of humanity, Interstellar Naval Command.

He whirled around with a precision and grace that very few possessed in this day. The skills of military drill were lost, even to most security professionals of his time but like all things military Kelly had studied the art and admired the personal discipline and physical precision it required. As his feet locked in place one hundred and eighty degrees from where they had been a moment before he came face to face with his future.

The Commander stared back at him and his comrades but yet not quite at them, more through them. He began to speak in a firm and resolute voice, quieter than before but still demanding of attention. Before the first words even left his mouth however, the cadets heard the sound of more doors quickly opening and closing behind them and the shuffling of several instructors entering the room from their rear. The experience that followed was mind-boggling.

"First, I want to welcome each of you to the INC cadet program," the grey-headed officer began.

"Something wrong with your eyeballs dirt bag?" a gruff voice yelled directly into the ears of the cadet to the right of Kelly. "Your Commander is speaking to you."

Clearly the cadet did not respond correctly, perhaps he jolted or turned his head. Kelly wasn't about to look over to find out. Whatever the reason Kelly heard the distinct sound of a closed fist striking the unfortunate cadet in the side, probably the kidneys. This was followed by the sound of his body slumping to the deck.

The significance of this moment was not lost on Kelly. He knew the levels within the government that things would have to go in order to authorize the use of physical force in training. He knew also that his time would come but he intended to do everything he could to delay that moment.

"Of course for most of you the experience will last only a matter of moments and that's for the lucking ones," the Commander continued.

The other instructors closed in on a female cadet toward the other end of the line and Kelly could hear the insults flying but tried to focus only on the voice in front of him. He couldn't help but notice this one was a fighter and stood and took it for a little while after the instructors found their reason to punish her. After several blows, she finally buckled and dropped to the deck. Kelly stayed frozen, focused on the gruff voice, and kept his heart rate under control. He had spent his life learning to control his fight or flight reactions, so that he could channel most of his energy to his most important weapon, his brain.

"I'm out of here," Came the sound of a third cadet who had decided he just wasn't up for the job. The instructors barely noticed as he bolted toward the door. The instructors didn't react at all. It quickly became clear they were free to leave at any time. Two more decided to make a quick exit.

"For the rest of you," the speech continued in the same firm and controlled voice maintained since it the beginning, "The experience will simply be an endless stream of painful tests; each one more excruciating than the one before and if you are successful at completing your training, we will reward you by putting you into an icebox and sending you out across space where you will meet a painful and inglorious death."

It was at that moment that Kelly knew he'd come to the right place.

The process continued until Kelly found himself the only one still standing at perfect attention in the line, the others were all sprawled on the ground or struggling to get back to their feet.

For the first time the Commander's eyes met Kelly's directly with a stare that could cut through steel. Kelly fought to hold his composure and focused on the man's final line. "A man would have to be crazy to join the Interstellar Naval Command."

Almost exactly as the last words left his lips he felt the crunching force of two large instructors punching him in his sides. He held his position for a few blows but then bent and went down to the floor. As he collapsed he felt a sense of pride that his adversaries had not bothered to find flaws with his posture, they had merely dealt him the test that everyone else had received.

He lay on the floor for a little while and carefully checked himself for injury. His ribs were bruised but nothing that wouldn't heal. The test had been executed with perfect care. He was tested, not broken.

As he checked himself over, he heard the Commander leave the room. It was at that point he realized he recognized the man's face. It was as if he had seen a ghost from the pages of history. He couldn't place it but somewhere somehow, he knew who this man was.

His thoughts were quickly interrupted when the other instructors began calling the names of the cadets and directed them through different hallways. Just as before everything was at double-time.

"Vasquez," he heard one of the instructors yell, as the tough female ran to the door he was pointing to.

"Kelly" another yelled, almost immediately after. "Third door, down the hall right, left, right again and second door on the left."

Kelly got the instructions and moved out. He felt the pain in his sides but tried not to let it slow him down. He came to the door in question and realized for the first time since he had entered the complex he was standing alone. He took a short moment to look around the hallway, noticing several small black smooth nodes lining the ceiling and realized these had also been in the room where they had taken the beating. Sensor nodes were taking visual, thermal and audio recordings of the cadets. Though they had been subjected to an old fashion physical indoctrination the very latest technology had measured just how much they had sweat.

He decided it wasn't wise to delay long, took a quick moment to straighten his appearance and knocked on the door.

"Come in, come in," came the response, from a polite voice as the door slid quietly open.

The room was a stark change from the Spartan surroundings in the rest of the complex. High definition three dimensional display panels covered all of the walls and ceilings and presented majestic mountain vistas in every direction. The result was remarkable. One might have easily thought they had stepped out onto a precipice where a simple desk was perched on top of a high peak in the Rockies or the Alps.

"Are the mountains Ok?" the small man behind the counter asked. "I understand from your file you're an avid outdoorsman."

"Yes," Kelly responded quickly absorbing the view as the man beckoned him to sit.

"My name is Michael Silversmith and I'll be handling your registration process," the man continued holding out his hand.

Kelly shook hands with the man and sat down. What followed was a pleasant conversation in which Mr. Silversmith confirmed the information found in Kelly's file, which was of course all correct. Kelly quickly sensed that much more was going on, however. He noticed sensors in the desk in front of him and was sure the chair he was sitting in was doing more than just supporting his weight. This was a character-profiling interview. By combining the expertise of the interviewer with sophisticated monitoring technology more was being learned about Michael Kelly than he even knew about himself. The interview lasted perhaps ninety minutes with Mr. Silversmith asking most of the questions. Kelly was able to ask a few questions of his own but wasn't really able to get a lot of information. He imagined that keeping him in the dark regarding the nature of the training was an integral part of the training process itself.

Mr. Silversmith closed the interview with a last friendly sounding question. "How about that Commander he's something isn't he?" as if to elicit some type of negative response from Kelly. Kelly answered the question with the same frank honesty he'd answered all the others.

"He's obviously an outstanding leader," Kelly replied. Few would have given that answer and been completely honest.

Mr. Silversmith smiled warmly and showed Kelly to the door, closing their time together with the only straight statement he'd made. "Good luck Mr. Kelly," he said, shaking his hand once more.

Kelly had no way of knowing whether he'd passed this test or not and wasn't given much time to think about it.

"What do you think this is social hour?" screamed one of the younger instructors who'd been waiting outside the door. Kelly was rushed down another set of long hallways to a new room. Where only one other cadet was waiting. He quickly put a name to the face, Vasquez. He thought perhaps they were the first two to complete the interview process and others would follow, but none came. It seemed they were the only two to have gotten this far. At that point, the process seemed to shift from obvious indoctrination to something more like in processing.

They were given haircuts, issued uniforms and went through endless streams of interview sessions both electronic and in person. They selected Birthright and financial beneficiaries, preferred transition rights and person to notify of assignment to INC. Biofeedback monitors were permanently attached to their wrists and measurements were taken of every internal and external feature and bodily metric possible. Throughout the entire process, they were rushed, screamed at and struck for every little slip up or error. Focus and attention to detail were the name of the game even when resting. They were given barely any sleep and kept on their feet all day, stressed to the limit mentally and physically. They saw very little of the Commander but were always being watched by one or more of his junior instructors. After several days it seemed their in processing was finally complete and the real training began.

It was at this point that they finally met up with some other cadets. Four other small groups joined them, bringing their total group size up to twelve. The training curriculum surprised Kelly. He had anticipated an extensive amount of technical and reflex training of which there was plenty but had not expected nearly the extent of physical training they were receiving. Day after day went by with almost an even split of what he might have considered interstellar combat training and physical survival training. The combat training consisted mostly of virtual reality simulations. In these sessions they were placed into a simulated combat pod, controlling a sophisticated weapons and sensor array. From this small floating pod that had been launched from a large interstellar Mother Ship, they commanded perhaps two hundred assets, all of which moved independently of each other as determined by instructions from the combat pod. The instructions given were not just provided by their human commanders but also by the artificial intelligence that sat both in the combat pod and in the weapons assets themselves. The weapons and sensor modules varied in both size and capability. Some had the role of detecting and tracking hostile entities. Others carried powerful beam weapons that could be directed at incoming targets. Yet others served the role of floating mines or torpedoes that when detonated would focus megatons of explosive force within their immediate vicinity. Finally an array of defensive units provided protection by acting as decoys against incoming attackers. The enemies they engaged in these simulated battles were mostly based on what was already known about the Intruder technology. Great invisible Mother Ships detectable only by the gravitational field they produced, making them hard to track and engage, would enter the battle area. Rarely would they even get a shot off against these monsters. Instead they were left to do battle with their spawn. Large numbers of smaller but equally difficult to detect, spherical orbs would be deposited into their immediate area and close in on them. Usually these adversaries would tear them to pieces. Occasionally, however, they would get a lucky shot in and take one out. They were quickly made aware though that there was really very little knowledge of what it would take to destroy an Intruder ship. None had been shot down yet. Any weaknesses the simulations attributed to their enemies were purely hypothetical.

Kelly found these simulations mostly tested his mental reflexes and his ability to quickly leverage a deep knowledge of physics and technology to deploy his assets most effectively.

The physical training was completely different, however, and mostly focused on their ability to survive in extremely hostile conditions. At one point in the training, each cadet was taken to the middle of a desert, which from the look of it was probably a wildlife reserve in what was once the Sahara, and left without supplies. Kelly was delirious from heat stroke and almost dieing of thirst by the time he was able to find a source of water, something he was only able to do by close observation of the few small creatures he observed during the exercise. During another drill, the same challenge of survival in extreme conditions was presented but this time it was the extreme cold of an alpine mountain pass they were forced to endure. Again Kelly's own training and experience paid off, allowing him to find shelter in the rough craggy landscape.

On both occasions Kelly wondered whether INC would just leave him for dead if he failed the mission. He knew of course he was being watched from afar but had no idea how close to death they would let him slip.

Though Kelly always relished the opportunity to improve his skills and increase his abilities, he was relieved when graduation finally arrived. He had been in training for twelve weeks and the experience had been far more challenging than any self-imposed test he had endured. He was thankful though that he had made it. Of the twelve in his group that had made it through in processing, only five now remained. Vasquez who had been with him since the beginning was still in and three other cadets that had joined them later, were also on the team. Five of them were left of an original group of probably one hundred and fifty.

The graduation event was short and included very little ceremony. The Commander, whose name they still did not know, spoke to them again, as if to give one last chance to change their minds. He closed his speech once again on a clear and somber note.

"You should all be very proud of yourselves for what you have accomplished. It's a real shame a cold and lonely death in the depths of space is the only reward we'll be giving you."

With that the group filed before the Commander and received a small pin that signaled their entry into this elite order. The pin was a simple one. Its background was a blue ellipse filled

with little white stars, in the foreground there was a silver
sword vertically placed such that it's tip and handle extended
beyond each side of the elliptical background. Kelly felt a chill
rush down his spine, as the pin was placed on the lapel of his
simple grey uniform.

"Welcome to the core Lieutenant," the Commander said
as he firmly grasped and shook Kelly's hand. Kelly strained
to remember where he knew the man's face, still with no
success.

Before long, the event was completed and they were standing
around congratulating each other, pleased that the challenge
was over, at least for now. Kelly felt a finger tap him on the
shoulder and turned to see Vasquez standing behind him.

"So, Kelly, where are you taking me tonight?"

Kelly hadn't given a single thought to how he would spend
his graduation night but the moment he saw Vasquez looking
at him and smiling, it struck him that though he may not
have realized it until now, he had given plenty of thought
to what a beautiful woman his fellow cadet was. More than
that, Vasquez was comrade in arms and probably the best in
the group. The combined feelings of deep respect and strong
physical attraction took him off guard and left him stuttering.

"What, I mean, where would you like to go?" he responded
somewhat feebly.

Vasquez was not so shy. She slipped her arm around his
waist and smiled.

"We'll figure it out on the way," she said.

Before long they were alone in a travel pod and heading
for the Greek islands. They only had a forty-eight hour pass
and they had their entire training pay to spend, so they were
heading for one of the most beautiful spots on the planet. With
only two days to spend three months pay, they were going to
spare no expense. Their time together flew by.

They rented the most glorious villa with a sunset view of the
Mediterranean and were at each other's side the entire time.
During the day they rented a yacht, sailed and dove among
the reefs. In the evenings they danced and dined in café's that
had barely changed in two thousand years. They spent the
night wrapped in each other's arms till the early hours of the
morning. It was the best time that Kelly had known in his

entire life. Kelly had always done well with the opposite sex, after all he was young, extremely intelligent and in excellent shape but he had never in his life bonded with someone the way he found himself entranced with Vasquez. They were both one in a million characters, lifelong soldiers in a world at peace, the first of many that would follow.

The last morning of their break they found themselves sitting together on the patio of their villa, looking down on the waves crashing against the cliff below. They hadn't talked about INC at all while they were together but their minds couldn't help but wonder what lay ahead.

"Where do you think we're going?" Vasquez asked.

"I'm not sure," Kelly responded, wondering what all the training they'd had was preparing them for.

They stared longingly at each other for a moment as if to ask if there was some way they could freeze time and make this day last forever but they knew they would have to head back within a couple of hours. Vasquez stood up, took his hand and led him back into the Villa to share there the rest of their time alone.

The trip back to the Alps was solemn; they barely spoke but rather held each other close and watched the scenery flash by.

When they arrived, INC headquarters seemed almost frozen. Everyone in the facility was glued to one of the many viewing screens spaced around the complex. Usually the screens would have been off, or providing information regarding training activities but today they were all on and tuned into the news feed. Vasquez, like Kelly, never stayed in touch with the news, so they knew nothing of the latest events.

What they were witnessing seemed almost unbelievable.

It had been over one hundred and sixty years between the attack upon Omega Theta and the destruction of Reykjavik colony and in that time the Intruders had moved only eight light-years closer to Earth. Now news had arrived of another attack and only a few short months after the last disaster.

Taos colony sat thirty-eight light-years from Earth and with over fifty-two thousand inhabitants was one of the larger colonies in the outer colonial rim. Like Omega Theta, she consisted exclusively of free orbiting colony stars and had no chance of surviving without power. She had chosen to bet her survival on defensive armament. With over seventy years of warning of the possibility of attack and an ample supply of raw materials available in her solar system, the colony had built an impressive defensive array to protect her. It was, of course, nothing in comparison to the magnificent if aging system that currently protected Earth but it was far more powerful than tho limited effort that Omega Theta had been able to construct. Fortunately for the military analyst back on Earth, she had also put together an impressive communications system, with redundant transmitters sending a constant beam of data back to Earth. It was on this transmission beam the images they were now seeing, thirty-eight years old, had been carried to them.

The horror of the catastrophe was unimaginable. Taos had over twenty-six large colony stars and one by one they were cut to pieces. Due to the dispersal of the colonies throughout the solar system, the attack had lasted almost two days. The final images had arrived a little less than an hour ago and they were now watching the news feed replays of what the media considered some of the most newsworthy scenes. Unfortunately, it mostly focused upon the suffering of the colony's inhabitants. All lives were lost. Some hit directly by the beams themselves, others consumed in the fires and explosions they caused and still others would simply have perished as the atmosphere of their colony started deteriorating without power.

Of much more interest to the new officers of the INC, however, were the details regarding the military capabilities of the Intruder ships and their attack orbs. They knew they would likely be facing these adversaries at some point in the distant future and wanted to learn all they could. Unfortunately, there was little new information provided by their attack.

Taos Defense Command had fought back with everything they had but hadn't seemed to even make a scratch on any of the attacking vessels. They had once again confirmed the Intruders could be detected by their gravitational field and by the shadow they left as they passed before any electro-magnetic force but getting a direct fix on them seemed impossible. Taos had also proved that hitting them with anything was even more difficult than tracking them. A wide range of energy beam weapons, as well as explosive mines and torpedoes were used but no conclusive evidence of damage to an Intruder ship could be found.

Some of the officers kicked off their own impromptu research as they looked up at the viewing screens.

"Give us a run down of all shots against Intruder ships?" a member of the audience instructed the system.

"You're all military analysts are you now?" a stern voice interrupted from behind and they turned to see the Commander walking up to them.

"Let's get to work, people. Form up," he continued.

With that the group snapped to order and quickly formed a neat line and froze at attention, as he continued his instructions.

"We depart for Saturn Station in two hours. Grab your gear. Mission briefing will be held on the way. Assemble in the launch area in ninety minutes. Dismissed."

Kelly and his fellow officers couldn't believe it. Their mission was going to get underway immediately. He had expected several more weeks if not months or years before they would be ready for launch. Kelly couldn't help but wonder how it had even been possible to ready an interstellar warship this quickly. There could only be one answer, The Avenger.

Within a couple of hours, Kelly found himself, strapped tightly into an orbital launch pod. He had experienced an orbital launch a couple of times before in his life but the exhilaration of the experience always made it feel like the first time. About the size of a standard transport pod but lacking in any viewing windows and cylindrical in shape, the pod would carry its six passengers into Earth orbit in a matter of seconds to their rendezvous with the awaiting interplanetary shuttle. Kelly felt the sharp jolt as his spine was compressed under the strain of four times his normal weight. At first, the same combination used in the transport tubes, of magnetic levitation and air flow would accelerate the pod through a long vertical shaft but upon its exit from the mouth of the shaft, that task would be taken over by a set of three powerful beams. The heat of the beams reflecting off the ultra-reflective base of the pod would explode the very air underneath the craft converting atmospheric gases into rocket fuel. Finally as the pod reached the extremes of the atmosphere and there was no longer any gases to burn her acceleration would stop and she would drift upward slowly loosing the speed she had gained in the first part of her flight. Then, right at the apex of her travel, just as she was ready to drop back to Earth, their little ship would be snatched up by the docking line of the orbital shuttle port. The docking line connected to the pod and pulled her in like a frog's tongue catching a fly.

Before long they had left the shuttle port and were aboard a passenger shuttle headed for Saturn. The journey would take six days. It was during this time they would learn the nature of their mission. Their questions would all be answered.

Their first surprise was the number of officers on the shuttle, at any one time they had never seen more than a handful of graduates during their training but now on board this shuttle, they had been joined by several more officers. They had been the last to reach the shuttle port, some had been there for several days and they had come from training facilities across the globe. All in all, Kelly counted sixty-four freshly trained INC officers onboard the shuttle, as well as four more senior officers that he had never seen before.

The next surprise came during their first briefing when once again they found themselves listening to the stern voice of their training Commander. They were seated in a small auditorium when the Commander entered and began to speak.

"Over the next six days, you will receive your final training for the first mission ever launched by the Interstellar Naval Command. Some of you may be wondering why this mission is being launched so quickly, the answer to that is simple, Politics. The government wants a show. Well, we're going to give them one."

At that point a large viewing screen dropped down behind the Commander and displayed a graphic of a solar system already familiar to Kelly.

"Reykjavik," the Commander continued.

"At this point the best and perhaps the only chance that any human has survived an Intruder attack and perhaps our best chance to gather intelligence about our adversaries, is here. Our mission is a simple one, to survive and to gather intelligence. Our voyage will take us out across the stars all the way to Reykjavik. The journey will last over two hundred and twenty years, during which time, if you survive, you will all be lucky enough to break the record for longest Cryo-sleep. Any questions so far?"

They were all a little stunned. It was the first time that the Commander had ever asked for their input.

"Yes Sir," a tall dark lieutenant in the back spoke up.

"What's the current record and who set it?"

"It's seventy-one years and you're looking at him," the Commander responded, as things suddenly fell into place.

Kelly now realized why that face had been so familiar. It wasn't anyone that he had known in his life. It was a face from the past, a face from the history books. Commander J. T. Stone had served as President Foresythe's top military Advisor and one of the founding officers of INC. It then struck Kelly, that Stone was a walking violation of the Birthright laws. Including his Cryo-sleep he must have been close to two hundred years of age. He also remembered reading that Stone had died as the Commander noticed the look of confusion on some of the faces.

"Yes, the rumors of my death were greatly exaggerated," he responded, smiling. "Cryo research was top secret during my time, so it was just easier to declare the first volunteers dead. Of course, I can assure you. I'm far from dead."

After a moment of laughter from the group, Stone continued, "when we reach Reykjavik, we will take every step possible to evade destruction by Intruder vessels, learning whatever we can during any combat that may occur, making our way down to the surface of Reykjavik. Once there, we will go clean, turn off our technology completely and test what we think we've learned so far, that the Intruders target technology not life. We will attempt to survive on the surface of the moon, seek out any other human survivors and periodically transmit our findings back to Earth. Of course, every time we transmit our transmitter will be destroyed, so we'll only do that sparingly. Any further questions?"

This time a series of questions came at the Commander, which he fielded patiently and intently. He was no longer training recruits. He was now commanding his own officers.

They learned a lot during their final six days awake in Earth's Solar system. They studied the combat systems they would be commanding when they came out of Cryo-sleep, which included the full spectrum of weaponry they'd learned to operate in training and more. They learned about Reykjavik, which was clearly a far crueler place than the locations chosen for their earlier survival training. Finally they learned about Cryo-sleep, the new and very dangerous technology that would get them to their destination.

It was six very busy days.

The final day of their journey they were once again given an evening's leave, onboard the shuttle. Kelly again spent the time with Vasquez. Of course, they didn't have the privacy they had found in Greece onboard a crowded interstellar shuttle but they still found a way to share each other's company.

Before long they found themselves drawing closer to the ship that would become their home for the next two centuries, The Avenger. She was a thing of beauty to behold. Long and sleek, her entire form slipping into the shadow of her forward shields. Like any interstellar ship, she was mostly fuel tanks but on the forward section, just behind the shields, the array of weaponry differentiated this vessel from her Generation Ship brethren. This lady was made to fight. At five million tons she was far from the largest ship to ever be built but she would be the fastest. At peak velocity she would reach a new record speed of thirty-five thousand miles per second, faster than the current record holder, the long departed generation ship, Foundation Voyager.

As the shuttle approached, Kelly and Vasquez could easily make out the original components of the ship and distinguish them from those that had been refurbished. The drive system was still completely original. There was no reason to change that; little had changed since her construction in drive technology. Her weapons systems, however, had been extensively upgraded. And the crew compartment was completely new. She had originally been built to carry only Artificial Intelligence command systems but the discovery of Cryo-sleep had made possible the inclusion of human intelligence. Kelly and his comrades would fill that role.

The shuttle docked with the great warship and the INC officers boarded her. With a last review of Cryo-sleep procedures, they each settled down into their Cryo-chambers.

Kelly gave a glance over to Vasquez as they entered as if to say I will be dreaming of you, though he knew there would be few dreams in Cryo-sleep.

Kelly felt a tinge of fear as the Cryo-chamber lid closed over him, wishing it was possible to perform sedation before beginning the Cryo-process but knowing the mixture of sedatives and Cryo-chemicals was fatal. He felt the needles of the chamber enter his arms and felt the piecing pain as the foreign fluid entered his veins. The fluid would not freeze his body completely, rather it would lower the temperature of his body to near freezing and bathe all the tissues of his system in a mixture that would keep them cold but alive. His life would continue but far slower than normal. He would only age a couple of years during their two-century journey.

He tried to drown out the pain with thoughts of Vasquez and the hope that they would be reunited again, somewhere out among the stars, on the surface of Reykjavik.

Chapter 11

New Home

3809
Foundation Colony
50 light-years from Earth

Sarah sighed with anxious anticipation as she stood at the doorway to the new lab. Almost six years in construction, she only wished her grandfather had been here for its first day of operation. She couldn't help but flush with a little family pride as she read the inscription on the door:

Carmichael Research Center
Dedicated to our dearly departed team member
Dr. John Carmichael 3610 – 3760
Authorized Personnel Only

Her facial scan completed, the door slid open. At first glance the room had more the appearance of an entertainment lounge than the control center of the most advanced Artificial Intelligence system ever created. The central element of the room was a large, high quality, viewing screen that took up much of the far wall. The rest of the room had the shape of a half ellipse stretching away from the screen and closing into the entry door at the far end. Directly in front of the screen were sets of very comfortable looking couches, arranged in a semicircular array. Around the walls sat the only clue of the room's true role. Several complicated instrument consoles lined the outer of perimeters, with simple swivel chairs in front of them. Sarah entered and the lights slowly came up to a soft relaxing level. She sniffed and inhaled a scent. It reminded her of a new shuttle ready for a test flight.

After surveying the room with a sense of satisfaction, Sarah walked to one of the consoles against the walls and touched one of the interface points.

"How are we feeling today Frank?" she spoke, directly into the console.

She then went back to surveying the lab as if she didn't expect a response at all. A full thirty seconds went by before a familiar voice came over the lab's speaker system. The delay was second nature to Sarah.

"I'm well Sarah, how are you?" the voice responded.

Sarah smiled warmly as she heard the voice. To Sarah Carmichael, it was a voice she had known and loved throughout her life. It was the voice of a soul that had been close to her family for three generations now, beginning with her grandfather's successful activation of the Founder simulation over a hundred and fifty years earlier, long before Foundation Voyager had reached the star that she and all of her children now orbited.

"Big day today Frank," she continued.

Again the silence seemed endless but Sarah thought nothing of it. She simply went on with her work. She had spent much of her life this way. Having an intimate working relationship with a partner who could only listen and speak with her at a fraction of the speed at which she could operate. Like her mother, Greta and her grandfather John before her. She had learned to multitask as she worked. She would carry on a conversation with her subject while performing the many tasks that came with being the team leader of the Founder Project. It was no coincidence that this role had been handed down in her family, for no other group in Foundation Colony had the attachment and understanding of the Founder that the Carmichaels had. As a child, Sarah had played in the lab while her mother worked. Frank's voice had always been a part of her life and as she grew older she learned quickly how to interact with him and care for him, as well as the systems that supported him. It was a proud day for the Carmichael family when their third generation took over the project shortly before Greta's transition ceremony. Sarah would be the first of her family, however, to be able to perform her mission without the restrictions of her predecessors.

From its outset, severe limitations were placed on the project. The Optio crystal that it depended upon for the construction of its main system was in short supply on Foundation Voyager. Its possession in large quantities was restricted by the terms of the Biotech Laws that amongst other things controlled the sophistication of Artificial Intelligence systems. Sarah's grandfather and mother had done everything they could do within these limited resources but their progress had been slow.

The first task had been stabilizing the neural network, which had depended as much upon the physical characteristics of the system as upon the inputs to it. The inputs to the human brain are controlled by the physical capabilities of its body. A simulation of that same brain required those same inputs.

The next challenge dealt with giving the system a purpose, a reason to stay viable. In the human body instinctive hard coding gave the brain direction, resulting, for most people, in behavior beneficial to the body and therefore the brain itself. Drives like find food, find warmth and find companionship were a built in part of the human programming. A similar set of drives, or directives, as they become known had to be written for the Founder, core goals that kept him going and gave him a link to his human past.

Once that was done, the team had focused on fine-tuning the performance and health of the system. They had been pleased with their successes thus far. The Founder was now comfortable and stable and able to operate at about five percent of human thought speed. He was able to receive audio input, which he heard as if it had come from human ears and he received limited sensory signals from other parts of his virtual body. The team had found that limiting sensory input and focusing much of the available resources upon simulating brain function had achieved much greater performance. The trade off was a limited ability to interface with the world.

The thoughts, feelings and memories of Dr. Frank Ryland were active, though they changed at a pace one twentieth of a normal human brain. He existed in a state similar to a blind and quadriplegic human who lacked any sense of smell and taste but despite these massive limitations he was able to think, hear the words of those that spoke to him through the lab's systems and feel simulated sensations upon his face. For many, enduring this existence for over one hundred and fifty years would have been enough to drive them to insanity. But Dr. Ryland had always been a patient man and in his new afterlife, that trait had served him well. He had benefited by being insulated from the endless stream of time by the operation speed of his neural network. For him only five years had passed since he had first awoken from that painful and black place that the neural interpreters had taken him, as they slowly but surely digested his human brain more than a century earlier. It had been an interesting five years and during that time he had become very close to the Carmichaels.

He felt a loss that he had not been able to get to know John Carmichael better. Many of his interactions with John were lost in the pain and confusion that came with existence in the earliest versions of the Founder Project's neural network. He spent much of that time dormant; his thoughts in a frozen state, while adjustments and fixes were made to the system. But while he was active, he had spent as much time as possible getting to know John. He remembered the first time he persuaded John to bring Greta to the Lab. She was eight the first time she visited him.

"Hello Uncle Frank? Can you hear me?" she had asked, nervously speaking into the console of John's Lab.

"Yes, Greta, it's so nice to meet you. Your father has told me so much about you. How are your fish?" Came his response after a nervous minute, in which John had assured his daughter she would need to be patient with Uncle Frank.

What followed for Frank was the sense of warmth that only a conversation with a child can bring. They had talked about Greta's fish and what she wanted to be when she grew up. She had told him.

"I want to be a doctor, like my daddy."

It was ten more years before Greta would learn the true nature of Uncle Frank, as she had only been allowed to interact with him on the condition that she not know his true nature. To the young Greta Carmichael, Frank was a medical patient and friend of the family being treated by her father. Though Foundation Voyager had been over thirty light years from Earth, there was still a wall of secrecy around the Founder

Project, the less who knew about it the better. The council agreed that interaction with a child would be a positive part of the project but secrecy would still be maintained.

It was this unique relationship between the Carmichaels and the Founder that made them so well equipped to care for him. They had come to know him first as a human being and second as what he was: a computer simulation of a man long since dead and gone.

Like her mother, Sarah had spent much of her life in the lab getting to know Frank. Growing to know him as family, friend and patient. She was a computer scientist by skill but she was a caregiver by nature.

And today she would give a great gift to her patient.

"Do you mean you're going to finally stop forgetting what we are talking about?" Came Frank's response over the speakers as the door at the back of the lab opened again.

"Well, at least we don't forget what day it is," interrupted Sarah's brother Tim has he walked into the room.

Sarah smiled at her brother and partner and gave him a kiss on the cheek. Not long after Tim's entrance, Chuck, the only member of the team who wasn't a Carmichael entered the room followed by the youngest member of the clan Jessica, Sarah's sister.

Tim and Sarah moved into the central area of the lab and sat down on the couches across from the screen. Chuck and Jessica sat down at two of the swivel chairs and began reviewing the data that flashed across the small control screen. Jessica looked over to Sarah and updated her.

"We're looking really good today," she signaled.

"Ok, let's get started," Sarah replied. "Frank, are you ready?"

They sat in silence waiting for his response, which seemed to take a little longer than usual.

"Yes Sarah, I'm looking forward to it, thank you."

Sarah turned to Chuck and nodded, who in turn turned to the console and began work.

"Freezing Founder system one," he updated them and continued.

"System Frozen, initiating data export." A short and tense silence followed then he proceeded. "Export complete, initiating import to system two."

Again a tense silence hung over the room waiting for Chuck's update. Then finally he initiated the last step.

"Import complete. System ready for activation."

At this point, Sarah gave some additional direction to her team.

"Ok, let's bring the screen up first," she indicated, turning to Jessica.

Jessica looked down at her console and made some slight adjustments. All four of them then turned to the screen and waited anxiously.

Like most viewing screens of its day, their lab's main monitor was a fantastic piece of equipment, though less than an inch in depth, its multidirectional pixels gave if the ability to project a perfect three dimensional image out into the lab. They had the ability to view any vista they chose in perfect clarity and depth. The image that appeared was instead a quite simple one but meaningful beyond words to the Founder Project team.

As the screen came to life, it displayed the image of a room, about the same size as the lab itself. In the center of that room, directly across from the couches of the lab, was a large and comfortable reclining chair, with soft armrests and a thick cushioned headrest. In the chair sat a man. He was lying back, still, with his eyes closed not making a sound or moving at all. Closer observation indicated that not even his chest was moving. He wasn't breathing, as if he sat in a frozen state. Yet he seemed alive somehow. The color in his cheeks was healthy and there was warmth in his face. He seemed quite serene.

"Go ahead Chuck," Sarah gave the final instruction of the process.

"Initiating system," Chuck responded without delay.

Again there was the same quiet and tense feeling hanging in the room as the system that drove the image before them came to life. Jessica provided the last update.

"Active and running at one hundred percent," she reported, as they all turned to the screen.

"Frank?" Sarah questioned.

For a moment it seemed something might be wrong, the man on the chair sat still as ever, but then it happened. At first it was just a twitch in his face that gave any indication of a response but then his lips moved and that so familiar voice came into the room again.

"Yes, I'm here," Frank replied with the sound of someone that had perhaps dozed off to sleep for a moment.

"How do you feel?" Sarah continued and was almost shocked when the reply came back to her immediately.

"Good, good," Frank continued, "how do I look?" still sounding a little groggy.

"Well why don't we let you see for yourself," Sarah smiled, turning to Chuck.

Chuck didn't need further instruction. He knew exactly what to do.

"Activating optical input," Chuck replied.

At this point, Tim, who had been quiet so far, sat up slightly in his chair and spoke.

"Very slowly Frank, see if you can open your eyes," he instructed their patient.

After another slight delay Frank's eyes began to twitch and then opened. For a moment he just sat and squinted, trying to get an understanding of his surroundings but as his little world came into focus he looked out and smiled at Tim and Sarah.

"Sarah? Tim?" he questioned. They smiled back in response.

"Jessica? Chuck?" he continued and the other two nodded back also, smiling.

"It's unbelievable," he cried, his face warming as if tears would well up at any moment.

"Once we had an abundant supply of Optio crystal, building a real time system for you was fairly straightforward given what we'd already learned in system one." Sarah began.

"And we knew the sensory input would be much more real if we put you into a virtual world, or at least a virtual room, that would allow you to interact with us directly," Tim continued.

"Yes, the screen in front of you is a three-dimensional viewing panel here in our lab. It's a two-way system, with multi-directional light sensors integrated amongst the pixels. Input from those sensors is translated into the image that your eyes would see based on your position in the room. We then project that image into your simulated optical nerves. This gives you a view into our lab. Likewise, our screen gives us a view into your world. The visual image of your virtual domain is projected onto our screen. Your body is driven, so to speak, by the reflexes emitted by your simulated brain. We hope you don't mind but we took historical medical scans of your real body from ships archives to make you look the way you might remember yourself," Sarah proceeded.

"There's a mirror in the arm of your chair if you'd like to take a look," Tim added.

Frank turned his head slightly and looked down at the mirror.

Somewhere deep inside the Founder Project's neural network a human feeling emerged: the feeling of a man looking at his own face for the first time in two hundred and eighty three years.

What proceeded might have seemed to an observer much more like a family reunion than a complex scientific research project. Frank had an endless stream of questions for the team and for the first time since his activation, talking to Frank was enough to keep them busy. They spoke to him in further detail about the system they had constructed for him. They almost apologetically explained that they were still working on giving him further ability to interact with his virtual world. He was still paralyzed, restrained to his chair and had no sense of smell or taste.

He would hear nothing of it.

"You can't begin to imagine how wonderful this is," he explained to them. "The darkness was the hardest thing to deal with and you've taken that away. To see your faces is a gift I never could have imagined receiving, thank you."

They blushed with embarrassment as the Founder of their world, the person they owed their lives to, thanked them for their work.

They talked on and on for perhaps two hours, before Frank began to feel strangely tired.

"The activity level of your network wears down the energy resources of the simulated neurons, certain areas of your matrix will periodically go into a dormant state. We have integrated this into your brain patterns as sleep. You'll need to take a nap every couple of hours," Tim explained.

"Just like a baby," smiled Frank as he drifted off to sleep. As he faded away Sarah turned to Tim and they hugged each other with joy. Chuck and Jessica came down from their consoles and joined them in the celebration. None of them could got more than a word in without a smile, tear or chuckle. Until Tim put his hands on Sarah's shoulder and spoke more seriously.

"Ok, now, you have somewhere to go don't you?"

"I know, I know, don't remind me." Sarah responded, her smile fading.

The sense of seriousness fell over the whole group as Sarah moved to focus on the next task. She stood up and walked to the exit, turning with one last comment as the door opened.

"Watch over our baby," she said.

As Sarah walked the hallways of Foundation Colony One, she wished she could jump with joy and let everyone she saw know about the wonderful thing that had just happened. She wondered if the council Chairman would see it the same way.

Twenty years ago, Sarah Carmichael wouldn't have had to worry about getting support for the Founder Project from the Colonial Council. As representatives of Foundation Colony the council was driven by the will of the people and the will of the people of Foundation Colony had always been very progressive. Frank Ryland had made sure of that over three hundred years ago when he had carefully selected the original inhabitants of Foundation Voyager. Her children were selected from families that not only were willing to place children on a generation ship, but also had progressive ideas about the future of Mankind, ideas that opposed the concepts laid down in the Biotech Laws. As the most blatant form of violation of the those laws, the Founder Project could only take place in the depths of space, far away from the prying eyes of the Unified Government, under the jurisdiction of a Colonial Council. But even here, light-years from Earth, in the most progressive colony in the realm of man, old fears persisted. Today, as Foundation Colony orbited her new sun, new challenges fed those old fears.

It was for this reason that the details of the Founder Project had always been kept a secret and ethical questions about its subject remained unanswered. Sarah Carmichael believed it was time to answer some of those questions but she feared the Chairman might have other objectives.

Chairman Spencer's office was on the outside edge of the innermost level of Colony Star One. This meant that Spencer was fortunate enough to have both windows and skylights in his office that gave him one of the best views in the colony. His door was open as Sarah arrived and he looked up from his desk and waved her in. Sarah couldn't help but look out over the view as she entered.

"Marvelous isn't it?" Spencer began looking out over the solar system that Sarah was captivated by.

The star of the show took center stage. Foundation Colony's new, young and brilliant host sun sat in the middle of their field of view. In front of it and far closer to the colony, sat the outer belt of asteroids. Some of them appeared quite large and distinct from their current position. Between them and the colony you could make out a few small mining drones shuttling back and forth between the asteroids and the colony stars.

"Too bad it's going to kill us," Spencer interrupted and turned to look at Sarah sternly.

"I'm sure we'll find it," Sarah responded, trying to dismiss Spencer's gloomy prediction.

"Oh we've already found it," he went on. "We just can't get to it. We hoped we'd find some in the outer belt but unfortunately we haven't found a single molecule, plenty of your precious Optio crystal, of course, but not much else."

They both knew what they were talking about, the one element that was essential to the growth of an interstellar space colony: Oxygen, the least plentiful building block of the cycle of life. Without oxygen the three most important substances, Water, Carbon Dioxide and Oxygen Gas, required to sustain life, could not be made.

"We've got Carbon, Hydrogen and everything else we need coming out of our ears but we can't get to the damn Oxygen. Of course, he knew that." He closed his focus on Sarah.

"Nonsense Bob, you don't believe that for one second," she rebuffed. "All the data from the Foundation Voyager pre-launch planning determined the supply of Oxygen was sufficient. There was an acknowledged risk that it may be harder to get to but that was factored into the final launch approval given by the Unified Government."

"Maybe they just wanted to get rid of him," he sneered.

"You can't possibly believe what you're saying," she continued. "You don't know Frank the way I do."

Bob Spencer huffed a sarcastic smile and turned back to the view, then after a pause he turned back to Sarah.

"I'm sorry Sarah, you don't deserve my abuse. It's the stress. You understand. Tell me, how did it go?"

Sarah didn't want to let him off that easy but didn't know what choice she had so she followed along with his change in topic.

"Flawlessly," she replied proudly, "we were able to bring him up to full speed, integrate him with the virtual environment and activate his visual abilities. We're working on extending his sense of touch and activating his smell and taste as well."

"Taste?" Bob questioned. "What exactly do you plan on feeding him?"

"Come on now Bob, you know from my past briefings that the best way to achieve stability is through normalized sensory interaction. We're trying to make his life as real as we possibly can. That brings me to the reason for my visit."

Bob looked up at her as if to wish her out of the room but he knew she wasn't going to let that happen.

"I want a motion put before the council to grant him citizen status."

Spencer pulled no punches in his response.

"And your intention is to allow him to live out the remaining eighteen years of his Birthright. Is that it? And how much time should we credit for the century and half he's already had?"

Sarah couldn't believe that he was taking such a hard position.

"That's not fair Bob, he places no strain at all on our organic systems, there's no reason whatsoever to impose Birthright restrictions on him," she responded.

"That may be so Sarah, but he is taking up more than half of the computational resources of this colony, resources we badly need to solve our real problems. You may not realize this but the very life of this colony is at stake here."

Sarah stuttered for the words but didn't have a response. "The council record is clear on this Sarah, the Founder Project was authorized, provided that it served the positive interests of this colony and posed no threat to the colony or to humanity as a whole. In fact I'm glad you brought this up, as I'm obligated to inform you that, due to current pressures, the council has reached a decision regarding your project. You have three months to submit a report as to how your project will support the needs of this colony and help us in our current predicament. If you are unable to show just cause to keep the project active, your work will be halted and the resources of your team will be devoted to other goals."

"You want to kill him?" Sarah said, with a tone of distress in her voice.

"No Sarah, calm down, of course not. Besides we can't exactly kill data, can we? But I will freeze him until we're out of the woods. Then perhaps, the project can be reinitiated."

Sarah looked down at her lap for a moment then looked up with a resolute look on her face. She knew there was no point in arguing with him.

"Then I guess I have work to do. Good day."

And she left the office without another word. She managed to hold back her tears until she was well out of sight of his office door, then turned into a doorway and let her feelings loose. She couldn't believe that they'd come this far only to face resistance from their own leadership. She couldn't give in though, so after a moment she wiped her eyes and made her way back to the lab.

She updated the team on the situation when she arrived in the lab and after some discussion she persuaded them it was best that they inform Frank of the situation. It wasn't long before Frank awoke and opened his eyes.

For a moment it seemed that Frank had forgotten where he was but soon seemed to recall his new gifts and looked around his room and smiled. Then he turned to the screen in front of him and looked out into the lab. He dropped his smile as he looked at the glum faces of his friends.

"Who died?" he asked, trying to make light of the gloomy scene.

"Frank, I'm not sure how to tell you this so I'll be as straight as I can," Sarah began.

"I asked the council Chairman to recognize your citizenship once again and he refused to even bring it to a vote."

"What did you do a silly thing like that for?" came back Frank's response much to Sarah's surprise.

"You don't want to be recognized as alive?" She asked.

"Do you think I'm alive?" Frank replied.

"Yes, yes, of course," Sarah continued.

"Well that's good enough for me. Now what else is bothering you?"

"Well it gets worse. The colony's in trouble and they're concerned about the resources the project is using up. We've got three months to prove our value, or the project will be frozen."

"I see," said Frank, pausing for a moment. "Look, it was always my belief while I lived on Earth that man could be so much more than he was through the creation of a more harmonistic co-existence with the his evolving technology. Every ounce of my research throughout my whole life focused on achieving that goal. The Biotech Era was a terrible experience for man and one that no one wants to see repeated. It created fears that have stood in the way of progress. I believe we can overcome those fears. I believe projects like this one, indeed my very existence, can benefit man. I wouldn't have embarked on this journey and Foundation Colony wouldn't exist if I didn't believe that. Now it looks like it's time to find out if I was right. Are you with me?"

"Yes Frank, of course," Sarah said, feeling that she was transferring from caregiver to student. "What do you need?"

"Ok, I need two things," Frank responded. "I'm going to need you to provide me with all the information you can about the status of the Colony and what we're dealing with here."

"I can some that up in one word," Sarah interrupted. "Oxygen."

"Yes, that would make sense," Frank replied.

"The Chairman thinks you planned it that way," Sarah continued. "He thinks your own rebirth came before the good of the Colony".

Frank smiled and looked back at Sarah. "No he doesn't Sarah. He's just scared and he's looking for blame. After all, I wouldn't have much of a life without the Colony. The fact of the matter is; I need you. The problem I have is that you don't yet need me and this relationship will only work if we need each other. Do you agree?"

"I already feel like I need you Frank," Sarah said smiling but knowing the seriousness of Frank's concern.

"And I'm grateful," he continued, trying to keep her focused on the issue. "But it would be a little selfish of you to take up all of those precious computer resources just to fill your needs. I, or perhaps we, if I can trouble you for your assistance, need to find a way for the whole Colony to need me. Which brings me back to my original request. I'll need to learn all the specifics regarding our problems."

"Yes, of course, and what's the second thing."

"I'll need to be able to work on the problem, that will require an interface to an Advisor with links into some form of analysis, design and modeling systems."

"That shouldn't be a problem," Sarah continued.

"Thank you," he concluded but noticed her face still looked discouraged. "Sarah?" he said somewhat sternly.

She looked up.

"Have Faith," he instructed.

With that, Tim moved up beside her and put his arm on her back. They turned to look at each other for a minute and after a moment Tim's confidant smile infected Sarah and she turned to her team.

"We've got a lot of work to do people, let's get on it."

Frank put his head back in his chair, closed his eyes again and drifted back off the sleep, exhausted from the exchange.

The next few weeks were a frantic time for the team. The focus of their efforts had shifted. No longer were they concerned with the quality of life of their patient but rather the rehabilitation of that patient as a contributing component of the Colony. The pathway to success was clear. They would seek to leverage the abilities that had always made Frank Ryland a powerful force of change in human society. Since his earliest dabbling in sophisticated Artificial Intelligence, Frank had always shown the ability to not only understand and

innovate technology but to apply a uniquely human creativity
to the process; to find new and innovative ways of looking at
and solving problems.

The team reconfigured Frank to maximize his ability to
function as a problem solver. Abilities that did not contribute
to this process were limited and those that enhanced it were
made the priority. Frank's visual abilities were maintained
but his peripheral vision was eliminated. His ability to sense
feelings on his face and upper body were sacrificed but he was
given mobility, in the form of a mobile chair and an acute sense
of touch in his hands and fingers. His sense of hearing was
preserved but sensitivity to the upper and lower frequencies of
the spectrum were removed. Improvements were also made in
his ability to stay awake.

The changes didn't only include Frank himself but were also
made to his environment. His comfortable chair designed for
interaction with the team in the lab, was replaced with the
smaller mobile chair, surrounded by a set of interface consoles.
Though the team was unable to gain access to Colony's main
design and command systems, they did have access to a wide
array of conventional computational applications that were
sufficient to give Frank an understanding of the problems
faced by the colony, but more importantly to test his ability
to interface effectively with the Colony's solutions design
teams. This process would require communication not only
with individuals in the lab but also directly with the colony's
systems. The new consoles gave him this ability.

The team was pleased as they watched Frank move through
his new environment and interact with the system consoles in
front of him and as things began to slow down a little, Sarah
again turned to the well being of her patient.

"How do you like it, so far?" she inquired.

At first Frank didn't hear her, obviously consumed gathering
data on the colony's host solar system from the virtual screens
in front of him, he apologized as he looked up.

"I'm sorry Sarah I was a little absorbed. You said
something?"

"Yes, Frank, sorry to interrupt you but I wanted to ask how
you liked the new environment," she repeated.

"It's unbelievable," he said, giving her his full attention and gesturing to the simulated equipment that surrounded him. "I was wondering one thing, however?"

"Yes, Frank what is it?"

"How fast can I go?"

The question didn't just grab Sarah's attention. The whole team seemed to freeze and look up at the lab's main screen. Tim stepped away from his terminal and walked toward the big screen.

Frank had been running at 100% since the initiation of the new system. No consideration had ever been given to exceeding that rate of neural activity. At this speed he was capable of interacting with humans in the lab as equals. With their initial focus on making Frank's life as real as possible, there was no need to evaluate changing that. Now, the goal had shifted.

"Well," Tim began slowly, looking first at Sarah, then back to Frank, "I did run a few numbers and we can probably get you up to about 140% with the current network. Do you want us to investigate that further?"

Frank responded in a matter of fact manner.

"It seems the council has made their position clear. I am a tool to be used to benefit the colony. It would seem to me I can be of most value if I am leveraged to my full potential. Wouldn't you agree?"

Tim looked at Sarah for a response; she remained silent for a moment.

"Yes, I agree," she responded, as a slight smile snuck across her face. She reached across and placed her hand on Tim's shoulder.

"Turn it up," she instructed.

The process that followed was a sequence of small increases in the processing speed of the system's neural network, each step of the way the health of the system was carefully checked and an archived copy of the system was created. Like any data system the Founder Project's neural network had layers of redundancy and the sensitivity of their activity simply increased the requirements for fallbacks.

As they stepped through the process Tim would update the team and Frank on how they were doing.

"104%, 105%, 106%," he continued in a steady and rhythmic voice but his confident tone couldn't hide the nervousness in the air, "121%, 122%, 123%."

The effects of the acceleration started to become visible in Frank's expression. The twitches in his face and movements of his hands began to seem unnatural and rushed.

"139%, 140%, approaching system thresholds and stabilizing," Tim sighed.

"All subsystems stable," Jessica quickly chimed in, reassuring the team.

"Frank, how do you feel?" Sarah inquired.

They chuckled at the response.

"I feel fine," came Frank's response in a squeaky and comically high-pitched voice.

"We can toggle his speed between normal and accelerated," Tim interjected, a little embarrassed at the side effects of his work.

"Yes, we'll do that," Sarah concluded smiling warmly at her brother and placing her hand firmly on his back.

In the following days, the final details of Frank's new world were fine-tuned. He was given the ability to set his performance to the task at hand: the ability to move at a pace that facilitated communication at one time, while moving at a pace that facilitated performance at other times.

With the task of maximizing Frank's ability to contribute to the colony completed, the task of finding the best ways for him to make that contribution moved into high gear. Watching Frank work was an amazing sight. Any scientist of the thirty sixth century was an expert at interfacing with computer systems through any of the available channels. The complex systems that Frank was working with could accept signals and provide data through any number of systems, visual, audio and tactile. The incredible thing about watching Frank work was that he was adept at using all of those channels simultaneously. Beyond these abilities Frank had other advantages. Of course, his rate of thought and interaction was accelerated beyond that of a normal human but his physical interaction speed had been sped up further. Because Frank's hands and fingers were virtual and not real, the restrictions of muscle reaction speed and nerve latency were removed. Frank could move his simulated hands every bit as fast as he could think about moving them. Tim was most interested in watching this amazing feat take place and estimated that Frank was working at about three hundred percent of normal human capacity. The weeks flew by and the team became more and more confident of their ability to prove their worth to the Colonial Council. After a few weeks, the critical moment arrived and Sarah and Tim found themselves talking to Frank. Watching the conversation you wouldn't have known it was Frank's future that was on the line.

"Don't worry Sarah, I'm sure you'll do fine," Frank reassured her.

"It's you that's got to do all the work," she rebuffed.

"Nonsense," he replied, "we couldn't have gotten this far without you."

With that he smiled and Sarah turned to leave the room. Only Tim was left behind.

"Tim," Frank questioned as Sarah left the room.

"Yes, Frank, what is it?" Tim replied.

"There's something that I want to show you."

"Sure, Frank."

Frank touched a couple of points on one of his consoles and a portion of the lab's main viewing screen was converted to an interface to Frank's design systems.

"This is a new design for the neural simulator." Frank stated, with a great degree of modesty in his tone.

Tim stared at the screen, not quite knowing what to say.

"I estimate its performance will be about fifty fold improvement over the current design.

"It looks very simple, does it work?" Tim questioned.

"I believe so," replied Frank, "of course more testing is needed. What I've attempted to do is map neurological activity at the logical level. As you know the current design mirrors a complicated chemical simulation of neural activity. At the time of its design, we had no data to allow us to pursue any other strategy. It was that early work that the system you have built is based on. But by monitoring the brain activity in my network I've been able to decode the neurological system. You'd be surprised how simple the basic codes of the human brain are once you dig down into them. This design simply stores and transmits those base code elements in its own native technology rather than simulate the chemical transactions that occur in a human neuron."

"It's amazing Frank. Simply amazing."

"Well let's hope we get a chance to see if it works. Just in case I find myself turned off any time soon, I've transferred my design data to you, I hope it all makes sense."

"I'm sure it will."

Meanwhile, in the council chamber, Sarah had just arrived and was finishing up pleasantries with the council members seated before her. The two main characters in the discussion were both at the far end of the table, Bob Spencer, the Chairman, who Sarah knew well and Frederick Reinhardt, who Sarah had only met on a couple of occasions. Reinhardt, in addition to being a council member, was the chief of Mining Engineering; the person whose unfortunate job it was to solve the colony's current problem and who most coveted the resources of the Founder Project. Though, like any space colony, Foundation Colony was essentially a closed system, there was always some degree of loss that occurred. Without a solution, the population of the colony would stagnate then dwindle as natural leakage resulted in the steady decline of the colony's precious Oxygen. The Oxygen they currently possessed had been brought all the way from Earth's system, in the water, in the air and even in the colonists themselves. Going back to get more was not an option.

"So tell us, Sarah, is he aware that this meeting is occurring?" Spencer asked, moving the discussions politely toward the matter at hand.

"Oh yes, it wouldn't have been practical for us to establish a basis for value without involving Frank in the process," she responded quite pleasantly, though the first response to pop into her head was a little less civil.

"I see," he replied, then turned the discussion over to her. "Well I think you understand our objective today, why don't we just let you get started."

"That's fine Bob thank you. I'm actually going to keep this short and then I'll be introducing another presenter to you.

"You all know who Frank Ryland is. As the owner and Founder of the Ryland Research Foundation he established tremendous wealth through revolutionary advances in Artificial Intelligence systems. Then in a decision that is the main reason we are all here today, he decided to invest that wealth in the creation of a generation ship; Foundation Voyager. It was that ship that carried our people across the stars to our new home. Frank Ryland himself was onboard Foundation Voyager when it left Jupiter's orbit in 3512 and he lived another twenty-five years on the ship until, in 3537, he died."

Bob Spencer's eyes widened just slightly, surprised to see Sarah so readily admit that Dr Ryland was dead. Sarah continued.

"He died during the execution of an experiment. An experiment designed to determine if it was possible to capture the contents of the human brain; the memory, feelings and thoughts a person. His purpose for conducting this experiment was simple, to explore the potential of the merger of human creativity and technology. Of course, this experiment was in direct violation of Earth's Biotech Laws and therefore could only take place somewhere like Foundation Voyager, somewhere far away from the jurisdiction of the Unified Government."

"Today, with the gracious permission of this council, we are continuing Frank Ryland's work, because we believe in his vision. The vision that Mankind can benefit greatly through the harmonious interaction between his creative process and the evolving and powerful technology that he has created."

"It is only because of the value we believe this process can create, that we feel justified in accepting the gracious use of the vast resources of this colony that you have placed at our disposal."

"With that said, I'd like to introduce you to someone who can articulate far better than I the value that the Founder Project can bring to our colony. With your permission, I give you the Founder Project's active simulation of Dr. Frank Ryland."

Fortunately for Sarah the council chamber included a quite large two-way viewing screen, though not quite of the quality or size of the screen in their lab, the system was nonetheless capable of providing a clear and deep image of her presenter. She turned to the screen and made a communications connection to her lab. The screen came into focus and Frank appeared, sitting in his virtual room looking back at the screen smiling pleasantly. The council was a little surprised by the image so human and so interactive.

"Hello Sarah, thank you, and thank you members of the council for giving me a chance to meet with you. It's really a pleasure. You can't imagine the joy I feel to be able to be of service to the colony that was my driving force during my life, but, let me get right to the point.

"Put simply the problem is that we need something that we can't get to. The simple solution to that problem is that we have to make that something come to us."

"Mr. Reinhardt let me compliment you on the fantastic job you've done leading the mining efforts of the colony. What I think you need is a little help. You need someone, or something, that can bring the Oxygen rich gas clouds of the inner belt out to you, so they can be effectively mined. Let me show you some of the concepts that I've been thinking of."

The screen in front of them split in half, half still showing Frank's face as he talked and the other showing three dimensional images of a complex series of theoretical events targeted to solve the colony's Oxygen collection problems. First an array of orbital devices were launched from the colony and spread into a wide orbit around the volatile star. Then particle beams were fired, converging at a point deep within the inner belt. The result was a intense energy burst that super heated the gases and sent them spraying out into the outer solar system, from there the gas mining drones would glide through the expanding and cooling clouds sucking up the available Oxygen. The audience stood in amazement at the solution being laid out before them.

Frederick Reinhardt turned to Sarah and asked. "How long would a system like this take to construct?"

Sarah almost wanted to laugh at the fact that the question was directed to her.

"You'd really have to ask Frank, it's all his idea," she responded.

Frederick turned to the screen, almost in a state of shock. "Um, I'm sorry, yes Mr. Ryland, how long would you think?"

"Well you have to realize I didn't have access to any of the main design systems to do all the modeling required and I'm a computer scientist not a mining engineer but I think the resources, construction and deployment could be completed within fifty years or so give or take. Oh and please, call me Frank."

"Would you be able to work directly with my team to assist in a project of this nature?" Reinhardt continued, his shock at talking to a simulated human quickly dissipating as he began to see the value that Dr. Ryland could bring to the colony.

"I'd be happy to," Frank responded, "of course, ultimately the decision is not mine, I am here at the service of the colony, as the representatives of the colony, that decision is entrusted to you and your distinguished colleagues."

"I'm set, let's get started," Reinhardt concluded.

Chairman Spencer, holding back his own shock, looked around the room for a questioning face. He found none. It was at that point, that Sarah finally felt she could take her eyes off the room and look back at Frank. What she saw surprised her. It wasn't the look of confidence on Frank's face, rather, tucked away in the corner of his virtual room she noticed something that hadn't been there before; a fish tank, a small octagonal fish tank. It was actually a nice touch but it was a touch she hadn't made.

She knew it meant nothing to the council but it meant the world to her.

With the presentation complete and the death of the project averted, Sarah made her way back to the lab. When she got there she found that Frank was tired and needed a rest. The rest of team was about to head to an entertainment lounge for a drink to celebrate. They gestured Sarah to join them.

"I'll be a long in a minute," she informed them.

Once they had left she took a quick look down at the console and there it was, as plain as day in the logs, the addition of a decorative fish tank to the environment. Her name sat next to the entry but she knew she hadn't made the change.

She looked up at Frank who wasn't quite asleep.

"Good job," she congratulated him.

"Thank you Sarah but you know I couldn't have done it without you and your team," he replied.

"You could have asked me if you wanted a fish tank you know," she boldly confronted him.

Frank woke slightly looked at her and smiled.

"Picking fish is such a personal thing, don't you agree?"

Sarah was quiet for a moment, then responded from her heart as her face flushed with the warmth of a trust that went deeper than words and computer security. Tears of pride welled up in her eyes.

"Yes, yes, I do, good night Frank, sweet dreams."

Chapter 12

Lost Children

3853
Reykjavik
42 Light-years from Earth

Taruk braced his feet against the sides of the shaft and pushed against the stone cover with his shoulders. The distinct sound of ice, cracking as the heavy cover shifted, brought excitement to the faces of the rest of the hunting party. Another winter in the dark caves of Reykjavik was coming to an end.

Taruk gave another shove with all his weight and the stone cover rolled over and flopped onto the slushy snow. The hunting party pulled their warm robes around them as the cold air of the surface rushed down into the cave. Taruk placed his large hands on the outer edge of the entrance and hoisted himself up. He turned and offered his hand to Mitak, then stood up and surveyed the surroundings as Mitak helped the other hunters to the surface. The warm volcanic air from the caves had melted the area near the entrance but winter still held its grip on the surrounding ground. They wasted little time, gathered their things and starting making their way along the side of the mountain range. The late winter sunrise gave an incredible show as they made their way along the snowy ridge path that Taruk had traveled many times. At first the edge of the sun appeared upon the horizon as it would on any other sunrise but then before much of it was visible, the form of the great green gaseous giant, Thor, which held Reykjavik in its grasp, rose above the horizon. It blocked much of the view of the sun itself and gave it a strange green hue. The light was enough for the hunters though. It would give them the guidance they needed to make their way to the surface caves their tribe would call home for the next few weeks.

Taruk was the oldest member of the hunting party. In a world far away from Reykjavik, he might have been considered a young man, only thirty-three years of age but amongst the children of Reykjavik he was a well-aged veteran, having lived over 60 winters. He was lucky to have survived as long as he had and even luckier to still be able to lead the hunt. Mitak had lived for about fifty-five winters and was Taruk's second man. The rest of the hunting party ranged from thirty to fifty winters in age. The hunters were all men. It was said that in earlier times the women of the tribe had hunted too but time had taught them that injuries and hardships the hunters endured often left female hunters unable to bare child and that had proved almost fatal to the tribe. The party was perhaps twenty members strong and spoke little as they strode along the mountainside. Though winter was waning, they knew that the night temperatures would be unbearable and they needed to finish their trek before sundown.

Taruk thought to himself as he trudged through the snow. He would make this hunt his best. He would make the old ones proud.

The great slow planetary sunrise that was playing itself out above them, was still well above the horizon when they reached their destination: a large cave opening that jutted out from one of the mountainsides. The hunting party moved into the cave, ignoring the distinct stench that filled the air. They moved toward the back of the cave where they heard the sound of large creatures lying in the darkness and breathing deeply This sound was pleasing to the hunters; their great hunting steeds had also survived the winter.

The first task was to warm the cave and there was no shortage of fuel for this chore. The dung that filled the cave and provided the source of the smell was quickly turned into a roaring fire near the entrance. The hunters then worked to build other smaller fires deeper in the cave closer to the great sleeping beasts. Before long the warmth of the flames had soaked into every corner of the cavern and the monstrous animals began to stir. This was a nervous time for the hunters but Taruk knew not to show his fear. He walked straight up to the largest of the creatures and stared at it sternly as its eyes opened and it awoke. For a moment it looked that it might devour Taruk whole but he held his position and kept his stare on the animal. It reared up, looked down at him and roared. He stared back and shouted out.

"Darkeye down!"

The great Snow Tiger hesitated then lay down before his master. It was easy to see why Taruk had named his mount Darkeye. The great lizard-like beast had two different colored eyes: one the more normal reddish brown and a second, jet-black. The other hunters worked to calm their waking mounts. Most found it more challenging than the veteran Taruk and it looked for a moment that they might loose a couple of their party before the hunt even began but the older hunters came to the aid of the less experienced ones and before long the entire pack of Snow Tigers, perhaps thirteen in all were awake and in the control of their human masters. Taruk worked to comfort Darkeye after the rude awakening from his winter hibernation.

"Soon my friend, soon, we will find flesh in plenty out on the plains."

The beast snorted in response.

They led the pack to the entrance to the cave and allowed them to drink from the melted snow. It would be a while before they could feed the animals though. The Snow Tigers would only eat fresh meat. Before long the sundown finally fell and they settled into the cave for the night, as the Snow Tigers lapped up melting snow and rolled and stretched at the entrance to the cave.

Much more of the sun was visible when daylight broke the following day, its planetary sunrise almost complete. The hunting party had much to do. Inside the cave was a wide array of tools they would use on their hunt. Long lance-like spears and shorter throwing spears lined the rocky walls. The group went to work checking that the weapons were still in good order. Strips of dried vines were used to lash the stone tips to the wood-like spear poles. As evening drew close, the group began to look anxiously toward the entrance of the cave, waiting for the others to arrive.

Their concerns were laid to rest, when rest of the tribe came around the outcropping to the right of the cave. Perhaps a hundred in all, the older men, women and children were pleased to see the site of the cave entrance. Taruk walked out, smiling and waving at his family who were leading the group. Taruk was fortunate to have a large family: two wives and eight children. In earlier times, men of the tribe would have had only one wife but as the hunt took its toll on the men some couples would add a second wife to their family. The survival of the tribe depended upon its ability to grow and that meant caring well for their mothers. He also cared for one of the elders, Patek, who had led the hunt before him. Patek was the oldest man in the tribe having survived eighty-three winters but still younger than the tribe mother, Paru, the very oldest amongst them, ninety-two winters in age and the tribe's leader.

After hugging his wives and his children, Taruk turned to Paru, bowing his head as he spoke to her.

"The hunt will be a good one, tribe mother."

"Yes, Taruk, I have no doubt it will be, come now, let's start the feast."

Taruk bowed again to Paru and turned to Patek and smiled.

"How is your leg, old man?" he joked as his older friend limped up.

"Still strong enough to keep up with you," Patek replied, pushing on the younger man.

Taruk gave way, pretending to almost fall; exaggerating the older mans fading strength.

"Darkeye looks eager." Patek said to his friend looking at the great Snow Tiger as it snorted and paced the perimeter of cave. "Come on, let's help with the feast."

From underneath the snow, the tribe dug out huge blocks of frozen meat that had been placed there at the beginning of the winter. The meat was smashed into a mush and placed onto a great hide blanket. Powdered mushrooms and spicy native herbs were added to the mixture. Then piles of snow were dumped on top. When the blanket held as much as it would fit, the whole thing was lifted over the fire and stretched across four stakes. The melting snow kept the hide of the blanket from burning. More snow was added as the earlier heaps steamed to the roof of the cave. Before long the blanket was sagging under the weight of a great steaming broth.

As the young adults of the tribe tended to the food, the others in the group celebrated around the fire. The children ran around the cave, pretending to hunt as the elders sat around and told tales of past hunts. Before long the feast was ready and the tribe began filing in as healthy helpings of tho rich meaty soup were dispensed into wood-like bowls. Soon the tribe had their food and began to form a semi-circle around the fire. As the crowd settled in their places and began to eat, some of them began a soft chant.

"The Story, The Story."

In a while the chant became rhythmic and members of the crowd began tapping on large bones and rocks creating a thumping that followed the rhythm. As the chant reached its peak Paru stepped to the front of the audience and raised her arms. The crowd grew silent. In a voice stronger than you might have expected from the slender woman she began to speak to the group. As she spoke many of the tribe mouthed her words in a whispering chant.

"This is the story of our tribe. We are born of the old ones, who came across the stars and made Reykjavik their home. The old ones lived in a great dome that kept them safe from the perils of our land of fire and ice but the black devils came and shattered the dome and the old ones fled to the caves. There they lived until the sickness came and took them from us, leaving only the young behind. ' You are young. You are strong. You must survive. You must make us proud, until we can return for you.' They said and taught us the life of the caves and the hunt. So we live and we hunt and we survive until the old ones return. In the times between the winter and the summer and between the summer and the winter we go out and kill the great beasts on the plains. At first the hunt was difficult we lost many brave souls. The Snow Tigers fed upon us and our prey eluded us but the old ones looked down on us from above and sent us a gift. We found in our caves young Snow Tigers and trained them to serve us. They grew and gave us their strength and now we rule the plains. We care for the pack and the pack cares for our

tribe. Soon another hunt will begin and we will make the old ones proud."

The crowd cheered as Paru finished the tale and the chant changed.

"The lines, the lines."

Paru continued.

"I am Paru, tribe mother of the children of Reykjavik, born of Tera. Tera wife of Mishak was born of Falu. Falu wife of Bantak leader of the hunt was born of ..."

Paru continued the chanting of her lines, giving the names of her female ancestors and their accomplishments, to the beginning of their tribe.

"Born of Jenfer who was born of the old ones," She concluded.

But before the words barely left her mouth, another woman stood up from the crowded and added to the chant.

"I am Lela, sister of Paru."

And so it continued long into the night, every member of the tribe, reciting their lineage before the group, the women tracing their mothers and the men tracing their fathers, until all the names of the tribe and their ancestors had been praised. Into the night, they ate and they drank and they celebrated the joy of simply being alive.

Before long most of the tribe was resting. Families huddled close together in groups around the cave floor; bundles of furs nestled close to small fires. Taruk was restless though, anxious for the hunt to start. He bundled himself up in his robe and walked to the cave entrance. Darkeye snorted and grunted as his master approached. The great beast walked up to his master and nuzzled his side. Taruk felt a strange sensation tingle through his veins. Something was different; something new was waiting for them out there on the plains of Reykjavik.

Morning broke and spring was bursting across the surface of the moon. The sun had completed its path across the planet and glared, full, round and brilliant in the sky. The snow on the mountains was turning to streams and cascading from the rocks above the cave. It was time for the hunt to begin.

Taruk and his band saddled their mounts. The sharp spikes that covered the animals had been removed from the center of their backs and hides were placed there instead. The hunters climbed onboard the creatures and settled into the makeshift saddles. They carried everything on the Snow Tigers, themselves, their spears and their supplies. They would live on the backs of these beasts for the next few weeks, becoming one with them. Before long they were making good speed away from the cave, out onto the plains.

Taruk was pleased with their progress on the first day. The mountains grew smaller in the distance and the streams running off them were turning into rivers that headed north, away from the ridgeline. The foothills gave way to the rolling plains.

The natural life of Reykjavik was an amazing thing. It had adapted to an environment with the harshest extremes. Less than half of the moon's cycle provided an adequate supply of water, sunlight and warmth to promote growth. The remaining time was divided between the extremes of heat and cold. The tribe had also learned to adapt to these extremes. During the spring and the autumn they would hunt and gather the needed supply of hides and meat to last through the hard seasons. During those difficult times they would eat the food they had gathered or hunted and survive on the plentiful mushrooms the caves provided.

Taruk was pleased by the rapid growth of the green spongy mass that grew all around them. Absorbing the moisture from the melted snow and soaking up the sunlight from above, the thick moss like plant life of the plains was doing well. Back at the caves the food gathering would be good and out here on the plains the herds would be eating well. Though the thick green carpet slowed their movement, before long they found what they were looking for; the trail of a large herd of Sloth Worms.

The origins of the name, Sloth Worm, were long forgotten to the hunters. They had never seen even a picture of a sloth or a worm and had never seen these creatures from far above. Originally named for their appearance as seen from a hover rover, these massive lumbering beasts, moved like great, flattened worms. Their bodies expanded and contracted in wave like motions that carried them across the plains of Reykjavik. It was the stringy appearance of their hide that had led the inclusion of the references to Earth's shaggy tree dwelling sloth.

Had they been viewed from a little closer, the term whale or some other reference to their size might have been included in their names. Measuring as much as a hundred feet in length, Sloth Worms were the largest living things on Reykjavik. Every spring they would migrate north, eating everything in their path. They would then spend the summer mating in caves near the moon's North Pole. In the autumn they would move south again eventually reaching the caves of the equatorial region before the winter struck.

The hunters had learned how to track and kill these giant beasts by mimicking their native companions. Though they would eat just about any large animal they could find, the most common prey of the Snow Tiger was the Sloth Worm. They were much to small to catch the largest animals but by working as a pack the ferocious predators could bring down a smaller worm and it would feed them for a season. The human hunters added their own skills to the process, including their spears and a little human creativity. Waking the Snow Tigers early with the aid of fire, gave them the first advantage over the worms, they hadn't previously possessed, a head start. The pack had done well sharing the hunt with the humans.

The Sloth Worm herd was not hard to track. They left a path hundreds of yards wide. Following this great road, completely cleared of growth, where even stumps and rocks were crushed into the surface, the hunters would catch the herd quickly, perhaps within a few days. The Snow Tigers moved much faster than the worms but, unlike their prey, needed to rest at night. The nights were still cold and the hunters and their mounts would huddle together on the plains each night, around a small fire until the sunrise of the following day. They would eat at night or during the day in the saddle; their supplies consisted of dried meat and mushroom paste, which they would mix with some of the moss like vegetation from the edge of the trail. They kept water in hide bags and would fill them now again from the rivers and streams that ran out onto the plains and crossed the trail from time to time.

It was after the third day of tracking the herd that they came upon a sight that caused them to pause. It was unusual for the trail to come this close to the ruins and it made the hunters nervous to see the site from their stories. They feared

the black devils might show up at any time. The circular
outline of the dome was still clearly visible, though the vine
like plants growing up its sides covered much of the structure.
The tallest remaining sections reached perhaps seventy feet
into the air and arched over as if their jagged edges were
reaching out to meet at some invisible point in the center of the
structure. Beside what remained of the dome, the shattered
hull of the power complex sat like a smashed box long forgotten
and covered with growth. Taruk urged his hunters to keep
up their pace so they would pass quickly from this forbidden
place.

The black devils were mostly the subject of the stories but
every once in a while one of the tribe would claim to have
spotted one. Orbs floating in the sky above them, with a
blackness that defied reality as if no light at all reflected off
their evil forms. Taruk was pleased that he had never seen one
and hoped he never would and he was pleased when the ruins
were far behind them.

On the afternoon of the following day, a more pleasing site
greeted them. Ahead, on the horizon, appeared a dust cloud
that could only mean one thing: the herd. They closed in
quickly. They would not hunt today. Instead they would look
to pass the herd and set themselves up for the kill tomorrow.

As they drew close the moving mass of gargantuan creatures,
the thick cloud of dust and the stench of the herd drove them
back out into the green carpet of the plains. Keeping up their
pace as they passed the herd, was essential. They wanted a
good lead on them before nightfall.

That night only the Snow Tigers slept. The hunters stayed
up all night sharpening their spears and wrapping the ends
with dried vines and coating them in fatty oil they kept in their
supplies. For the first time on the hunt, they would leave much
of their supplies behind, tightening the straps of their saddle
and mounting their steeds with only their spears in hand.

Each one lighting the end of their spears so that it doubled
as a torch, they began to move out in a large U shape before
the herd. As the sun poked over the horizon and the massive
form of their host planet followed, they leaned to the side of
their mounts, placed their flaming spears to the undergrowth
creating small fires around the herd and began to yell and

scream as the beasts approached. Fire again proved a great
gift from the human hunters to the Snow Tiger pack.

The fires quickly joined and spread into a large burning dead
end directly in front of the herd and the lumbering animals
slowly came to halt. At the head of the herd, there was a large
male, at least one hundred feet in length. At the sight of the
flames and smoke he reared up on the hind section of his body
and swayed about, perhaps forty feet above the floor of the
plains. The Sloth Worm had only the most primitive eyes but
they were sufficient for him to find a path around the obstacle.
This was the moment for the hunters. As the lead male signaled
the change in direction of the others, the disruption in the
group created gaps for the hunters to penetrate. They moved
in quickly from both sides, focusing on the younger smaller
animals in the center of the group. They quickly found their
targets. Two smaller females, each perhaps fifty feet in length
became the prey for the hunters. It was now time for the Snow
Tigers to do the work. The pack closed in on both animals.
Leaping onto the center portion of their prey. The hunters
held onto their mounts with all their strength occasionally
assisting with a jab of their spears into the thick hide of the
Sloth Worms. The worms writhed and bucked their attackers
and swirled in their own defense. The safest place was to stay
in close to the body of the worm, avoiding the lashing tail and
head of the massive animal.

Darkeye was in his glory. He showed no fear of his victim,
though she was four times his size. He climbed completely
on to the back of the animal, sinking his teeth into the softer
upper portions of the hide. Taruk grasped his saddle straps
with all his might to stay on Darkeye's back. From this new
vantage point, Taruk was able to glance around and get a view
of how the hunt was going. Though the scene was jolting and
shifting as the Sloth Worm tried to buck its attackers, he was
able to gather enough information to make the critical decision
of the hunt.

First, the prey, his quick observations showed him that the
required damage was done. The animals were a long way from
dead but they were injured sufficiently that they would not be
able to keep up with the herd. Next, the rest of the herd, the
element of surprise had now been lost and the larger worms

were moving in to clear their midst of the unwanted intrusion. The large lead male was directly in front of Taruk and closing in quickly. Finally, his hunters and their pack; they had spent their greatest energy and would be best served by getting out with their lives.

With his quick and skilled assessment complete, he did what his team depended upon the leader to do. He called off the attack.

"Darkeye off!" He yelled to his mount. "Hunters, retreat!" he called to his group.

With that command, the Snow Tigers and their riders broke from their prey and retreated to outside the herd. Only the great speed and agility of the Snow Tigers kept them from getting crushed as the larger worms closed in. Taruk watched as Mitak found himself charging directly under the falling mass of an eighty-foot long female coming to save her companions. He passed directly under her body and heard the massive thud as her weight hit the ground behind him. Before long he joined Taruk and the rest of his team at a safe distance from the herd.

A quick count of the group helped him assess their losses. He was pleased to see that all the hunters had made it clear. Though some of them had obviously taken some serious falls. They were short two Snow Tigers, whose riders had been lucky enough to escape death and hitch a ride with another hunter out of the mêlée.

It was clear the herd was also assessing their losses. The larger worms were prodding the victims of the hunt, trying to get them going. The injured beasts just moaned in response unable to move again with the rest of their group. Before long the survivors began to move on, making their way around the edge of the fire that blocked their path and turning north again to continue their migration. They left behind the carnage of the hunt, two fifty foot Sloth Worms, slowly bleeding to death and two large dead Snow Tigers crushed under the weight of their foes.

Taruk was pleased. It was a good hunt. The old ones would be proud and the tribe would eat well for another season.

They had also made good time. They had caught the herd quickly and weren't far from the home caves. This time advantage would mean more of their kill could be brought back to the tribe. With the rest of the herd clear of their wounded prey they moved back toward the beasts. They dismounted from their Snow Tigers and climbed upon the backs of the worms. The creatures were still alive, their backs rising and falling slowly with every labored breath. With a moment of homage to the old ones, the hunters plunged their spears deep into the brains of the wounded animals. Their suffering ended.

They labored for over a week, processing one of the kills, while the Snow Tiger pack devoured the other. First the hides were carved off the animal. Then the meat was cut away in strips over six feet each. Each strip was then stretched to dry over a slow smoldering fire. Meat of the spring hunt was always dried, smoked and treated to preserve it through the summer season, while the product of the autumn hunt was always frozen to preserve it through the winter. By preserving the food, the tribe had an ample source of protein in each of their moon's seasons. With the meat cut and dried and the hide divided into usable sections, they were ready to start their long trek back to the spring caves. Their spear poles were tethered together and used to create long lean-tos that carried the goods. Their faithful hunting mounts were now beasts of burden.

Before long the hunters were heading south. The slower pace of the return journey gave the hunters more time for conversation.

"Will Fera have given birth before we get back?" Taruk asked of Mitak.

Mitak and Taruk had grown close on their many hunts together. Mitak learned everything he could from the older leader, in the hopes that he would someday lead the hunt.

"I hope that we will back before the baby comes." Mitak responded with the pride only an expectant father could express.

Mitak was old enough to have many children but his first wife, Melu, had grown sick and had been unable to carry a child. Mitak could have taken in a second wife. Melu had urged him to but he had chosen to focus his energies on caring for her instead. It had been difficult for him adjusting to life without her but Fera had been a good wife and helped him recover from the loss. Mitak knew that his expected child was a gift for his patience.

Taruk admired his younger friend greatly and hoped to teach him the same patience and understanding on the hunt that he showed with his family. Mitak was a risk taker and that worried Taruk. He hoped that fatherhood would cure him of that.

The two friends talked endlessly as the miles passed away but as they drew close to the old ruins, their conversation was interrupted. Ahead, in a shallow valley, strange creatures moved on the surface of Reykjavik. They were unlike anything they had seen before, with bodies similar in size to a man's but much rounder. In every other way they were foreign from anything they knew. Dark brown, almost black in color, they were moving quite slowly along the center of the valley. They moved on a multitude of long thick tentacle legs that stretched out from their body. There were perhaps ten or twelve of these strange animals and each one appeared to have a different number of tentacle legs. The smaller ones had perhaps eight, other larger ones had as many as sixteen. Though there seemed something intimidating about the site that they couldn't quite define, Taruk called the hunting party to a halt and beckoned Mitak to join him to investigate further. They unhitched their Snow Tigers from their loads and moved down into the valley.

The image of the creatures became even stranger as they drew close. For each tentacle leg they had a matching eye; a large cold black eye. Taruk and Mitak drew even closer to the creatures, who seemed unconcerned with their presence. They were easy to catch up with, as their many legs flowed over each other causing their round bodies to almost glide across the surface, their pace little more than a man's walk.

Taruk and Mitak drew closer and closer and still the creatures ignored them, simply making their way down the valley as if oblivious to the approaching hunters. Mitak called his mount forward and came alongside the group perhaps only twenty feet away. From up close Mitak could see their skin, rough and abrasive like the surface of a rock. Their color seemed black at times and brown at others almost changing as they moved.

Mitak's Snow Tiger snorted and snarled at the strange visitors, who had finally decided to respond to the attention they were getting. One of the creatures stopped and began to move toward Mitak and his mount. Mitak held his ground but the creature kept coming. Dwarfed by the massive Snow Tiger, the stranger seemed little of a threat but also seemed completely unafraid of the far larger predator. Mitak raised his spear as if to gesture the creature to hold its position but the animal kept coming. As it came close it began to reach up with its forward tentacle as if to touch the great face of Mitak's Snow Tiger. Mitak knew his mount would not allow the contact and instinctively thrust down with his spear, striking the creature firmly in its outstretched tentacle.

The response was instantaneous.

From above, beyond the view of Taruk and Mitak a searing white beam came down on Mitak and his mount. Taruk watched in horror as both Mitak and his Snow Tiger were slashed in half by the powerful ray from above. He looked up to see the origin of the destructive force but the beam just disappeared into the sky above. In another moment it was gone.

Taruk just froze as the reality of the moment sank in. The smell of burned flesh hit his nose as the eerie squeal of the many-legged creature before him hit his ears. Mitak's spear had broken the flesh of the creature's leg and brown ooze was seeping out but the animal was otherwise unharmed. It drew back from the burnt carcass of the Snow Tiger and Taruk's friend, while the others came up behind it.

Taruk wondered if he would be the next struck down from above but nothing happened. Some of the creatures gathered around their injured companion while others investigated the victims. Taruk's mind swirled with anger, shock and relief that he was still alive. For a moment he wanted to charge the group and let Darkeye tear them to shreds, Darkeye's snorts told him that his mount had the same idea but something inside him held him back. As he regained his awareness, he realized that the same fate that had met Mitak would greet him if he harmed these new visitors to their world. Instead he backed away from the scene and returned to the rest of the hunters.

They all watched over the area from the ridge above the valley for some time, saying little. Finally the creatures moved on, seeming to have had enough of the scene of the carnage. With the danger past, the group moved down and recovered the body of their fallen friend. They stared in disbelief at his fallen mass and the incredible power that had killed him. After some words to the old ones, they gathered up his body and placed it on one of the lean-tos and made their way out of this horrible place. Tears flowed when the hunters reached the caves again and news of Mitak's death spread through the tribe. Taruk told everything to Paru, fighting to hold his anger back. The women of the tribe attempted to comfort their men, many of them secretly glad their loved ones had not confronted the visitors. Paru turned to Fera and tried to bring her solace for her loss but Mitak would not easily be forgotten. That evening Paru again addressed the tribe.

"The old ones have again blessed us with the return of our loved ones from the hunt. The hunt was good and food will be plenty in the hot days to come. We will return to our cool summer caves knowing we will be safe till Reykjavik's autumn arrives but a new chapter has also been added to the story of the children of Reykjavik. Dark visitors have come among us, visitors who are protected by the black devils above. The loss of our brave brother, Mitak, must not be forgotten. >From here on let it be known to all the children of our tribe: do not harm or touch the evil many legged ones. Hold back your anger and your pain, until the old ones come and show us the path to revenge."

Taruk clenched his teeth and stared out at the plains of Reykjavik. Yes, someday, when the time was right vengeance would come, for the tribe, for Mitak and for the old ones.

Chapter 13

New Mission

3864
Foundation Colony
50 light-years from Earth

Years earlier, Sarah Carmichael wouldn't have been at all happy to be visiting the office on the Colonial Council Chairman but much had changed since Foundation Colony's first decade. Foundation Colony had become the most successful example of a deep space colony in the thirteen hundred year history of Mankind's ventures beyond Earth's solar system. Since the solution of the Oxygen harvesting problems, the colony had already completed its first new colony star and was already building its second. All her inhabitants knew the reasons for their success. Once again they owed their very existence to their Founder and the innovation he had given them and as the key force in the Founder Project the Carmichael family had rose significantly in prominence and status as a result.

Although the reasons for its successes were still a secret to far away Earth, Foundation Colony had become the most advanced civilization in the history of Mankind.

Since the very earliest origins of man's technology, on the far away plains of southern Africa, where man's ancestors, not far removed from their ape cousins, began exploring how stone tools made their lives easier, several key factors had dictated how quickly man's technology advanced.

The size of the human community had always played an important role in man's progress. Each new addition to the human race was a new set of eyes, eager to learn how they could manipulate the world to their benefit.

The ability to communicate their observations had also been fundamental to the advancement of the race. From the earliest mutations of the human vocal cords to the advanced interstellar communication beams that kept humanity linked across the depths of space, man's communication ability drove human advancement.

Finally, man's ability to store and retrieve information allowed each day's work to build upon the lessons of the past. >From the first stone carvings of written language to the advanced virtual libraries of Earth, the extent and access to records of information formed a foundation of advancement.

When all of these factors were layered on top of the natural intelligence that man possessed, they formed the engine of human achievement.

On Foundation Colony, however, the rules of the game had been changed. A single human mind, Frank Ryland's, was now able to drive innovation at a pace, faster than ever achieved before. First, his own natural intelligence made him one of the greatest innovators ever born. When added to the fact that Frank's brain now operated at up to one hundred and fifty times normal speed, the Founder had become a formidable force of change in his realm. Frank also possessed the ability to interact with his artificial intelligence Advisor systems at his own speed, creating the perfect marriage of human innovation and computing power. This partnership had enabled him to not to only solve fundamental problems facing the colony like Oxygen collection, but also design vast improvements to the systems and processes that kept Foundation Colony healthy. The colony's decisions were still made by the council but the innovation and implementation behind many of those decisions was Frank's job. As a result Foundation Colony was unlike any other interstellar settlement.

Most colonies became frozen at a certain point in technological evolution. They carried with them the technology of Earth at the point of launch but from that point forward were able to invest very little in the generation of new technology. Occasionally a breakthrough from Earth would come over the beam and, if they were fortunate, they might have the systems and raw materials to take advantage of it, but more often they would simply be left behind. The oldest colonies in the realm struggled by, on technology now over thirteen hundred years old. Even the colonies of Foundation Voyager's day were already three hundred years behind the times. Foundation Colony however, had not only been able to keep up with Earth but had achieved much advancement not dreamed of far away, in the cradle of humanity. Frank Ryland himself was one of those advancements and Foundation Colony's willingness to throw out the Biotech Laws had been a critical to his existence. The very laws that Earth created to protect itself had become its own handicap.

Life on Foundation Colony was good. Most colonists, like their counterparts on Earth, no longer had jobs to do as part of the operations of the colony. They were free to enjoy their lives, learning and celebrating the joy of living.

Sarah Carmichael considered herself the fortunate amongst the fortunate, as a pioneer in the Founder Project, she was a celebrity in the colony and could easily have won an election to Colonial Council Chairman, had she ran, but she had felt others were better qualified to do the job.

"Hey there brother!" she exclaimed as she entered the Chairman's office.

Tim looked up and smiled briefly, but a moment later a look of anguish returned to his face.

"What's wrong?" she asked immediately.

"You haven't seen?" he replied. "Come here, sit down."

Sarah joined her brother on a large and comfortable sofa that sat directly in front of a large viewing screen that formed the centerpiece of the back wall of Tim's office.

Tim looked at the screen and spoke.

"Earth News."

Upon his command the screen came to life and began displaying images selected from the data beam that connected Foundation Colony to Earth. The scenes were shocking.

New London colony was one of the largest that Mankind had yet created, with over three million inhabitants. Her planet bound configuration had given her close contact with the necessary raw materials needed to expand. A complex series of transparent domes interconnected and spread across the equator of her home planet. About the same size as Earth, she differed from her inhabitant's native world in just about every other way. First the planet was completely dead. With an atmosphere rich in Sulfuric Acid, she had not produced nor would ever be able to sustain any native life. The humans on the planet lived only under large thick shells of structural crystal that withstood the hostile atmosphere. Perhaps the most startling thing about New London, however, was her proximity to Earth. She sat only twenty-two light years away and now she was the twenty-second colony and the closest to Earth to fall victim to the Intruders.

The significance of her loss was not lost on Tim and Sarah, though not military experts by trade, they, like most of humanity had become very familiar with the military realities of the ongoing war with the alien invaders. The further away from Earth an attack occurred the less the chances of a victory for Mankind. It was hoped, however, that as the Intruders grew closer to Earth and encountered the larger more advanced colonies with their sophisticated defensive arrays that the tide of the war might begin to turn, that some weakness might be found in the Intruder's war machine. The battle of New London had once again shown that hope to be fleeting. Like so many colonies before her, she had been torn to shreds without mercy or pause.

Experts on Earth had debated back and forth over whether it might be possible for some of the inhabitants of New London to have survived. If they could have kept one of their great domes intact, to keep out the poisonous atmosphere, some of them might have lived. There really was no way to tell for oure. The signal from the colony had gone.

All that was known is that most, if not all, of the colony had been lost before the signal went dead. The sketchy information seemed to indicate that most of the colonists would have taken a suicide pill after the loss of their internal atmosphere, but nonetheless, the images of New London's last hours were traumatic to watch.

The terrible white beams, now an all too familiar fixture of the last three hundred years of human history, first cut through the colony's defenses. The colony struck back with powerful beam generators that it hoped would have the strength to break the Intruders attacking orbs into pieces, but the attackers just kept coming. There was still no evidence of even one successful kill against the enemy.

After breaking the colony's defenses, its domes were easy targets. One by one they were shattered, as horrendous fires broke out in the buildings below. The colonists, sheltered far below the surface, had little choice but to wait for death, or take their own lives painlessly.

Tim and Sarah just shook their head in shock at the images before them.

Tim broke the silence.

"They'll reach Earth by the end of the Millennium."

"Earth will stop them," Sarah replied trying to be reassuring.

In times past, it might have seemed strange for so much attention to be paid to events that would not affect Earth for several hundred years and wouldn't affect Foundation Colony for perhaps several hundred more years. During the twentieth and twenty-first centuries for example, Mankind squandered the natural resources of his home planet, with little regard for what the unbalanced state of the energy and chemical cycles of the world, might have on the future. The price of these practices was not fully known until the crises of the early twenty-second century. Since that time man's awareness of his future had grown. This was even more true in the tenuous environment of colonial life. No colonist could accept the prospect that their colony might someday fail, whether that was for local reasons or due to broader events in the galaxy. That growing sense of anxiety that the future was uncertain now hung over the entire race.

"I'm not so sure," Tim replied in his typical technical way. "Although New London was an old colony, originally based on ancient technology, she had received several secondary colonization missions in more recent history and had access to much of the advanced technology from Earth. As I understand, the power and accuracy of her weapons systems weren't far behind Earth's and they didn't appear to make a scratch."

"Earth's defenses are hundreds of times the size of New London's. You can't possibly think the Intruders will have it as easy as they have with the colonies," Sarah responded, always trying to be the optimist.

"Do you know what even one of those attack orbs would do to Earth if it got through the defenses?" Tim pressed on.

Sarah had no reply. She simply smiled and placed her hand on Tim's shoulder, refusing to accept defeat.

Tim turned away from the screen and changed the subject. "I'm sorry to rush off but I have a council meeting in a couple of minutes. Can you walk with me?"

"Yes, of course," she said as they both stood. "I'm stopping in at the lab and you're on my way."

Their conversation during the walk was more pleasant, Tim updated Sarah on how the grandchildren were doing and ribbed his sister for never marrying. Before long, they reached the door to the council chamber and they hugged goodbye as the other council members arrived. They greeted Sarah with reverence and friendship as they all filed into the council. Now alone in the hallway, Sarah decided to go along with her fib to Tim and visit the lab after all.

The lab was quite as she entered, as it was rarely used any more. Frank took care of much of his own maintenance and monitoring and any communication with him could now be made from any console in the colony, though still considered a system and not a citizen of the colony, Frank had been given the same communication access as everyone else. The colonists of Foundation Colony now thought of Frank as a living being who they had ongoing communication with on a regular basis, though the legal questions regarding the status of his existence had never been addressed. Though it seemed strange to Sarah, Frank was the least concerned of all of looking at the issue. He preferred to be appreciated for his value to the colony rather than because of some legal doctrine. Regardless, his survival was now assured. He was as essential to the colony as the structural hulls of the colony stars themselves.

The old screen was a blur when Sarah entered the room. Frank was working at his own pace and though the view was still projected out in to the lab, its shear speed made little sense to the human eye. Before Sarah got comfortable, the blur came into focus and Frank's image appeared in the screen. Frank slowed his pace, to converse with his old friend. Sarah was

one of the few people who Frank would interact with at real
time. Most of the colonists who worked with him, were used
to seeing messages recorded by Frank in a microsecond but
minutes in length to the listener.

"Hello Sarah. How are you?" Frank asked.

"I'm well Frank, how are you?" she replied.

"That's funny you look troubled?" he continued, demonstrating
his uncanny ability to read the people he dealt with. Having one
hundred and fifty times longer to examine facial expressions,
gave Frank a distinct advantage in conversation.

"Yes Frank, I'm sorry. I am troubled. It's the news regarding
New London. I just can't believe it."

"Yes, very tragic, I was shocked when I first learned about
it," Frank responded.

Sarah had gotten used to working with Frank and his way
of taking something that happened only moments ago and
talking about it like it was part of history. Of course, to him,
it was. Whereas everyone else on Foundation Colony had only
had a few hours to absorb the news, Frank's accelerated mind
had the equivalent of nearly a month to think about it.

"I've been looking very closely at what data I've been
able to extract from the feeds. Unfortunately its limited but
nonetheless concerning."

To Sarah, the whole thing was concerning, but she knew
Frank and he had something very specific in mind. She let
him continue.

"By my calculations, the energy level of the Intruder's
attackers are about one thousand times more powerful than
anything we could create with a similar mass and one hundred
times more powerful than the most powerful energy beam we
are able to create."

"Is there anything we can do?" she questioned.

"Possibly, but not here," he responded.

"On Earth?" she questioned, hopefully.

"I can't say," Frank replied.

Sarah's troubled expression grew and Frank continued.

"I've been doing some modeling on the theoretical possibilities
for energy beam generation and the related technologies.
Specifically, those required to produce the raw energy and
those required to direct and control it. When combined with the

ability to absorb energy and maneuver their weapons systems, this represents the core of the Intruder's advantages over us. Currently, those advantages are significant. It's possible that we can improve on what we have now and perhaps we can put something together allowing us to put up a fight. But we can't do that here. The materials required to even explore the possibilities don't exist in our system and I don't even know if they exist at all."

"What do we do Frank?" she questioned.

"If you're asking my opinion, then I have to tell you that a fundamental shift in the focus of this colony is needed. We need a new mission. We have to join the war and we have to do it now," he concluded.

"We're over sixty five light-years from the closest battle what good can we do?" she pleaded.

"Like most of the wars on Earth before our time, the outcome of this conflict will be determined by science. The side that is able to bring the more advanced technology to the battlefield will ultimately be the victor. Right now, that reality does not bode well for the future of humanity."

"What do you propose?" she further questioned.

"Foundation Colony is uniquely qualified to help shift the balance but to accomplish that we must change the rules a little."

"The Biotech Laws?"

"Yes, ultimately we cannot help if we keep the details of life in our colony confined to this system, keep things a secret."

"You mean keep you a secret," Sarah confirmed.

"Exactly, everyone on Foundation Colony now knows the of my existence. It may be time for that knowledge to extend beyond the colony, but ultimately that is a decision for the council. It's my belief that with the Intruders approaching, my existence will be considered much less of a threat, however, ultimately that is not my call." Frank replied.

Sarah smiled and touched the console button in her chair and created a message for her brother.

"Tim, when you're finished with your meeting, can you come down to the lab," she instructed, reassuming her role as her brother's boss and the leader of the Founder Project.

While they waited for Tim, Frank politely changed the
subject. Asking about Tim's flock of grandchildren, the most
recent generation of the Carmichael clan. The two of them
were lost in laughter and fond memories when Tim finally
arrived in the lab.

"You called, boss," Tim joked as he opened the lab door.
He smiled as he entered the room, pleased to see Frank
operating at human speed.

"Hello Frank," He smiled.

"Hello Mr. Chairman," Frank joked back.

"Come in, sit down we need to chat," Sarah instructed
getting right to business. "Frank and I have been discussing
recent events on New London and what we should be doing
about it."

"The council just voted to expand our investment in our
defensive array," Tim responded. "What else do you have in
mind?" he questioned, turning to Frank.

"There's an old saying on Earth, 'The best defense is a good
offense' and that's exactly the philosophy I propose we follow."

Tim paused, unconvinced. Frank continued.

"My calculations show that Mankind's colonies will continue
to fall one by one. Earth will be attacked around the end of the
Millennium and will most likely be overrun."

Tim knew there was no point in arguing with Frank and so
he didn't try, instead he looked to find where Frank was going.
Frank understood this and continued.

"What's needed is the silver bullet that will allow us to
inflict real damage on the Intruder's ships. So far we haven't
come close to finding that and I believe that if it exists, it's
somewhere else, not here. We need to focus on research and
exploration of alternative weapons technology, then attacking
the Intruders with a new sword, so to speak."

Tim's response was as expected

"The council won't support anything that makes Earth
aware of our violation of the Biotech Laws."

"Yes, I agree," Frank replied to Tim's surprise. "Who would
you consider the deciding votes?"

"It would probably go nine to three against. I can't vote
unless there's a tied vote. Jenkins, Dubois and Smith would go

with us. Thomson, Schroeder and Chin would probably be the easiest votes to swing but it's unlikely we could get them all."

Frank looked back at Tim through the lab's screen and smiled.

"Put forward a resolution and call for a vote, perhaps our good councilmen will have a change of heart."

It was much later that evening when Councilman Jeff Thomson received the notification of the next day's meeting.

"What's Carmichael up to?" he questioned himself as he read the notification on the terminal. He was even more surprised to find the attached draft resolution.

"In acknowledgement of the approaching threat of the Intruders to the future of Mankind, in acknowledgement of the superior technology developed by this colony, with deepest respect to the jurisdiction of the Unified Government of Earth and the Biotech Laws enacted and enforced by that government, yet acknowledging that the external dangers facing Mankind exceed those posed by the human technology integration within this colony, this Council hereby resolves to attack the forces of the Intruders beyond the boundaries of this colony, knowing that this resolution may result in the disclosure to our brethren on Earth of our decision to overturn the Biotech Laws in the jurisdiction of Foundation Colony and to extend that jurisdiction to all domains where our influence may serve to defend Mankind as a whole. From this day forth this resolution shall become the new mission of this colony. We shall focus every available resource to the exploration, research, development and use of new, yet unknown weapons capable of saving Mankind from the terror that has befallen us. Agreed to this day, by the Council of Foundation Colony".

Thomson was shocked by the resolution. He respected Tim Carmichael, most of all because he was a good politician and rarely brought up legislation that was doomed to failure. His style was rather to build consensus through compromise. He knew, at best, this piece would get three or four votes but it wouldn't get his. He couldn't fathom what Carmichael might be up to. He turned off his terminal, turned down the lights and made his way to his bed. Tomorrow was going to be an interesting day.

His sleep was interrupted, however. Just as he had dozed off, his terminal sprang back to life. Images he had seen earlier in the day flashed across the screen. It was the news data he had watched from New London. He froze for a moment as he watched one of the white beams slash into one of the great domes of the massive colony. For a moment Thomson couldn't decide if he was dreaming or not but regained his consciousness and ordered the images away.

"Terminal off," he snapped.

The only explanation he could come up with was that perhaps he'd made a sound in his sleep and accidentally instructed the terminal to come on. He lay back down and tried to forget the interruption. He soon fell back asleep. His sleep was soon interrupted again, however, but this time by a more pleasant image. His terminal once again flicked before him, he looked up to see some of the footage he'd watched recently of his ancestral home in North America. Jeff Thomson's family had maintained a tradition of remembering their origins on Earth; he smiled quizzically at the images before him. Picturesque residential domes lay against beautiful green hills, where wild mustangs ran in the valley below. It was here in the foothills of the Rockies that the first of his family to set foot on Foundation Voyager had been born. Daniel Thomson had loved the home he grew up in almost as much as he'd loved the prospect of being part of Foundation Colony but like his fellow travelers he knew he owed his very life to the Founder and shared his vision of the future. Jeff Thomson smiled at the images, almost drifting back off to sleep as he sat up looking at the screen. Suddenly the image changed again and the terrible pictures of New London filled the screen. Children were falling as an Intruder's energy beam cut through the gangway that they were fleeing down. The changing image sent a jolt that struck right to his heart. He snapped back in reaction.

"Terminal off."

He rubbed his forehead again, not willing to let it go this time.

"Advisor, explain terminal activation," he requested.

"It appears a request to transmit data was sent to your terminal by the colony's central defense Advisor."

"Excuse me? Get me Frank," Thomson gestured in disbelief, knowing that a quick message to the Founder would get to the bottom of this mysterious and unexpected malfunction. In a moment the image of Frank Ryland appeared on the councilman's terminal. Frank responded to the councilman politely.

"Yes, Councilman Thomson, how can I help you?"

"Can you explain to me why the terminal in my room has gone nuts?" Thomson asked.

"I'm sorry Councilman, what do you mean?" Frank replied. It suddenly struck him that he was actually talking to Frank Ryland. This was a first for him. In his tenure as Councilman he'd had many conversations with Frank but they had always come in the form of video messages that Frank recorded in his own accelerated time and then sent to him. Never before had the Founder slowed down enough to speak to him directly. He suddenly felt nervous.

"May I ask why you are talking to me directly?" Thomson inquired.

"Well Councilman, I understand you have important work to do tomorrow. I want to make sure that you have everything you need?" Frank responded.

Thomson's nervousness grew, he could inquire with Frank about the problem he was having but he suddenly realized that would be futile, he sensed clearly what was going on and it frightened him terribly. For over fifty years, the Founder had served the colony faithfully and given them a life they could never have imagined without his help and he had never, at least to Thomson's knowledge, imposed his own will upon the colony in any way, form or manner. Is that what was happening now? Could it be? Jeff Thomson decided he didn't want to know.

"I see, thank you Frank, never mind."

"There's nothing I can do for you, Councilman?" Frank continued in his polite tone.

"If you could get my terminal working right, I'd be grateful," Thomson closed.

"Of course, Councilman, pleasant dreams," Frank concluded.

Jeff Thomson's dreams weren't pleasant though. He found himself trapped in a whirlpool of uncertainty trapped between two choices that both scared him, he just couldn't decide which scared him more.

When the morning arrived, Thomson was exhausted from a very restless sleep and arrived at the council meeting with his head hung low.

The Chairman kept the meeting brief. He had sent the resolution forward out of loyalty to Frank and his shared belief in Frank's point of view but as a politician he wasn't going to waste his time trying to debate for passage of legislation that didn't have a chance in hell. He'd rather just get it over with and go tell Frank he tried.

He was surprised by the result. The vote was tied six to six. He looked up at his swing voters. Thomson, Schroeder and Chin all looked back at him as if they had just made a deal with the devil. He cast the tiebreaker vote and the resolution passed.

It was as if the whole council was in the shock, all six of the councilmen voting against the resolution, just sat dumbfounded staring at the swing voters but they just walked out with their heads hung down.

It was a couple of hours later when Sarah sat once again talking with Frank in the lab.

"How did it possibly pass?" she asked.

"I think our good Councilmen had an opportunity to sleep on it," Frank responded.

"What now?" Sarah continued.

"The journey ahead will be long and the outcome is uncertain," Frank responded.

"I wish I could take it with you," Sarah replied, in one of the more frequent references she had been making to her upcoming transition ceremony. Though still several years away, the upcoming event loomed on the horizon for Sarah.

"Perhaps you can," Frank said, in a response that Sarah had not expected.

"What do you mean?" She inquired, curiosity surging through her veins.

"Well, you are still the leader of the Founder Project are you not?" Frank inquired.

"Yes," Sarah responded, not sure where Frank was going.

"Do you consider your project a success?" Frank continued, confidently.

"Yes, Yes I do," she responded, smiling proudly.

"Well then, perhaps it's time to repeat the experiment. Of course that's ultimately your decision."

"Yes, I understand, do we, I mean do I, have the time?"

"Oh Yes, in fact I've been spending an extensive amount of time looking at a new neural interpreter design. I believe we can do it much more easily this time around. I'm ready when you are, Sarah. Are you ready?" he questioned.

"Yes, Yes Frank, I am," she replied.

Chapter 14

Falling Star

3938
Reykjavik
42 light-years from Earth

Agony swept slowly across his body, as Michael Kelly struggled into consciousness. Every beat of his heart felt like a great pounding drum exploding in his chest. He could feel the blood surge through his veins, as the Cryo-chemicals drained from his body and the new blood was injected in. His body temperature continued to rise and finally he opened his eyes. The image above him was blurry but he could make out the shape of the Cryo-chamber lid folding slowly away from his body. He tried to move his arms but the initial response was nothing more than a stinging pain in his extremities. The torture of Cryo-recovery was moving from his central body to his limbs. Eventually movement began to creep back into his fingers. He tried to lift himself out of the chamber but still could barely move his arms. A familiar and firm voice began to coach him through the process.

"Take it easy Kelly. Let the strength come back to you," Commander Stone instructed him.

Kelly was impatient.

"What's our status commander?" he mumbled, barely able to move his lips.

"All systems are operational and combat status is green," Commander Stone replied in a strong but calming voice. "Take your time, soldier."

Finally, his vision began to come into focus and he saw Stone looking down at him. The scene was surprising. Stone's face was thickly bearded and his grey hair hung long around his shoulders. Then he realized, hair growth continued during Cryo-sleep, he probably didn't look to good himself. He reached up and felt his face, feeling a full beard covering it for the first time in his life. Priority number one was a shower and a shave.

It was two hours later when the entire crew was awake, cleaned up and gathered for their first briefing. He looked across a couple of seats at Vasquez and gave her a subtle smile, many of the crew, women and men, had shaved their Cryo-sleep hair growth but Vasquez had found herself attached to the long flowing dark mass and had just tied it back. Kelly liked the look, it was a change from the short military cut she'd had at the academy. Out here in the dark depths of space, there was no question of their loyalty to the core and uniform regulations didn't seem to matter even to Stone, who wasn't wearing any command insignia, as he stepped to the front of the group. The room became quiet and focused on Stone as he began to speak.

"Ok people, listen up. Here's our current position." As the screen in the back of the main briefing center came to life and showed a three dimensional image of the Reykjavik system, with Avenger approaching from outer space.

They were still in deceleration. Avenger's engines in full burn, slowing the ship down from the peak velocity she had reached in open space. Just as during their acceleration, the great accelerator shaft of the ship was streaming accelerated sub atomic particles into space but now the beam extended from the front of the ship, from the large hole in the particle shield that housed the forward accelerator shaft opening. The drive had been burning for the last 15 years of their Cryo-sleep and would finally shut down in about two days, shortly before colliding with the system's sun. Avenger was on a one-way mission and wouldn't give up her secrets to the enemy. Before her impact, however, her crew and the combat armada they would command, would jettison from Avenger and make their way down the surface of Reykjavik. That is, if the Intruders let them.

"So far no sign of Intruder activity but it's early yet," Stone continued. "Affective immediately we are all on scramble alert. If we're lucky we'll get close enough to the moon to launch at the optimum point but unfortunately our enemy may not cooperate with those plans. Once you launch you know the drill. Fight your way through any resistance, using whatever assets you need to use. Then get to the surface. Go power clean as soon as you land and make for the caves. Once you're on the surface your mission is simple. Survive and perform reconnaissance as possible. The most important data to get back to Earth is anything that will help us survive and win against this enemy in the larger battles to come. We want to know if there are any human survivors, how they survived and anything else we can learn about our enemy, including any lessons from the journey in."

Stone paused for a moment.

"One more thing. When we left Earth, three systems had been attacked. That count is now at least twenty-four and that information is forty-two years old based on our distance from Earth."

He paused again.

"New London is history," he stated, plainly but with the slightest hint of anger in his tone.

Even as professional soldiers the loss of such a large system still brought gasps from the audience.

"When you look at the data there are some things become abundantly clear: this war is progressing faster than we thought and we are way behind enemy lines."

His tone returned to matter of fact instruction.

"The ship's data library now has a complete download of all the available data from Intruder attacks. Study it carefully. Best case we have two days to prepare before we launch for Reykjavik, use the time wisely. Dismissed people, get to work."

For Kelly and most of his comrades, their first priority was to check the system status of their combat pods. The combat pods were small single seat spacecraft built for maneuverability and communication. They had only minimal armament of their own. They relied on other assets that would be launched with them to attack their foes. Avenger carried sixty of the small combat pods and provided an additional two thousand assets to make up her combat armada. Only the combat pods had human pilots, the other craft relied on a combination of

Artificial Intelligence, central command input and remote instructions from the combat pods to determine how best to engage their targets. While flying his combat pod, Kelly was not responsible for command of specific assets but rather would be granted command over the appropriate resources dynamically, depending on how the combat progressed.

Kelly's pod checked out fine. As he sat there, he paused in amazement at the engineering of the great warship, Avenger. She had managed to carry her precious cargo across forty-two light-years of space in a journey lasting over two hundred years and everything worked flawlessly. She would be thanked with a fiery death in Reykjavik's sun.

After checking out his combat pod, Kelly retreated to the training area to start catching up on two hundred years of military history. The lesson was a hard one. In all of the destruction that the Intruders had unleashed on humanity, very little had been learned about their vulnerabilities that was not already known after the attack on Omega Theta. They had received over thirteen confirmations via burst transmissions of colonists surviving the initial attacks. It was believed that perhaps two or three of the colonies in question had any real chance of survival for any extended periods of time. The INC warships that had followed Avenger would focus on those systems. Some of them would have already reached their targets despite being launched decades after Avenger. Unfortunately, however, no data had reached Earth yet to be of value to Avenger. She was now the deepest penetration, into Intruder held space. There was no way to even know if the ships that followed had shared Avenger's luck and made it all the way. They believed that Avenger's path, one that had steered away from other systems, might have been a critical element in their survival so far.

The data available on the strength of the Intruder's weaponry was perhaps the most disconcerting. Sufficient imagery had been received to allow for endless analysis of the strength of the energy beams that the Intruder's possessed. Avenger's most powerful beam was barely one two-hundredth the power. If they encountered even a handful of Intruder attack orbs, they were massively out gunned. The latest information on detection and targeting was not much more encouraging. Gravitational tracking was still the only way to get a fix on an Intruder ship. Fortunately that fact had been known prior to Avenger's launch and her entire sensor array was primarily gravitational in design. This had meant that a large percentage of the total mass of Avenger's attack armada had been taken up with sensory equipment.

The rest of the day went by with no sign of Intruder vessels and Kelly found a moment to catch up with Vasquez.

"What do you think?" he asked her as they both chatted in the hall outside the training center.

"It doesn't look good," she said, as straightforward as she'd been two hundred years ago when they left Earth.

"Maybe they've left," he replied, smiling at her.

"That's probably our only hope," she responded, smiling back.

Then quite suddenly, realizing they had the hall to themselves, she grabbed him and tugged him into a storage alcove. She squeezed him so tight he thought he'd burst. Then she looked at him and reiterated Stone's order.

"Survive, remember, survive," she instructed.

"You know me, I always follow orders," he replied, as she grabbed him and held him again, before the approach of another crewmember, interrupted their moment alone.

At the end of the day the group lay down in their bunks but unfortunately, they didn't get much time to rest.

The scramble siren blasted through the sleeping quarters jolting them awake. Within moments the entire crew of Avenger was scrambling for their combat pods. Kelly slid into the seat of his pod and began his pre-launch check, the onboard Advisor responded positively to each item on the list. Finally Kelly gave the instruction.

"Launch."

The interior of the pod shuddered as he was shot out into space, away from Avenger. He felt his body float up in his chair as he gave up the rotational gravity of the Mother Ship. He tightened his harness to secure himself in the seat. Then he began a review of his instruments to get his bearing.

Almost all of the attack armada had successfully launched and was forming up around him. The command pod fell in behind them and Stone's voice came over the pod's speaker, directing their attention to the cause of their scramble. A single Intruder orb was closing in fast, headed straight for Avenger. It might have seemed the tiny invisible sphere was vastly outnumbered by its foe, but Kelly knew the reality of the situation. This single killer would probably cut right through them. A quick calculation showed him that, if there was any combat, it wasn't going to last long. Their combined closing speed was almost two thousand miles per second. Though much slower than their peak speed, the armada had retained Avenger's velocity at the time of launch, which was still considerable. When combined with the speed of the approaching Intruder orb, this made for an astounding closing velocity. In a few moments they would shoot past each other, without the possibility a second run.

"Power up weapons," came Stone's voice. "We only get one shot people, let's make it count."

Unfortunately they didn't get the first shot. Before their sensor arrays even got a clear fix on the incoming target, a piercing white beam began to cut through the forward elements of the combat fleet. In bursts, each lasting no longer than a microsecond, the beam targeted one component after another. Within less than a second, over five percent of the fleet was converted to dead space junk, streaking lifelessly toward the center of the solar system. Though only moments had passed it seemed an eternity before the fleet was able to return fire. The results were not encouraging. There was no visible sign of even one hit against the target and a moment later the orb slipped right through the middle of the armada, taking more victims as it passed. In another second, it was gone. Screaming onward toward Avenger.

"Stat Rep," Stone's voice came over the speakers in Kelly's pod, unshaken by the fly-by and the damage it had done.

Kelly quickly scanned his instruments and confirmed his ship was untouched. He tapped at the console to report his status back to the command pod. Thinking for a moment whether the others had been as fortunate. He checked his panel and quickly confirmed that all the combat pods had remained unharmed. It appeared the sensor arrays and beam generators had been the preferred targets of their adversary.

He turned his attention to Avenger and pulled her status up on his display. His fears were realized a moment later. The large ship was a sitting duck when the Intruder orb reached it. Targeting the main Fission-Fusion reactors, the orb tore the aging lady to shreds in no time. The impact of the deadly white beam triggered a reactor overload and Avenger blew herself apart, leaving only an empty hulk of the front end of the ship still streaking toward the system's star.

"Prepare for debris field," Stone's voice instructed as the expanding cloud of microscopic debris spread away from the point of detonation.

Kelly spun his pod about to point it into the approaching cloud. The front end of his ship provided the best protection against impact. His defensive shield beam generators were designed to destroy debris from his pod's path but could also be used to protect him against more rapidly approaching objects when required, by turning the vessel into the threat. The maneuver reminded Kelly of steering an ancient sailing ship into a massive approaching wave. His ship shook as the generators strained to eliminate the hazards. Some of the smaller particles made it through and scarred the front end of the pod. Kelly sighed in relief, realizing his hull had held.

Again Stone called for a status report and Kelly was pleased to learn that most of the fleet had survived the blast wave, unhurt. All the pods were still intact.

With the action of their first attack behind them the fleet settled into the journey that lay ahead. Without Avenger's engines to slow their velocity, they would now have to rely on the atmosphere of Reykjavik's host planet, Thor, to control their speed. Slight adjustments in their course put them right on target for a close orbit of the planet.

They had been lucky. Had they been forced to launch from Avenger even a couple of hours earlier, their velocity would have been too great and they would have had no chance of making it to the moon's surface. Their small ships' drive systems allowed for maneuvering only. Large adjustments in velocity were the responsibility of Avenger's larger interstellar drive. At the wrong speed, even if they were able to survive the Intruders, they would have found themselves unable to escape the fiery clutches of the system's sun. Even now their chances were slim. Their velocity at contact with the atmosphere would be extreme and the stress of the slow-down would push the heat resistance of their ships' hulls to their limits.

Kelly knew there was nothing much he could do about the orbital mechanics of the slow-down. He would simply have to rely on the accuracy of the atmospheric density data and the hull design of his ship.

He chose to focus his attention elsewhere, on the Intruders. There had to be a way to hurt them. He thought about their powers, energy production and energy absorption. The subject reminded him of his studies in energy absorption and resonant frequencies.

"Frequency," he said to himself as he thought out loud about the problem.

Perhaps that was it. For any system, certain pitches of energy couldn't easily be absorbed due to the system's characteristics and in some cases would even be amplified by the system itself. Perhaps this was the key to hurting the Intruders.

His theory would be easy to test, if the armada's command intelligence would cooperate; it would be a somewhat expensive experiment. What they had been doing wasn't working, however, so Kelly couldn't see the harm in trying.

He quickly went to work loading up his request. He asked the beam generators to fire at their next target across the full available spectrum, adjusting frequency as they fired, instead of only in their optimum frequency. The result would be severely reduced power output but the beam would determine the effects of a range of frequencies against the target.

He spent most of the rest of the journey fine-tuning the request, ignoring the primary frequencies that had already been tried without any luck. He prioritized the remaining frequencies in accordance with the power level at which the beam generators could produce them. Before long he had completed the request and was bracing himself for atmospheric entry, wondering if he'd even get to try his little experiment out.

They made it as far as the planet's atmosphere with no further interruptions from the Intruders. Reykjavik lay on the other side of the planet and that is where they expected to meet their adversaries in a final show down.

Kelly couldn't believe the site before him as he penetrated the outer layers of Thor's atmosphere. He had never imagined so many shades of green could exist in one scene. At times seeming almost blue and others almost yellow, the entire planet was a swirling spectacle of gaseous interaction. His craft began to jostle as the bands of gas became thicker. His viewing screen went darker as less of the system's sunlight reached it and the jostling turned to thudding that felt it would rip his whole pod to pieces. The density of gas interfered with his communication systems and he lost contact with the rest of the fleet that had plunged into the soupy sea along with him. The thudding became a rapid vibration and Kelly felt for sure he was doomed. His ship couldn't possibly take much more. His instrumentation indicated his hull had reached 113% of maximum heat tolerance. There was no way to know how far beyond its design threshold his ship could be pushed. Kelly couldn't believe his luck when the vibration finally began to subside and the hull temperature began to drop. Kelly quickly checked his velocity and confirmed the slow-down had worked. They would come out of the planet's atmosphere at a velocity slow enough to pull into orbit around Reykjavik and then descend in for a landing. That was, of course, if the Intruders let them.

As he came out of the emerald mist of the planet's outer atmosphere, his communications came back on line and immediately his alarm sounded the detection of multiple Intruder attackers ahead. The entire fleet was emerging back into space only to be hacked to pieces by a small cluster of the invisible orbs. At the rate they were loosing resources, the entirety of Avenger's attack fleet would be gone in less than a minute, not nearly enough time for them to make it to the surface.

But there was no time to panic. Kelly had a job to do. He scanned the console quickly, to see if any of the beam generators had been tasked with his request. He couldn't believe his luck. Two of the surviving generators had been resourced to him and were firing as best they could at anything they could get a fix on. Kelly took a recording of one of the shots and in less than a second played it back under the careful scrutiny of his onboard analysis system.

There it was, exactly what he was looking for. At a single and defined point in the spectrum, the beam generator's impact on the Intruder ship had generated something not yet seen by Mankind's warriors, an image of the Intruder ship. It was fleeting; gone again in a moment but nevertheless, Kelly had made them do what he wanted, fail to fully absorb the energy cast at them.

He quickly made note of the successful frequency and entered another combat request. This time he asked all available beam generators to launch a coordinated strike against the closest Intruder target, firing, at the specific frequency he requested, at the same time.

His heart raced as the instruction was entered and he realized the closest Intruder ship was heading straight in his direction and was cutting through the resources between them like a hot knife through butter. Mine layers, sensor drones, beam generators and torpedo ships were one by one being rendered useless before him and he was next.

Suddenly the dark orb in front of him lit up like a new star, as four surviving beam generators behind him blasted it with everything they had. Kelly didn't know whether his pod or his enemy would burst to pieces first and gasped with relief when the attacker split before him, the two dead halves falling toward the moon below. It was the first known kill in over four hundred years of fighting the Intruders. Perhaps now humanity had a chance. He recorded the track of the Intruder orb's debris, wanting to confirm his kill.

There was little time, however, to savor the moment. Kelly still had to make it to the moon's surface alive. He issued a "fire at will" request to the remaining beam generators to continue the attack strategy he had devised, automatically. He then checked the status of the rest of the fleet. He was shocked. Over ninety five percent of the fleet had now been destroyed and the command pod was gone. His heart froze as he realized Commander Stone was probably no more. Only six combat pods remained and they had only eight beam generators left. He wondered for a moment if Vasquez was alive but communications were too disrupted to get a fix on which combat pods were operational.

He programmed a landing track into the pod's navigation system and hoped for the best, carefully watching the combat continue to unfold behind him. One by one the remaining components of the attack fleet dropped off his console screen. The sensor arrays were already too depleted to give him any kind of fix on the Intruders. What was left of the fleet was now blind. All that Kelly had left was his ship and his guts and they both told him there was no way he would make it to the surface in one piece with his power systems active. He took a quick look at his angle of decent, extended his atmospheric entry stabilizers and cut his power, hoping to render himself a non-target.

It was going to be a rough landing.

Kelly could see the effects of the spring thaw on the surface of Reykjavik as he broke through the cloud layers and streaked down toward the surface. A large lake had formed directly in his path and Kelly couldn't determine if that was good news or bad, as the water below rushed toward him. He hit the surface fast, at a shallow angle, and bounced off like a skipping rock. His whole ship rotating rapidly as it climbed back up into the air then descended again toward the water. The sensation was disorienting and Kelly had little sense of where he was. Things got really clear again when he felt the sharp jolt of the ship once again hitting the surface of the lake. He felt the pod rock back and forth for a little while. Then he began to feel the heavy hull descend into the water. He knew he didn't have much time. He grabbed his survival pack from his left side and turned the release lever on the escape hatch above him. Water immediately began to rush into the ship and a foul sulfurous smell penetrated the cabin. He made it out just in time to avoid the massive rush of water as his pod sank to the bottom of the lake.

With the expectation that much of Reykjavik's surface would be covered in water at the time of their arrival, Kelly's survival pack had been fitted with flotation capability. A quick pull of a release cord inflated the pouches attached to the pack allowing him to float for a while and get his bearings.

He couldn't help but look up, curious if there were any signs of the combat he had just left. The sight was stirring. The sky above was ablaze with fiery streaks of debris falling to the moon's surface. Kelly knew that every bright yellow line represented a component of the fleet burning up in the atmosphere. He could only hope that at least some of the other combat pods had managed to settle into a survivable descent.

His next priority was to survey the scene around him. He was a little surprised by what he saw. He had studied Reykjavik in detail in his preparation for this mission. He knew its features as if he had lived here all his life. He also knew that he might expect to find a technological presence associated with any ground landing the Intruders might have made. But nothing had prepared him for the scene before him.

Surrounding the shore of the lake, in every direction, there were clusters of primitive stone domes; clearly not something a technology as advanced as the Intruder's would build but there they were. Kelly dared not believe it, but perhaps these were the homes of human survivors of Reykjavik. In his excitement to find out, he began to swim to the closest shore. Before long he pulled himself out of the water on to the shore and heaved his soaking wet pack onto his back. He had barely left the water, when the inhabitants of the strange domes came out to meet him. He was shocked to learn they were far from human. They rather more closely resembled octopuses, each having at least eight long tentacles, some much more, perhaps as many as sixteen. Unlike Earth's large multi-legged creatures, these had an eye for each leg. It was the site of those eyes that made Kelly most nervous. They were large and lifeless in appearance, just staring blankly at Kelly as they approached and they were now approaching from every side.

Kelly had studied all of the native life of Reykjavik and he knew without a doubt that these primitive looking creatures, who were apparently the builders of the strange stone domes before him, were not natives of the moon. The Intruders must have brought them here, perhaps as livestock or for some other unknown purpose. Regardless of their reason for being here, Kelly felt uncomfortable with his presence getting such attention. He reached into his pack and pulled out his hardened crystal survival blade and prepared to defend himself. Larger than a knife but smaller than something you might call a sword, the large blade was the best tool for survival in a world where any more advanced technology would probably get you killed.

Perhaps eighteen inches in length with the sharpest cutting edge available, it would cut through almost anything and would be more than adequate to slice one of these lumbering animals to pieces. His adversaries, however, showed no fear whatsoever and kept advancing on him. Before long, he was surrounded as they moved in on him from all sides.

He picked an escape path that would give him the least trouble and raised his blade to hack through the closest beast. He expected the creature to real back in fear but still, it advanced on him, unaffected by its own certain doom. Kelly suddenly felt uncomfortable about his situation and the possible results of killing this creature and so at the last moment he decided not to execute the strike that would have surely carved the creatures body in two, instead he raised the blade above his head, ready to use it at any moment and made a break, through the sea of tentacles that were reaching out for him. For a while he thought he might not escape and would be forced to bring down his blade but by turning and shifting his weight he was able to elude their grasp and break free. The creatures turned to follow him but their slow lumbering pace was no match for his athletic speed. In a short while he found himself on a ridge looking over the cluster of domed buildings and the lake beyond. His adversaries seemed unwilling to pursue him much further and turned back toward the buildings.

Kelly sat down on the ridge side and watched them disappear out of site into their strange little village. A quick survey of the perimeter of the entire lake told him there were probably thousands of these creatures living just around this one lake and the extent of their construction indicated they probably lived here throughout the seasons. He considered how hardy they must be to survive the moon's harsh winter and summer with only those primitive domes to protect them. He had learned all he could here, however, and decided it was time to move on.

His priorities were clear. He would first focus on trying to find the downed Intruder orb and see what he could learn from it. Then, when the moon moved into line-of-sight with Earth, he would make his transmission to INC. He had critical data to transmit and the position of Thor during his decent had made transmission impossible. He pulled out his Mechtab, a small mechanical device that allowed him to record and review data without the use of electronics. The device already contained two notations; one regarding the frequency he had used to kill the orb and the second gave the orb's trajectory down the moon. He pulled out a map of the moon's surface from his pack and planned his trek. He determined that the orb was probably three days hike to the west and the caves that he hoped would provide him a chance for long term survival were another four or five days south from there. Hopefully he would reach shelter before the summer heat made survival on the surface impossible. As his last task before leaving he pulled a collapsible pole out of his pack, assembled it and attached it to his blade. Once connected, the device made a lightweight spear. This would be his only defense against the predators of Reykjavik.

Kelly made good time as he hiked across the surface of the moon. The temperature was comfortable and the spongy mass of green that covered the ground didn't hamper his progress too much. He snacked on food from his supplies as he walked and occasionally tried some of the native plants that his training had taught him might be safe. There were plenty of signs of the moon's abundant seasonal life but fortunately he did not encounter any of the large predators. He did notice a herd of Sloth Worms but they were far to his North and no danger to him. He would have loved to see them up close but his mission did not include further study of the native life. As he came across small rivers and lakes and refilled the water pouches in his pack, he would frequently notice more of the strange stone domes and their alien inhabitants. He had decided he would investigate them further at some point but not before he had found the destroyed Intruder orb.

He found the largest section of the downed sphere exactly where his data indicated it would be. It sat at the base of the small crater formed by its impact. Kelly made his way down into the crater to examine his fallen foe more closely. He was surprised by its small size, perhaps twenty feet in diameter, about the same as his own combat pod. Its energy-absorbing surface, perfectly black in all prior observations, was now a dull grey. With the killer now cracked completely open, he could observe the five-foot thick diameter of its outer shell. He couldn't see any visible disruption in its surface. The shell itself was most likely responsible, not only for the device's energy absorption capabilities but also its deadly beam weapon and its propulsion. He wished he had the tools available to perform a more careful analysis of this powerful material, that obviously held the secrets of much of the Intruder's Technology. He entered his initial observations into his Mechtab and focused his attention on the inner core of the orb. This central section of the object was much more complex than the outer shell. It housed a series of chambers and tubes apparently designed to carry and process various types of fluids, intertwined with thin fibers probably designed to carry instructions or power around the system. This complicated series of devices all seemed to lead to a central chamber. This chamber was the only section of the sphere that was intact. It consisted of a membrane sack perhaps six feet in diameter. Kelly paused for a moment to consider the possible hazards of opening this membrane but decided it was important for him to understand its contents. He reached forward and touched it, finding it soft and slimy. He then brought forward his survival blade and cut it open. It sliced open easily, revealing the inner contents.

Kelly stumbled back in a moment of shock as the inhabitant of the central chamber slumped halfway out. The familiar site surprised him. Inside the chamber sat one of the strange creatures he had already encountered on the surface of Reykjavik but reconfigured in a horrible way and now completely lifeless. Its tentacle legs had been removed and were connected to artificial interface points that linked them with the rest of the orb. Its eyes also had been removed and were connected to large fiber bundles that were tied directly into the super structure of the rest of the ship. Large tubes connected the abdomen of the creature with the fluid systems of the ship itself. The revelation sent chills through Kelly's body.

The Intruders were Biotechs. They were the product of the integration of biological evolution and artificial technology. The site brought back a flood of feelings and memories into his mind. He wandered back through his history lessons to some of the more tragic times in Earth's past; The Great Wars during the late Biotech Era. He remembered the pictures he had studied of humans with their eyes removed, replaced with direct optical nerve integration. These ghosts of man's past had given up their human vision in return for direct sensory integration with powerful weapons systems. They had traded in their human limbs for the ability to directly control those systems. They were half human and half machine. Their bodies and their way of life became very different from the Natural Humans, those who had no technological enhancements. During the Great Wars, a period brought about by a series of changes designed to protect the rights of Natural Humans; the Biotechs had rebelled and almost succeeded in gaining permanent control of human society. Their defeat had resulted in the Biotech Laws, new, stricter regulations, which permanently outlawed the direct integration of humans and technology.

It seemed things had gone differently for the Intruders. It appeared that the more powerful members of Intruder society were those who were integrated with their technology. The realization was a frightening one for Kelly and raised critical questions about Mankind's future. Had Mankind made a terrible mistake? By suppressing the evolution of changes in the human form, had they left themselves unable to compete with other intelligent life in the galaxy? Kelly tried to put the thought out his mind, as he continued his investigation of the wreckage. He took a sample of the tissue of the lone pilot of the craft but couldn't remove any of the orb's grey shell. He took what other information he could and made plans to move on.

The daylight sun was getting hotter and Kelly knew he would not be able to remain exposed on the surface of the moon for much longer. It would be a couple of days before he would be able to make his transmission to Earth and staying here to do it would place him at danger of not making it to the moon's equatorial caves. He began his trek south.

As he traveled, he again sampled the natural vegetation on the way. He quickly learned the plants that were edible from those that were not. His hope was to find additional supplies in the caves that would ensure his survival long enough to perform further reconnaissance in the moon's autumn. He knew his chances of any long-term survival were slim though and he began to wonder how long the moon's colonists themselves had survived after the attack.

He rested at night, sleeping as he could and at other times staring up in amazement at the great green giant that dominated the sky. Her reflection onto the moon made the spring night brighter than full moon on Earth. The green light reflecting off the carpet of vegetation created a strange green world that reminded Kelly just how far from home he was.

The night before he planned to make his transmission, he found himself sleeping more soundly than he had in the past evenings, perhaps growing more comfortable with the strange environment of this moon and its foul smell. His rest was interrupted, however, when he was awoken by a strange sensation.

At first it was as if he felt a warm moist breeze on his face as he slept. Then, in a startling realization, he heard a snorting sound interrupt the rhythm of the air movement. He looked up with a gasp, staring at a set of massive teeth, only inches from his face. In fright, he reached for his survival blade only to find it was caught under the beast's massive paw. In all his adventures thus far, he had never felt so close to death as he did at this moment, staring into the glaring eyes of a massive Snow Tiger.

What came next was even more surprising.

"White Claw, back!" a gruff voice grunted and the Snow Tiger reared away from Kelly's face.

With the large vicious head no longer blocking his view, Kelly was now able to view the source of the life saving instruction. The beast had a rider, a human rider. Kelly was speechless. He just lay on the ground in shock. The rider seemed equally as surprised to be looking at Kelly. He dismounted the Snow Tiger and walked up to him. At first he just stared down at Kelly with a look of confusion on his face. Kelly began to wonder if he was still in danger but the look on the man's face began to change. Confusion turned to wonder and wonder to a look of embarrassment. He reached an arm out to him in a clumsy and apologetic manner. Kelly took the arm and stood. Soon he was the victim of embarrassment as the man quickly knelt before Kelly and bowed his head deeply, almost touching the ground.

Kelly grabbed the man's shoulder gesturing him to stand.

"Please don't," Kelly instructed as the man stood again. "Tell me, who are you?"

The response came in the same gruff voice. Kelly could barely interpret the strange dialect but with concentration was able to decipher the man's speech.

"My name is Katak, leader of the hunt. We followed the falling star and it brought us to you. It is an honor to greet you 'old one'?" Katak responded with wondrous questions in his eyes.

"Well Katak, you're a sight for sore eyes, you can't imagine how happy I am to meet you. Tell me why do you call me 'old one'?" Kelly asked, smiling and wondering if perhaps his two centuries of Cryo-sleep was showing more than he thought and thinking how this weather beaten hunter looked far older than he. The answer he got was more than he bargained for.

Katak proceeded to give Kelly, the history of his people and his ancestry.

"...*Son of Taruk* ..." Katak was reciting as Kelly began to notice the rest of the hunting party approaching him in wonder.

"... And so we have been waiting for the arrival of the old ones from beyond the stars are there more to come?" Katak concluded, after finishing his chant.

Kelly decided the truth might be too much for his new friend, so he decided to let them down gently.

"Yes, but I am the first. Will you show me the way to your homes?"

Before long Kelly and the hunters were saddled back on the Snow Tigers and were on their way. Kelly rode with Katak and spoke with him as they traveled. He quickly learned how they had survived on the surface of Reykjavik, living in the caves during the summer and winter and hunting in the spring and autumn. He also learned that Katak was far younger than he might have imagined, approximately twenty-eight, based on the number of winters the hardened man told him he'd lived. He learned more about the strange, many legged, visitors to the moon and how they had first come to the surface almost eighty years ago. Kelly felt lucky he had not struck any of them when he learned of the deadly consequences to one of the tribe's well-remembered heroes and how they had been strictly avoided after that. He was surprised to learn how much the visitors had reproduced and how they were able to survive out on the plains with only the makeshift stone domes as protection, becoming dormant in the coldest and hottest parts of the moon's cycle. It seemed the greatest problem for the tribe, had been in their interruption to the migration paths of the Sloth Worms and how many of their prey had just rotted on the plains, sliced to pieces by the deadly beam from above when they had stumbled into villages of the visitors. It was only now that the great beasts seemed to be adapting and avoiding contact with the new comers.

They were making good headway toward the equator, when Kelly asked Katak to stop for a while. Reykjavik had finally moved clear enough of her host planet to give her line of site access back to Earth's system and Kelly didn't want to delay his transmission any longer than he needed. He smiled to himself as he realized what a treat his new friends would likely get, from his burst transmitter.

Setting up the transmitter was a fairly simple task. The device was amazingly compact, perhaps only eighteen inches in length and six inches in diameter. It would rely on the vast size of the INC listening arrays in Earth's system to receive its weak signal. In forty two-years, an antenna over three hundred miles in length and tightly focused on Reykjavik's location would hopefully receive the signal he was about to send. It almost made him feel important that such a vast machine would be listening for his tiny voice in the cosmos.

He pressed a small button on his Mechtab and out popped a small foil sheet. The metallic film, with a series of small perforations in its surface, contained all of Kelly's notes since his launch from the Avenger. He hoped the data he had gathered would prove valuable to the war effort. From his experiences, Earth would learn the Intruder's ships could be shot down and how. They would learn the Intruders were Biotechs whose natural cousins had been brought to colonize Reykjavik and finally they would learn that, amazingly, Mankind had survived on the harsh surface of this moon, so far away.

With the data film loaded into the transmitter and its tripod legs extended the device was ready for activation. Kelly let Katak know that once he activated the device they would need to get far away from its location before it actually launched. A simple pull of a mechanical cord started a chemical fuse as Kelly remounted White Claw and he had Katak darted away from the site. When they were perhaps one hundred yards away, Kelly turned around to watch his message go off.

The transmitter operated flawlessly. First a small antenna dished popped from the top of the device as the transmission began and then small rocket engines in the base of the device fired. It would transmit the contents of the data film repeatedly as it climbed in the atmosphere. Kelly was pleased to see it climb high in the sky before meeting its inevitable doom. White beams from far above, sliced it out of the air, shattering it into pieces like a great firework. The beam then turned to the launcher still sitting on the ground and turned it to a charred hole on the Reykjavikian plain.

Katak stood in awe at the site. He had never seen the black devils at work and though the scene frightened him, he had confidence that his new friend knew how to taunt these demons and yet keep him safe.

Soon the hunters and Kelly found themselves approaching the cool protective caves and Kelly couldn't believe his eyes. There, amongst the women of the tribe walking out to meet the hunters, Kelly saw a face he never thought he'd see again. At the sight of him, Vasquez rushed out to him and embraced him with a love he felt would last forever.

They were together, their duty done, free to share the rest of their lives, here on the surface of Reykjavik.

Chapter 15

Departure

4011
Foundation Colony
50 Light years from Earth

The councilmen chatted pleasantly, as the twelve of them filed into the room and took their seats. The large oval viewing screen at the head of the room was still dark as they sat down. Slowly the conversation lapsed and one by the one the group turned their attention toward the screen. It slowly came to life, revealing, at first, only a blur. Then it slowly took form, displaying a crystal clear image of their Founder. Frank Ryland sat before the group with a pleasant and businesslike expression on his face.

"Good afternoon gentleman," Ryland addressed the group.

"Good afternoon Mr. Chairman," an older member of the group replied, as the others nodded and smiled to welcome their Chairman and good friend to the meeting.

The older council member continued.

"Frank, our agenda for today is pretty short but nonetheless important. First we'd like to review the final status of Foundation Explorer in preparation for launch. As a second, item we need to look very carefully at the cross-over request for Lucas Cranford. I think you're familiar with the case," the man continued.

"Yes John, thank you. Can we take a look at that issue first, as I'm certain it will produce more debate amongst the council members than the Explorer update," Frank responded.

Since assuming the role as council Chairman, Frank Ryland had been known for attacking the difficult issues head on. It wasn't that he didn't realize the realities of politics. He just seemed to be capable of dealing with them much faster than most.

Anywhere else in the colonized galaxy, it would have seemed bizarre for a man who had been dead for almost five hundred years to have assumed the leadership of a governing body. Only thirty years ago, the thought would have been poorly received even here on Foundation Colony but much had changed in the last thirty years. The first change had come in the refocus of the colony toward the goal of counter attacking the Intruders that were sweeping across human space and the subsequent decision to construct Foundation Explorer. The second change had come with the dramatic and secret crossing-over of Sarah Carmichael, the leader of the Founder Project.

In crossing-over, as the act had now become known, Sarah had ended her human life as microscopic neural interpreters recorded and then digested the contents of her brain. Her memories, feelings and personality had become a data file, kept in storage and protected by the Founder himself. The Founder's focus on the rapid construction of Foundation Explorer had dictated a strategy of not activating Sarah until some point in the future when resources were available for the task that would not slow their critical operations against the Intruders. This had not, however, dulled the effects of her decision on the colony.

Though it had previously become a matter of tradition that the Founder was considered a computer system, not entitled to human rights, it was impossible for the colony to justify this philosophy for Sarah. She was perhaps one of the most respected members of the colony and a member from their own time, as the leader of the Founder Project much of the appreciation the colony had for Frank's work was displaced to the closest human and that was Sarah. So, shortly after her experiment was completed, the Colonial Council had voted unanimously to change her official status from deceased to 'crossed-over'. Her birthright was not transitioned. Instead it was preserved indefinitely for the living mind of Sarah Carmichael to will as she saw fit at some point in her future yet to come. The reclassification of Frank Ryland was almost automatic following the vote on Sarah.

After Sarah's crossing-over, colonists partitioned the Founder in droves to follow in her path. At first Frank was reluctant to let so many give up their human lives with no guarantee of any future at all. It would be perhaps centuries before sufficient resources could be allocated to support the activation of so many others but the dream of immortal life as a human spirit living in the virtual realm, was too enticing for a dieing human to resist and the requests kept coming. Eventually guidelines were setup for the process.

It was decided that any colonist who had reached their maximum human age potential while still maintaining their mental integrity would be eligible to cross-over. This meant that candidates were only giving up the last waning years of their life. Thousands took the deal. Even though it gave no guarantee of anything other than an early death. Lucas Cranford was a more interesting case, however, and challenged these simple guidelines.

"Yes Frank I think you're right. We should get to the bottom of this as soon as we can. The family is anxiously awaiting a decision," Councilman John Alexandria continued but was soon interrupted.

"He's a child," blurted out a red headed councilman at the far end of the table. "I don't understand how we can consider letting him cross-over. He's simply not old enough to understand the consequences of the decision."

John turned to the man politely and responded.

"Simon, your concerns are well founded, however, we cannot dismiss the fact that he is terminally ill and the request has been made by his parents not the child himself. Which reminds me," John continued turning back to Frank, "as part of the request they have asked that upon their own transition, guardianship of the boy be granted to you, Mr. Chairman. Do you have any input for the council on that aspect of the request? I do believe the decision of the council would have to be contingent upon your agreement to that stipulation."

"I would prefer not to comment directly upon that until the council has had an opportunity to fully debate the matter, but I agree that any final decision should be contingent upon someone who fully understands the consequences of crossing-over becoming guardian to the child," Frank responded.

"What is the exact medical status of the boy?" a younger councilman sitting directly across from John inquired.

"Good question Jack. His medical team has indicated that he is most likely to die sometime within the next one to two years. His chances of surviving more than five years are less than one percent. It's really very tragic. Thompson's syndrome is one of the very few diseases that medical science has not yet been able to tackle," John responded.

"How sad, the parents must be devastated," Jack replied.

"Look, we all agreed that if a person had lived all their useful years, taken full advantage of the gift of life and still had a high degree of mental integrity left, they were eligible for cross-over. It sounds to me like little Lucas meets those criteria. I support the request."

"I can't see how you can define an eight year old boy as having the required mental integrity to get sucked into a computer," Simon continued to protest, then went a little red as he looked at his Chairman. "No offense Frank," he paused. "The whole thing just doesn't make any sense to me."

"It would seem the mental maturation process, would be able to continue after his activation in the virtual realm," John answered and once again turned to Frank for guidance. "Is that not the case Frank?"

"That is something that I would have to fully evaluate if I were to decide to take on his guardianship. I was one hundred and thirty-two when I crossed-over and the decision was completely my own. Though completing the mental maturation process within the virtual realm is entirely possible, it is, of course, completely new territory and not a decision that should be taken lightly," Frank replied.

"From my standpoint, I trust your judgment in this matter and am prepared to grant the request subject to the guardianship of our Chairman and Founder. If there are no other questions, I call for a vote," John concluded, making his position clear.

Within moments by a show of hands the vote carried, eight to four. Frank closed the issue.

"Thank you gentleman. John could you let the parents know the council's decision. Please make them aware I will review the situation very carefully before making a final decision on guardianship. I will contact them directly at the appropriate time. Shall we move on to our next topic?"

"Sure Frank, let's have it," John responded.

Frank smiled and began his presentation. As he began to speak, his image shrank into the right side of his screen and a live three-dimensional view of the construction of Foundation Explorer swept into the open portion. Her slender form had a similar appearance to a large generation ship but looked the telltale colony stars, in her forward section. In their place, banks of instrumentation and equipment gave away the fact that she was a ship designed for research and robotic colonization not the support of human life. Construction drones hovered around like tiny sculptors all working in unison to finish a massive work of art.

"As you can see, construction is almost complete. We have finished testing of all six reactors and are presently calibrating the main accelerator shaft. The central neural network has been tested and I will be transferring to the ship two days before launch to give a thorough going over. Any failure will cause the automatic reactivation of my system here in the colony," Frank explained.

Again Simon jumped in from the end of the table. "Are we going to be breaking any records Frank?"

"Most definitely Simon, most definitely," Frank replied, grinning. "At peak velocity we expect Explorer to hit fifty-three thousand miles per second. She'll also reach this speed in a fairly short burn cycle, only five years. The fastest ship Earth has built was the INC Warship Enterprise. As you know she was obliterated in deep space by the Intruders but not before reaching her peak speed of forty-one thousand miles per second."

The group responded with the wide smile of proud colonists.

"Of course, the fact that Explorer will not carry any human passengers helps. We can push the systems to greater limits without the requirements of functioning bio colonies."

"Have we completely ruled out the option of a Generation Ship to follow Explorer to her destination?" John inquired.

"I'm afraid so John. The destination system is extremely hostile to biological life but hopefully it will provide the resources we need to make a real difference in this war," Frank replied.

"I see, and how are things progressing with the custodian?" John continued.

"Good question John, thank you. Yes, the custodian will be activated and tested in parallel to the testing of my new system on Explorer. He will use many of the same sub-systems that I currently use to assist in the management and monitoring of the colony but keep in mind, he is an Advisor not human intelligence," Frank clarified.

Simon's voice chimed in again from the back. "Can you tell us again why we can't keep you? Again, no offense Frank, but you are essentially a computer program. Can't we just make a copy of you?"

"Technically yes, but I must be honest with you. It is a purely selfish decision to not allow a replication of my own program. I'm not sure how having another one of me running around the universe might affect my decision-making capacity. Of course, there's always several backups of me available at one time but I've have gone to great lengths to ensure that only one copy of me is active at one point in time. I can assure you though, the custodian will take very good care of the colony," Frank replied politely.

John rallied to his Chairman's defense. "Come on Simon, how would you feel if we made a copy of you?"

"Are you kidding me, this colony can barely stand one of me," Simon replied, jokingly conceding the point. "Go on Frank, sorry for the interruption."

Frank continued his presentation, giving further technical details about the ship and the huge and volatile system that she was destined for. Her journey would take her another twenty-six light years away from Earth, where it was hoped she would lay the seeds of the new technology that would give humanity a weapon against the Intruders. Ironically, the hopes of humanity might depend on a system colonized entirely by machines.

As the presentation drew to a close obvious questions cropped up in the minds of the council.

"What about Earth?" John inquired, jumping right to the point.

Frank's response sent cold chills through the room.

"It is most likely, already, too late for us to assist in any initial attack on Earth. Our best hope is that either the INC can withstand the first attack or that Mankind can survive beyond the Intruder's destruction of Earth's technological infrastructure. We can still only hope that our efforts will be successful and we can be of some help in the future. I don't want to create any false expectations gentleman We will do what we can," he stated in somber tone.

"God's Speed then Frank," came John's reply.

The rest of the council nodded in agreement and the meeting drew to a close. As the meeting ended, each of the council members pondered the topics that had been discussed and some of them chatted intently as they left the room. Frank Ryland also went on with his day, but for him, that process was very different.

First, the cycle speed of the massive neural network behind the Founder System began to spin up to full speed again. While interacting with the council, Frank's simulated mind operated and processed information at a speed that allowed him to interact with them in real time. When he was no longer in communication with the human residents of Foundation Colony, however, he operated much, much faster. Today, two centuries after first giving him the ability to interact with his human companions in Sarah Carmichael's lab, the Founder Project's network now ran at over one thousand times the speed of normal human thought. Within minutes of the end of the meeting, before his fellow council members had even finished saying their goodbyes, Frank had already had several hours to ponder the challenges that lay ahead. His artificial home also gave Frank other capabilities beyond its sheer speed. Where once it had only been able to produce a simple virtual room that mirrored the control center of the lab, the system could now produce a wide variety of different environments and the associated sensory inputs to Frank's artificial brain. In each of these virtual worlds Frank experienced everything with stunning reality. Every sense that a normal human would experience, Frank also enjoyed. Sight, sound, taste, touch and smell were all produced to perfection each one as a simulated sensory stream directed into Frank's neural pathways. In exchange, signals sent by Frank's simulated brain gave him the ability to interact with his virtual world. The system gave Frank a complete virtual body in which to experience his vast virtual home. Unlike it's first incarnation his virtual body was fully functional, fit, young and having lived for over two hundred years at a vastly accelerated pace, near immortal. Frank and the world he lived in was, by far, the most advanced computer generated environment ever created. Beyond interaction within the environment, however, Frank also had control over the system itself, which he controlled in any number of different ways. Furthermore, as he was the inventor of much of the innovative technology that made life on Foundation Colony so simple for it's residents, he also had a great degree of control over the colony itself.

Frank had learned to make the very best of this new existence, and took advantage of its capabilities to counteract the loneliness that came with being the only immortal occupant of his virtual realm. While the other members of the council walked the corridors of Foundation Colony, Frank Ryland could choose from a large selection of locations to spend his next few hours.

Today he chose one of his favorites.

He stepped out of the council chamber onto a large open stone patio. A warm Caribbean breeze struck his face as he strode out and placed his hands on the decorative stone railing. The radiant blue ocean stretched out before him. There were, of course, no oceans on Foundation Colony and none of the other council members had ever seen one, but Frank Ryland had lived much of his physical life on Earth, and the islands of the Caribbean had been one of his favorites places to spend time.

About seventy feet below, at the bottom of a rocky bluff on which Frank had chosen to place his villa retreat, there stretched a long yellow sandy beach. In the center of that beach a wooden pier stretched out toward the reefs and a large octagonal gazebo sat over the water. A similar gazebo sat on the left side of the stone patio seven stories above its beachfront cousin. Frank made his way over to this closer structure and took a seat in the comfortable couches that surrounded its outer perimeter. As he sat enjoying the ocean, a man, carrying

a tray with two glasses on it, came across the patio and spoke
to him.

"Some lemonade Frank?" the man asked smiling.

"Yes Thomas, thank you," Frank replied taking a glass,
"Please sit."

It might have seemed strange to an observer for another
person to show up in a world that only had one resident, but
Thomas was one of Frank's many inventions to make his own
world more pleasant. Thomas was an advisor, a computer
generated intelligence, not in any way human. For the purpose
of easy interaction, however, and perhaps to keep him company,
Frank had chosen to give his advisor a completely human
appearance. For the virtual world created by the Founder
Project's system, this was no trouble at all. Thomas appeared
to Frank, in every way, human. Though he, of course, knew
better.

"Is something troubling you Frank?" Thomas asked as he
sat next to his master in a way that might have made you
think the two were best friends.

"Yes Thomas, thank you for asking," Frank replied, "The
boy's parents have formally requested, he be allowed to cross-
over."

"I see," said Thomas, in a serious tone of voice, "and you
need to understand if it's the right thing to do."

"Exactly," responded Frank, with just a hint of pride at how
well his advisor companion did his job. "We need to research
this extremely carefully. I was nearing the end of my natural
life when I made the decision to cross-over. The boy is only
eight. His parents have requested the procedure, but they also
don't fully understand what they're asking. I'd hate to get this
one wrong."

Then Frank sat silently for a moment.

"The possibilities are fascinating though," he concluded.

With that conversation Frank Ryland began to research
how an eight-year-old mind would be affected by crossing over
into his world. In his time that work would go on for decades.
Outside the system, in Foundation Colony, only a couple
months would go by.

Though nothing in comparison to the events in Frank's world,
that time was a busy one for Foundation Colony. Cross-over

ceremonies were frequent as the last to have their data images travel with Foundation Explorer met their fate with the neural interpreters. Several of the colony's transition chambers had been converted for the purpose. Since the beginning of the cross-overs, more than three thousand of the colony's citizens had given up their last remaining years to take their memories into the virtual world and now one last cross-over ceremony remained before the launch of Foundation Explorer. This ceremony required that Frank once again interact with his human friends.

It was the first time in many years that the procedure had been performed in Frank's old lab. Frank sat watching from the screen as Lucas' parents led him to the front of the lab and helped him lay down on the lab bed in front of Frank's screen. Frank looked directly down on the boy and spoke to him as an assistant began to make preparations for the procedure.

"Are you scared Lucas?" Frank asked.

"No uncle Frank, I think I will be Ok," Lucas replied, with a nervous look on his face.

"I've really enjoyed getting to know you over the last couple of months Lucas and I'm looking forward to shaking your hand soon," Frank responded with a warm smile.

"Is it cold in there?" Lucas asked.

"Oh no, Lucas, it's as warm as you want it to be," Frank replied.

"Now remember Luc when you cross-over to Uncle Frank's side of the screen, he's in charge. You do everything he tells you to do, ok, and mind your manners," His father instructed fighting to hold back the emotion of the moment,

"I'll miss you Luc," his mom followed "but you're going to have lots of fun with Uncle Frank."

Lucas smiled as he began to fade away under the cross-over sedation. His father looked up at Frank with anguish in his voice.

"You take care of my boy, Founder," he ordered.

"Lucas will know wonders that no young colonist has ever known, that's my promise," Frank reassured the couple.

They both turned to leave the lab, unable to watch the life drain from Lucas' body.

It was a week later when the two of them stood with many of their fellow colonists, on the observation deck, watching as Foundation Explorer's main engines fired. The brilliant blue beam tore away from the elegant lady, pushing her out into the darkness of space. As they watched, they couldn't help but feel that this one ship held the best hopes for the future, for Lucas, for three thousand frozen souls, for Foundation Colony and perhaps, for all of Mankind.

Chapter 16

Their Finest Hour

4123
The Surface of Mars

The memorial tower of INC central headquarters was a stunning structure, reaching over two thousand feet above the surface of Mars. The marble tiled observation deck stretched out over four acres under a perfectly transparent dome. In the center of the deck, bronzed statues of the four 'heroes of humanity' stood gazing defiantly into the Martian sky.

Colonial Commander Luis Rodriguez had been the first to be granted the highest honor that INC could bestow. Over six hundred years ago, he had been drafted into the war by the circumstance of being the first to discover the approach of the Intruders. Once in the fight, he had given everything, right to the end, when he died delivering vital information about the enemy back to Earth.

President Joanne Foresythe was the next to receive the recognition. As the Founder of INC, she had fought tirelessly through Earth's political jungles to ensure the defense of the planet and the colonized galaxy. After the fall from grace of the "hawks", Joanne gave much of her personal wealth and energy toward the goal of maintaining preparedness for a war she had felt was inevitable.

INC Commander James Tiberius Stone stood sternly looking to the stars, the third member of the elite group. Stone had the unique distinction of living longer than any other human being. Including his two Cryo-sleeps, Stone had lived almost 400 years. As commander of the first and most successful Interstellar assault mission ever launched, he had died leading his troops toward the surface of, enemy controlled, Reykjavik.

As for the final hero, his fate remained a mystery. What was known was that he was the man who had been responsible for finding the "chink in the armor" that the INC now hoped would give them final victory against the Intruders. In his burst transmission from the surface of Reykjavik, Lieutenant Michael Kelly had proven that Mankind could survive indefinitely in Intruder controlled space, provided they avoided the use of the advanced technology that drew attention to them. Perhaps more importantly he had given INC a weapon to use against their enemy. He had found a single energy frequency that the Intruder's technology seemed unable to absorb.

It wasn't that these four individuals were the only heroes of man's long running war against the alien invaders. In fact, there were thousands listed in the annals of the INC. It was these four, however, that had been selected as the ones that had had the most impact on the war during their lives. Others were remembered in the carvings etched into the tiles of the viewing deck. In addition, the eighty-six short stone memorials that surrounded the outer perimeter of the deck paid tribute to all the colonies the Intruders had destroyed or forced into a stone-age existence.

This had been Admiral Jackson's favorite place to think during his time on station and today he walked the deck in solitude one last time, wondering if he would live up to the heroic precedent of those who went before.

His contemplation was interrupted by a friendly but respectful voice.

"Admiral are you ready?" Ensign Jeffries inquired from the terminal on Jackson's wrist. "Your shuttle will be arriving in a moment."

"Yes Ensign, thank you."

Before the words left the Admiral's mouth, a small shuttle rose up along side the dome and docked in one of the several docking points around the perimeter. The Admiral walked over and stepped in. The passenger compartment of the shuttle consisted of a spherical transport pod that could be detached from the shuttle if desired. Its transparent outer wall gave Jackson a view of the INC headquarters complex as he headed up into orbit. The memorial tower sat almost in the center of the array of buildings that spread out in every direction. Of course, the buildings on the surface represented only a small portion of the complex itself. Much of the critical infrastructure and command facilities sat deep under in the crust of the planet.

As the Admiral's shuttle climbed into orbit, his destination rose over the planet's horizon. The largest spaceship yet built; quietly waiting for her inaugural launch, the INC Gunship Bismarck was an incredible site. At fifty million tons, the great dreadnought dwarfed anything that had come before her. Surrounded by her construction framework, she looked like a wild predator tied in a cage not strong enough to hold her. Unlike the ships of the INC's past, Bismarck would not travel far from home. Her mission would be fulfilled within the solar system, defending Earth against pending attack. As the largest of the thirty-two Gunships INC had constructed, Bismarck would use her massive drive systems to accelerate rapidly across the solar system and intercept an Intruder Mother Ship before she could threaten Earth. Bismarck, her smaller sister ships and the Fleet Ships that protected them, formed the first line of defense for Planet Earth. If they failed in their mission, it would fall upon Earth's orbiting defensive array to protect the planet. As INC fleet commander, it was Admiral Jackson's job to ensure that failure did not occur.

His heart quickened as the massive ship came into view. Much wider than her Interstellar cousins, Bismarck was powered by nine huge accelerator shafts, six of which ran the length of ship and provided forward and reverse thrust. The other three extended laterally in a three-pointed star configuration from near the rear of the ship and were designed to provide rapid maneuverability. Along the forward section of the ship, in three groups aligned with the lateral thruster shafts sat her main weapons systems. Her huge beam generators could be targeted accurately and inflict damage on targets up to ten million miles away. Mounted in pairs on individually controlled turrets, the eighteen great guns had given rise to the tradition of naming these ships in the memory of the Battleships of old.

Their massive size and large guns made the Gunships vulnerable to any Intruder orbs that escaped from their prey. They would depend on the Fleet Ships to target the smaller adversaries. Each Fleet Ship carried into combat a large armada of small combat interceptors designed to attack the enemy orbs.

Jackson caught sight of the other shuttles nearing the ship, like tiny gnats approaching a sleeping crocodile. He wondered if there was any way he could get out of the ceremony over which he would soon preside. He hoped his time with his distinguished guests would be short. Jackson was a military man. He didn't care for politicians.

"Is that you Jackson?" came a jovial voice over his shuttle's intercom.

"Yes Senator, good to hear from you," Jackson lied.

He was always thankful that the Senate was only one house of the Unified Government's legislative branch and the second house, the people, were there to keep the politicians in check. Jackson didn't participate in the legislative process himself but he knew many who did and he was thankful for that. Every Senator represented one hundred million people on the Senate floor but everyone represented themselves, through virtual voting, in the second house. It may not have made politicians honest, but it made them act it.

Jackson laid in a course to bring him into the construction framework's main viewing deck and turned to enjoy the view of his new flagship, as the shuttle glided in and docked.

As he stepped off the shuttle the Admiral was shocked to find he was immediately accosted by a swarm of media representatives and political aids. For a moment he wished it were only the Intruders attacking him as he tried to make his way through the crowd.

"Let's give the Admiral a little space," came the familiar voice of Senator White, who made his way through the throng and put his arm around the Admiral.

Jackson felt like things were just getting worse as the Senator shook the Admiral's hand and turned toward one of the image scanners, smiling widely. Admiral Jackson never liked attention and the thought of his live and three-dimensional image beaming to every news media outlet on Earth made his stomach turn.

"Let's let the man speak," the Senator continued.

Jackson was surprised to find that he'd already been maneuvered to the podium and was now facing the group directly.

"Thank you Senator," he responded clearing his throat and holding himself steady on the podium. "In a moment I'll be asking my good friend Senator White to launch the bottle officially christening this magnificent ship that you all see behind you. In the mean time, however, I'd just like to say a few words."

But before he even began his speech his wrist terminal flashed the signal.

"Priority Interrupt."

With only a quick smile of apology to the audience, he looked down at his terminal to see the message.

"Admiral we have new bogie. She's big and coming in fast," came Ensign Jeffries voice beaming up from the surface. "And Sir, this is not a drill," he concluded.

Jackson feared for a moment that his prayers had perhaps been answered. The nervousness disappeared from his face.

"Senator, I'm afraid I have to ask that we skip with formalities and get this ship into service. It looks like she has a job to do," he said turning to the Senator with a confident and commanding look in his eyes.

Now it was the Senator's face that became nervous. Jackson kept control.

"Just press the button Senator."

The Senator pushed the small button on the podium with his finger and a small and ancient glass bottle shot out from beneath the viewing deck and zoomed down to the super structure of the Bismarck. As an intra-stellar ship, Bismarck had no high velocity shield beam generators to smash the tiny bottle. Instead it simply crashed into the hardened forward hull of the vessel and shattered into pieces.

"Sorry to cut the ceremony short, best of luck to all of you," the Admiral said concluding the event and heading back to his shuttle.

A few moments later Jackson was standing on the command bridge of the Bismarck easing the massive warrior out of her construction dock.

"Take her out," he instructed his helmsman.

"Eye Sir," the helmsman responded.

"Strategic View," he ordered the ship's main Advisor system.

"Strategic View Active," a voice from the ceiling responded. The entire front wall of the bridge was one large high definition three-dimensional viewing screen. It quickly came to life and displayed an image of the entire solar system, giving the position of every ship in the fleet. Thirty-two Gunships and Forty-one Fleet ships scattered about the solar system covering the various angles of approach for an attack on Earth. The new visitor was clearly displayed on the screen, still outside the outer perimeter of the solar system but closing in on Saturn at about one sixth light speed. Using the control pad in his seat, and a series of verbal commands to the strategic Advisor, Jackson was able to divide his force into three attack groups that would intercept the invader at various points in her track.

Unfortunately more than half his fleet would not be able to intercept the Intruder ship before it reached Earth but that was the nature of naval warfare. Defending all possible approaches meant only a portion of the available resources could attack any single target. The alternative, pulling the fleet closer into Earth would have left the planet in extreme danger of direct damage during the battle. The intent was to destroy the enemy before it reached the home planet.

There were six ships available to launch a coordinated attack on the enemy vessel before it reached Saturn. The Gunships Missouri and Victory would engage the enemy first escorted by the Fleet Ships: Taos, New London, Alpha Centauri and Zion. The second attack group would be prepared for the enemy to sling shot off Saturn directly for Earth and would be lead by Bismarck. She would be backed up to two more Gunships; Constitution and Yamamoto. They would be light on escort, protected only by the Fleet Ships Hercules IV and Silver Sun Colony. A third group, slightly smaller in size and including the older Gunships Hood, Arizona and Graf Spe would be prepared for secondary slingshot off Jupiter. Only one of the second two groups would actually be able to meet the ship.

The remainder of the fleet would close in on Earth in case they were needed for secondary action in support of the orbital defense array.

"Lay in the course and get orders to the rest of the fleet," Jackson instructed his helmsman.

"Eye Sir, Full thrust, 3G for seventy-one hours," the helmsman responded.

"So much for breaking her in gently," the Admiral replied. "Prepare for full thrust."

On his command, the small twelve-man crew of the massive warship prepared for a long and difficult ride. They harnessed themselves into their force tolerance seats and felt the sting of the injection needles hit their arm. Each of them gave a slight wince as a concoction of foreign chemicals surged through their blood. Intrastellar combat was a matter of acceleration not velocity and these precious fluids would keep them all alive and healthy during the stress of extended rapid acceleration.

The ship itself also made her adjustments. Bismarck's bridge, a small circular room, was mounted within a spherical housing that sat just in the front dorsal area of the ship, just below the first dorsal gun turret. As Bismarck's acceleration slowly increased to maximum thrust, the bridge moved within it's spherical housing. Its normal position, inverted within the sphere, with its ceiling closest to the main accelerators, slowly tilted upward. During this process the rotation of the ship that normally provided artificial gravity came to halt, slowly being replaced by the force provided by the sheer acceleration of the ship. That acceleration increased until the force on the bodies of the crew reached three times their normal weight.

With the engines now burning at full thrust and his crew regaining their composure from their force tolerance injections and the transition to full force, Jackson began a series of recorded messages to his other commanders.

"Hiro, Bismarck here," he began his message to the commander of the Missouri. "You already know now that you and Victory have the unfortunate duty to lead our attack. This little devil is going to come at you fast and will have a full complement of attack orbs when you meet her, so make sure your fleet escort deploys early. You know what you have to do, blast her to pieces. Our prayers are with you, Bismarck out."

Despite his optimistic message, Jackson knew the reality of what his comrades were up against. The INC had never gone head to head with an Intruder Mother Ship and there was simply no intelligence on her firepower. In all the combat that had taken place thus far, humanity's forces had only managed to engage the attack orbs and only managed to destroy a total of four. The first had been killed in the assault on Reykjavik and Alpha Centauri had taken out three in her valiant stand against the enemy. The good news was that the Kelly frequency had proven a reliable weak point. Alpha Centauri had only a limited time to refit her defensive array and wouldn't have made a single kill without doing that. A kill on a Mother Ship was the Holy Grail for INC. If they could succeed in that mission, then humanity had a chance.

Over the next several hours, response reports came back from the fleet. The battle groups of Constitution and Yamamoto were the closest and first to respond. Captain Wallis of the Constitution was the first to give his report.

"Our group confirms the Rendezvous Admiral, if she goes for Earth straight off Saturn, she's going to get quite a welcome."

Jackson hoped that Wallis was right. He wanted to get a shot at her himself. If there was anything that could crack open this dark invader, Bismarck was the lady for the job. Jackson was proud to see that the whole fleet had responded immediately to his deployment and all of his captains were upbeat and ready to do their jobs. He had trained them well.

His thoughts then turned to Earth and the events that would be transpiring at home. He hadn't seen his wife, children or grandchildren in two years but he knew they would be working together to stay safe on the home front.   Earth would have received word of the Intruder ship a few minutes ago and right now the entire planet would be moving to yellow alert. Ten billion humans were now all making their way to their homes and preparing for technology shut down should that be necessary.

Over the last two hundred years, Earth had quickened the pace of her preparation for the possibility that she may one day have to get by without the technology she relied on for the last twenty-two hundred years. Massive changes had been made across the planet to prepare for this possibility and routine drills were conducted to test preparedness. For as much as a month at a time, the entire population would practice life without technology. The biggest changes had been in the way that food was grown and distributed and in the manner that that heat was provided. Large scale, highly automated, food management systems were replaced by localized alternatives. Mechanical windmills had cropped up across the planet and were the main source of power for irrigation and other activities such as wood crafts and clothing production. In colder climates, excavations into the ground and wood burning hearths would provide heat. Local trade between villages and towns replaced global trade and distribution. The democratic system once centralized, automated and involving the entire population at one level would now become distributed. Local councils would manage residential settlements or villages of approximately one hundred people. Those settlements would periodically send representatives to Market Towns, those in turn to District Capitals, finally to Regional Capitals and then once a year representatives of those cities would journey to single point on the globe and meet to make law that would rule the planet. These five levels of government each representing one hundred times the population of the preceding level would form the backbone of democracy should the Intruders succeed in overcoming the planet's defenses. Mankind had even had to rediscover the entertainment and education methods free from technology. Chalkboards, books and board games replaced interactive viewing screens. It had not been possible to test life without technology completely but it was believed that the entire population of the planet could be preserved in this carefully designed and distributed society. It was medieval technology designed and implemented with fifth millennium sophistication.

Jackson was pleased that his family had been able to create a power free environment in their own home and in the event of the shut down his extended family would all end up living under his roof. His wife had become quite proficient at cooking in their new stone oven and the young children seemed to enjoy reading books. Jackson's family lived in a fertile region of North America and the adults of his family would work with the rest of their village to maintain a large farm with livestock and cereal grains. It would be hard work but life would go on.

Despite his confidence that his family would endure, he hoped that Victory against the enemy would make that possibility unnecessary. It was not that the thought of his own death concerned him, or even the thought of his family struggling by without technology. It was more the thought of his loved ones living under the good graces of the cold will of the Intruders that he could not bear.

He, like many of his comrades in INC, felt that survival was not living. As Bismarck surged toward her destination, he and his crew shared their thoughts of events on Earth and their families back home.

Their focus turned back toward their mission when the first reports from Missouri came in. They were still at least a light-hour away from Missouri when she met the enemy. In order to ensure Bismarck received the most information possible, Missouri had left their transmission channel open during the engagement. Bismarck crew could see the viewing screen and the crew of the vessel and witness first hand the events that had occurred just an hour ago, farther out in the solar system.

Captain Hiro Kimato who commanded Missouri was an experienced naval commander. He had been training under Jackson for more than five years and the two had become good friends. Jackson was confident Kimato and his crew would make the INC proud. It was going to be first engagement with the Intruders within the solar system and its outcome was critical.

Weighing in at thirty-two million tons, Missouri was smaller than Bismarck. She carried twelve large beam generators mounted in pairs on mobile turrets. She could target an enemy at over eight million miles and was perhaps the most tested Gunship in the fleet. Victory who had joined her battle group was a smaller ship weighing twenty-four million tons. She was one of the oldest Gunships in the fleet. Each of their escorting Fleet Ships weighed between five and ten million tons each. They had already launched their combat fleet and now over 2,000 combat interceptors protected the two big warriors, each weighing about one hundred tons.

The entire task force was now streaming laterally into the path of the oncoming Intruder Mother Ship at nearly three thousand miles per second. Their enemy, weighing the same five million tons, the ship that had first attacked humankind had, was inbound into the solar system and decelerating. With her estimated velocity at rendezvous of fifteen thousand miles per second, the combat timeframe as she passed the task force would be short. The whole battle would probably last less than ten minutes.

The crew of Bismarck cheered as they saw Missouri was the first to fire. She had turned her nose to her foe as she moved across her path, minimizing herself as a target and giving all twelve of her guns a crack at the enemy. The shots missed as Missouri's gravity sensors struggled to get a fix. She fired again as the enemy got closer. The second time she struck a glancing blow and the Intruder ship lit up as the Kelly frequency shot through her hull and burst out from her surface in every direction. The target went black again as the beam slipped off the mark. The enemy was making evasive maneuvers. They hadn't made their kill yet and could not even assess if the hit had caused any damage but it was the first time we got the first hit and that felt good.

The telltale bursts appeared on the sensors as the enemy ship began to launch her attack orbs. INC still had no way to know how many attackers their enemy carried or if the Mother Ship itself had any weapons, so the nervousness began to grow as the enemy began to deploy its weapons against them. They counted the launch of only thirty attackers before the bursts came to a halt. Things still looked good for the task force.

Victory fired her first salvo and scored a hit on the first try. Again the black ellipse turned to a bright white, as the energy poured out of her, in every direction. The beam held on to her target for longer and the entire crew of the Bismarck thought for sure she would burst into a million pieces, any second. Finally their enemy once again eluded the stream of fire and went dark. Surely one more good hit would do it.

Missouri took her turn as the distance continued to close, they were less than a million miles apart now and the gravitational readings were making their prey easier to track. This time the bright white turned to a brilliant purple and it seemed for sure they had her.

The observers jolted back into their seat when the Mother Ship opened fire in response. The massive bright white beam cut through Victory like a hot knife through butter. All of the starboard turrets and her entire starboard lateral accelerator shaft were severed from the hull and drifted off into space.

With maneuvering limited, she was unable to train her guns on her quarry and was effectively taken out of the fight.

"Crew alive and ship operational but rudder control limited," Captain Pierre Mont Blanc reported from the bridge of the Victory. "Good luck Missouri".

Their foe did not close in for the kill but rather continued on her track, closing in on Missouri. Missouri fired again and scored another hit, again the target glowed bright purple. They were now less than five hundred thousand miles apart and the Mother Ship now fired on the larger of her two attackers.

The entire ship shuddered as the incredible heat of the enemy's beam cut into Missouri's hull, then a sharp jolt rocked the bridge and gravitational rotation was suddenly lost. The instrumentation went wild and for a moment the viewing screen went dim. When functionality was restored, the damage report was horrifying. The beam had struck the forward port side turret. The power of the ray had caused the turret's upper beam generator to completely overload and explode. The blast had decapitated the ship. The forward section of the main accelerator shafts with the bridge still attached was now drifting freely away from the rest of the ship. The remaining portion of the ship, the vast majority of its original form, including most of the main accelerator shafts, the fuel tanks, reactors, lateral accelerators and remaining turrets were drifting away in the other direction like a great fighting knight beheaded in a joust that had not gone his way.

The crew of Bismarck reeled in shock. In two shots the Intruder ship had disabled both of the Gunships in the task force. The Fleet Ships were now sitting ducks to the Mother Ship's powerful ray.

It was now the turn of the Intruder's attack orbs to do their part. In an eerie display of fireworks they began to cut through the sea of combat interceptors that surrounded the two wounded hulks of Victory and Missouri. The interceptors fought back and the occasional orb would burst in a cascade of brilliant purple but it was the INC interceptors that suffered the most losses.

Unfortunately the Mother Ship showed no mercy either despite her assured victory at this point in the battle. New London and Taos were torn to pieces by blasts from the Mother

Ship as she passed right through the task force. The crippled Victory fired a response but it went way high of its mark.

On the free floating bridge of Missouri, Commander Kimato tried to establish a com link to the other section of his ship to see if he could bring the guns around but it quickly became clear he would not be able to respond in time.

As the Mother Ship passed out of range, only Alpha Centauri remained unscathed. Victory and Missouri were crippled and would be out of commission for months. Zion was also crippled and Taos and New London were gone. They had also lost several hundred combat interceptors and had not even slowed down their foe. They could claim perhaps ten to fifteen attack orbs and possibly some damage to the Mother Ship.

"It's up to you now Bismarck. Good luck my friend," Kimato signaled to Jackson as he ended his communications.

The shock of what they had witnessed took a little while to sink into most of the crewmembers of Bismarck but Jackson went right to work. He began the process of analyzing the footage they had just watched. Before long the rest of his team joined the process.

"Missouri got three shots before they were able to return fire Sir. It looks like we have them on Range," Weapons Officer Rankin chimed in.

"Our range, sensor accuracy and firepower are all superior to Missouri's. We should be able to give her a good smack before she can touch us," Helmsman Smith added.

"The Fleet Ships were sitting ducks Sir. Is there a way they can be protected?" Medical Officer Jacobson joined the chorus.

A moment of silence crept over the bridge as Jackson sat and thought over the situation. Then finally, he gave direction to his team.

"Give orders to the rest of the task force. I want Constitution and Yamamoto in close with us. We'll get strength in numbers and force the enemy to spread her fire. Have them link into our targeting systems also. We should be able to extend their range to close to ours. Hercules and Silver Sun should deploy their interceptors ahead of the Gunships and then fall back behind us. The only hope we have to protect them is if we can take that Mother Ship before she gets to them. Now, let's hope they come to us and not Arizona. We've got the firepower.

Speaking of Arizona, get a signal out to her and make sure she's prepared for a similar deployment."

"Eye Sir," the crew responded and turned to their consoles to execute their orders.

For the remaining hours before their adversary reached Saturn they analyzed the specifics of the combat, looking for any further clues that might be helpful but before long the moment of truth arrived.

The gravitation sensors onboard Bismarck and additional sensors scattered out through the solar system tracked the Mother Ship as she closed in on Saturn. The entire crew of Bismarck froze in silent anticipation as she rounded the planet. The slightest adjustment in her course would determine whether Bismarck or Arizona would be the next to meet this incoming angel of destruction. Visual image sensors, positioned on the now long deserted Saturn colonies, watched as the dark shadow moved into view, close to the giant planet's surface. The entire solar system outside of Earth itself was now a military zone and the solar colonies now stood as silent floating ghost towns sometimes used as listening posts and layover stations.

The images beaming onto the deck of the Bismarck were eerie. It was as if a strange elliptical hole had formed in the side of the planet and was moving rapidly across its surface. As she cut under the planet's rings and reached the edge of the large disk of the planet's main body, the trajectory data came in.

"She's headed straight for Earth, Sir," Helmsman Smith indicated.

"She's got to get through us first," Jackson responded. "Have Arizona break her course and join the Earth task force. Weapons, give me a complete system status."

"All generators fully charged and operating at optimum state," Rankin replied.

"Good. How are our friends doing?" Jackson continued.

"Constitution has already fallen into position, Yamamoto is coming up along side us now Sir," Smith informed his commander.

"Bring us head on and cut forward thrust. Go to battle stations," Jackson ordered.

On his command, the Bismarck's massive main accelerator shafts fell silent and their acceleration, almost constant for the last three days came to a halt. The bridge fell into zero gravity. It was Jackson's intention to keep Bismarck as steady as possible during combat. He did not want either forward acceleration or rotational gravity to have an effect on the accuracy of his shots. Only the crew's harnesses kept them secured to their seats.

"Wait till we get a solid fix," Jackson instructed his weapons station.

"I've got her Sir," Rankin responded.

Jackson looked coldly into the young officer's face, carefully measuring the confidence in his eyes. Then he smiled and gave the order.

"Fire at will," Jackson instructed, turning back toward the viewing screen.

On that instruction all eighteen of Bismarck's guns opened fire scoring a direct hit on their opponent. What was once a black gap in the star field on their viewing screen became a bright purple glowing ellipse, headed straight for them. Constitution and Yamamoto open fire as well, following their bigger sister's lead. Their guns also scored a hit on the target.

Jackson's heart froze again, as he waited for their target to just crack wide open but it held together as the beam generators reached full discharge and had to disengage. The image on the screen faded and went black again.

Jackson uttered new instructions to the whole task force.

"Recharge fully and fire again simultaneously," he instructed.

Rankin coordinated with the other ships and they let loose another blast on the enemy. Again she lit up in response. The viewing screen became so bright the crew turned their heads from the blinding image but again she withstood the blast.

They recharged their guns and prepared for the third shot but theirs would not be the next volley.

The Mother Ship finally responded, directing her white beam at Bismarck's dorsal guns. Jackson and his crew felt lucky to be alive, as the beam surged just above the bridge and devastated the middle turret and everything above it. The dorsal accelerator shaft was half severed and twisted loose, clanging against the port side of the ship, as it hung by a few remaining structural beams. Frustration raced through Jackson's mind as his ship jolted sharply downward in response to the impact. As he surveyed the room to check over his crew, thoughts flashed of how easily the five million ton Intruder ship tore through an opponent ten times her size and how he would ever defeat this foe.

"Damage report," he yelled, over the sound of the creaking structure of the ship and the flashing of the power systems trying to stabilize.

"We've lost our dorsal accelerator and four of our guns," Rankin responded.

"Can we get a bead on her," Jackson continued, desperate to get one more crack at the black menace.

"Yes sir she's still in our field of fire and our guns held their charge."

"Fire!" Jackson yelled.

Bismarck's guns unloaded as Yamamoto took a direct hit right down her main central accelerator shaft. The blast shattered the entire ship to pieces. Constitution was also damaged but she was still in the fight and her volley joined Bismarck's at near point blank range.

Finally the familiar purple glare of their enemy under fire began to change. The point blank impact from twenty six of INC's biggest guns was taking its toll. Long black cracks in the elliptical form of their adversary began to form. Then suddenly, the entire Intruder Mother Ship shattered into millions of pieces.

Bismarck had done her job. The dragon had fallen.

The burst of celebration on the deck Bismarck was cut short by the sudden peril their foes demise had left them in.

"Blast wave incoming," Rankin's warning rang through the bridge.

This was one storm that Jackson was happy to endure. The ship shuddered as hundreds of tiny pieces of the shattered ship clashed against the sides of Bismarck's hull. Fortunately no further significant damage was done.

The crew watched with joy as the escorting combat interceptors cleaned up the few Intruder attackers that had escaped their host's death. Like little wasps whose nest had

been destroyed, the black orbs lashed out wildly, taking down
many of the combat interceptors that came to engage them but
one by one they each met their doom.

Jackson felt that the weight of the world, perhaps the weight
of the galaxy, had been lifted from his shoulders.

Interstellar Naval Command had paid heavily for their
victory but nonetheless victory had come. Two Fleet Ships
and one gunship were lost. An additional fleet ship and four
more Gunships, including Bismarck, were badly damaged.
The fleet was weakened but the enemy was vanquished. More
importantly, however, a formula for victory had been defined.
The massive beam generators deployed on the new Bismarck
class ship had done the trick.

Jackson smiled deeply in the knowledge that Bismarck was
the first of eight in her class and more could be commissioned
soon if needed. He didn't know how long it would be before
they would again have to battle the Intruders but now he knew
that INC was up to the task.

He was overjoyed to give the final order of the day to his
crew.

"Make Course for Earth, standard thrust," he instructed.

On his command, Bismarck opened up her main accelerators
in reverse thrust. At standard thrust it would be four days
before the great ship would shake off her current outbound
velocity so that she could begin the journey home. Then a week
of inbound acceleration followed by a week of deceleration and
she would finally pull into Earth orbit for shore leave and
repairs. Constitution and their escorting Fleet Ships soon fell in
behind. Yamamoto was lost but her crew would be rescued.

Jackson couldn't believe that in less than three weeks he'd
be holding his grandchildren. He thought of them often as
the time drifted by. The bridge was a quiet place for the next
couple of days. The crew spent most of the time resting in
their quarters immediately below the bridge, exhausted from
the prolonged exposure to excessive acceleration and the
exhilaration of combat. It was just Jackson and Rankin on
duty on the bridge on the third day of their journey.

"You must go there," Jackson was advising his comrade.
"You can't help but be amazed by the hardships those old sailors
endured. They were no more than a few thousand miles from

their homes but their journeys lasted months and they had no contact whatsoever with the outside world. Navigating by the stars and sailing by the wind. True adventurers, they were."

Rankin was smiling and nodding as his commander ranted on about his fondness for the history of Earth's sailing ships and his visits to the old naval museums. He almost didn't hear the beep from his console over Jackson's flowing narration but the blinking indicator caught his eye.

"If that's another politician calling to congratulate us, tell them to leave a message," Jackson joked.

Jackson's tone changed, when he saw Rankin's face turn pale.

"It's another one Sir," Rankin indicated.

"What's her position?" Jackson queried, fastening himself into his command chair.

Rankin activated their strategic view and displayed the position of the enemy ship. She was coming in from the other side of the solar system and would make Earth long before Bismarck could, even at full thrust. Jackson quickly went to work.

He once again plotted out the position of the fleet and this time called upon many of the ships that had been furthest away from the fray the first time around. A task force of four Gunships escorted by three Fleet Ships would be able to meet the new attacker just inside Saturn's orbit. Jackson couldn't help but realize that if two Mother Ships had arrived in the solar system within less than a week, then this was a coordinated attack planned and launched from systems far away decades or perhaps more than a century ago. It had been hoped that like the other systems attacked, Earth would be visited by only one Mother Ship at a time. That assumption was now proving false. There was no way to tell how many enemy ships were on their way to Earth.

It was two days of agonizing wait, watching his task force move closer to the incoming target, Bismarck unable to assist. His heart sank even further when a third ship was detected before combat with the second had even began. Jackson turned to his communications officer and instructed him to prepare a message to the fleet.

Jackson spoke with a solemn but resolute voice to the forces under his command.

"To all my brave comrades of Interstellar Naval Command, my thoughts and prayers are with you as you face the difficult days that lie ahead. You have all received your orders and you know your mission. What I want to impart to you now are some of my thoughts as we, the core, face this great test. I want you to know that though our enemy is strong, we have shown they can be destroyed. Though their approaching strength may seem daunting, we know they are finite, set in motion against us many years ago. Victory can be ours. Most of all, I want all of you to know that it has been my greatest honor and privilege to serve with you and no matter what history writes of Interstellar Naval Command I know that it will tell that this was our finest hour. God bless and God's speed."

The battle for Earth would rage on for three more months. INC would fight valiantly but eventually the superior firepower and resilience of the Intruder ships would get the better of them. After some makeshift repairs, the great ship Bismarck would meet her death in a fiery plunge into the surface of Mars, her accelerators destroyed while making her third and final kill. In all, seventeen Intruder ships would enter Earth's system. Six of them would survive to claim the prize. As the dark victors descended into Earth's orbit and tore apart the remnants of the defensive array, the lights below began to go out. It was as if the world stood still. The people of Earth plunged into a world of darkness, under the shadow of the Intruder's dark orbs.

Chapter 17

First Adventure

4194
Neo Prime
76 Light-years from Earth

Lucas blinked his eyes and looked around. The blurry image of the lab slowly came into focus. Above him, a familiar face emerged, smiling warmly. At first he thought it must be his father, still standing beside him, providing comfort during the procedure, but as the scene cleared he was surprised to find that it was Uncle Frank's soft eyes looking down at him.

"How are you feeling Luc?" Frank asked.

"I feel great Uncle Frank, where's mom and dad?" The young boy responded.

"They had to leave, but they've left you some messages, maybe we'll look at them later?" The older man responded.

Then it struck the boy that Frank was now in the lab with him, not looking at him from the other side of the screen. Was it over already? That was easy, he thought.

"What's this?" Frank asked, in a comforting tone, pointing to the youngster's soft toy dinosaur.

"That's Hank," Lucas replied, proudly holding up a little brown stuffed animal that vaguely resembled a prehistoric Saurapod, but with big friendly eyes and a wide happy smile.

"He's wonderful," Frank continued, "Do you like dinosaurs?"

"You bet, they're the best," Lucas exclaimed, "I know all their names."

"Do you really?" Frank responded, beaming warmly. "Would you like to see some?"

"Yes, I'd love to you," Lucas said, sitting up on the table and looking at the lab's large screen which had a dull grey color as it sat silent and inactive.

Frank smiled and put his hand on the boy's shoulder. "Oh no, not there," he explained. "We can do much better than that. You remember, I promised you real adventures right?"

"Yes, are we going to take one already?" the boy replied, his eyes growing wider every moment. "I thought there'd be more doctor stuff first, you know?"

"Oh no, we're done with all of that, no more needles and lights, I promise." Frank replied, lifting him off the table and setting him down on the floor, facing the door to the lab, "Shall we go then?"

Frank took Lucas' hand and walked toward the door. It opened, displaying a breathtaking vista, where once a simple hallway had been. The youngster gasped in amazement.

"Welcome to the late Jurassic," Frank exclaimed, proudly.

The view before them was astounding. The doorway had brought them through to a cave opening in the side of a large mountain ridge. To their left, volcanoes spewed molten lava down ravines out onto a large flat plain. Immediately in front of them, in the distance, the plain met a dense green jungle, where a large river ran into a massive sea that stretched out to their right. Steam rose up from the swampy estuary, obscuring the view of the far side of the massive valley.

Far more amazing than the terrain, however, was the wildlife. In front of them, immediately before the beginning of the dense jungle, a herd of Camptosauruses grazed on the water plants that thrived at the edge of the swamp. Further up the plain, closer to them, a small group of Stegosauruses lumbered slowly along, heading toward the coast. Then closer yet, small long necked creatures poked around the rocky slopes, looking for worms and insects. Above them, winged Teradons ruled the skies, swooping down from the mountains into the sea, bringing up large scaly fish and carrying them back to their perches in the rocky cliffs of the ridgeline.

Lucas just stared in shock.

As a child of the fortieth century, born to the most advanced colony in human existence, Lucas had experience many wonderful things. He had become accustomed to viewing entertainment and educational materials in three-dimensional reality on advanced viewing screens. He was used to systems that could even simulate the smell of an environment and produce totally realistic sounds, but nothing had ever compared to this. He was here. He was standing on mountainside looking over Earth, as it had existed over one hundred and fifty million years ago. The hot steamy air made him perspire almost immediately, but he didn't care. This was just unbelievable. His young mind couldn't even begin to comprehend the true nature of the sights and sounds around him. To Lucas, he had simply stepped back in time.

The pure excitement of the moment and the unbounded curiosity of an eight-year old overcame any fear he might have felt. He turned to his new guardian with a gleam in his eyes.

"Can we get closer?" he asked, wondering if the whole thing would break if he even moved.

"Oh, of course," Frank replied, "but let's go there in style."

With that the man looked up into the sky and smiled, as a large Pterodactyl came swooping down toward them.

For the first time, Lucas was suddenly afraid and his whole body stiffened. Frank rested his hand on the boy's shoulder and eased his fears.

"Don't worry Luc, nothing can hurt you here."

The boy looked over and saw the pure confidence in his protector's eyes, then looked back at the massive beast that had settled less than ten feet from them. It dwarfed any living creature he had ever seen take to the air. Its wings were still stretched as it focused in on the two humans. What once had been a vast panorama of ocean was now thirty feet of skin stretched almost transparently over long thin bones that looked like they might snap at any moment. The creature slowly folded in the massive flight surfaces and looked at the two humans intently. Then, as if bored by the momentary delay, it leisurely began grooming the back of its wings with its long pointed mouth.

Luc looked back at Frank again, still unsure of what to do next. Finally the warmth of the man's face won him over and he grasped his hand tightly. It was as if something inside him knew that this was his uncle's world and he had to trust him.

As an eight year old he knew that there was something wrong with climbing on the back of a massive flying lizard that had been extinct for over one hundred million years and lived on a planet fifty light-years from his home, but there was a strange magic at work in this place and it was clear to Lucas that Frank controlled that magic.

The great beast seemed totally unconcerned as the two approached and it slowly rotated its body to save them the trouble of walking around. Lucas didn't know what to expect as he climbed up the animal's back and was surprised when it didn't so much as flinch. Frank climbed up behind him and placed hands firmly around the boy's waste. Then the ride began.

It felt at first that they would just plunge to their death as their mount took a few steps forward and just slumped off the edge of the ledge to their right, but then its massive wings opened and they swooped out over the plain below. Lucas had ridden simulations of Earth's old roller coasters on Foundation Colony and he guessed this is what the real thing might have felt like. At first they dove down fast and hard, then as the creature picked up speed and found the thermal currents rushing up the cliffs, their flight leveled off and then they began to climb. Before long they found themselves in a steady upward spiral, riding strong warm air currents up high above the cliff tops. The view from up here was even more panoramic than from the ridgeline below.

Lucas could now see much more detail in the ocean. Great shapes moved just below the surface, some massive and fishlike in shape, others had long necks and tails that stretched out from rounder bodies with large flippers on each side. Large schools of smaller fish shimmered in the sunlight and provided ample food for the bigger creatures. Then Lucas realized that it wasn't only the marine predators below that had spotted the feast. Their Pterodactyl mount was obviously hungry as well.

"Hold on tight," Frank yelled over the rush of wind as they dove rapidly toward the ocean below.

Lucas thought for sure that they were just going to plunge into the sea and disappear below the waves, but just as he felt the spray of the surf on his face their enormous flying steed spread it's wings wide and pulled up. Only the creature's giant pointed head broke the surface of the water and came up with a fish the likes of which Lucas had never seen. It was almost three feet in length with a rounded face that looked like it was made of solid bone. It thrashed about for a while in its captor's mouth as they swooped out to sea and began to gain altitude once again. Once more they circled up into the sky as the Pterodactyl gained full control of its meal and swallowed it whole in flight.

Its hunger satisfied, the animal seemed more willing now to follow their bidding, and Frank leaned around the boy's shoulder and spoke to him.

"Well, where shall we go now?" Frank yelled over the rush of the wind.

Lucas' heart was still pounding from their close encounter with the ocean and it took him a while to respond, but then the vista below came into view and he picked his target. They were now flying along the coastline, directly in front of a large river mouth surrounded on both sides by the thick swampy jungle. From their airborne vantage point they could see directly up river and it was there that the young boy noticed the most exciting sight yet. Close to the left bank of the river, their long necks pulling branches down from the fern like trees, a pair of large Apatosauruses were feeding leisurely.

"Down there, in the river," he yelled, pointing at the massive creatures and smiling.

"Is that a Brontosaurus?" Frank asked, quizzing his companion.

"The proper name is a Apatosaurus," the young boy bragged.

"Ok then, here we go," Frank replied as their Pterodactyl again began to dive.

This time, however, instead of dropping straight for the ocean surface, the creature swooped inland and came to rest on a small bluff that jutted out into the river, just upstream from the long necked saurapods. Frank and Lucas dismounted and looked around. Lucas felt funny standing on firm ground, as if he'd been living on a ship for a week and the solid ground felt wrong, lacking in some natural rhythm that the motion of the waves, or the air might provide. He grasped Frank's arm to steady himself.

Frank kept the adventure moving.

"There, down stream a way, see them?" he asked.

"Yes, yes I do," Luc replied, finally getting his footing, and looking out at the lumbering animals as they waded slowly along and fed.

They climbed down from the bluff that sat about twenty feet above the rest of the riverbank and felt a rush of wind as their winged friend swooped over their heads down river and back to the skies.

The young boy became nervous as they hiked along the riverbank, moving closer to the pair of ancient monsters. Frank again looked down at his companion and smiled.

"It's completely safe," he reassured the child.

But Luc had noticed something new that had taken his mind completely off his fear.

"Uncle Frank, look!" he interrupted the older man.

About thirty feet into the jungle, tucked away in the darkness provided by the thick green canopy that hung over head, Frank could make out the shape of a large nest like structure, it was probably fifteen feet in diameter and was formed by large stones and branches constructed into a crude circle. Through the gaps in the branches the two human visitors could barely make out movement.

"Shall we get a little closer?" Frank questioned, obviously enjoying his companion's excitement.

"Yes, yes," the boy responded, "what do you think they are Uncle Frank?"

The answer came quickly.

The two climbed onto a tree stump that sat just outside the perimeter of the nest, clearly broken off when the primitive circle was built. From there they were able to see directly into the interior of the nest. The creatures inside didn't even notice them.

"Frank look!" Lucas proclaimed, standing as tall as he could and supporting himself on Frank's shoulders.

"Yes, yes, what do you think they are?" Frank enquired, testing the boy.

"Baby Apatosauruses!" Luc replied, glee shining in his eyes.

They sat; quietly watching the small creatures play in the nest. There were six of them in all, averaging perhaps three feet in length. They were quite mobile but not quite agile enough to climb out of the nest. Instead they rolled over each other and fought over the scraps of green vegetation that were scattered around the soft interior of the circle. For several minutes the two observers just watched, neither of them saying a word.

The serenity was broken suddenly by the powerful sound of the river sloshing around behind them. They looked over to see one of the massive adults moving closer to the nest. They froze as the long neck of the parent extended directly over them and deposited a large bundle of fresh vegetation right into the nest. The youngster's responded with a flurry of motion as they battled over the choicest pieces.

Lucas looked up at Frank and gasped, then turned back to watch the scene some more.

"Do you want to get in there?" Frank asked, surprising the child yet again.

"Can I?" Luc responded.

"Sure, they won't hurt you." Frank replied, helping the boy down from the stump.

A pathway into the nest wasn't too hard to find, with a little help from Frank, Lucas was able to stand on one of the larger boulders on the perimeter and straddle the logs and branches that formed the top part of the outer rim. Stumbling slightly as he dismounted Luc soon found himself sitting in the middle of the nest, surrounded by baby dinosaurs. He tried to stand, but three of the babies jumped on him and began licking his face, pinning him to the soft dirt floor. Frank made himself comfortable watching Luc play, sitting down on a well worn spot on the stump.

Lucas was surprised by the feel of the young animals. First, instead of being cold and scaly like the snakes and lizards he had petted in Foundation Colony, these creatures were warm and almost soft. Though not furry like a puppy dog or a cat, their hide had a soft leathery feel to it that was quite pleasant to the touch. Lucas sat and played with the little sauropods for at least half an hour, while Frank just sat and watched him. Periodically an adult Apatosaurus would return and leave more food in the nest and the babies would leave Lucas alone for a moment, but after a short while they'd be back again, licking him and tugging at his clothes. Lucas seemed to never want the adventure to end. He felt totally at ease in this world, knowing that Frank would never let anything bad happen.

His confidence was suddenly shaken when he looked up from the nest and saw two eyes looking in at him from the jungle.

"Frank, Frank!" He whispered over his shoulder, not wanting to take his eyes off the new intruder.

"I see it Luc. It's okay. Stay calm," Frank cautioned, as if they might actually be in some real danger. "Climb out of the nest and come to me." He continued, stepping down off the stump.

Lucas now felt really afraid and he clamored clumsily out of the nest and into Frank's arms. Frank picked up the child and held him tightly.

"Hold still now." He said quieting the boy's nerves, but the child went totally stiff, as the jungle suddenly seemed to come alive.

The Allosaurus charged in on the nest with lightening speed and it looked for sure that one or two of the babies were done for, but as suddenly as the attack had began it was halted. From above the massive tail of one of the large Apatosauruses came swinging through the jungle, knocking down saplings on its way to its target. The undergrowth did little to take force out of the swing, however, and the two legged predator was knocked twenty feet away from the nest onto its back. It writhed in the bushes trying to get its footing and address its adversary. It was barely on its feet, however, when another swing came down from above and knocked it back down.

Itself a youngster, the Allosaurus was perhaps twenty feet in length. No match at all for the eighty foot long adult Apatosaurus, it began to retreat into the jungle. Lucas realized the battle was just beginning, however, when a much larger predator emerged from the trees. At least thirty feet in length the adult Allosaurus posed a real threat to the Apatosaurus. If it got inside the larger creature's striking perimeter to the vulnerable flanks its dagger like teeth would tear the plant eater's flesh to shreds. The two monsters stood their ground facing each other down. The Apatosaurus let out an ear-piercing squeal and the Allosaurus responded with an earth shattering roar. Its younger companion now feeling bolder came to its side and added to the chorus.

Lucas felt his heart would explode as the lives of his new little friends were held in the balance between the two combatants. A sigh of relief came over him when the balance of power shifted and the second, larger, adult Apatosaurus arrived. The predators still appeared determined though. It was as if their hunger burned like a fire in their eyes. Their need for food overrode any fear they had of the massive prey. Again the world seemed to freeze as the predator charged. This time the larger adult, heading straight for the smaller adult Apatosaurus. The creature writhed trying to get its tail into position and fend off the attack but it was too late, The Allosaurus was inside and bit into its left shoulder. Lucas knew if the attack lasted too much longer, the proud parent was doomed. Salvation came from the larger Apatosaurus, lifting its tail completely over the top of its companion it cracked down the attacker like a giant whip. The first hit didn't shake the predator off, but the defensive barrage continued. The smaller Apatosaurus knew how to help and slumped to its knees to give its partner a better crack. Then it came; a solid blow directly to the top of the head of the sharp-toothed assailant, breaking his grip. He stumbled slightly back. The distance was enough to give its victim a chance to retaliate and the tail of the smaller Apatosaurus lashed up and struck the roaring creature broad side, knocking it to the ground. The smaller parent used the time to its advantage and bounded out of the fight. This left the struggling Allosaurus completely exposed to the larger saurapod, which didn't delay in taking advantage of the moment. It turned completely reverse to its target and smacked it repeatedly with all thirty feet of its massive tail, knocking the creature senseless. The Allosaurus barely had the strength to stumble away back into the jungle with not so much as a morsel for its struggles. The smaller Allosaurus then squealed away after its companion. The battle was over. Luc's new little friends were safe.

He jumped back into the nest and hugged the little sauropods who had all been frozen in the soft dirt during the entire fight. Lucas could never have known that the outcome of events was all predetermined, that though Frank may let Lucas know fear, he would never again experience real danger. Though nature's outcome might have been different, in this realm, a simulated world controlled completely Frank Ryland, the true nature of which Lucas would not know for some time to come, a happy ending was a guaranteed gift for his young companion. He would learn the meaning of disappointment but not this early. For now, the focus was showing him the wonder of his new world.

Lucas lost himself in the joy of that moment. He wrestled around with his little friends for almost another whole hour, as Frank watched quietly, smiling. Eventually, with very little fuss, the excitement of the adventure got the better of the young boy. He laid down in the soft dirt of the nest, using one of his new friends as a pillow and as the other young dinosaurs snuggled up to him, he slowly closed his eyes, went to sleep and began to dream of endless adventures in Earth's distant past.

After a little while, the boy opened his eyes again, stirring slightly to get comfortable. As he shifted around he realized he was now in his bed in his own room. He couldn't recall whether he had journeyed back there with Frank, or if somehow Frank's strange magic had brought him home, but he was happy to be in the calm comfort of familiar surroundings. Everything was exactly as he remembered it, except now on his table next to his picture of his parents sat a picture of Uncle Frank. The same warm face was sitting by him smiling down on him as he snuggled up in his bed.

"Did you like our little adventure?" Frank asked as the boy squeezed his toy dinosaur and buried his head in his pillow.

"Oh Yes, Uncle Frank, can we take some more?" The boy replied closing his eyes again.

"More than you can imagine." Frank replied. "Have you ever been for a ride on a Wooly Mammoth?"

"That sounds fun," the boy replied, squeezing Hank tighter and dozing back off the sleep.

Lucas would indeed know many more adventures. More than any human child had ever known. His adventures would not be restricted by the physical limitations of the human body or the physical world in which that body existed. Lucas' adventures would only be limited by his own imagination. The realm that Frank Ryland had created for Luc could produce any world and time he desired, and this wondrous realm was Luc's playground.

More than adventures though, Lucas would learn lessons. He would indeed ride a Wooly Mammoth and he would fly in the sky with the Eagles. He would hunt Bison on the plains of ancient Europe and help in the construction of the Pyramids. He would ride the plains of Asia with Ghengis Khan and cross the Delaware with George Washington. He would learn more about the universe, Mankind and its history than any human had ever known and, unlike most humans, he would not forget the lessons he learned, his mind would not fade with time. Instead it would grow stronger and wiser with every lesson.

And time would pass very quickly for Lucas. In just days he would live a lifetime of experiences and eventually he would come to know the reality of who he was and the world that he lived in. He would learn all of Earth's history, of Foundation Voyager and the Biotech Laws. He would learn how Frank had died over six hundred years earlier, and the nature of his new realm. He would visit Frank's room in the lab on Foundation Colony and learn of the day he himself had crossed over. He would come to understand the incredible computing power of Frank's realm and how it made possible the recreation of a myriad of worlds and times that he had experienced.

Ultimately, however, having experienced its wonder in such a personal way, he would learn to love humanity, even though in some ways he was no longer part of it. It was that lesson most of all that would prepare him for the great responsibility his future would hold. A responsibility that Frank knew Lucas alone was uniquely qualified to take on.

Chapter 18

The Last Outpost

4321
The Outer Banks
17 Light-Years from Earth

Commander Nathan Jackson stared out of the window, completely unaffected by the astounding view before him. His thoughts were elsewhere. As was often the case for Jackson, his thoughts were far away, on Earth. It might have seemed strange for someone who had spent his entire life living in an asteroid belt that orbited a star seventeen light-years from Earth to be so consumed with the long since conquered origin of human society, but Jackson always felt his destiny awaited him far away, on that warm blue planet.

For any other observer, the view would have been hard to overlook. For there was no question that The Outer Banks was the most beautiful location in the galaxy that Mankind had yet found to colonize. Most human colonies were typically built as free orbiting colony stars, manmade structures that typically resembled great floating drums and used rotation to create the artificial gravity for human life. Others were built on the surface of available Earth sized moons and planets and relied on good old-fashioned real gravity. The Outer Banks fit neither of these categories. It was unique in that it was one of the few colonies actually built into an asteroid belt.

Normally, the very structure of an asteroid made it unsuitable for the construction of a colony. Their low mass meant they were held together loosely and lacked the structural integrity required for construction of a space colony. Their habit of colliding with each other also served as a problem to potential colony builders and usually was the driving force behind placing colony stars some distance away from the asteroid belts that their mining operations relied upon. As a result the belts were more often used as a source of easily accessible raw materials than as a building platform themselves. The Outer Banks were different. Formed by remnants of the core of a gas giant planet, after its impact by a huge comet, several hundred million years ago, the asteroid belt that housed it consisted almost entirely of crystallized carbon, called diamond, when found naturally on Earth. Unlike the typically white or clear appearance of its normal form however, the asteroids of The Outer Banks shined with the all the colors of the rainbow. Many of them were perfectly clear, made of almost pure carbon crystal, others had hues of red, green, blue, purple and turquoise created by the inclusion of various trace elements into the crystalline structure. The site of all that free-floating crystal gleaming in the sunlight of its host star was stunning.

It was here, amongst this massive celestial treasure chest that, for the last six hundred years, the citizens of The Outer Banks had made their home. Arriving in one of the earliest colonization missions launched from Earth with less than a thousand souls, they first took on the ambitious project of stabilizing the asteroid belt itself, giving the inhabited asteroids rotation of their own and protection against collision with their cousins. The whole belt was now tamed. It was a living example of the most complex yet peaceful work of orbital mechanics that Mankind had ever achieved. With their rock solid foundation in place, The Outer Banks had since grown to be the largest still surviving human population outside Earth with over six million inhabitants.

It was often pondered why such a beautiful colony had received such a non-descriptive name and the common theory was to keep their trove of gems to themselves. The boring reality that the first captain of the generation ship that gave birth to the colony was originally from its namesake islands off the eastern coast of North America, just didn't seem to have the sticking power.

More recently The Outer Banks had become home to a new set of visitors, Interstellar Naval Command. Arriving in the very last interstellar mission to leave Earth before the fall of the home fleet, INC now claimed The Outer Banks as their last outpost and lived amongst the native colonists.

The Intrepid, the very last interstellar warship to leave Earth had journeyed, not on assault mission against the Intruders as most of its predecessors had, but on an escape mission from Earth. It brought with it over a hundred of the brightest minds that INC could spare, all safe in Cryo-sleep and the very latest in weapons technology. Its mission: to build a last castle beyond Earth where INC might finally find victory against their enemy. To the colonists of The Outer Banks it was a welcome arrival, boosting their chances of survival by giving them the tools and know-how to strengthen their defenses and hopefully hold out against the Intruders.

With its arrival, however, The Intrepid had sparked off a political debate that still shook the colony today, almost a century later. The question was simple: whether the mission of INC was to defend the remnants of human civilization here in The Outer Banks or to strike out and liberate Earth from the Intruders. Jackson sat at the center of this controversy.

Jackson was the youngest son of one of the original travelers onboard Intrepid, and more than that was a direct descendent, the grandson of the now Infamous Admiral Jackson who had commanded Earth's home fleet in its last valiant moments. It was the general consensus that the elder Jackson had died a hero, doing everything he could to save Earth from domination by the Intruders, but for Nathan his grandfather's failure burned like a hot iron through his soul. Nathan Jackson believed it was his life's mission, his destiny, to take retribution against the Intruders and in so doing to liberate Earth. Much to his frustration, his command authority didn't agree.

"Commander the Admiral will see you now," came a young female voice from behind Nathan, breaking his vengeful contemplation.

Startled slightly, he turned around gathered his composure and responded politely, "thank you Jennifer."

Admiral Montage smiled warmly and stood as Nathan entered the room, stepping out from behind his desk and walking to meet the younger officer.

"Come in, come in," the Admiral grinned, shaking Nathan's hand and gesturing him toward some comfortable chairs that sat along the wall of the office.

As the two of them sat, a viewing screen rose out of the low table in front of them, and the Admiral continued talking, "fantastic work Commander, truly revolutionary".

The design of a new starship appeared on the screen in front of them. Its shear length and the massive fuel tanks stretching along its exterior clearly gave away its interstellar capabilities but the large beam generators that lined its sides gave away the additional fact that, like the old Gunships of Earth, this lady was not afraid of a fight.

"Do I understand she'll make the trip in less than seventy years?" the Admiral continued, "it took Intrepid over a hundred."

Jackson couldn't take the small talk any longer, he knew his design was good and he wasn't in the mood for compliments, even from his superior officer.

"Did they approve her?" he asked jumping right to point.

"Nathan, you have to understand it's a very complicated issue," the Admiral began.

"I knew it," interrupted Jackson, "all they can think about is their own precious little skins."

"Watch your self Commander," the Admiral warned, dropping his polite tone.

"I'm sorry Admiral, I mean no disrespect. It's just that," Jackson began to explain.

This time it was the Admiral that interrupted.

"Nathan, it's not just about protecting the colony verses launching a counter attack. There's no question that liberating Earth is at the heart of INC's mission. It's a question of timing."

Jackson wasn't buying it.

"How many generations shall we wait Admiral?" he asked with fire in his eyes.

The Admiral would not back down either.

"Our gun designs are not even tested in battle and we have no way of knowing whether the Kelly frequencies will still work or not. The enemy will adapt you know."

"But Admiral," Jackson began to plead.

"The decision of the council is final Commander. It will be reviewed again in a year if nothing changes in the meantime," concluded the Admiral. "Now, do yourself a favor and use the time wisely, refine your designs and for god's sake take some time off. Get married or something," he jested, trying to mend the fences.

"Yes," Jackson interrupted, displaying little emotion.

"Yes what?" The Admiral asked, not sure what Jackson was replying to.

"Yes, she'll make the trip in less than seventy years," Jackson responded, maintaining a dry tone that made it very clear he wasn't going to let go, no matter how long they pushed him off.

The Admiral sighed and became quiet for the remainder of the briefing, his apparent excitement over the new ship's design now more difficult to maintain. Jackson, however, refused to skip the details and made it clear to the Admiral how his planned creation was more than ready for the mission it was to be built for.

Retribution, were she to be built, would become the first manmade Interstellar Ship to travel to Earth. Bringing with her the most sophisticated firepower that had yet been created. Like the Gunships that preceded her, she relied upon the Kelly frequency to engage and destroy her enemies, but with more than a century of additional development work, and the vast raw materials of The Outer Banks at their disposal, INC could now give her a much-improved weapons system. First, learning from the lessons of the Battle for Earth, she would engage her victims at a range that exceeded that of the Intruder's Mother Ships. Her beam generators were specifically designed to maximize their effectiveness at two to five million miles. Furthermore, they were designed to fire short extremely accurate and high-energy bursts that would rapidly overload the defensive capabilities of their adversaries. INC had high hopes in this new gun design, but they remained untested in combat.

The colony's own defensive perimeter relied on the same systems and it was thought that the inevitable attack on The Outer Banks would prove their effectiveness. The commanders of INC remained conservative in their thinking and wanted to wait until the technology was tested before investing their resources in a counter attack on Earth. Retribution would not be built until The Outer Banks itself had been tested in combat. It was this strategy that most frustrated Jackson.

In other respects Retribution was much like other interstellar vessels, she was designed for peak velocity not acceleration. Once she reached Earth's solar system she would have no intercept capability. She would instead fall into a simple orbit around Earth and wait for her enemies to come to her, a great floating gun platform that, it was hoped, could regain control of the Earth's destiny.

"If I can provide any further information please let me know," Jackson concluded in the same dry and frustrated tone. He refused to hide his distain for the decisions that command had made.

The Admiral looked hard at Jackson as he stood to leave.

"Be patient Nathan, the time will come," he gestured sternly.

With the briefing complete Jackson decided to make his way to one place on the ship where he felt his ideas were more readily accepted. The moist chilly air felt good hitting his face as he entered the Cryo-sleep facility.

"Good evening Nathan," a soft voice greeted him from a small desk at the entrance to the long hall.

"Is it?" Jackson replied, still in a somber tone.

"Oh come on, don't be so down," the young redheaded woman continued, standing and walking toward the Commander.

"Rebecca, they turned me down again," Jackson confessed.

"And that surprises you?" her smiling face responding in a comforting way.

"It just doesn't make any sense Bec," he continued, "we have to find out once and for all if we can beat them. We just can't sit around and wait. Who knows what's happening on Earth while we're sitting on our butts out here in the cosmos. We may already be an extinct species on our own home planet. We have to act."

"We will Nathan, we will, you just have to give them time to gain the confidence, they need to know The Outer Banks is safe first," Rebecca responded, placing a hand on his shoulder.

"You sound just like them," he replied, looking up at the ceiling and running his fingers through his hair in frustration.

"Nonsense," she said, "if it was up to me, I'd give you your ship and let you run halfway cross the galaxy chasing those monsters. I'd give up everything, you included, to see you happy."

She pulled him closer and put her other hand on his chest.

"You don't have to give up anything," he replied, looking down at her. "You know you're more than qualified to join the academy. Even if they approve Retribution today, it will be years before she's built. I'm sure you'd make the crew."

"There you go talking nonsense again. Do you have any idea the competition you'll have for a crew when the project gets approved? The command council may not want the mission to happen yet, but there are plenty of people ready to join it when it does. There's you and perhaps and handful of others on this colony who have the experience to guarantee a spot. Everyone else will have to scratch and claw their way on board. I wouldn't stand a chance. No, this Cryo facility is the closest I'll ever come to sailing to Earth."

She waved her hand down the long hallway, at the lengthy row of Cryo chambers that lined the wall.

"Don't kid yourself, you have every bit as much chance at making it into one of these chambers, as I do," Jackson scoffed, taking her arm and walking down the hallway with her.

She smiled up at him thoughtfully.

"So what else did the Admiral have to tell you?" she asked.

"He told me to get married," Jackson laughed.

"Now there's an idea you should take him up on," she said, turning toward him and grasping both of his hands.

He smiled at her warmly and slowly kissed her lips.

Their moment together was interrupted by an unexpected sound.

The combat early warning sirens rang through the chamber and the flashing light cascaded off the walls. They looked at each other intently. It must be a drill, they both thought. Jackson looked down at his wrist terminal for more information and to his amazement found he was a mistaken.

The status message on his screen read:

Multiple incoming targets detected, all personnel report to your posts. This is not a drill.

"This is it," Jackson exclaimed, with an excitement that would have seemed misplaced to anyone but Rebecca.

For Rebecca the reaction was closer to how the rest of the colony was feeling at that moment and the fear quickly showed in her eyes.

"We're going to kick their ass," he stated confidently, reassuring her with his absolute confidence and kissing her passionately one more time.

"Go," she whispered wishing she could share his elation.

The central defense control facility of The Outer Banks looked much like control centers had since the dawn of the computer age. A large central viewing screen took up much of the center of the room, standing perhaps twenty feet high and sixty feet in length. In front of it sat three rows of consoles where all of the defense command officers monitored their stations. Each station had its own integrated viewing screen and command console. Instead of a separate set of controls, the stations were capable of sensing the positions of the hands and bodies of the operators and were controlled by manipulation of three-dimensional images that the screens themselves projected. Each station was semicircular in design and surrounded its operator. Only the operator's heads showed above their positions, allowing them to communicate with each other and view the central screen as well as their own stations. The facility was the most advanced command center ever created.

In the center of the room, raised perhaps four feet above the level of the other stations sat the Admiral's post. His station was slightly bigger than the others, but also lower so that more of his body was visible and he could more easily survey his staff in the room below. As the central facility this one center would control the entire battle. In the event it was damaged any of five others elsewhere in the asteroid belt could take over its mission.

At the rear of the room above the level of the control stations sat the center's viewing gallery. Three rows of comfortable chairs awaited INC officers, like Jackson, who were authorized to enter the facility as observers, but did not play a direct role in the colony's defenses.

When Jackson entered the facility, Admiral Montage was already in his station and giving orders to his defensive forces.

It didn't take Jackson more than a few seconds to take a look at the massive three-dimensional image on the main viewing screen and assess the situation.

A single Intruder Mother Ship had entered their solar system and was rapidly approaching the asteroid belt. It had already launched over thirty-two attack orbs that were spreading out to attack the asteroid belt at various points. It immediately occurred to Jackson that the Intruders had learned little from their hard fight for Earth and had, by the look of it, drastically underestimated the defensive capabilities of The Outer Banks. They were coming with only one Mother Ship, despite defenses that were even stronger than Earth's, a battle that had cost the enemy eleven of their vessels. It seemed to indicate that such great attention had been paid to Earth primarily because of its role as Humanity's planet of origin rather than any ability to measure the defensive capabilities it possessed. The Outer Banks was just a colony, what could it possibly do.

The perimeter sensors that had picked up the Intruders were currently under attack and they were being picked off one by one. That did not concern any of the officers manning the consoles of the command center. The sensor arrays of The Outer Banks were considered expendable. INC now had a new weapon in her arsenal to track and engage the enemy ships. With the colony now at battle stations, the main guns that were distributed throughout the asteroid belt, one hundred and eighteen of them in all, had been brought to ready status. Though massive in size, the largest beam generators ever created, they were still finely tuned instruments, and as such even when only in ready mode they gave off a hum, in their signature Kelly frequency. Instruments integrated into the guns themselves used this background hum and newly created hypersensitive receivers to their advantage. At this one frequency the Intruder ships reflected energy and the reflection of that hum could be used to track the targets as they approached with far more accuracy than the gravitational sensors that had traditionally been used. It was like painting a bull's eye on a target with a laser spotter. The incoming ships were sitting ducks.

The Admiral was biding his time. Jackson quickly noted that some of the attack orbs were already within range of the guns, but the colonial forces were holding their fire. It quickly became evident that Montage intended to let the entire Intruder attack force including the Mother Ship come within range before he opened fire. This was a bold strategy, one designed to achieve absolute victory, not just scare the enemy off. Jackson was surprised by the Admiral's courage.

The tension in the control center was unbelievable. It felt like the air had turned to stone and nothing could move. Each one of the defense officers sat glued to his station focused on his own mission. One by one the enemy targets would come into range and more and more of the colony's guns would zero in on their prey. In all, sixty-two of the guns would be able to engage in the first volley. Every single one of the Intruder's attack orbs would take at least one shot and thirteen guns were aimed at the Mother Ship.

Jackson couldn't help but think back to a time almost two hundred years ago, when his own Grandfather at witnessed a similar sight. He thought back over the recorded footage he'd seen time and time again to the moment when Bismarck had taken down the first Intruder Mother Ship. His heart began to pound as he remembered recounting those seconds of anticipation as each volley left Bismarck's proud guns. His mind did some quick rough calculations and he realized that the ship that was approaching them now faced a much stronger adversary. When the improved accuracy and the increased amplitude of the new guns was factored in, this enemy was about to take a shot ten times stronger than Humanity's first Mother Ship victim had felt. Adrenaline surged through Jackson's veins as the moment of truth drew near. Slowly he sat up in his chair and gripped the railing in front of him tightly.

"Come and get it you bastards," he whispered under his breath.

Then the trap was sprung.

"Fire at will," the Admiral called out across the room, breaking the icy silence of the moment.

The quiet visual of the solar system on the great screen in front of them slowly transformed before their eyes. A scene unfolded before them like a great slow moving fireworks display. At first bright lines indicated the energy beams of the colony's

great guns began to spread out from various points along
the asteroid belts. Even at the speed of light it took several
seconds for the beams to hit their mark, but one by one each
one did. Several more seconds past before any confirmation
was received back to the center of the results.

Cheers rose from every corner of the room as the first images
came in. Scene after scene blazed across the screen of Attack
orbs shattering in a blaze of purple light The guns of The
Outer Banks had worked flawlessly.

Tension returned for a moment as the room waited for the
results of the strikes against the Mother Ship. A deafening roar
shook the place as everyone cheered the long awaited outcome.
The Mother Ship was torn to pieces after being struck by only
the first two guns. The other eleven beams had shot right
through the empty space left behind.

The Intruders had finally met their match. After eight
hundred years of conflict that had began, so long ago, over
sixty light-years away with the destruction of an insignificant
interstellar space probe, humanity had finally achieved a
victory. A human colony had withstood attack and lived to tell
the tale. Billions of lives had been lost, and almost every
settlement of humanity had been destroyed but now, after
being pushed to the edge, after retreating to their last outpost,
Mankind had triumphed. Now there was hope. Now there
would be retribution.

Jackson looked again at the main screen. Not a single
Intruder target had survived the onslaught. Not a single shot
had missed its mark. His attention now turned to the Admiral.
He smiled watching his commander have his moment. The
entire center had broken from their posts and was surrounding
the Admiral's station, shaking his hands and patting his back.
He deserved the moment. They all did. Jackson was happy to
let it happen.

He sat back in his chair and smiled, putting his hands behind
his head and stretching out. His time would come now. His
moment was drawing near. Above the sea of heads surrounding
him, the Admiral even glanced up at the gallery behind him
and nodded as if to say. It's your turn now Nathan.

In the elation of victory, it was hard for him to comprehend
what his eyes were now witnessing. One of the officers on the
control floor below made the same observation.

"Incoming Debris," the voice from below warned. Within a second the attention of the entire control center was once again fixed on the main viewing screen and everyone was securing themselves back into their stations. At five million tons, a devastated Intruder Mother Ship produced a whole hell of a lot of wreckage but in the vast dimensions of a solar system the chances that any of it might strike an inhabited asteroid was considered unlikely and for that reason the staff of the command center hadn't given it a second thought.

Luck had frowned on them.

Not only was a large piece of debris going to make impact with a colonized piece of the asteroid belt but that piece was the command center itself. The debris elimination protocols were in place but this particular piece was just too large. Unfortunately because it was now dead and inert, hitting it with the Kelly Frequencies had no further shattering effects. It just continued to break down like any other piece of floating junk a little bit at a time.

There was nothing that could be done. Now they were the sitting ducks.

The whole room jolted wildly as the impact came and pieces of the ceiling structure began to give way. Jackson looked up in slow motion as a large beam came falling toward him. He unclipped his harness and dove for the floor next to the railing as the beam slammed into his chair smashing it. His instincts told him to feel for rushing air, thankfully there was none. The structure had held its seal. They were still holding their air. Next he surveyed the room. The sight shook his senses. The same beam that had crushed the chair he'd been sitting in had pulverized the entire central control station, where Admiral Montage had been standing a moment ago.

Jackson climbed slowly over the railing and dropped to the main floor below, hitting the ground hard as he realized their asteroid must have entered an uncontrolled spin. He was feeling at least twice normal gravity. Thankfully the force was downward, keeping everything firmly grounded to the floor. He made his way across the room, removing debris as he went and mounted the Admiral's station.

The Admiral lay before him barely breathing, the end of the beam lying straight across his chest.

"Medtech," Jackson cried out hoping to get some help but there was little hope.

"I'm done Nathan, don't waste your breath," the Admiral hissed below him, spitting out blood as he spoke. "Just do me one thing," he continued to sputter.

"What's that?" Jackson asked kneeling closer to his commander as he felt the spin of the asteroid come under control.

"Build your damn ship," the Admiral replied as he hissed his last breath.

Chapter 19

Shining Light

4424
Earth

Otter was determined to continue his observations, despite recent developments. As the only remaining member of the core within Riverhead it was his responsibility to maintain a watch for any sign of an end to the Intruder's reign of Earth's skies. The icy cold night was making it difficult to focus the telescope. So he blew into his hands and rubbed them together to try to get some of the feeling back. On his second try the metal dials loosened and he was able to clear up the image in his eyepiece. Tonight's reading would be a good one; the moon was bright and clear. He looked over at the sandglass and noted that the first passing was still a few minutes away.

For over three hundred years, members of the Interstellar Naval Command's Ground Observer Core had watched the skies over Earth. A team had once worked at every District Capital or larger city since the defeat of the INC's home fleet. They were looking for any sign that the Intruders had left or perhaps been attacked by INC forces from outside the solar system. Unfortunately, in that entire time, no such event had occurred. Instead, things had just gotten worse and now time was running out.

It had been hoped that, even without advanced technology, stability and peace on Earth could be maintained. Things had not gone as planned. The three centuries since the defeat of the INC home fleet had been perhaps the most difficult in the planet's history. To begin with, the Intruders had not behaved as expected. At first their destructive rays, focused only on systems that utilized power technology, as they had in other star systems but their attacks on humanity didn't stop there. No one could be sure why. Perhaps it was the vast population on Earth or perhaps it was simply phases of destruction that just hadn't been seen yet in other systems. Whatever the reason, the white beams continued to whittle down the tools that man used for his survival, for several years after the first attacks.

It had been hoped that sophisticated steam engines that used only heat and mechanical technology would escape destruction but these workhorses were the next in line. From there the Intruders turned their attention to any complicated mechanical device, especially those made of dense materials like structural crystal or hard metals and those with many moving parts. It was during this phase of the downfall of man's technology, that the greatest loss of life occurred.

The power free Earth had relied heavily on sophisticated steam engines, windmills and waterwheels to drive complicated irrigation systems. These vital components of Earth's life giving agriculture were systematically destroyed. Millions of square miles that, since the dawn of the industrial age over two and half thousand years ago had served to provide food to Mankind, were reduced again to their natural form. The ancient deserts and barren grasslands of Earth's past re-emerged from the fertile farmlands that had taken their place.

Billions starved.

Those that survived did so by returning to ancient technology. The areas of the planet's surface that could support agriculture without complicated irrigation systems became a haven for the remnants of man's civilization. People flocked into the river valleys and estuaries. Fishing communities survived on the fruits of the ocean and held onto the shores of much of the world. Large numbers also got by, managing the livestock that fed upon the vast grasslands. Though their density was greatly reduced by the loss of irrigation, these creatures kept a widely dispersed population of herders alive. Mankind returned to the roots of his civilization. We had become a race of hunters, gatherers, river valley farmers, fishermen and herdsmen. For the survivors, life was hard and it left little time to think about holding onto the dreams of the past.

Things had only gotten worse when the Crawlers arrived. Seemingly primitive creatures with eight to sixteen sets of large dark eyes and large tentacle legs that had been brought to the planet by the Intruders; the Crawlers were now everywhere. They posed little threat in and of themselves but were protected by the Intruders and therefore made even more space unusable to humans. Mankind was being squeezed from every side.

Democracy survived only in the most fortunate of groups. For others, despot leaders sprang up and proclaimed themselves chieftains or kings. The multi layered system of management instituted by the Unified Government crumbled quickly, leaving behind only small pockets that tried to continue the democratic traditions and hold out for hope that someday the magic that was technology would return.

Riverhead was one of those places.

Perched upon tall rocky cliffs that overlooked the shores of the Delaware River, on the North Eastern edge of North America, Riverhead controlled a sharp gap in the hill line that the Delaware cut through on its way to the sea. Directly below the cluster of stone fortifications sat a large concrete dam that had been built just before the fall of the INC home fleet as part of a large power free water management project. The resulting lake sat behind the dam and fingered out down the valleys that joined the Delaware, providing life giving fresh water throughout much of the region. Control of the lake and the food production it supported kept the people of Riverhead alive and united but now even this bastion of civilization was threatened.

Like many of the river valley towns, Riverhead had been able to maintain a reasonably stable life for its citizens. It had been unable to help those around it, however, and they had fallen into a desperate state.

Mankind had lived in peace on Earth for over fifteen hundred years under the rule of the Unified Government. With food and prosperity for all, sophisticated education practices to detect and correct aggressive behavior and highly advanced technology to provide security, peaceful coexistence had been easy to achieve. Things had changed with the arrival of the Intruders. Mankind had been separated into thousands of individual communities each fighting for its own existence and if they couldn't find the means of survival from their environment they would quickly turn on each other. Warfare between men, again, returned to Earth.

Riverhead could not escape this tragic repetition of history. Faced with starvation, the communities around the lake had turned on their larger neighbor. In response, Riverhead had formed its own militia legion and went on the attack. With its vastly superior resources and supplies, Riverhead had easily achieved a victory and subdued the surrounding communities, at least until the arrival of General Kurn.

Like many of the ruthless despots that had sprung up around the planet, Kurn was a new breed. He had never had exposure to a formal education or been taught to manage the aggressive side of human nature. Instead he had learned that killing was means of survival. It was believed he had actually been born in Riverhead thirty to thirty five years ago. His exact age and birth name were unknown. What was known was that at a young age, while hunting on the perimeter of the town's territory with his father, he had been captured by bandits and taken as a slave. He was only five or six. He had been beaten and abused and witnessed terrible things during his time in bondage and when he reached his teens he made his captors pay. While the small group of cutthroats holding him slept, he awoke and, with nothing more than a slither of broken rock, cut the throats of his sleeping keepers. It was rumored he survived on the flesh of those first victims for a short while. This began the wild period in Kurn's life. He lived by himself in the woods sometimes surviving by killing wild animals at other times stealing from outlying communities. He would hide from the adults but liked to make his presence known to the children. Often he would befriend them by bringing them gifts and telling them stories of life in the wild. Those that showed strength and aggression he encouraged to join him. Soon he became leader of a wild and ruthless gang of killers and thieves.

It was at this time that his presence became known to the council at Riverhead and they made their first attempt to put an end to Kurn's destructive ways. A posse was formed and a reward was placed on his head. He proved elusive though.

Despite numerous attempts, he remained at large and with each failed pursuit, he grew stronger.

Soon his gang became an army. Many from the outlying settlements joined his group. Others who remained loyal to Riverhead paid for their decision. Villages that resisted him were eradicated, every inhabitant killed and every home taken to pieces stone by stone, often by the villagers themselves before their death.

Riverhead sent force after force out to find and destroy him, without success. It seemed his entire army would just vanish into the trees as their attackers approached, never engaging the numerically superior Riverhead legions. Then when the armies were forced to return to Riverhead, supplies exhausted, his attacks would begin. Coming in rapid and fleeting strikes that stung at the backs of their retreating foe, Kurn's forces would wear their enemies down, never giving them a chance at victory.

Riverhead grew frustrated and decided to amass an army that could finish the job. Twenty thousand strong, the Great Northern Legion would be the force that would finally destroy Kurn. The army was well equipped and would be able to pursue Kurn far beyond the Pocono range. When it became known that Kurn was massing his forces for a strike on the far end of the lake, the new legion moved out. It had now been ten days since the army had marched.

The first news of combat to come back was disturbing. It appeared now that a large army, perhaps commanded by Kurn himself had somehow slipped through the borders of Riverhead and was moving up along the river from the South. Riders had been sent north to bring back the legion but it might now be too late. The early reports were that Kurn had formed a decoy force in the north of freed slaves and starving peasants that the legion was most likely slaughtering right now, meanwhile his main force of skilled killers was closing in on Riverhead. A scouting party had been sent south, along the river, to find Kurn's force but they hadn't yet returned.

For Otter, however, these events did little to change his job.

As he saw the sandglass reach the designated point, he turned to his telescope and put his eye to the eyepiece. Now over three hundred years old, his reflective scope still worked as it did the day it was made. It was a precision instrument but simple in design with few moving parts. It had successfully avoided drawing the attention of their foes. Sure enough there it was, right on time. A small black spot moved across his field of view, as if there was suddenly a hole in the moon. Without a solid understanding of the nine-hundred-year-old war between man and the Intruders, Otter probably wouldn't have had an explanation for what he just saw. For a well trained observer like Otter, however, the predictable precision of its path, the shape of the shadow and the pure darkness of its form told him exactly what it was; an Intruder orb, orbiting silently above.

He turned the sandglass and recorded the observation. He now had over two hours to kill before his next sighting. He surveyed the battlements of the town's defensive wall that stretched away along the cliff line parallel to the river. His telescope was mounted on the main watchtower of the wall and he hoped the militia would leave his position alone as they prepared for a possible attack. He doubted he would be that lucky though and feared that tonight might be his last chance to make his recordings. He refused, however, to give up his post. The young soldiers working on the defenses looked scared. They were far from being the best the town had to offer. The garrison was perhaps two thousand strong and mainly comprised of troops too young or old to move with the main Legion. The leadership of Riverhead had never imagined Kurn would try to strike against the town itself and had left themselves poorly defended. Of course, this had been Kurn's plan all along. Though their troops were scared the council remained confident the walls would hold until the Legion returned. They remained convinced this bold move by Kurn would be his undoing.

Otter turned his attention back to the sky. He didn't quite know why he chose that particular spot to look at in the sky and, for a moment, he thought he must be mistaken. There, far above him, something new had appeared, a shining light streaking across the sky. It was long and perfectly straight in form and moving sideways across the field of view. Light blue in color, it wasn't very bright and would have been missed by anyone not looking directly at it. Otter knew in a moment this was not a natural sight but he wasn't sure what it was. He turned to try to get the attention of one of the soldiers further down the wall but before he was even able to utter a word, the light was gone again, fading slowly and then disappearing completely.

Otter had to figure out what this had been. He rushed down from the battlemento through the narrow stone hallways and into his library in the lower floors of the watchtower. He scanned the titles of the old books on his shelf and found what he was looking for. The title read:

INC Observer Core
Catalog of Potential Observations
Last Revised 4121

He flipped the tattered pages passed the pictures of black orbs and ellipses and ancient Interstellar Warships towards the back of the book. There he found it, a picture of a bright shining trail moving through the night sky, with a caption alongside.

"Particle Trail – Will appear as a long glowing line in the upper atmosphere. May indicate the arrival of an incoming ship venting a particle beam during deceleration. After making such an observation special attention should be paid to Intruder orb activities. Do not open vault unless orb elimination is confirmed."

Otter couldn't believe it. Were they here? After three hundred years had they finally come back?

He had to get back up to continue his observations. He grabbed some candles and the catalog and headed back up to the battlements. His next observation point was getting closer. He had to hurry.

When he arrived back on the rooftop of the watchtower he couldn't believe the commotion he saw and only had a moment to take in the reason. There, on the far shore of the river, was a trail of torches leading along the bank. Kurn's army was now in sight and moving into position, perhaps to cross the river and attack. Otter had no time to worry about it now. He made for his telescope.

The soldiers scurrying along the battlements had other priorities, however, and one of them bumped Otter as he carried a bundle of large spears along the walls.

"Out of the way, idiot," the lanky young soldier yelled as he passed.

Otter's telescope was knocked completely out of alignment and he looked over at the sandglass realizing he'd never get it back in time. He tried, quickly, to make the adjustments but time was running out. He looked down the eyepiece as his moment came and grunted with frustration when he realized he still wasn't even pointed at the moon. The next thing he saw sent his whole body into shock. There, right in the center of his field of view right where he expected he wouldn't have a chance in hell of seeing the passing orb, he saw an explosion, a shattering purple blast. That was it. He couldn't believe it. The battle had already started.

He yelled out at the soldiers down the way in his excitement.

"We're at war!" he screamed. "We're at war!"

The two soldiers who were looking down at Kurn's troops, moving along the river, turned to him, with a puzzled look on their face.

"You reckon?" they replied, then turned back to each other and laughed.

Otter didn't have time to explain. He grabbed his notes and headed back down into the building. He had to get to the Mayor as soon as possible. The Mayor was busy meeting with his militia commanders when Otter burst into the room.

"Mr. Mayor I have some great news," Otter blurted out, not even waiting to be noticed.

"What you've finally decided to give up your crazy notions and join the militia. We need that blade of yours you know," the Mayor replied, looking down at the highly prized INC survival blade hanging at Otter's side.

Almost everyone in Riverhead knew of Otter's blade, forged before the collapse, of a material that could no longer be made. It was rare treasure indeed. Though Otter was considered a little eccentric, everyone knew he was handy with that blade and would make a good soldier if he'd just give up his crazy ideas about old myths. Otter looked back at the Mayor a little confused.

"No Sir, not that. It's the INC. They're here. We can open the vault," he replied.

"Have you gone completely mad?" the Mayor replied. "I've got Kurn breathing down my neck, my Legion is probably still several days away and you think I need Intruders taking their turn as well? I'd sooner slit my throat."

The technology vaults were secured locations in every former district Capital that contained information and items that could be used if it was ever determined it was safe to turn advanced technology back on. Most doubted anything in there was of still of value. Otter, however, had confidence the tools to unlock three thousand years of lost technology lay behind the vault door.

Otter continued to press his point, "Mr. Mayor, it's my obligation to inform you that as a representative of the INC, I do not need your approval to open the vault. I am merely required to inform you of my intention to do so."

The Mayor had been pushed to far. "Otter I have tolerated your refusal to serve your obligated term in the militia and allowed you to enjoy your little fantasies but now you have gone too far. Sergeant, arrest this man."

On his master's command an older militiaman stepped forward and drew his blade on Otter. The younger man responded swiftly. He drew his own and sliced right through the soft metal of his opponents weapon, leaving him defenseless, a sharp edge pressed to his throat.

The soldier smiled and challenged Otter confidently. "You gonna' kill me then, Starman."

Otter's reputation preceded him, everyone in the room knew he was quick with his blade but would never kill in cold blood. The mayor stepped in to ease the moment.

"Otter stop this nonsense," he said as he took Otter's blade from him. "We'll hold onto this till you cool off and change your mind. Lock him up," he instructed, turning to the guard and handing him the blade.

"Think about it Otter. We need you here, not with your head in the stars," the Mayor closed, as the young man was lead from the room.

Otter was led down another set of stairs and shoved into a storage room.

"Let us know when you're ready to grow up. Until then I'll hold on to your toy," the militiaman jeered, holding up the blade.

Otter surveyed the room. It was fairly typical of the rooms on the exterior of the watchtower. It had one small barred window and was filled with old wooden furniture. Otter decided the least he could do was keep up with events outside. He pulled over one of the wooden chairs and stood up on it. It was just tall enough to reach the window and he was surprised by the quality of the view. The room sat on the river-facing side of the watchtower and the small window looked directly out over the canyon below. He could see the campfires of Kurn's army perched on the far hillside. He wondered what they were doing. Surely Kurn didn't intend to set in for a long siege against the town. The Legion would return long before the winter's supplies ran out. Time was on Riverhead's side. If Kurn was going to be successful, his attack would have to be quick and decisive. Right now it didn't seem clear how he might achieve that when faced with the cliffs of Riverhead and the steep walls of its fortifications.

Otter turned his attention skyward. He so wanted his telescope, but what he really wished was to be part of the fight up there in space. Otter had always longed to return to the old days. He felt that he was a man from a different time, mostly self-educated in understanding orbital mechanics and the fundamentals of interstellar drives, sciences long forgotten to most. Yet now, here he was, a prisoner in a castle. Suddenly something in the sky caught his eye. It was a falling star. Then there was another one. He knew the meteor shower schedules well and there was nothing expected any time soon. These flashes in the sky could only be debris from the great battle that must be raging in the sky above. He looked back down at the campfires of the approaching army. Something was happening there to. Fires were moving up the rocky slopes of the opposing side of the canyon. Could Kurn's army be retreating?

Otter watched events unfold for much of the night. He counted the falling stars he could see from his tiny little window and did the math to determine the total quantity of debris falling in the whole sky. Several thousands pieces fell throughout the night judging from the duration of the burn they ranged in size from small specs of dust to large blocks perhaps 20 or 30 feet across. Some looked like they were reaching the ground.

Activity proceeded across the canyon as well. The main body of campfires remained at the base of the hillside but a small notch of moving torches and activity indicated that Kurn was doing something on the opposing hill. Every once in a while, a flaming arrow would surge out from the walls of Riverhead. The militiamen were tooting their range to see if they could hit Kurn's troops. Their shots fell short; extinguishing themselves in sparks as they hit the ice of the mostly frozen Delaware. Finally, as the night drew to a close, Otter grew tired and stepped down from his chair. He found himself some old blankets tucked away in the pile of junk furniture and made a makeshift bed.

He awoke again with the sun high in the brilliant blue sky. He came again to the window and looked out on the landscape. The blue sky made it impossible for him to get any clue as to what was happening high above but the scene on the ground was much more clear.

A wooden structure was beginning to take form on the hilltop across from the watchtower. It looked like some type of tower, or perhaps an archery stand. He was surprised how quickly the structure, whatever it was, had been erected. Kurn's troops must have cut the timbers previously and brought them in during the night. They had probably brought them with them up the river. Throughout the day figures moved like little insects up and down the structure securing beams with ropes and pegs. As nightfall fell again it was still unclear what the purpose of the assembly might be.

During the following night, Otter again turned his attention to the sky. Again the occasional falling star gave a hint at what might be going on above but without his telescope Otter couldn't learn much more.

The morning brought much more clarity to events across the river. During the night, Kurn's forces had brought a large beam into place in the center of the wooden structure. The beam was attached to the rest of the structure by a central axle, which was able to rotate freely within sockets on either side. It extended perhaps twenty feet from one side of the axle and perhaps sixty feet in the other direction. The beam itself was clearly cut from a single massive tree and measured at least four feet in diameter at its widest point. Hanging from the shorter end of the beam was a large net filled with rocks, on the long end of the beam was a lengthy sling that held a single large boulder.

As the sun rose over hills to the east and shone down the canyon, all of Riverhead gasped in fear as they looked upon Kurn's massive Trebuchet.   In one sudden moment, the townspeople knew their time was short. Their leadership has misread Kurn horribly, mistaking him for little more than a ruthless and mindless barbarian who had to this point been lucky. Now the reality seemed clear. He was ruthless, yes. But his ruthlessness was matched by his cunning and wisdom. His assault on Riverhead had been planned to every last detail. From the creation of the decoy force, the bribing of border posts and the creation of ready to assembly war machinery, Kurn was a juggernaut and he was now poised to roll over Riverhead.

The battlements of the town were so quiet that Otter could even hear the commands yelled back and forth between the Kurn's engineers as they slowly wound back the massive war engine.   Time seemed to shift into slow motion as the tether was cut and the first projectile came hurtling across the canyon. The massive boulder seemed to hang in mid-air as if to soak up the warmth of the morning sun. Even in his makeshift cell, Otter felt the thud as the boulder fell low and hit the Cliffside at the base of the watchtower. He knew the next shot would not miss.

As the second round came hurtling directly toward the tower, Otter dove for the floor of his room and buried himself under a musty table. The crash behind him was deafening. The other side of the room had been pummeled. What was once his tiny window was now a vast gaping hole in the side of the room. What had once been a locked solid wood door to his cell was now a smashed in, half arch, exposed to the cold winter air. Otter wasted no time, he ran right through the opening. On the other side he found his guard, now crushed under the rubble of what was once the wall, his dead hand still clenching Otter's blade. Otter took his weapon and looked through the open whole at the Trebuchet. Another massive rock was arching toward them. He made for the stairs. This one hit the upper part of the tower and brought much of the upper battlements crashing down into the rooms below. Otter barely missed some of the falling debris as he charged down the stairs.

He made straight for the vault. Before long he found himself in the base of the main tower, in what had been, before the construction of the tower above it, the Observer Core station. He began to cross the room to the vault but was suddenly knocked off his feet. The wall along side him had received a direct hit from the Trebuchet and the floor was breaking away beneath him. It tumbled down to into the canyon below. Otter grabbed onto what was left of the far wall and pulled himself back up. He tried to get his bearings to make another run on the vault but it was too late. The stone roof of the room caved in, blocking the entrance to the vault permanently.

Otter couldn't believe he could get this close, only to be stopped at the threshold. He believed in his heart the Intruders were gone, or at least preoccupied. He also knew that there were weapons and tools behind that door that would allow them to repel Kurn's forces in no time. One small hand held beam gun would put an end to that Trebuchet in a matter of seconds but now he was shut out. Imprisoned in the dark ages until a way could be found to get to the vault.

He slammed his fist against the wall. Then realized, he couldn't stay here, the whole tower would come down any minute.

He turned and exited the room. He went straight up the stone steps and through the doorway in the rear. From there he climbed an exterior set of stairs that spiraled around the side of the tower to the battlements that ran along the ridge. He reached the top, just as another large boulder slammed into the lower portion of the tower. This time the tower itself began to give. With much of the outside face of it's structure smashed it could no longer support its own weight and the upper floors, rising perhaps fifty feet from the top of the ridge, began to slide away from their base. It held its shape at first but then began to crumble into an avalanche of stone that careened down the cliff side into the valley below.

The significance of the loss was not lost on Otter. Without the main watchtower, Riverhead had lost its view of the steeper portions of the cliff below. One of the main roles of the tower had been to prevent assault up the cliff face. Archers on the top of the tower would have been easily able to pick off any invaders trying to make their way up from the river. They were now blind to any attack until the enemy crested over the top of the ridge and by then, with the numbers Kurn had amassed, it would be too late.

With the tower gone, there was a lull in the firing from the massive war engine that had brought so much devastation on their defenses. Otter took a moment to watch the movement of Kurn's troops down the valley. They were beginning their assault. Groups of rafts moved out from the far shore and formed themselves into a line across the river. He watched as the well-disciplined attackers worked furiously to tether the rafts together creating a floating bridge across the unfrozen portion of the center of the river. Quickly the attackers began to cross.

Riverhead could finally strike back. A volley of arrows soared up from the battlements and rained down on the crossers below. The few that hit their mark made it known by the quick screams as the bodies fell off into the freezing river. The successes were few though and the majority of the force was making it across.

Otter heard the gasp from the archers along side him that turned his attention back to the Trebuchet on the opposite hill. Its target and ammunition had changed but its contribution to the battle was far from over. The image seemed to freeze as the missiles arched toward them. The projectiles were simple in form; large clay pots with their tops on fire. The enemy was firebombing the ramparts of Riverhead.

Otter gritted his teeth with visions of what he would have done to that wooden monstrosity if only he'd gained access to the secrets hidden in the ancient vault now buried in rubble. Instead he could only watch in horror as his countrymen fell burning alive from the battlement walls. Those that had survived the assault continued to try to pick off the attackers from the river below. Some of the braver bowmen climbed over the rubble of the fallen tower and leaned over the cliff, firing down the Kurn's troops as they advanced up the rocks. Arrows quickly picked them off from below. Before long the fur

clad warriors of Kurn's assault force came over the top of the
ridge. At first, it seemed the flow might be stopped as arrow
and spear brought down the earliest ones over the top but soon
their numbers exceeded the defender's missiles. They surged
right over the rubble pile that was once the tower and began
to attack the battlements from behind. Otter knew he was a
sitting duck here on the wall and decided to make his escape.

He yelled in rage as he jumped directly onto one of the enemy
soldiers and rolled to the side drawing his blade. His enraged
adversary regained his footing and came at Otter. His attack
was halted when Otter's blade sliced his shield in two and took
much of the man's arm with it. A second swing severed his
head.

Otter didn't stop to think about his first kill of the battle.
Instead he moved quickly through the attacking force staying
close to the group to avoid their deadly arrows and using
the advantage of his superior blade to keep him alive. Soon
it seemed Kurn's men learned to let him pass and focus on
the wall. Before long, Otter had escaped the battle and was
moving through the narrow streets of Riverhead headed for
the lake. Reinforcements were climbing up the sloping streets
headed for the battle. Otter gave no mind to their fate. He was
fighting a different war.

It was several minutes later when Otter reached the lake.
Looking back at the wall from the icy shore, he could see Kurn's
troops waving in victorious celebration at the capture of the
high ground above the town. They were now moving out along
the rest of the walls and down into the town itself to impose
their control over the entire area. Otter knew enough about
warfare to understand their intentions. They would fortify
their positions within the town and prepare for the inevitable
counter attack by the returning Legion. With the entire winter
food supplies of Riverhead at their disposal they would be well
equipped to withstand the siege. The returning Legion on the
other hand, would be short on supplies and exhausted from the
fast march south.

Otter had to think quickly in order to escape the scene before
the town fell completely. The lake presented his best chance of
escape. It was mostly frozen except where water moved more
swiftly, immediately in front of the dam's sluice gates. Some

of the town's canoes were sitting alongside the dam and would take him across the water. He decided to make his move.

Near the shore the ice was solid and he made his way as fast as he could across it, half sliding, half running. Some of Kurn's men, moving along the dam, noticed him and pursued him from the shore. Arrows bounced off the ice around him, as his foes tried to put an end to his escape. He made it to one of the canoes as one of the arrows pierced the hide skin. Before long he was in the water, crashing the canoe through the thin ice, near the gates. He paddled hard to escape the archers who were now moving down the dam. He felt the sharp bite, as a single arrow caught his arm. With no time to tend to the wound he kept paddling trying to ignore the pain.

He hoped that he would be safe once he had paddled out of arrow shot but he glanced back to see that some of the attackers had also grabbed two canoes and were now paddling after him. With more rowers in each boat, his pursuers were gaining on him and he was running out of open water to row through. As he got further from the dam the water was moving slower and the ice was closing in from every side.

Then he thought of it, the Crawlers. The one thing that Kurn's men would be afraid of was the Crawlers. Riverhead had been fortunate and not encountered to many of them so far but a small group had formed a colony on the western shore of the lake and with the threat of the Intruders from above the citizens of the town had learned long ago to stay away from them. Otter headed his canoe right toward the forbidden shoreline and pushed it as far as he could into the ice line. He had hit the ice about twenty feet before reaching the shore and lunged out of the canoe on to it, hoping to stay out of the freezing water. It was no good, the ice was still to thin. His weight crashed through and into the water. He reached down to his side and pulled out his blade and flailed it onto the ice trying to get a grip. The ice shattered with the blow but he was able to swim in closer and felt his feet touch the muddy bottom of the lake. It was his confidence in water that had earned him his name when he was a child. He needed that confidence now.

He pushed hard off the bottom and stabbed again at the ice with his blade. This time the ice held and he was able to pull

himself free from the water. The other boats were close now
and another arrow zinged past his ear. He stumbled to his feet
and lunged for the shore loosing his footing just as he hit the
cold dry land. Several of the strange domed structures, the
Crawlers had built, were directly in front of him and he charged
into the midst of the little village to conceal himself from the
attackers in the boats. He stopped for a moment and peeked
out. It had worked. The soldiers had an amazed look on their
face and broke off the pursuit, leaving him to certain doom at
the hands of the deadly white beams from above. Otter hoped
for a different outcome.

He turned to take in his surroundings and saw the strange
looking beasts coming out to investigate his presence. The site
of them repulsed him. Their long dark tentacles reached out
for him and he felt their cold ends touch his body. His repulsion
turned to anger and the anger turned to rage. It was as if nine
hundred years of groveling were welling up inside him. He felt
as though every defeat Mankind had known since they first
encountered the Intruders, in the far away depths of space,
were weighing on his shoulders. He reached for his blade and
let the rage loose.

He hacked at the dumb and curious creatures with all his
might. Tentacles fell lifelessly to the floor all around him, as
the strange animals squealed in agony. Those squeals were
the sign that death would come from above at any moment
but there was no retribution, only more terrible squeals. He
continued his rampage, stabbing at the eyes of his victims,
which popped violently as his blade ruptured their shiny black
surface. The creatures were helpless. They were far too slow to
flee and had no ability to counter attack. Otter didn't care. He
had to know. He had to find out if Earth was finally free of the
chains that had held her in bondage for so long. When there
were simply no more left to slaughter, Otter finally stopped his
attack. His chest heaved up and down with the exhaustion of
the onslaught and his blade hung loosely at his side, dripping
with the slimy brown ooze of his victims.

Otter turned his head to the sky and spoke to his invisible
adversaries far above. "Come on, I'm here, take me you
bastards." There was no response, only the cold wind rushing
off the lake against his wet and exhausted body.

As he began to shiver, he looked again to the sky and wondered to himself what was next for Earth. How would he now unleash the technology of the past? Would this new found freedom from their bondage last? And was there any other soul on Earth that even knew it was here.

Chapter 20

Retribution

4424
Earth

Jackson surveyed the proud expressions on the faces of his crew. He couldn't blame them for being ecstatic with their performance so far. He himself had never felt more fulfilled in his entire life. It had only been four days since they had come out of Cryo-sleep and they had already proven their ship's battle worthiness twice over. They had claimed two Intruder Mother Ships and countless attack orbs without so much as a scratch on Retribution. Their first adversary had intercepted them as they passed Jupiter and the second had tried to prevent them from taking up a planetary orbit around Earth. The debris of that second victim had made quite a show as it rained down on Earth's atmosphere.

Retribution had performed flawlessly.

The site of his crew looking so confident, Earth sitting below them now liberated from the grip of the Intruders and the memory of his ship tearing apart their enemies without breaking a sweat, gave Jackson a new vision of Mankind's future. He saw a path of conquest ahead. He felt assured that after the liberation of Earth's solar system was complete, Mankind would be able to strike out from home and regain the territory that they had lost to the Intruders. Humanity would again prosper and he and his crew would go down in history as its greatest heroes. The legacy of his family would be redeemed.

Long-range scans of the solar system on their hyper sensitive Kelly Frequency scanners indicated that at least one more Mother Ship was still on an intercept course with them and would have to be dealt with for the liberation of the system to be complete. Jackson knew that soon that ship would attack but it might be several more hours before it arrived. He decided to put the time they had to good use. With Retribution now stable in a wide orbit around Earth it was time to find out what was going on down below.

"No sign whatsoever of a surviving INC presence on the surface commander," his communications officer and wife, Rebecca Jackson, replied.

"Any signals at all Ensign?" Jackson responded, maintaining a professional tone.

"Not a whisper, Sir," she replied.

"Ok, let's open up the visual scope and see what we can find, I want to know if there's even anyone alive down there."

Before long the main viewing screen of the command bridge had come to life. Retribution's sophisticated scopes began surveying the surface of the planet. It wasn't long before the images started appearing on the screen before them. The scenery was a little surprising but comforting nonetheless.

A healthy human population still thrived on the planet's surface below. It was difficult to estimate its size and the great expanses of unpopulated areas clearly indicated it had declined significantly since the Intruder's occupation had begun. However, it was there and the images gave the crew of Retribution a great sigh of relief.

The scopes zoomed in and showed details of life below. Farmers worked riverside fields with primitive horse drawn ploughs and wooden boats fished on the rivers, lakes and shorelines. Stone and wood houses had replaced the sophisticated structural crystal buildings of the Earth's golden times. Everywhere they looked they saw evidence of how ruthlessly the Intruders had suppressed human technology, but equally intriguing, they saw how the planet's inhabitants had adapted to the challenge and survived.

"Ok, let's find out if there's any Intruder activity on the planet anywhere?" Jackson indicated to Ensign Thomas, his reconnaissance officer.

"Yes sir," replied the young woman manning the scopes.

Before long she'd found what she was looking for. Images began to appear on the screens of the Crawler's strange and primitive domes.

"Amazing," Jackson commented at the view before him, standing and stepping away from his command chair toward the screen, "just like the records from the Avenger."

"The Kelly records leave us with the understanding that these are the biological cousins of the Intruders, who themselves are actually Biotechs," Thomas interjected.

"So vulnerable," Jackson replied, and then paused for a moment looking closely at the image.

"Ok, if we can't communicate with our comrades below, let's give them a sign that we're here. Let's start targeting some of these dome villages and see what that does for us. Weapons, find your targets and fire at will," he instructed walking back to his command chair and taking a seat.

Ensign Zakura was pleased to have something new to shoot at.

"Yes commander," he responded eagerly.

Before long the ship's gunnery officer had found his targets and began firing at the planet below. The energy beams created blazing bright purple lines as they penetrated the planet's atmosphere. The entire crew couldn't help but feel a sense of satisfaction as the ships scopes displayed the exploding domes below.

"Continue your barrage for several orbits, I will be in my quarters if you need me," Jackson ordered, standing and leaving the bridge.

Lieutenant Robertson, the ship's propulsions officer stood from his console and made his way to the command chair as the barrage proceeded.

Otter woke suddenly as a huge explosion shook the entire village. He thought for a moment he was doomed. Large pieces of stone flew into the air and came careening down all around him. By pure luck none of them hit him. Adrenaline surged through his bloodstream and his mind spun into action. He knew he had to get out of the Crawler complex immediately.

Knowing it was the one place that Kurn's forces wouldn't come looking for him, he had made a home out of the now deserted Crawler settlement. It had given him an opportunity to heal his wounds and think about his next steps. Now, the village that had provided him with sanctuary for the last couple of days had suddenly become a very dangerous place indeed.

The sudden assault from on high had told him that it was now time to make a decision. Once he was clear from the village he flopped down to the ground and turned to watch the domed structures burn.

He quickly assessed what might have happened and his first thought was that the Intruders had finally targeted him for his vengeful slaughter of the Crawlers. That explanation didn't seem to make sense though. First, the beam clearly targeted the buildings not him, and he noticed that the beam was a distinct violet or purple color not the white beam he'd always expected from the Intruders. No this had to be INC. They had taken care of the Intruder orbs orbiting the planet and now they were eliminating the Crawlers down here on the surface. Liberation was near.

The elation of the realization made him soon forget how a moment ago he'd thought his life was over. It also made the decision on what to do next clear to him. He had to get back to the vault. It wasn't going to be easy though.

He took a moment to examine his wounds, which were almost healed. He tightened the bandages and came to his feet. Before he'd even decided what direction to head in, a plan of action was formulating in his head. The only way he was going to get back into Riverhead was if he blended in with Kurn's Army. Skirting around the burning village he made his way through the woods to the shoreline of the mostly frozen lake.

Peaking out from behind the trees, he noticed he wasn't the only one affected by the attack on the Crawler village. Two of Kurn's men, who were patrolling the lake by canoe, were now coming in to get a closer look. Between his own disappearance into the village and the attack from above, it was clear they were getting braver. This would give him the chance he needed. He quietly found himself a hiding place in the trees as his adversaries brought the canoe up onto the ice.

They were big men, clad completely in furs. Otter reached for his side and gripped the handle of his blade tightly. The men were on guard as they approached the tree line. Otter studied their weaponry as they came closer. Fortunately neither of them had a bow. They both held long wooden spears with sharp metal heads. They were also protected by primitive armor. Through the front opening of their long dark fur cloaks, Otter could see a chest plate, fashioned from scrap metal. They were poorly prepared however, to face Otter's superior blade. As long as he didn't have to take them both on at the same moment, he felt confident of victory.

He sat quietly, barely even breathing as the two made their way through the woods, walking directly toward him. Otter's heart rate quickened, praying they would not see him together. Then his moment came. One of the men turned to the right, and took a few steps away to get a better look at the burning village. The other man broke to the left coming closer to Otter.

He took the moment, springing from his hiding place and charging the closer man. A vengeful and confident smile beamed across the barbarian's face as Otter attacked. Kurn's warrior was larger than his attacker by at least a foot and the smaller man was just armed with what looked like small sword. He stood his ground and lunged his spear forward as Otter reached him. His confident smile disappeared in an instant when a defensive swing of Otter's blade completely severed the head from his spear. Before he even had a moment to react, the second swing struck closer, breaking what was left of the spear in two and amputating his hand just above the wrist. He began to step back in retreat and shock, but it was too late. Otter lunged the blade straight into his chest. His armor barely slowed its penetration. Otter looked right into his eyes as he sputtered his last breath, the look of shock at his sudden demise still burned in his eyes. Otter pulled the blade back, as the limp body of his victim fell to the ground.

His second adversary had been approaching from behind as the melee proceeded, but stopped suddenly as his saw his companion fall. The ease of his partner's defeat struck fear into his heart and he turned for the lake and ran, dropping his spear as he fled. Otter couldn't let him escape. His plan depended upon surprise.

He made a desperate but calculated move. Quickly he measured the man's distance and speed and deliberately threw his weapon. The blade turned twice in the air and hit the fleeing man squarely in the back. Otter sighed in relief as the man fell to his face in the snow covered ground.

He dragged the second body back behind the tree line and laid it down next to its dead companion. He stood over them for a moment trying to pick the man that most closely matched his size, but neither fit the bill. He'd have to make do. He took the cloak and armor from one of the men and threw down his own woolen cloths. The cloak felt warm and heavy on his body. It was mostly bearskin but trimmed around the hood with grey wolves fur. Kurn's men prided themselves on their furs, which had to be made from their own kills. Otter had found himself a nice one. Searching the inside, he found a pouch in the left side of the cloak. In it he found some dried meat wrapped in leather and a small tinderbox. The find was a blessing. He'd had nothing but berries to eat in two days, and starting a fire had taken most of his first night. He had left Riverhead with nothing but the clothes on his back and his blade. Simply surviving had been a challenge.

He tucked his own weapon under the thick cloak and picked up the intact spear. He could only hope that he could pass himself off as one of Kurn's own, as he made his way toward the ice. Before long he was in the canoe and paddling slowly through the chilling water back to his home.

The town was bustling with new activity, as he got closer to the outer buildings. Kurn's men were busy refortifying the town to prepare for the upcoming assault from the returning legion. The townspeople themselves were doing much of the work driven by the whips and prods from fur clad warriors. Kurn encouraged no restraint in the cruelty inflicted on his enemies. The women and the children of the town were working right along side their men folk. They hauled large bundles of stone and supplies up to the battlements, where angry shouts instructed them where to place their loads.

Otter was pleased that no one paid attention to him, as he drug the canoe up onto the ice and made his way up toward the city.

"Back to work woman," he was forced to snarl at one of the newly bound slaves who recognized him as one of their own. She bowed her head and returned to her task realizing that Otter didn't want to be recognized.

Kurn's attack on Riverhead had proven brilliant, but his forces lacked experience in maintaining a secure perimeter.

Otter was able to slip into the town without being challenged. His foe was more concerned about the vast approaching army than about implementing tight security procedures. Before long Otter had worked his way around the outer wall of the town and was overlooking the ruins of the main watchtower. He couldn't believe his luck.

In their efforts to rebuild the defenses of the town, Kurn's men had been ordering the enslaved citizens of Riverhead to gather up loose rubble and use it to reinforce the walls. In the process, they were uncovering the entrance to the vault. Otter could already see much of the great door, now exposed to him. A few more stones and the lock itself would be accessible.

He needed a distraction.

It didn't take him long to find one. Stacked against the wall behind him, sat a pile of clay pots. Each one filled with oil and sealed with an oil soaked cloth. Looking at them he remembered the firebombing of these very same battlements just a couple of days ago. Kurn's army had been preparing more of the rudimentary bombs. They would suit Otter's needs nicely. He pulled the rags from one of the pots and splashed the contents over the whole pile. Then he began tearing the rag into strips and binding them together. Before long he had a primitive fuse. He laid one end against the pile and the other he stretched away from the fuel. He took out his tinderbox and went to light the end.

"What the hell do you think you're doing," he was interrupted from behind.

Otter decided to reply with his blade. Quickly he turned and drove the sharp tip into the man's abdomen. With his other hand he blocked his victim's mouth to prevent a scream. Fortunately, no one else had noticed the activity. He carefully laid the man's body against the stack and covered his face with his cloak.

Otter smiled for a moment thinking how his victim looked just like he did the first night he had tried ale, slumped lifelessly against the walls of Riverhead. There would be no waking from this hangover though.

Otter lit his little fuse and walked slowly away from his distraction toward the vault. He was almost there as the stack of pots exploded into flames behind him. Just as he had hoped, the crowd around the vault door scattered. Some headed toward the fire to try to put it out. Others headed the other way to safety. Otter felt the heat of the blaze against the exposed back of his neck. He didn't let the danger deter him from his mission.

He quickly removed the last few stones required to expose the lock, and before long was turning the large metal dial to open the door. The lock to the vault was a very old-fashioned combination lock, something that would not attract the attention of the Intruders as long as it was left still, but would keep the contents of the vault secure. Otter had memorized the combination to this vault long ago when he'd taken the oath to join the observer core. It was not written or recorded anywhere but in his own head. He was the only one that could open this door.

He pushed down on the handle and sighed with relief, as the large door swung open. He pushed a couple more rocks aside to make the opening large enough and he entered just in time.

"Hey, what are you doing?" he heard the shouts behind him as Kurn's men put out the fire and returned their attention to their surroundings. It was too late. Otter was in.

The great door closed behind him with a thud. A loud click told Otter the mechanical lock had closed again. He knew he was safe now, without the combination there was no way Kurn's men would be able to open the vault door. As long Otter didn't need to leave he was in no immediate danger.

The vault was dark, completely dark. It was the kind of darkness that you only find deep in a cave when all the lights are out. Otter couldn't even see his hands in front of his face. He fumbled in his pocket and once again found his tinderbox. He struck the side with the flint and watched the oil wick flicker slightly and then light. The small flame illuminated the interior of the vault and Otter was able to look around.

The sight was a shock. He had waited his whole life for a chance to open the vault and he'd expected to find it packed full of gadgets and gizmos from a forgotten age, technology that would solve all his problems, instead he found a very simple room with very little in it. Behind him, sat the massive vault door now shut securely. The other three walls were bare and grey. In the middle of the room sat a large chair with no controls or devices around it. The entire room was no bigger than ten feet by ten feet. This was perhaps the most surprising thing to Otter because he knew the physical dimensions of the vault itself measured at least twenty feet by fifty feet.

There was only one thing to do. He sat down in the chair.

At first nothing happened, then he heard a quiet clicking sound in the base of the chair below. His weight in the chair had activated some type of mechanical switch. There was an eerie silence in the room for a moment or two then he began to hear a whirring sound. At first it seemed to come from the floor below him, then it grew louder and moved into the walls and the ceiling, then began to fade away again as a light began to illuminate the room.

Otter looked around for the source of the light, there was none. Then it occurred to him, it was the walls themselves that were glowing. He looked around him and below and the floor and the ceiling were emitting the same strange grey light and seemed to be fading away from him. Only the chair he was sitting in and the vault door behind him remained solid. He gripped the chair tightly not sure what to expect next. For a moment he felt like he was falling and had to close his eyes. After a while with his eyes tightly closed, it became clear he wasn't going anywhere. He opened them again. Now things were coming into focus again.

What once had been a ten by ten room was now a vast panoramic view stretched out before him. He recognized the view immediately. It was Riverhead. He was looking down on Riverhead from directly above the exact location of the vault. He sat suspended in a chair perhaps fifty feet in the air looking down on the battlements surrounding the vault. Kurn's men were swarming all around him. Some were pulling back their bows and shooting arrows up at Otter. Otter tried to duck to the side as an arrow shot toward him.

"Don't worry you are in absolutely no danger," came a voice to his right.

"What?" Otter exclaimed turning directly toward the voice.

A young man sat next to him perhaps eight feet away, just beyond where the wall of the room had once been. The man looked very relaxed sitting in a chair identical to Otter's.

"Please don't be alarmed," the man continued, "you are completely safe."

"What is happening?" Otter questioned, still confounded by the sights around him.

"That's a very good question," the man smiled, "and one that I think we can both answer for each other."

"I don't understand. Who are you?" Otter questioned.

"Yes, that's probably a very good place to start," the man began. "My name is Simon. I am an advisor."

"What does that mean?" Otter interrupted.

"I'm sorry. Let me step back a little bit and try to explain. I'm a computer program, do you know what a computer is?"

"I think so," Otter replied, "a sort of thinking machine?"

"Pretty much," Simon responded, "Although it's a little more complicated than that."

"But how is this possible. You don't look like a machine?" Otter sat up in his chair and looked intently at the man.

"I'm a part of a very complicated machine. As I understand it you've lived some or all of your life without any exposure to technology as sophisticated as me, so this may all seem a little strange to you." Simon explained sympathetically.

"You can say that again," Otter retorted.

"Tell me, what year is it?" Simon requested, trying to get a bearing on where things stood.

"It's 4424," Otter replied.

"Oh my, well yes, that would make sense, the astronomical and physical data I can gather supports that assessment," Simon paused. "That means that for over three hundred years I've been inactive. Have the Intruders been here that entire time?" he questioned.

"Yes, Otter replied, but it looks like they're gone now. That's why I opened the vault," Otter gestured proudly.

"Well let's hope you were right because if you're not this conversation will be a short one. Anyway, as I was saying I am a computer program, and the room you are in right now is my interface to you."

"I'm still in the room?" Otter questioned.

"Oh yes, in fact why don't you see for yourself. Get out of the chair and reach toward me."

"I'll fall," Otter replied looking down out of the chair.

"No, that's an illusion. Just reach out with one foot you'll see."

Carefully and slowly Otter put one foot down in front of him. He felt the solid ground of the floor beneath him despite the fact that it looked like he was floating about fifty feet above the ground, Kurn's men still yelling up at him. Slowly, like a cat walking on glass, he stepped across the room and reached out to touch Simon. Before his hands made contact, however he felt the wall.

"Three dimensional viewing screens, state of the art, I might add", Simon explained. "Or at least they were, three hundred years ago."

"Like a mirror, but different," Otter queried.

"Yes, very good, just like a mirror. Except instead of reflecting the image it receives this mirror gives whatever image I ask it to give. Right now I'm showing you the image of the sensor beacon that I've erected above us. Your friends below seem quite upset about the whole thing."

"They're not my friends," Otter interrupted.

"I see, that explains a lot," Simon replied, "not to worry though, they won't be able to hurt you. At least not easily."

"I think I'm beginning to understand, please go on." Otter requested, now feeling more comfortable to ignore the arrows and rocks flying up toward them.

"Very well, as I said my name is Simon and I am an advisor. A very sophisticated computer program," Simon smiled, "I was originally activated in the year 3553 and assigned to the Unified Government's Security Administration. I once served as the Advisor to Joanne Forsythe and became her personal advisor upon her retirement. Upon her death I became the curator of the Foresythe Presidential Library until my reactivation to military duty in 3735, eventually becoming the vault custodian for the district capital of Riverhead. I was deactivated in 4123 when the Intruder's assaulted Earth. I remained dormant until you reactivated me a few moments ago. I will therefore apologize if I have little data to offer you of what's happened in the last three hundred years. Although from what I can tell it seems there's clearly been a tremendous amount of technology deterioration. It's good to see that humanity has survived though."

"Yes, we're still here, although I'm not sure I'm going to be around for much longer," Otter interjected and motioned at Kurn's men gathering curiously around them.

They had stopped their assaults on the sensor beacon and the mast that supported it and were gathering in groups to determine what to do next. They were clearly trying to figure out how they could open the vault.

"Yes, it doesn't look like they're going to leave us alone for long. We'll just have to see if we can get some help. Tell me why, specifically, did you open the vault?"

"My most recent observations, a few nights ago now, indicated that the orbs were being destroyed," Otter replied. "Then it seemed that Interstellar Naval Command was attacking the Crawlers as well. I had to open the vault. It was difficult because the town had been taken but I managed to sneak back in."

"Very brave of you, well let's see if there's anyone out there looking for us. Cross your fingers," Simon gestured smiling and turning to a small console that seemed to magically appear before him.

Jackson sat at his desk pondering his next move, when the good news came.

The tone at the door indicated someone wished to enter; Jackson waved his hand over the console to authorize the entry.

"Sir, a signal from below," announced Rebecca, keeping her professional demeanor in all but her beaming smile.

Jackson jumped from his chair and strode to the door wrapping his arm around his wife as he re-entered the bridge.

"Let's not keep them waiting," he announced, "on screen."

Rebecca gave him a subtle squeeze to show her pride then returned to her console and activated the signal. Two men appeared in a clear three-dimensional visual on the large screen in front of them. It looked as if two new crewmembers had just joined the bridge and were sitting there with the rest of them.

There appearance was as striking in its clarity as it was in its differences, both men were quite young. One had the neat appearance of an INC officer, but the lack of insignia gave him away immediately as a human simulation advisor. The second looked quite different. Unshaven and worn out, the man looked quite stunned by the whole experience.

The advisor spoke first.

"My name is Simon, INC advisor assigned to the district Capital of Riverhead, it's good to see you. My friend, Otter here, is the last remaining member of the Riverhead observer core and he's in need of some help, would you be able to assist us?"

"Commander Nathan Jackson of the INC Battleship Retribution at your service and let me say, the pleasure is all ours," Jackson replied proudly. "We'll launch a recover team immediately."

"Be advised that we are surrounded by hostile forces," Simon warned.

"We'll take the necessary precautions, thank you," Jackson closed.

"Ready the shuttle and assign a team of security droids," he instructed his crew.

A little less than twenty tons in mass, Retribution's scout shuttle number six resembled a large beetle. Mostly oval in shape, it had six large landing pads protruding from its belly, three from each side. On its back sat two small fusion drives that provided simple but efficient propulsion in space. Once in the atmosphere, decent and accent were controlled by six electro turbines that sat in each of the legs of the landing pads.

The journey down the surface lasted about two hours, and Jackson stayed in contact with Simon and Otter during the voyage. Kurn's forces had given up on their attempts to destroy the sensor beacon and were now focusing on the vault door itself. Having given up on opening the lock, they were now hammering the door with a large battering ram. Simon had assured Otter that their current tools would not be capable of penetrating the vault door, but nevertheless the constant thudding was making Otter very nervous.

Otter had actually gotten his first look at Kurn himself, who had now arrived at the scene. He was a surprisingly small man, covered completely in a silvery grey wolf's fur coat. His face was cold and scarred and his eyes seemed empty and dark. He seemed to show no sense of frustration or impatience with the situation but rather a constant burning persistence to defeat and destroy any adversary. Every time Kurn looked up at the sensor beacon Otter felt that the stare alone would cut through the walls of the vault and rip his very heart from his chest. Immediately upon his arrival the attempts to penetrate the vault had taken on a new level of organization and seriousness. None of Kurn's men dared show any sign of surrender to the impenetrable barrier, they just kept trying to find new ways to break through.

Inside the vault, Otter's nervousness continued to grow. Even if he was safe inside, he could not stay here forever. Jackson was his only hope.

Jackson was accompanied by three other crewmembers on the shuttle. Zakura, his weapons officer, managed the tactical display and Johnson, a junior Lieutenant, manned the helm. Finally Ensign Schultz had charge of the four security droids. The droids were spherical in shape, perhaps three feet in diameter. Like the shuttle, their motion was provided by electro turbines built into their structure. Their surface was covered in various sensors and weapons systems.

Before long the shuttle was approaching Riverhead along the Delaware from the south. Kurn's men just stared in shock as the bug like craft appeared over the ridgeline and bore down on the location of the vault. Kurn himself glared at the machine with a burning anger in his eyes and held his arm up in the air to instruct his men to hold their fire. Each of them brought their bows and spears to the ready in case they had to engage the monster.

The shuttle moved in and hovered directly over the battlements, just above the vault. A small metallic box lowered itself from the center of the craft and touched the ground. A door opened in the front and Jackson and Schultz stepped out, surrounded by the hovering droids.

Jackson seemed to completely ignore Kurn's men as he began to make his way down to the vault door.

At a nod from Kurn, one of his men stepped forward and addressed the team.

"Bow to Lord Kurn, or die where you stand," the man shouted.

With that the remainder of Kurn's men standing around the area, raised their bows and aimed them directly at Jackson and Schultz. The two men just ignored the whole scene and continued their stroll toward the vault door. A chorus of twangs followed as more than a score of arrows streaked in toward the two of men.

The response was startling.

Without any instruction from Schultz his droids eliminated the threat. Well-aimed beams cut each and every arrow from the air and turned it into a shower of ash. In the same instant high-pressure air, blasted the debris back, leaving Jackson and Schultz without even a stain on their uniforms. Kurn's men were also unharmed save the ash on their faces and the stunned look in their eyes. Their greatest fear was now how Kurn would react to their failure.

The warlord just stared intently at the team as they reached the vault door.

"A pleasure to meet you," Jackson gestured, as Otter opened the vault door and peered out at the scene. The dumbfounded look on the faces of the barbarian attackers astounded him.

"What about them," Otter queried, not sure what to do.

"We have no business with them," Jackson replied, completely dismissing the throng. "Our first priority is to make contact with remaining elements of INC and then we can define a strategy for the rehabilitation of the general population. Come the shuttle is waiting."

As they stepped away from the vault, Jackson turned to his wrist and spoke to Retribution.

"Rebecca, can you take care of our friend Simon please, his current location will not remain secure for much longer," he requested.

"Not a problem sir," came the response from his wrist terminal.

The walk back to the shuttle was less eventful. Kurn's men parted before them without quarrel or comment. Kurn made no attempts to attack them again. He just maintained his intent stare as they boarded the shuttle; his wicked mind formulating how he might deal with this new and powerful force in his world.

Within another two hours, the shuttle was entering its bay onboard Retribution.

"I'd like to introduce you to the crew of the Retribution," Jackson announced to Otter as they walked onto the bridge. Members of the crew came up to Otter and introduced themselves, shaking his hands vigorously. They were beaming with pride for having made contact with the remnants of Earth's INC core. They hoped that Otter would be the first of many to join their ranks and help them with the liberation and reconstruction of Earth's civilization.

"Have we had any further contacts?" Jackson asked Rebecca, hoping for some more good news.

"Unfortunately not Sir," she responded, "our friend here is the only one so far."

"Very well, keep trying I'm sure they'll be others," he closed optimistically.

"We are tracking the remaining Intruder ship Sir," Ensign Thomas interjected she'll be coming into range of our weapons in a few minutes.

"Excellent," Jackson responded, then placed his hand on Otter's shoulder. "You're about to see an amazing sight," he smiled at the young man, who had changed on the shuttle and was now wearing a brand new INC uniform.

Otter took a seat in an unmanned tactical console and surveyed the room in amazement. A couple of days ago, he'd been looking up at the skies from his almost medieval home town and now, here he was; in orbit of Earth onboard a great Battleship, about to witness a direct engagement with an Intruder Mother Ship.

"That's interesting," Thomas noted, almost speaking to herself.

"What is it Ensign," Jackson inquired.

"Well Sir, I'm not sure if I'm reading some kind reflection or a new reading but I'm picking up second a gravitational anomaly directly behind the target. I'm not picking it up on the Kelly Scanners though," she mused.

Jackson was the first to realize the seriousness of the observation.

"Eliminate the first target immediately," he barked at Zakura.

"Yes Sir," Zakura responded and fired all his weapons on the first Mother Ship.

Once again the massive purple explosion filled their screens and the crew cheered in celebration, as they'd done before.

This time Jackson ordered silence on the bridge.

"Is the second target still there," he questioned Thomas.

"Yes, Sir," she responded again, "but still nothing on the Kelly Frequency."

"Zakura, hit it with a full spectrum burst as quickly as you can," he ordered, then turned back to the Reconnaissance station, "Thomas what's the range?"

"Six million miles and closing Sir," she replied.

At this point, the crew began to sense the jeopardy of their predicament. This new ship wasn't responding to the Kelly Frequency. They were in serious trouble.

Retribution was a finely tuned instrument of war. Tuned for one purpose: to exploit the vulnerabilities of their adversary, vulnerabilities that had been discovered long ago and far away in the skies above Reykjavik. Today for the first time in almost five hundred years, those vulnerabilities were gone.

The entire crew froze, awaiting word from Zakura.

"It's reflecting at a new frequency Sir," Zakura pronounced.

"Retune the guns as quickly as you can and give me an efficiency rating," Jackson shot back.

"Retuning," Zakura replied, "efficiency at one point six percent."

Jackson's face turned pale with dismay as he gave the next order.

"Fire, all guns."

Otter sat motionless, barely aware of the happenings around him, but clear something wasn't going as planned.

Everyone on the bridge fixed their eyes on the viewing screen in front of them as the image of the new enemy taking the hit appeared before them. The elliptical shape of the ship appeared, glowing a faint green. It was easy to tell by the intensity of the glow, however, that they were nowhere near cracking this one open like they had the last.

"Do we have a good beam," Jackson inquired of his wife, wanting to know if everything they were seeing was making it back to The Outer Banks.

"Yes Sir, we have a good homebound transmission," she responded. At least INC would learn from this if nothing else. "Repeat fire at will," Jackson ordered, "give it everything you've got."

Zakura fired another volley and again their adversary showed no sign of breaking. Jackson readied his crew for the inevitable.

"Prepare for incoming fire," he ordered as Thomas added new information.

"Sir, we're picking up another ship approximately ten million miles behind the first and closing in fast," she informed her commander.

Their predicament seemed hopeless and Jackson did not have an opportunity to respond before Retribution took her first hit. The deadly white beams lashed out from the forward Mother Ship and tore into the Battleship's hull. The weapons turrets were the primary targets. The forward dorsal turret was hit first and exploded into a billion shards of shining structure as the main energy reservoir overloaded. The barrage did not stop there though. Their opponent also took out the right front turret before Retribution could fire again.

The distance was closing and Jackson hoped the new range would help them inflict more damage on their target. No such luck. The volley barely seemed to make a dent.

Their enemy wasted no time in returning fire. This time the white beams shifted their focus to the ship's internal systems. One cut right through the bridge and shattered several of the consoles.

"Rebecca," Jackson screamed as his wife disappeared into a shower of sparks and flames.

Otter quickly realized he was the only one on the ship who didn't have a job to do, and jumped up to tend to the wounded communications officer.

"She's Ok," he cried back to Jackson, bracing the wounded women in his arms.

Otter had learned much about first aid in his time in Riverhead and knew exactly how to handle his patient. Robertson, who had the least to do at his post, stepped away for a moment to assist. Schultz moved over to the communications console.

Retribution continued to return fire with little effect as the new Intruder Mother Ship slowly tore her to pieces.

Robertson's console was the next to go dead, noting that Rebecca was in good hands, he returned to assess the damage.

"We've completely lost propulsion and we're falling out of orbit," he reported.

"Power systems failing Sir, the ship is dying," Thomas updated them, "and the second ship is now closing in fast, I should have a visual in a minute if the systems hold."

Unfortunately the next moment, the power went completely dead and the bridge went dark. Within seconds the faint green light of chemical sticks shone eerily across the bridge.

"Propulsion what's your guess on the status of our orbit," Jackson inquired of Robert's glowing face.

"It's just a rough guess Sir, but I'd say we're going to come down somewhere over central Asia within an hour. Unfortunately without power we can't activate the shuttle either. We'll survive the decent but we don't have a hope of surviving the impact," he replied. "If we can't get power and propulsion back within the next twenty minutes, we're doomed."

"That's if the Intruders leave us alone even that long," Thomas added.

"Let's see if we can't get something back online," Jackson responded optimistically, "Ensign, Propulsion would obviously be our first choice," he continued smiling to Robertson.

A busy silence fell on the group as each of them went to work on their consoles to see if any of the critical systems could be brought online somehow. Every possible bypass and backup was explored. As his crew worked, Jackson broke from his command chair and went over to his wife. She was now sitting up on the floor propped against the side of her console, her eyes were closed and her faced grimaced in pain. Otter sat beside her holding her wounded arm.

"Can she be moved?" Jackson asked.

"I wouldn't risk it," Otter replied. "It looks like her back is injured. If we can stabilize our orbit and get out of danger, then we can carefully move her to a more comfortable location."

Rebecca opened her eyes and turned to her husband.

"Worry about the ship Nathan, not me," she wheezed. "Everyone's doing what they can, you just try to rest," he replied then turned to Otter. "Some rescue, my friend?" he said, as if to apologize. "Nonsense, I would have given a thousand life times to see this wonder," he replied gesturing to Retribution.

"Soon to be a wonderful crater in Central Asia," Jackson replied, quietly resigning himself to a defeat he was not ready to admit to the rest of the crew.

"Don't be hard on yourself Nathan," Rebecca sputtered, "You have saved humanity today."

"That is exactly, what I've failed to do," he exclaimed to the both of them.

"Don't you see," his wife insisted, "The Outer Banks now knows of the new frequency, they'll have time to prepare. What would have happened if we had waited and one of those new ships had arrived there before you got here?"

"Yes," Otter added, putting his hand on Jackson's shoulder "Your friends will send more ships and some day we will win."

Suddenly it struck Jackson, like Michael Kelly many years before, he had found a chink in the armor, one they were not ready to exploit today, but one that would save humanity in the battles to come.

The hull of the ship began to shudder as Retribution fell into the upper atmosphere. He looked out across his crew with a new sense of pride. Every member of the crew knew they were facing immediate death within the hour. Yet the green glowing chemical sticks continued their activity, without pause, as everyone tried to bring their systems back to life. Jackson squeezed Rebecca's hand and wondered: how long before real retribution would be theirs?

Chapter 21

Distant Murmurs

4424
Neo Prime
76 Light-years from Earth

Sarah felt a wonderful warmth on her face as she awoke from a strangely restful sleep. She slowly opened her eyes and squinted at the brightness around her. She closed them again wondering if she was still dreaming. The distinct and peaceful sound of waves lapping against the soft sand of a beach struck her curiosity and she opened them again, this time with her hand raised, to take away the sharpness of the glare.

She sat up and looked around, still trying to get her bearings. The scene was stunning and surreal. Sarah found herself sitting on a comfortable lounge chair perhaps twenty feet away from a warm blue sea. A gorgeous yellow sun was the only interruption in a bright blue sky that stretched away from the ocean in front of her. To her left, she could see other lounge chairs, each spaced out quite comfortably. There were others on the beach, enjoying the sun, but quite far away so that she had her immediate surroundings completely to herself. Down the beach to her right, there was an ornate wooden pier, with a hexagonal, pointed roof gazebo at the end. She tried to grasp an understanding of how she could have found herself in this marvelous place.

Sarah had spent her entire life over fifty light-years from Earth in Foundation Colony. She had never seen a beach or an ocean except in entertainment simulations and she could immediately tell this was no simulation. This was real in every way. She reached down and touched the sand. It was course and grainy, every bit how she imagined beach sand might really feel. Her confused absorption of these strange and wonderful surroundings was interrupted by a new but familiar sound from behind her.

"Hello Sarah," the familiar voice greeted her.

She turned and looked at the man standing behind her. He had a tray in his hand and on it were a pair of sunglasses and what looked like a glass of lemonade. She understood that she knew this man but in the confusion of the moment she couldn't quite place him. The man seemed unaffected by her lack of recognition and simply reached out and handed her the glass. Sarah put the glass to her lips and tasted the cool refreshing sweetness of the liquid. On Foundation Colony, lemonade had always been one of Sarah's favorite drinks but it had never tasted quite this good. She reached for the sunglasses on the tray and put them on. The bright glare of the sun was immediately eased and she looked around to take in her surroundings more carefully. She had never seen such a beautiful place in her entire life.

Then, suddenly, the man's identity hit her.

"Frank?" she questioned, as the puzzle began to come together.

"Yes, Sarah, how are you?" Frank replied, smiling at her recognition.

Sarah didn't know quite what to say, how to describe how she felt.

"I feel wonderful," she finally replied after a long delay. "I feel wonderful. This is simply amazing."

Frank reached down and held out his hand to her. Sarah felt her heart pound as she reached out to hold the hand of a man she'd never known as anything more than reproduced voice or an image behind a screen. Now he stood in front her, real in every way. She took his hand and stood up. It felt strong and warm and comforting to hold as the reality of the moment began to come together.

"Come, let's walk a little," Frank requested, helping her out of the lounge chair.

Frank let her take her time to get her bearings. They held hands and walked down toward the shore. She looked over at him and smiled as they walked. He was wearing a comfortable

white jacket and looked quite at ease is this wonderful new
world. The questions began to emerge in her mind.

"Where are we?" she asked first.

"The Caribbean," Frank responded in a matter of fact
manner. "Beautiful, isn't it?" he continued.

"Yes, yes it is," Sarah replied, still very confused by the
images around her.

They reached the shoreline. Sarah noticed her feet were
bear and something else; her feet were young. The stiffness
that had begun to show up after she passed one hundred and
twenty now seemed to be gone. In fact, her whole body seemed
younger. She looked down at her arm and stroked her skin.
It was the smooth skin of a woman in her twenties or perhaps
her thirties. She simply couldn't get a full grasp of what was
happening to her.

They stepped into the water and the waves began to lap over
her feet. The ocean was warm and the feeling was wonderful.
She giggled as she felt the tickling sensation of her feet sinking
into the soft wet sand.

Frank smiled at her and began to speak again.

"I used to love to come here. Of all the places I knew on
Earth, this was the hardest to leave. I always found it a great
place to come and contemplate things more carefully."

Sarah looked back at him ready to dig a little deeper.

"Where are we really?" she asked, clarity coming into her
soft eyes.

"Come with me," Frank responded. "I'll show you as much
as I can."

They began to walk along the beach toward the pier. Sarah
turned and looked out over the ocean. She still couldn't believe
how serene things were and how real every sensation was.
After a few moments, they reached the pier and Frank led her
out to the gazebo.

"What do you remember?" he asked her, as they sat down on
the couches that circled the perimeter of the structure.

Sarah looked down into the water, where stingrays glided
in and out of the beams that held up the structure of the pier.
She tried to clear her thoughts.

"The last thing I remember, I was in the lab preparing for
the procedure," she recounted.

"Oh, Yes," chuckled Frank, as if someone was reminiscing about something that might have happened long ago in his childhood. "Thank you for the lab. You gave me back so much."

Sarah refused to accept the compliment.

"We just got you started, you took care of everything from there," Sarah responded, modestly, and then turned back to the matter at hand. "And by the look of things, you just kept on going."

As she spoke she turned back to the view of the ocean and opened her eyes wide, in an expression of amazement, then turned to Frank and smiled. A look of embarrassment came over his face.

"Well I wanted your awakening to be a pleasant one," he responded modestly.

"Better than yours?" Sarah replied, almost apologizing.

"Now don't be critical of your grandfather, Sarah. He was a wonderful man and he gave me everything he could with the limited resources he had at his disposal. Remember, I had a lot more to go on than he did. I want you to be proud of your grandfather. In fact, I want you to be proud of everything your family did for me," he politely scolded her.

"Frank, please tell me more. Where are we?" She continued, pleading for more information.

He looked back at her intently as if to measure what she was ready for. Then he began.

"Everything you see before you is an elaborate simulation. It's constructed of billions of separate data elements all interacting with each other based on their own set of complicated rules. The stingrays you see below you, the birds flying in the sky up above. None of them really exist. Yet to you, right now, they are as real as anything you may have ever known, perhaps more real. Input to your senses is calculated based on your own interaction with the simulation. If you look up, you see the sky, if you look down you see the ocean. That's because, like everything else in this world, the body you feel yourself inside is also a simulation. It works very much the same as the room you gave me in your lab, just on a larger scale."

"You can say that again," she interrupted again looking around in amazement.

Frank smiled in reply and continued. "You see me in front of you because my body is not only a data element in my world but also in yours and visa versa. You can see me, hear me and touch me just as if I were real. I call this world 'The Realm'," he said and paused for a moment.

Sarah smiled in awe.

Frank continued. "Your thoughts and feelings exist no longer in your biological human brain but in an artificial simulation of that brain, which interfaces directly with The Realm. It's similar to the system you built for me but again, somewhat refined."

"Refined how much?" she asked, her curiosity growing.

"The thoughts you are having right now are occurring at approximately fifty thousand times the speed of normal human thought. You can now live an entire lifetime in a day and you can live as many lifetimes as you care to," Frank explained.

"Wait, did you say fifty thousand?" she questioned. "How is that possible?"

"The hardware is somewhat different than the systems you are used to. Its circuitry is based on flow of pure electro magnetic energy. There is no latency associated with electrical, magnetic or chemical storage and transfer of data. Your new brain, if you will, is in fact about the same size as your human one was. It just moves things around much, much faster."

Sarah again looked out at the ocean stunned at what she was hearing. She then looked back at Frank and asked him to continue.

"And where is all of this taking place?" she asked, almost frightened by the reality of what she was learning.

"Let me show you," Frank continued. "Hold on now," he said, standing up in the gazebo.

Sarah grasped the wooden beam along side her tightly, not knowing what to expect next. As she tightened her grasp, the ocean, the sky and even the pier disappeared. Leaving them on the gazebo floating freely with a black background all around. Then slowly, in front of her, where the ocean was a moment ago, the image of the Milky Way galaxy emerged. Sarah tried to fight back the sense of vertigo the change in scenery created. As she looked at the scene, the whole thing zoomed closer in. It was as if she was traveling through hundreds of thousands of light-years of space in a few seconds. The picture before her zoomed in to a part of the cosmos she knew well, Earth's neighborhood.

"Here's where it all started," Frank began to narrate. Then the picture scanned over to Foundation Colony's system, fifty light-years further out in the galactic spiral.

"And here's Foundation Colony," he continued as the scene moved again to a new and turbulent system thirty light-years further and seventy-six light-years from Earth.

"And here's where we are now. I call it Neo Prime. It's a very hostile system, biological life would struggle to survive here but for us. It's perfect, rich in everything we need."

The scene zoomed on the large barely formed star, still swirling in a cloud of volatile gases and unstable clumps of material.

"And here's where we are now," he concluded, as the scene zoomed in further on a small solid object in a slow and wide orbit of the center of the system. "I call this a 'Mindstar' and for us, it's home."

Sarah could easily see the origin of the name. The object had a star like structure with four three sided points, each one pointing one hundred and twelve degrees from the other three. The more interesting thing about it though was its color, or more accurately, its colors. The object was quite dark but every once in a while it would shimmer and each shimmer seemed to be a different color. The effect was quite beautiful.

"So far I've built six of them," Frank continued "and each one can be a home to hundreds of us, if necessary."

"Hundreds?" Sarah questioned.

"Yes Sarah, but of course you don't know. You started a trend. The promise of immortal life brought thousands flocking behind you."

"Are there others awake?" she asked.

"Yes, there is one other and I hope that you will meet him soon," Frank replied.

"The others on the beach?" She clarified.

"Simulations, I found it much nicer to see others enjoying the scenery as well," he commented.

"What else have you been up to?" she inquired.

"Quite a lot actually. Let me show you," he continued. "Perhaps the most important mission has been making sure I can tap the vast resources of the system. That required a mining operation."

The scene before Sarah, panned in closely to the dust clouds of the system. At first she thought she was missing something. She was looking for a mining drone and there was none to be found. Then, as the dust streams got closer and closer until they appeared to be passing right through the gazebo, she saw them, like tiny little honeybees. One drifted right before her eyes and she saw it slowly consuming the particles of dust it passed through. Much was ejected from the tiny machine like unwanted peanut shells but clearly some of the elements were retained, in little sacks that hung underneath. The ejected materials seemed to serve as a primitive form of propulsion keeping the little devices in the thick parts of the clouds. Then she noticed the true miracle of these little workers. Some of them looked like two stuck together but they weren't sticking together. They were dividing. Like the little insects they resembled, they could reproduce.

"By utilizing a self replicating technology, I was able to exponentially accelerate the rate at which I absorb the raw materials available in this system. When they are needed for other purposes, the drones break down easily into their component materials. Then I can refashion that into whatever I need. Since arriving here, I've managed to mine over ten billion tons from the dust clouds. Most of it is still floating freely in the form of these tiny little 'Bugminers' but not all of it. Let me show you my greatest accomplishment."

Again the gazebo seemed to float through space. This time away from the thick dust clouds to a thin triangular object floating in the distance. As they grew closer it was clear the object was quite large, perhaps ten million tons or more.

It was simplistic in shape. Its cross section was a three-pointed star, tapering to a point at both ends. In what appeared to be the back of the object it tapered from its wide midsection to its pointed tail quickly. The front tapered much more slowly, giving it the appearance of a sharp three bladed spearhead as they drew along side. Beyond its simple and elegant shape, its surface also gave it a mystical and powerful appearance. Like the Mindstar, it seemed to glisten different colors. "This is how the rest of the galaxy shall come to know us. These ships will serve as our ambassadors. Of course, the Intruders may come to know them differently," he exclaimed, as Sarah sensed an undercurrent of vengeance in his voice.

"The shimmer, it's beautiful," she stated, simply amazed by the appearance of the elegant ship.

Frank smiled and explained. "A pleasant side effect of the technology. You see, when I first arrived here, I began to experiment with new technologies that might do us some good against the Intruders. My initial track was based on size and power and produced much the same results that Earth achieved. I was able to build massive weapons that were capable of bringing down the enemy but they proved to be too unwieldy and vulnerable to be an effective offensive tool. They would work fine, provided the enemy did not adapt, but any changes in their technology and we would be doomed. So I began to focus on breaking the secrets of the Intruder's own technology. The best clues came from the discoveries on Reykjavik. The first orb we shot down was weak at a certain frequency and its structure was made of a solid material. It had no separate weapons, propulsion or sensor systems. I was intrigued by this fact and decided to pursue it further. Where it took me was astounding. Here, let me show you."

As he spoke an image appeared in the middle of the gazebo. The object reminded Sarah of her molecular studies long ago but this was more complicated than any molecule she had seen before.

"What is it?" Sarah asked

"You might call it a 'Nano-Reactor'," Frank continued. "It's a single molecule with amazing capabilities. It's the holy grail of human science, a cold fusion engine capable of changing its make-up and producing nuclear power in the process. Its wonder doesn't stop there though. Not only can it convert matter directly into energy but it can also do the inverse. It can convert energy back to matter. Believe it or not, that's not all. If loaded with enough juice this baby will actually multiply and inversely, if you suck it dry, it will break down and be absorbed by its neighbors. It's much like a virus, but instead of manipulating chemical energy, it does the same thing with nuclear power. It's the perfect energy management tool. The science required to produce the first one was mind-boggling. It made the neural interpreter look like an abacus. The shimmer comes from slight improvements I made in the structure shortly after the discovery. You see the Intruders version is pure black. It absorbs everything that hits it but it fails at certain frequencies, they can change those frequencies but the limitation remains. The technology that I developed leaks energy across the spectrum, reducing its vulnerability at any given frequency and," he paused, "giving it the shimmer. The result is a structure that is practically indestructible. Almost all of the ship's structure is made of this substance and it provides the propulsion, weaponry, sensory and structural requirements of the vessel. I've launched eight. You are looking at the ninth. Like the Mindstar, they can carry us but only one of the first eight voyages was commanded by one of us."

"The one you want me to meet?" Sarah interjected.

"Yes," Frank replied, "the others, were piloted by advanced Advisors. This one will leave soon for Reykjavik."

"Very impressive Frank," Sarah responded, in awe. "Have you been able to track their progress?"

"Oh yes and much more," Frank replied. "Let me show you one more piece of Neo Prime."

Again the gazebo seemed to float through space and this time arrived at a seemingly endless veil of free-floating objects each spaced perfectly from its neighbors. She recognized its purpose immediately. It was a massive listening array.

"There are over a billion listeners, providing an array over 10,000 miles in diameter and the sensitivity is far greater than anything ever erected before. You won't believe the wonders we've heard. Let me start here" Frank explained, pointing out at the new images unfolding before her.

They were now zooming back away from Neo Prime and the shape of the complete galaxy was re-emerging. Frank looked at Sarah and asked her, "Can you hear it?"

Sarah stared out at the image before her and began to hear something emanating from the stars, a distant murmur of something intelligent and distinct.

"What is that?" she asked.

"It's them," Frank replied, "or at least their communications as picked up by our listening array and distilled down to something tangible to the human senses. We've been listening to the stars for over two thousand years and in that time found no trace of what is out there. The signals were simply so faint or configured in ways we wouldn't have expected. Now, however, with the sensitivity and pattern recognition capabilities of this array, we can finally here the voices of the beyond."

Sarah was puzzled by what she heard but knew it would take time for the sensations of this new realm to come together in her mind. She let a vision unfold before her. The signals started to paint a picture in the stars, mapping out the space occupied by their long time foes. She was astounded by the size of the image. It stretched out across the three of the closest arms of the spiral galaxy for at least ten thousand light-years. It looked like a giant ameba eating up great chunks of the surrounding space.

"At its peak Mankind spread out over a diameter of over one hundred light-years and colonized over two hundred systems. The Intruders have control over two million systems. To the center of their civilization we have not yet built the great pyramids and we are also seeing them now, as they existed thousands of years ago. Mankind will be dealing with the Intruders for hundreds of thousands of years. The millennium of war that we have known is just the beginning of a very long journey. It began long before we knew it, when the Intruders first heard our earliest radio signals and were drawn our way, to destroy every new emerging technology as they've been doing for millions of years."

"Is there any chance of peace?" Sarah asked in desperation.

"From what I can tell it seems unlikely. It is bred into the very nature of the Intruders to destroy any sign of emerging technology in their sphere of influence. It's interesting to note how parallel their history is to ours. Like us their intelligence emerged as an adaptation to the threats of their environment and like us it gave them a technology that soon threatened their own world. They learned how to integrate their technology with their biology and like us this brought conflict to their culture. Unlike us, the biotechs won. With their victory, came the burden of controlling the rest of their culture. They did this by violently subduing any access to technology that their natural ancestors possessed. They doomed them to an eternal existence as primitive Stone Age creatures, maintained for no other reason than to provide a gene pool to their technologically integrated masters. There was, however, a catch. By subduing the technology and protecting their captive predecessors, they have suppressed the intelligence of the entire species. That suppressed intelligence is passed on to them when they take new blood into their ranks. They have de-evolved and become technologically advanced but mentally crippled. They are little more than a piece of their own machinery. For us to make peace with such a culture may be impossible. It would be like trying to negotiate with a ticking bomb."

"Is that what our future holds then, to wage war against a thoughtless destructive machine for hundreds of thousands of years?" she questioned her heart sinking.

"It's a part of our future and one that can't be ignored if Mankind is to survive but other discoveries await us out in the stars. Let me show you what I mean," he continued.

As he spoke the image of the galaxy before him slipped back to reveal its entire form. Other shapes began to emerge to join the sprawling mass of the Intruders, some smaller, some larger. In places great black gaps existed between the groups, in others the groups merged and joined together.

"Intelligent races of all shapes and sizes have made their mark on the cosmos. As varied, as the race of man was when his tribes began to meet each other, the diversity in the galaxy goes far beyond that. Some meetings will be violent, as was our first contact. Others will surely be more peaceful. And look it goes on."

The vision of the galaxy before them shrank away and other galaxies began to emerge. Some of them were also filled with the crackle of intelligence. These images also began to shrink away and a new and distant one appeared.

"A whisper from before the dawn of time," Frank interjected, then paused. "This is my most recent discovery, another universe, hundreds of billions of light-years away. It sits far beyond the reaches of anything we've seen before and we see it now as it existed long before our universe even came into being and there's no reason to believe it's the only one."

"It's like looking through the eyes of God," Sarah whispered in pure amazement.

"Oh no, I wouldn't say that," Frank replied. "I've now seen more than I ever knew possible but to compare that with the power to create such a marvel, well, to me that's unimaginable. Although," he smiled as if he might almost laugh, "a good friend of mine might disagree."

"So there is no God?" Sarah asked wondering if Frank's perception had reached that far.

"Of that I cannot say," Frank replied, turning toward her. "I can say only this. I have looked across the universe with a clarity of vision that Mankind has never before known and one thing still puzzles me."

Sarah looked at him intensely.

"Why?" Frank continued. "Why, of all the possible structures that this universe, this existence, might take on, why is it made in a way that allows us to exist? When the answer to that question is known then the nature of God will be revealed and with all the advancement we have made, the answer to that question still lies far, far away."

"What about humanity Frank, what about Earth?" She asked in near desperation, hoping for some good news.

"That is a question we can answer together," he responded, "and I'll introduce you to that friend of mine I mentioned. Are you ready?"

"Yes, Frank, I want to know," she replied.

"Then I must ask you to close your eyes for a moment," he instructed, "and trust me."

Sarah closed her eyes and felt a new sensation overcome her, the sensation that she was falling, that she was suddenly fading away, the feeling frightened her and she tried to open her eyes, but she couldn't. She was disappearing, disappearing into a world of blackness she wanted to fight it but she couldn't. She had only one choice she had to trust Frank so she held her breath and let the darkness take her.

Chapter 22

The Guardian

4424
Earth

"Sir, I have sensors and communications," Thomas announced proudly, "shall I activate them?"

"Any luck with propulsion?" Jackson inquired, looking at Robertson.

"I'm afraid not sir, no luck with the shuttle bay power either," he replied.

"Very well Ensign," he signaled, turning back toward Thomas, "let's take one more look before we go down."

The screen came back to life and the image before them sent a wave of shock across the entire bridge. The second ship had now closed in tightly on the Intruder Mother Ship that had taken them down. It was a mystical sight. It was larger than the first ship by at least twice and completely different in shape. From their near head on view, it appeared as an almost perfect three-pointed star. Its center, however, was extended far toward them more like a three bladed spearhead. Far more striking than its shape, however, was its glimmering structure. Waves of different colors flowed across its surface like the reflection of a rainbow cascading off a shimmering brook. For a moment it reminded Jackson of home, of the shimmering crystal asteroids of The Outer Banks. He had no idea where this strange ship had come from or what its purpose was, but it warmed his heart to see it. Something inside him told him, it just wasn't an Intruder Ship.

His instincts were confirmed when their own adversary fired on it. The piercing white beam that had devastated Retribution let loose on the new ship. Everyone on the bridge gasped as they saw the result. The new visitor just seemed to absorb the Intruder's beam as one might soak up the sun on a warm day. It had no effect at all.

A moment later the new arrival returned fire. The blast emanated from the entire surface of the ship. It had the same light green color as Retribution's most recent volleys, obviously set to Intruder's vulnerable frequency, but it was hundreds of times brighter in intensity.

Their enemy was vanquished in a moment. The Intruder ship shattered into millions of tiny glowing green sparks and disappeared from their scopes completely.

The crew of Retribution stared in silence, thinking for a moment they might be next, but the screen before them changed quickly as they received a new incoming signal. A young man with strong shoulders and long wavy hair sat before them. He was dressed most unusually. He wore long white robes fastened by a broach on his shoulder. His surroundings looked more like an ancient palace than the bridge of a starship.

The man spoke first.

"My name is Lucas. I have been sent by the Founder to serve as the Guardian of Humanity. What is the status of your ship?"

Jackson was stunned by a million unanswered questions that shot through his head, but knew there was no time now to question this new ally. He decided to trust him with everything.

"We have lost propulsion and will impact Earth in approximately thirty minutes," he responded.

"I see," Lucas replied, "Unfortunately there is no way for me to save your ship, but all is not yet lost. I cannot explain to you what will happen next but you must not resist. Do you understand?"

"Yes," Jackson replied.

"They have launched a projectile and it's headed toward us fast," Thomas interjected.

"Let it come," Jackson ordered. "Nobody do anything."

They all trusted their commander, and knew they had nothing to loose. So they sat still and waited for the incoming missile to strike the ship.

It slowed as it approached the ship and hit with a thud directly on the exterior of the bridge, right behind the position of the screen. Before long the screen began to spark and fizz as something began to cut through. They reached for their atmospheric masks but the breach occurred with no loss of pressure in the hull. The device had created an outer seal before breaking through the hull itself. As soon as the hole was opened several small objects broke through. They looked like large flying ants each one perhaps twelve inches in length. Jackson and his crew couldn't help but feel frightened as they buzzed around the bridge, but they held their positions.

The insect like machines fanned out and each landed on the head of a crewmember. Jackson looked straight at his injured wife as they both felt the strange invaders make contact with their scalp. He grabbed her hand and squeezed it tight as he felt thousands of tiny needles penetrating at different places in his head. He couldn't begin to understand what was happening but had to trust their new friend. Some type of medical procedure was clearly being initiated.

Otter looked over at Jackson and his wife and tried not to rip this new and strange device from his head. He looked at Jackson and realized his only choice was this or death. He grabbed Jackson's shoulder and gritted his teeth as the needles dug into his skull.

The pain was intense but lasted only a few moments. Before long every member of the crew began to relax as a warm and soothing feeling crept over their body like liquid.

Jackson slumped forward and nestled his head to Rebecca's chest, unable to consider whether he might damage the device on his skull. He did not. It simply continued its work.

Jackson's last thoughts were of his wife and his crew as the world around him faded to black.

Chapter 23

The Return

4501
Earth

Sarah regained consciousness. Once again, she felt strangely well rested. She wondered for a moment if her experience with Frank had been a dream and almost didn't dare open her eyes to find out. She felt a strange warm breeze on her face and hope returned that everything she had seen was real, or at least existed within The Realm.

She opened her eyes. She found herself still sitting in the same gazebo looking across at Frank.

"I'm sorry," Frank apologized, "It's always a little scary."

"What is," Sarah asked, "what happened?"

"You died again."

"Oh, I see," Sarah replied, still somewhat confused.

"Yes, unfortunately there's no way to freeze our neural image without freezing brain activity and to the human brain stopping is dieing. It's not capable of comprehending that it's now a digital image that can be copied and restarted, or, as in this case, transmitted to a new host."

"A new host? Where?" Sarah inquired.

"Here," Frank gestured, toward the sky.

For the first time since reawakening, Sarah looked around at her surroundings. She was on the same gazebo, but much of what lay beyond, had changed. They were still sitting out over the ocean, but no longer were they looking at the gentle waters of the Caribbean. Now lively waves crashed white against jagged rocks that surrounded them. Behind them a small pebbly beach replaced the long sandy one that had been there before, and steps led up to an ancient looking structure that sat on a bluff, overlooking them. Most amazing of all, up above them where Sarah might have expected to find the sun, sat something unexpected and soothing. Earth filled the sky like a great blue moon, warm and serene.

"We shall soon both know what has become of our ancestral home," Frank informed her. "Though you felt only an instant pass, seventy-six years have gone by and in that time the image of your mind traveled seventy-six light-years from Neo Prime, home, to Earth."

Sarah just stared back in awe, until her thoughts were distracted by a new sound from behind.

"Welcome, welcome," came a young and confidant voice. Sarah turned to look.

An interesting looking man was pacing down the pier towards them with a beaming smile on his face. He was young, tall and proud looking and his long wavy hair bounced as he walked. He wore a long white robe that looked Greek or Roman in appearance, fastened by a small broach on the shoulder. As he drew closer Sarah immediately saw a wisdom that went beyond his years, gleaming in his eyes. Like Frank, this man had experienced many lifetimes in the Realm.

"Founder, it is so good to see you," the man beamed as he embraced the older man. "You must be Sarah Carmichael. What a pleasure to meet you. The Founder has told me so much about you. It is truly an honor to welcome you to my ship."

He reached out and shook Sarah's hand firmly.

"Let me introduce you to Lucas, he will be able to update us on happenings on Earth," Frank noted.

"All in good time Founder," Lucas replied, "Let's allow the lady to get her bearings first."

"As I said, welcome to my ship, I hope you like it," Lucas began, "I call her Pegasus, and she was the first Ambassador ship to leave Neo Prime. I'm quite proud of her. She's performed flawlessly. Of course, you can't really see that much of her from inside my Realm. Let me give you a better look."

Lucas waved his arm and several things occurred all at once. First a grey fog quickly swirled around the gazebo. Then, as quickly as it came, it dissipated. When the new vista emerged, the gazebo was now perched on the hillside beside the building that Sarah had noticed earlier. She smiled to herself, thinking how useless the steps were when you could just travel by magic if you wanted to.

The scene above them had also changed. The Earth still dominated the sky, but it now had a companion. An ambassador ship, identical the one that Frank had showed her earlier, hung above, watching over the planet like a vigilant falcon.

Again Sarah was stunned by the ship's beauty, shimmering in the heavens above them. She was particularly warmed to see it sitting in Earth Orbit with no sign of the Intruders at all.

"How are things up there?" she asked.

"Very well, very well indeed," Lucas responded. "I arrived here just behind the first counter attack from Interstellar Naval Command, Retribution, commanded by a Nathan Jackson, fine ship and a fine crew. They had already taken care of most of the Intruder force in the solar system, but unfortunately they weren't equipped to deal with the very newest Intruder ships. I wasn't able to save their ship or the crew, but I was able to save their mind-images."

"Lucas, we agreed no crossing over from Earth," Frank interjected somewhat concerned.

"They were not on Earth, Founder and I felt their bravery earned them a chance at Immortality, but I have not woken them yet. See for yourself," Lucas gestured.

In the building behind them, which Sarah realized now had more the appearance of a temple than anything else; lay the bodies of the crew of the Retribution and their guest from Earth's INC observer core. Each one was lying completely still on a marble pedestal, looking serene and peaceful. She was reminded of that day long ago in her lab when she stared at Frank's peaceful virtual body ready to give the command to activate him.

"I understand your decision, you did the right thing," Frank conceded.

They walked between the great stone columns that held up the roof of the building and looked more closely at the crew.

"Do they have any idea what has happened to them?" Sarah asked.

"Unfortunately there was no time to explain anything to them. I barely had the time to perform the procedure," Lucas explained. "We will have to wake them very carefully. This one in particular will be in for a shock."

"Why is that?" Frank inquired.

"Well, I learned later that he is from Earth. The crew of Retribution recovered him before it went down. His name is Otter. The last few days of his life must have been quite disorienting in and of themselves. Living on Earth left him without any exposure to advanced technology, he's had only what he learned from INC manuals to prepare for the changes he's seeing, and there's nothing in those manuals about the Realm. He was the only surviving member of INC on Earth to open a vault. That's why Jackson went and got him."

"We'll take things slowly with him, with all of them," Frank replied.

"What about the rest of Earth?" Sarah asked, eager to learn more.

"Yes, yes," Lucas continued. "As I said they are doing quite well. They don't know all the details of what's happened above them, but they figured out that something changed. It appears that during Retribution's brief but impact-full visit they attacked the Crawler villages below. This sent the message to everyone down there that the Intruders were gone. In the seventy-six years that have followed Mankind has began to crawl his way back from the dark ages. Much technology has been rediscovered; hard metals, steam engines and internal combustion are already in wide spread use. They are beginning to play around with powered flight. The population has doubled. Four billion humans now inhabit the world. Their social and political structures are beginning to re-evolve as well. Democracy had almost vanished completely when I arrived. It is now flourishing everywhere, trade and culture are awakening as well."

"Do they know anything of us or INC?" Frank inquired.

"They know nothing of us and they know very little of INC," Lucas replied. "Our good friend here, appears to be almost all that remained of INC on Earth and the Retribution was unsuccessful in contacting anyone else. They know from her fiery crash that there was a fight above them and items pulled from the wreckage told them it was INC, but they know little more than that. They've seen Pegasus too."

"Have they had any other contact with you?" Frank inquired quite sternly.

Lucas looked back at his old friend solemnly and replied.

"No Founder, I have not, and I must tell that I've come to agree with your feelings on this matter. They must define their own path now."

"I'm pleased to hear you say that Lucas," Frank confessed. "I know that my wishes in that regard were difficult for you."

"Yes, but watching them all these years, I see what you mean."

"Help me out here," Sarah interjected.

"I'm sorry Sarah. I know that you're learning a lot here," Frank replied. "Let me explain. Lucas and I talked at length before he left for Earth. Before he took command of the Pegasus. It has always been my feeling that we have an obligation to liberate Earth, but we should not do anything more. We do not have the right. We have no mandate here. I am just one man and I left Earth almost one thousand years ago. Not to mention that I'm not even really human any more. What right do I have to direct humanity's future? No, I decided that we must leave them alone. They must learn for themselves."

"I didn't always agree with Frank. I care about these people deeply, though I was only one of them for eight years," Lucas added. "I felt they needed and deserved our help. Watching them learn here on Earth though I've learned what a mistake that would be. Frank's right, it's not our place. Beyond that, who would we help? They are no longer one people, there are over a hundred different nations down there now, fewer each day as treaties and alliances bring them back together but it's still a complicated world. How do we know we'd be helping the right ones? No, it's better this way."

"What about INC?" Sarah asked. "They'll be back right?"

"Yes, they'll be coming. Very soon in fact," Frank confirmed. "I'm not sure their mandate is any stronger than ours though. INC is the military branch of a government that was destroyed almost four hundred years ago. How will they choose what side to take in Earth's quarrels?"

"If we are not going to interfere with Earth's rebirth, then we shouldn't let INC interfere either." Lucas added resolutely. "Yes, when the time comes we will need to speak with INC about several things," Frank followed up. "To them, we are a violation of their most sacred laws. Though ironically, it is our existence and our ability to advance technology far faster than they can, that has saved them and saved humanity. They must learn to reconcile themselves to that and that will be difficult for them. Once that is accomplished, I hope that we can work together to defend what remains of humanity. Mankind once numbered almost eleven billion and inhabited over two hundred solar systems. They felt invulnerable. That growth came from the realization, after the Great Wars that Earth was a single point of failure for the very existence of Mankind. An unspoken fear of our own extinction drove us to the stars. Then the Intruders arrived and everything changed. Though they've come far in a short time, they still have a long way to go. If Mankind is to be truly safe again they must be allowed to once again spread across the galaxy. Protecting them will be vital for many years to come. INC can help with this, but they cannot do it alone. They will need us."

"What about us Frank?" Sarah questioned. "What lies ahead for us?"

"A good question Sarah. Our evolution must also continue. One thing I've learned by observing this universe of ours is that all things evolve. We are nothing more than a step in that process. Whether it's the very matter that makes up the universe or the life than sprang forth from it, everything seems to follow an evolutionary path. Even the technology that both Humans and Intruders possess evolved slowly over time. Ironically, it was the clash of those two species and their technology that produced our most recent evolutionary challenge. It is the ultimate challenge that nature imposes on all of her creations: evolve or perish? Humanity chose to evolve. We are the result of that evolutionary step. We must protect our human ancestors we have that obligation, but what lies ahead for us remains to be seen, and is not up to me."

"What do you mean Frank?" Sarah asked.

"It's up to you Sarah." Frank replied, surprising her with the answer.

Lucas smiled and turned toward Frank to let him explain. Frank began.

"I was born almost eleven hundred years ago, before we even knew of the existence of the Intruders, in a time when Mankind thought the Universe was ours for the taking. I always believed, however, that new challenges would lie ahead and that the solution to those challenges would come in the evolution of our technology and our ability to harness that power. That belief led me on a journey, a journey that has led me right back here, to Earth. I could not have known that the challenges we would face would almost cost Mankind his future and that the discoveries we have made would salvage that future. It's been my honor, truly my honor to have played a part in this."

"It wasn't always by choice though. Was it?" Sarah asked, now realizing what Frank was talking about.

Frank smiled at her and continued.

"No Sarah, you are right, it has not been by choice. You remember the gift your grandfather gave me?"

"Yes," Sarah replied. "Your prime directive."

"Yes, my prime directive, to protect Mankind. Your grandfather was a brilliant man. He worked tirelessly to bring me back from the frozen mind recording I had turned myself into it. He worked against technical and even political challenges to accomplish that goal. I am grateful to him. He knew one thing though and that one thing scared him. He knew that we were taking a dangerous path together. He protected us against those dangers by giving me my prime directive. That above all else, I would protect Mankind. It is good that he did that, because ultimately Mankind would need protecting in ways he could never have imagined."

"What about Lucas? If the prime directive was yours, then why did you give the job of defending Earth to Lucas?" Sarah asked.

"That's one of the little ironies of our story Sarah," Frank replied. "Because of the prime directive I couldn't ultimately take on responsibility for protecting Earth. Do you know why?"

"Yes, Frank I understand. The prime directive can be changed or deleted?" She replied, now smiling back. "By the leader of the Founder project."

"And that is you," he concluded. "You see as long as the prime directive could be changed, my role as Mankind's protector was always flawed. That is why I chose Lucas for this role. He has no prime directive; he is free to choose his own destiny. He chose the role of Guardian for himself."

"And I am honored with the role," Lucas chimed in proudly.

"And you have done well," Frank congratulated his student.

"Lucas lived only eight years as a human, then transitioned over to the Realm," Frank began.

"I had a terminal illness you see," Lucas added.

"Lucas' parents were good and caring people and they chose to give Lucas a new chance at life. They allowed him to crossover and made me his guardian. I did everything I could as his new parent, to instill in him a love for humanity. In the three hundred years since he came into my charge we have lived thousands of lifetimes together in all that time I hoped he would take the burden, but I never forced it upon him. When I felt he was ready and willing for the task I granted him his own Realm and gave him Pegasus. He now serves as the Guardian of Humanity, leaving me able to wake you."

"So that if I change the prime directive, Mankind is still protected," Sarah realized.

"Yes Sarah, you are the custodian of the Realm," Frank beamed. "You will decide our destiny. For all of us but Lucas, you will decide where the future takes us."

Sarah fell silent at the realization of the role she would now play. The three of them walked out from the temple and stood on the edge of the Rocky Bluff.

Sarah gazed up at the warm blue vision of Earth floating above them, so still and peaceful. She felt she could reach out and hold it in her hand. She couldn't help but wonder what lay ahead. Her mind was filled with visions of the future, for her, for Lucas, for the Founder and for all of Mankind.

The future will continue...

Printed in the United States
26370LVS00003BA/346-360